LORD BLACKWOOD

Realms ♥f Man

C.M. CONNEY

Published by
Ace Lyon Books
LLC

Published by
Ace Lyon Books
Acelyonbooks.com
First Edition
Editor Name
Cover Design by S. M. Savoy
Lord Blackwood/ C.M. Conney
ISBN 978-1-947122-53-6

BOOKS IN THIS SERIES

Seethe

Lord Blackwood

Upcoming Book: Anima Whispers

RELATED BOOKS SET IN THE *REALM OF MAN*

Moon Caught

Heaven Scent

*

Qarahpyr

Contents

Chapter 1

A dimly lit, twelve-foot-tall, metal gate swung open as our car approached. Trees shaded the narrow driveway, blocking the moonlight. Iron posts holding decorative lanterns were spaced evenly the length of the drive. Each one flickered to life as the car approached and went out when we'd passed.

Ryu said, "You know what they say about curiosity…"

I lifted an eyebrow.

Julia patted my hand. "It kills the cat," she said absently, peering over her shoulder at the lights flickering out behind us.

"This place is creepy as shit," Ryu said.

A single small light lit the front steps of a large house tucked into thick trees. The home was very grand with flower edged paths that disappeared into the woods.

The driveway wound around the house to a small parking lot that was partially filled with expensive cars with black coverings over their license plates. It was all meticulously kept but had an abandoned air because it was so dark and quiet.

Candlelight lit a few of the windows on the top floor. Red light shone through partially closed curtains on the bottom floor.

"'Tis the home of a vampire," I said.

Ryu laughed.

I hadn't been jesting.

He said, "It does look like the sort of joint Dracula would dig."

Julia clasped my hand hard. "Let's go back to the hotel."

"And let it come upon us unexpectedly? Nay! 'Tis folly."

"This is folly!"

"Mayhap."

Julia said, "I shouldn't have agreed, but I didn't really think she could be here..."

"Lady Delphine has no reason to wish me ill."

"Pip, she can't know it's you!"

"It was her who named me so. She was my first real friend, mayhap my only one... but I'd not ask you to face her. Ryu can take you back."

"And let you go in alone? Don't be silly!"

"I'll be perfectly fine."

"It isn't a risk I'm willing to take! Besides, you might need Ryu."

"I'd not risk him—there is no risk."

"Don't try to pretend you're not uneasy when I know you are!"

"'Tis the... ambiance, nothing more. She has no reason to harm me—and I'm not powerless."

"Please, Pip! She could be much more powerful than us! Our little lights might do nothing except piss her off!"

"Your anger isn't helping... it might be turned against us."

"Then stop being such a dunderhead!"

I said, "Ryu, let me off here and take Lady Blackwood back to the hotel."

"Don't be ridiculous!" She took a deep breath, exhaling heavily.

"Ryu, I think you should wait in the car. Keep the lights on inside and outside. We won't be long. Don't leave the car even to piss."

"I'd not leave him ignorant of the danger."

Ryu pulled up parallel to the wide front steps.

"He'll never believe you—but go ahead."

Ryu said incredulously, "Are you telling me that you really believe a vampire lives here?"

I said, "I know not. I know not how to kill one or hold one at bay with any certainty. I only have hearsay to guide my actions. Light is the only thing that I know of that might repel a creature of the night."

Ryu snickered. "Man, all those books you read be giving you the jitters. This place was made to fool suckers like you."

Julia said, "He could be right, Pip."

"She could be the one friend I have left in the world…"

Julia heaved a heavy sigh and kissed my cheek. "She won't be the person you recall even if it is her, but I suppose I can't blame you. I'd want to speak with her too if the tables were turned. But don't get your hopes up, darling. She might know nothing of your family."

Ryu said, "I thought you didn't remember your family?"

I exited the car without answering.

Julia followed me out.

It took more willpower than I liked to admit to myself to mount the steps and ring the bell.

A handsome, middle-aged man wearing a dark blue suit answered the door. The faint sounds of a woman singing a sultry song accompanied by a piano reached us.

He looked perfectly ordinary, which was very reassuring. Julia's tight grip on my arm eased.

"Good evening, Lord and Lady Blackwood," he said in heavily accented English. "The mistress is expecting you. Please ensure your cell phones are off. We don't allow pictures. Normally, it's my job to search the guests to ensure that no such devices are brought into the house, but I'm sure you'll abide by her wishes."

As he was speaking, a woman wearing a gold evening gown and a black mask glided down the stairs behind him. Her hair was up in an elaborate braid studded with gems that sparkled in the red light. She wore gloves and carried a small white dog that she set down when she reached the bottom.

Soft talk, laughter, the clink of glasses, and low moans were coming from a room on our left. The décor, what I could see of it, had an oriental flavor.

The woman ignored us, entering a door on the right. The room was darker than the hall. Just a few small candles lit it.

I caught a quick glimpse of a dining table set with crystal glassware, white China, and men and woman in formal wear and masks before the door closed behind the woman.

The man who'd opened the door for us said, "My name is Renee. Please, come with me."

We passed an open archway from which the music originated.

A group of elegantly clad men and women wearing masks were playing roulette while sipping drinks and nibbling canapés, served by waitstaff in white jackets and black pants. Couples, in varying stages of undress, lounged on velvet settees. We passed the doorway before I got more than a quick glimpse.

That one glimpse made my cock throb.

Julia whispered, "Maybe we were mistaken?"

Renee led us passed a closed door on the right and opened one on the left.

He knocked once on the next door then opened it and ushered us in, bowing deeply as he said, "Madam, your guests have arrived."

"Bring us drinks, Renee, and see that we aren't disturbed."

She sounded like I remembered Delphine but a hair higher pitched or maybe breathier, or maybe I was misremembering her tone. It made my eyes fill with tears though to hear a voice I'd thought never to hear again.

He bowed again, gesturing us to enter as he headed to a sideboard that I could barely see in the gloom of the room. A single candle sat on a small table halfway between us and a grouping of chairs. A woman wearing a long gown sat in the chair farthest from us. At least I thought it a woman by the faint silhouette of upswept hair and graceful arms.

"*Mon pépin, tu as beaucoup changé et pas du tout. c'est si bon de vous revoir!*" she said with deep affection.

"It's good to see you also. But, please, speak English. My wife has no French."

"Please, you must tell me how you came to meet!"

Julia said, "It was our fate."

"How did you know to send for me?" I asked.

"I have long been searching. Please, sit. We have much to discuss."

Julia and I sat together on the small settee directly across from her. Renee handed us both wine glasses. I couldn't decide if Delphine wore a gown or was a shadow in the shape of a woman wearing a gown.

She said, "It was purely by chance that I got word of you. I have a friend of a sort, Vitus Athinganoi, although he seldom uses a surname, having no need. He travels more than most of our kind and had recently had dealings with another... you might be unaware but it's common practice for us to seek safe passage when traveling through another's territory. It's a mark of... prestige to be able to host another well and an act of disrespect to venture into another's territory without making the proper introductions."

"I know nothing of your kind... or mine own."

5

"*Mon cher pépin,* say it isn't so! Have you wandered all this time with no knowledge! Why, he was more of a bastard then I thought him!"

"I hadn't been wandering but trapped."

I told her my story, which made her weep. Her graceful hand movements became formless wisps of darker black in the dark room.

Her voice was rough with emotion when she said, "I am truly sorry, *mon pépin.* I'd thought you were safe from him when I left. I'd come to your house in search of a mate. I was a seethe but not a very strong one. I'd inherited the power from my father, you see, so while I had some inkling, I'd also had the misfortune to be a woman."

Julia said, "He'd told you what you were?"

"He did. I'd known, of course, that he wasn't a man to trifle with, but I didn't know how he managed to best men twice his size or convince thick headed scoundrels when others could not, but when I was a woman grown, he told me of our true nature. Not that I possessed his power, but he knew that if he was to perish and I were nearby that I would inherit it, and he wished me to be prepared. I was also able to help him—the family—more effectively. But the true reason he'd told me was he loved me and wished us to remain close when he eventually must switch hosts.

He'd been searching for another, seeking out men with reputations as fierce warriors and shrewd bargainers, until he met my mother that is. He truly loved her, and he truly loved me. Once they were wed, he stopped seeking another and instead spent his efforts on building a defendable estate that would support us. He traveled a great deal fearing his methods would become known and might make the locals act against us, so I rarely saw him when I was a child.

My mother never knew he wasn't of this realm. He died soon after her. I like to think they travel the bardo together..."

"The bardo?"

"The blackness that held you. A soul that has sinned mightily can take eons to cross. *Your* soul was pure, but your father's was most assuredly not. I think it safe to assume that your cousin Edmund's soul was as corrupt as a person's could be, and it's entirely possible that Edmund was already hosting a fragment of Blackwood's anima. 'Tis a common practice for a seethe to infuse their anima into a potential host as a means of paving the way, so to speak.

"When my father died, I went through his notes, hoping he'd left me some clue as to where to look for another, someone I could love as he'd loved my mother. Someone I could trust who could be a partner through the ages. My father had thought Lord Blackwood might be such as us, so I offered my services as governess and went to get his measure.

"I knew almost immediately that he was a powerful seethe, but I also saw that he was an evil man. He was grooming his son and his bastard, and not like my father had with the intention of preparing me for what might be my fate, but to use their bodies if the need arose."

Julia and I exchanged horrified glances.

Delphine continued, "Part of the problem in being so long lived is keeping what you've worked for. In the general course of things, a seethe will marry a younger spouse and transfer themselves into that spouse so as to keep their home and belongings. Or they will gift or sell their host body's properties or in some way pass on their wealth, but marriage is easiest to arrange, although easiest is by no means easy. The host body needs to be full of rage with the correct form of skandha, but it also needs to be weaker willed than that of the seethe trying to possess it. It's much easier to find males with the correct attributes than females, or at least it was.

"My father had successfully switched bodies four times. The first time he'd picked a young man who fit the criteria and had a small holding. He kept the holding by finding a younger woman to wed and arranging who she wed on the event of his death, which gave him plenty of time to prepare that body by infusing his essence until the host body had no real will of its own. It instantly did whatever it was told.

"There was still a chance that person's dormant spirit might rally and resist but the older a seethe grows, the better it becomes at judging whether its victims are agreeing because they lack the will or because the seethe's will is forcing their compliance.

"Seethes can live a long time, but people *will* notice, so they can't use their power too often or they won't age like they should. He kept his holding but wasn't able to use the same technique again because the laws had changed and he had no way to ensure his widow would marry the correct man, so he married a young woman and became his widow.

"Life as a woman wasn't at all to his liking, not the woman shape but the restrictions women lived under, so he transferred into a man again, but this time he didn't care about his holding. He wanted to find another seethe. Another seethe would make life simple. They could build an empire and hold it indefinitely with one just marrying the other, switching from man to woman as needed. He was hoping to find one he could love but instead met my mother.

"When I met Blackwood, it was clear he would never be content in a woman's body. He despised them or maybe he despised wanting to be one, but whatever the reason he was determined to hand his estates to himself through his own son."

I was horrified. I hadn't been close to my brother, but I'd been fond of and had admired him. I hated to contemplate that my father had been abusing him his entire life.

She continued, "I *was* a seethe and reveled in rage, but I also knew love. He used lust as a weapon, not that he wasn't capable of acting the perfect gentleman. He presented a charming façade, but he was monstrous to his sons. He had many bastards and he taught them to hate and urged them to murder and kept them handy to snack upon..."

"Why did you stay?" I asked.

Unspoken was my real question, *why did you leave me there?*

She laughed and it rose the hair on my arms.

"I feel your anger seethe. You're right that I could have saved you, but you had no need of saving. He intended you and Violet to have good marriages, not for your sake, but still, he would have arranged the most advantageous matches he could have. I did intend to return if I'd been able but then you died and he died soon after, so there was no need for me to return. In all honesty I was glad of it because he was much stronger than I. I was a new seethe and not at all in control of my whispers.

"It would've been difficult for me to kill him. I could send an assassin but if he'd lived and caught the man, he could make the assassin say who had sent him. Not to say I was glad you'd been murdered. Far from it. I was furious. You should have been safe... my affection for you was very real. I'd hoped to grow in strength and be able to murder him in such a way that I could pick who inherited his power. It would've had been a very difficult task fraught with danger because his will must have been murdered as well or it would be him who took your body."

She said wistfully, "You were smart and sweet. I truly loved you..."

Julia said fiercely, "*We're* in love and she'd never forgive you if you harmed me."

Delphine said softly and with regret, "The dream of a life with Pip died many years ago...."

Her sorrow was clear in her voice and the gold flecks that lit the darkness by her face.

I said, "You can't transfer to another body?"

"I could but doing so would likely leave me powerless for a time. Besides, I quite enjoy this form. It has drawbacks but also compensations. I no longer worry about material things, except for my family's sake. I do my best to see that they need for nothing. This is only one of my homes. I have many in many places. I *was* weak but now I'm one of the most powerful of my kind."

"Can you tell me how to safely transfer?"

"I shall do all that I can."

Julia said, "And what would you want in return?"

Delphine laughed again. This time the sound was light and musical. "Your company occasionally would suffice. There aren't many who can reminisce with me. There aren't many I call friend— who I love."

I said, "Warn me before coming to visit because I have lights inside the walls."

"You'd allow me in your home?"

Julia squeezed my arm hard enough to bruise.

"Of course. I loved you then and have no reason to think our friendship wasn't real. Your shape might be different but you're still the same"—I laughed in embarrassment— "I was going to say person, but I suppose being is closer. I have no wish to offend you and no notion of what your form is called."

"This form is called many things, most commonly vampire. I prefer Tulpa but 'tis just a word. Call me whatever you wish."

"Then I shall call you *mon professeur bien-aimé*. I missed you dreadfully, but more than that, I savored every word you ever spoke to me while I was trapped beyond the veil."

"The bardo can be a perilous place. We cross it quickly, stepping in and out before we can become lost. I hadn't realized a seethe could become trapped there, which in hindsight... I think it a miracle you emerged at all."

"I hate to remember. I hate to think of myself as that hideous thing, although now seeing you, maybe I wasn't as hideous as I imagined."

She laughed again, the sound like bells tinkling.

Julia said, "You weren't hideous, Pip. Lou was hideous. You were a shining bright light. I thought you an angel and while it scared me to death it wasn't because of your shape. You were always beautiful—always."

Delphine said softly, "So sayeth true love." She clapped once. "I shall have my books brought. It's been many years since I wrote in them and many more since I read them, but perhaps they'll have more insights for you."

The door opened and her form fluttered and resolidified.

A man stepped into the open doorway, but I couldn't make out if it was Renee or another.

Delphine said, "Gather the books from the red trunk and send them with all dispatch to Lord Blackwood. Ensure they're delivered safely into his hands and no other.

I said, "If I can be of service…"

"I have many servants. You can be a friend."

She cocked her head to the side, a silhouette of curls tumbling over a graceful shoulder. "Your companion grows restless."

I said, "I'd forgotten we'd left him in the car."

"You're welcome to stay as long as you wish but the entertainment might not suit…"

She giggled and stood, gliding slowly to the door.

Despite my very real affection for her it still rose the small hair on my arms.

Julia said, "Thank you for the offer but we aren't yet accustomed to ourselves."

Delphine nodded slowly. "'Tis wise to know it. Don't think of yourselves as human because you are not. Human morals have no place with you. I don't mean that you should forget love or laughter, but you can't live your life like a human male because you won't always be such and those who can't adapt die… your outward shape has no bearing on who you are, except in the very minor detail of physical sensation. I have worn a human male shape and quite enjoyed the strength of my arms and the strength of my penis. I prefer this form as its most familiar to me, but occasionally I adopt another."

She fluttered closer, her hips swaying the way I remembered her, elegant and graceful in her beautiful gowns.

"I wish I could hug you," I said.

Her shadow leaned close, stirring the air by my cheek. Her presence was warm, not cold, which surprised me.

"You do hug me."

Her voice was a whisper of sound.

"I feel your affection and fear. Go now, *mon cher pépin*. We will speak again."

She'd said the last bit so quietly that I wasn't sure I heard it with my ears.

"*Au revoir.*" I kissed the air by her face.

She turned until I could see the glowing orbs of her eyes.

Julia said, "You're terrifying and beautiful."

"As are you."

Before we could answer, she spun and was gone. I wasn't certain if she'd left the room or was hidden in the darkest corners.

We let ourselves out.

Chapter 2

"I was getting worried. What took so long?" Ryu asked as we got into the car.

I said, "A friend I hadn't seen in ages."

"Is she though?" Julia whispered.

"I have no reason to believe otherwise. She was always kind even to those who were less than kind to her. I admired her greatly. She was everything I aspired to be, strong, independent, highly educated, well read, beautiful... my heart was broken when she left and not just because she left but because that was the moment that I was certain that my parents didn't care a whit for me."

Ryu said, "Parents... who needs *'em*! I did better without the bitch."

Julia said to me, "I don't think you can blame your mother. Your father was certainly controlling her."

"I suppose not..."

"You didn't ask about Violet."

"I'm not certain I want to know.... Delphine said my father died soon after me. She didn't say who inherited..."

"We could go back and ask..."

"We could but we shouldn't. At least not yet. I think we should read her books and think on it a while. I'm not sure I want to know. Violet was beautiful and sweet. I can't imagine how horrible it would have been for her to suddenly have him in her head."

"Dear god."

Julia's voice shook with loathing.

"Thank god it didn't happen to you!"

"But it did happen to Lou. I saw that child being abused and did nothing…"

"You were dead! What we're you supposed to do?"

"What the hell do you mean he was dead?" Ryu asked.

His tone was caught between worry and disbelief as if he couldn't decide if it was a figure of speech, a joke, or a horrible truth.

I laid my hand lightly across Julia's mouth.

"Mayhap 'tis time to tell him some truth?"

She shook her head.

I said, "How then can he protect himself?"

"He'll freak."

"I'm right fucking here! What the fuck are you talking about? You been smoking or some shit? Vampires, dead… what the fucking hell?"

"See!" Julia said.

I said, "Ryu, if someone told you that vampires were real and there were other things, scary things, roaming around and they could prove it, would you want to know?"

Julia said hastily, "Before you answer, would you want to know if you also knew you didn't know everything. That you'd never know everything?"

He pulled to the side of the road and turned to stare at us.

"Are… you a vampire?"

Julia said, "I think it's a mistake to tell him, Pip. We can't tell him everything. He's bound to worry about it. It might worry him so much that he does something that we'd have to do something about."

"Ryu wouldn't turn us in. Not that there's anyone to turn us in to. But he isn't a rat."

Julia giggled. "You're getting better at slang all the time. No. He isn't a rat, but he *does* feel obligated to his crew."

Ryu's eyes narrowed and I could practically hear him wondering if I planned to drink their blood.

I clasped her hand as I said, "Isn't he more to us than he was?"

"I guess," Julia said unhappily.

"I think he deserves a choice. He can choose freedom."

"You like him more than you should," she said.

That was true and made me flush.

I said defensively, "He's done evil, but haven't we? Had he more or less choice than we? How then should we continue to use him when our need is no longer urgent? 'Twas one thing to take him so unwillingly when we knew no better, but now…"

"Don't kid yourself, Pip. You want to tell him because you like him. It hasn't a thing to do with right or wrong."

Ryu snapped, "Somebody better fucking tell me or I'm outa here! What the fuck do you mean unwillingly?"

I met his eyes squarely. "You know exactly what I mean if you stop lying to yourself."

We stared at each other for a minute before he nodded slowly. "I seen some shit…"

He turned back and began to drive again.

"So, you gonna tell me, or what?"

"There isn't much to actually tell that you haven't deduced already. I'm not a vampire but I'm not of this realm either. My kind isn't native to the realm of man. I believe we're very rare here, but I could be mistaken."

"So what are you then? Like a demon or something?"

"No. Demons are from a different realm."

Julia said, "Actually we have no proof of anything. We can only speak factually about what we can do or have seen. The rest is things we were told. For all we know, it's all a pack of lies."

"So what are you then?"

I said, "A seethe, a creature that survives on the anger of others."

Julia said, "We can eat any strong emotion. But, yeah, it's mostly anger because there's lots of angry assholes out there."

Ryu huffed a sharp bark of laughter.

I said, "We can use a person's anger to control them, and if they're angry enough they won't even remember we did it. People who've murdered develop a sort of rind around them that makes them very easy for us to manipulate."

"So you've been doing that to me...."

"No. Or at least not often and mostly not on purpose. Your rind is growing thinner. I used it when I was injured to heal myself. I might have murdered you. I *would* have if you hadn't had that rind..."

Julia said, "Please stop beating yourself up over that, Pip. You didn't hurt him."

Ryu eyed me in the rearview mirror with deep displeasure. "You'd have murdered me..."

Julia said, "No, she wouldn't. She might have killed you, but it wouldn't have been murder."

"Gee, that's so reassuring. And what do you mean—she?"

"Pip is a woman."

I said, "I'm a man now. Let's not confuse things. I wouldn't have purposefully harmed you, or maybe I would have. I was scared and wanted to live. I ate your anima before I could stop myself. I didn't plan it and I stopped as soon as I could, but I had wanted someone—anyone—to come within reach. I think I'd have eaten anyone. Maybe even you, Jewels."

"Whoa, whoa, whoa, let's go back to Pip being a woman."

16

Julia said, "She was a human woman whose father was a seethe. She didn't intend to come back but she was there as a sort of ghost when Lou tried to murder me, so she possessed him to stop him and now she owns that body."

"That is... are you for real with all this? I mean, I know you have some serious mojo. I seen you spoof your way into places and shit, but this..."

"We're for real," I said dryly.

Julia said, "Our only proof would be seeing it—but that wouldn't actually prove anything because we could make you *think* you'd seen anything we wanted."

"Maybe we could get him an amulet," I said thoughtfully.

Julia pursed her lips.

I said, "I want to get him one that will protect his anima just in case I'm injured again."

"He has extra."

"I know we picked him because we thought he was expendable, but he isn't. I'm sorry, Jewels, I know it makes things difficult, but he isn't!"

"I sure as shit ain't! You can't just eat me if you get a little peckish!"

Julia said, "We can find another, but you have to stop... liking them!"

Ryu glared in the rearview mirror at Julia. "So let me get this straight, you're picking us not to help us or even give us a chance but to fucking eat us?"

"Don't act like you're all innocent. I know you aren't! You've murdered more than one person! It's your own evil deeds that let us control you!"

"He has a right to be angry, Jewels."

"This is exactly why I didn't want to tell him! Of course he's angry about it! Anyone would be. He's not going to be okay with us using his buddies, no matter how evil they are!"

17

"They ain't evil, lady, you are!"

I said, "Most of them aren't. They might fight or steal but they don't take pleasure in it. But some of them enjoy hurting others. Some of your friends are very dangerous and they like it. They look forward to murder."

"You mean Birdie."

"And Bent."

You're nuts! Bent's just bored. He likes the nightlife. He'd ain't no pussy but he ain't no murderer neither! He's kilt but just those who had it coming. In our world, you know when you crossed a line and the price you pay when you cross it. It ain't murder, it's the law of fucking nature!"

Julia said, "Bent's a rapist who likes watching the girl be killed. Just because he doesn't do it himself doesn't mean he isn't responsible. He might get Smalls to gut the women, but he gets off on it!"

"No fucking way!"

Julia sighed hard. "They can't fucking lie to me, dumbass! I ask them and they answer. I can give you a list of names, but do you really need it? You're going to sit there and tell me you had no idea that the two of them would slip away for a bit of mayhem?"

Ryu said slowly, "I know they're pals and neither had any respect for women, but I never saw them do anything. It was all talk..."

"It was more than talk. They both make my skin crawl." She turned to glare at me. "It's why we shouldn't feel at all bad about using them! That anima rind is anima stolen from their victims! Using it helps us and it helps keep them from making more victims! If we kill them using it, it's more than they deserve!"

Ryu said, "We—my crew—wouldn't put up with that shit. We're not fucking animals. If we knew he was killing his ho's, we'd have taken care of it."

"We're taking care of it," Julia said firmly.

She was angry enough to make the air by her mouth sparkle as she spoke.

I said firmly, "We have no intention of murdering anyone."

Julia grimaced at me, glaring at the back of Ryu's head.

I continued, "We're careful to eat only what we need, but accidents *could* happen."

Ryu said, "What happens when you've eaten all of the extra anima or whatever it is?"

"We don't know. I don't think anything because we've eaten the anima of people who have no rind and they didn't seem to have any ill effects. We're trying to eat them slowly enough that they'll be ready to leave."

Julia shook her head. "Bent will never be able to leave. I couldn't take the chance our control wears off. We'll have to deal with him."

Ryu flicked me a glance in the rearview mirror.

"You mean kill him."

Julia said, "Or have him turn himself in. Or are you saying he should get off scot-free for murdering five women and raping eighteen? Eighteen women, Ryu! Most of them were barely women at all. You can call it date rape or whatever you want but he wanted to hurt them, to humiliate them, to leave them terrified of him and he did. That isn't okay! I'm not just going to let him waltz away! It pisses me off that we're so nice to him... He might get all of the shit jobs, but he deserves them!"

I said, "I agree, Jewels, but they *are* his friends. He's bound to see it differently than us."

"Which is why we should make him forget this entire conversation!"

"I—he isn't like them. If we make him forget, then we need to find him a new place to work, one where no one knows he was ever connected with us."

"So you *do* think Delphine is dangerous!" Julia said triumphantly.

"Of course she is! But I wasn't thinking of her in particular. I don't think she's dangerous to me, except that our acquaintance could draw others. I trust her, Jewels. I don't trust what other creatures of the night might do."

Ryu's eyes widened and his voice trembled when he said, "We really just visited a vampire? I feel like I've been drinking or some shit. This whole conversation is surreal."

I said, "It isn't just for his benefit but for ours too. He'd be much better equipped to guard us and the house if he knows what he supposed to be watching for."

"What am I watching for?"

"I don't know because I know almost nothing about the creatures from the other realms, but if you saw something odd, you'd at least know enough not to ignore it."

He said, "Should we stop and get some holy water or some shit?"

Julia said, "I doubt it would work. We don't know what would work. We've been told light will work on a vampire but they're unbelievably fast."

I said, "They might be able to use knives or guns. They can pass through walls, which is why we put lights in the walls of our home."

"Couldn't they just flip the switch and turn them off?"

"Yes, which is why our lights work independently with no switch. They come on automatically and have backup batteries."

"I'll never be able to enter a dark room again..."

To my surprise Julia laughed.

"Me too. I put a LED under my bed even when I have a light on in the room."

He said, "But you can make amulets to repel them?"

I said, "I have no idea. We know a professed mage. I saw a few magic spells work, so it's probable that others would."

"Magic as in real magic?" Ryu asked doubtfully.

Julia said, "The mage became invisible, but it's possible it was a mind trick like we do."

I said, "Finding those pictures was no mind trick. That spell definitely worked."

Julia shrugged at me. "I'm just saying that we don't really know how magic works. The mage said they'd show us and warned us that we might not be able to use mana, which is what she claimed to use to cast spells. Not all creatures use the same thing to power their spells and even the same types of creatures sometimes never learn to do it."

"Will you show me too?"

I said, "Yes, but it has to be kept secret."

Julia said, "And we'd know if you tell. We'll know if you lie to us."

"Would you let me go if I asked?" he asked with obviously forced casualness.

I said, "Yes, but we'd have to make you forget this conversation."

"Damned if I do, damned if I don't..."

We were all silent until the lights of Paris appeared in the distance.

He said, "This is crazy as shit! I shouldn't believe a word of it, should I? I should get on the next plane home and never look back. You all be crazy mother fuckers—but I don't want you snacking on my crew neither..."

Julia said, "You make it sound like we eat them. We eat their rage. They never even notice it."

"But you're making them stay there to be your tasty little pick me ups."

"As opposed to turning them into the police for the crimes we know they've committed?"

I patted Julia's hand. "'Tis unfair but life oft is. We need the anima, but we do our best to let them retain what freewill we can while still keeping them as law abiding as we can."

Julia said, "Consider them in our jail—a prison of their own making."

I said firmly, "One we hope will rehabilitate them into productive members of society."

"As your fucking slaves," he muttered.

Julia snorted. "I suppose it could be considered slavery but what would you do if you were me?"

He didn't speak until he parked at our hotel.

"I'd probably do a lot worse," he admitted.

She said, "You can't mention this or anything that we tell you to anyone. And I mean anyone! I'll be checking, Ryu, and there won't be a second chance if you break your word to us."

"I'm going to want a bigger paycheck..."

To my surprise Julia laughed. "We already pay you too much, but I wouldn't be opposed to you riding our investment coattails as it were. What you need is starting capitol." She shot me an anxious glance.

"I think I have a good way to get some but you're not going to like it."

Chapter 3

We exited the car in the hotel garage.

Julia said to Ryu, "Bring the sweeper to our room and we can talk there, or you can head home and get your things together. Don't try to disappear on us. We have ways of finding things."

"There's no need to threaten him," I said. "He's smart enough to see it's in all of our best interest to work together. If you need some time to think things through, go home and take a few days. But please don't talk to anyone because we *will* know it and we'll be forced to take action."

"I'm not sure I believe all this shit, but if it's for real, I want to know what's what. I'll get the gear and be up in a few."

Julia and I headed to our room without speaking. I knew she was annoyed and likely marshaling her arguments like I was mine.

She surprised me again by saying, "Order us room service, Pip. I'm going to take a quick shower. I stink of sweat. She scared me half to death. I don't know how you're so calm about her."

She kicked off her shoes and began undressing.

I headed to the table beside the window to use the hotel phone, stopping to check that our alarm hadn't been touched. It was exactly where we'd left it.

I said, "You wouldn't have been as scared if you knew her like I do. I was scared, don't think I wasn't, but not really of her. She has absolutely no motive to want to hurt me."

Julia went into the bathroom and closed the door.

I ordered room service for three, steak dinners, an assortment of pastries, a bottle of wine for Julia, a pot of tea for me, and three bottles of beer for Ryu.

Ryu knocked before Julia was out of the shower.

I let him in, and he swept the room for bugs.

"It's clear. Nothing is transmitting but that doesn't mean there aren't passive receivers."

"No one came inside." I picked up the small gold owl that housed the alarm. "If it's moved, the color inside the eyes changes, which means if someone turned off the alarm, we'd know they picked it up."

He rolled his eyes at me, saying, "Or they picked it up and set it down again until the color matched."

"Not likely because it would turn back on after it's set down again, and if you turn it off three times in a row without letting it dial through, the eyes turn black.

"Then why am I sweeping again?" Ryu asked.

"Because Julia is paranoid."

"Not paranoid, prudent," she said as she stepped from the bathroom wearing a silk robe and toweling her hair.

"Close the blinds and turn some music on."

I hung up my jacket and removed my tie while Ryu did as she bid.

She said, "I know you want to believe Delphine is your friend, and maybe she is, but we have no idea what motivates her. It's been hundreds of years, Pip. Just please keep an open mind and try to see her without the bias of past friendship. I'm not saying she means us harm, but I do think she has an agenda besides getting reacquainted. The risk of contacting you—a seethe—is pretty high if the mage is to be believed. Delphine might remember you fondly, but how could she count on you remembering her the same way?"

"True…"

Julia gave me a quick hug.

Ryu said, "You knew the vampire before you became this seethe thing?"

"She was a human woman," Julia said.

"Humans can become vampires," he said thoughtfully.

Julia shook her head. "Delphine's father was a seethe. Vampire is just a name but it's misleading. They drink blood but they're a lot different than Dracula."

"Not really," I disagreed. "It's possible a really old one could go into a candlelit room. Or maybe there's spells that could let them enter a lighted room. They move so quickly that they could be mistaken for bats. And mirrors wouldn't reflect them if they were just shadow."

Julia sat at the small table to brush her hair.

I could tell by her expression that she disagreed with me.

She said, "You really think that was a true story?"

"I have no idea. I was just pointing out that the popular myths could be applied to Delphine."

Julia said, "First thing tomorrow we're going out to buy silver crosses and find someone to make us silver bullets and then we're stocking up on holy water. No offense or anything, Pip, but I want water from a real priest."

"None taken. I'd prefer the water be blessed by a priest as well. I think we should make a trip to Lourdes and maybe Rome."

"Will a cross work?" Ryu asked.

"It can't hurt," Julia said as I shook my head.

"'Tisn't for vampires but demons."

Ryu closed his eyes, pinching the bridge of his nose and nodding. "Of course, demons... You've run into a few of those, have you?"

"Just one and that was more than enough."

Julia said, "She chased it away by her faith..."

"I don't think I had a thing to do with it," I disagreed.

Ryu gaped.

Julia shook her head. "It felt your faith, Pip. Maybe that held it at bay and maybe not, but it for sure felt it. We're testing everyone when we get home."

I said, "More than that. We're insisting on regular church attendance."

"I doubt that would work unless we really forced them," Julia said. "And do we have the right to force them to be religious?"

"'Tis our duty to see that all in our charge are afforded the light of God's grace. How then shall they learn of him if not through priestly ministrations?"

Ryu said, "Can we get back to the demon for a minute? You really saw one? How did you know it was one?"

Julia snorted, "Horns, a tail, eyes that could make you piss yourself, you know, the usual stuff."

"But... that's impossible!"

She'd paled despite her flippant tone and was rubbing her arms.

I hated that I'd brought her to that place as it would assuredly give her nightmares too.

She said to him, "I assure you, it was all too real."

I said thoughtfully, "Perhaps we see them because of what we are?"

"I hate that idea," Julia said. "Unfortunately, I think it might be right. Because I'm sure Pete isn't the only demon-possessed human to be shot, and that's the sort of thing that would get talked about."

Ryu said suspiciously, "So you're saying I won't be able to see them?"

"Since we don't know how or why it manifested, I couldn't really say. Maybe it showed itself because it knew what I was? Maybe they always show when not possessing a host? 'Tisn't something I know much of."

Julia said, "The mage might be able to make us an amulet to see them. She did say she could give us one to see hidden things."

He said, "The mage… do you not know his name, or you just don't want me to know it?"

A knock on the door interrupted us.

Ryu answered it and let in the waiter with our dinner. The two of them set the plates on the table and then Ryu tipped the man and escorted him out.

I said, "You're really getting very good at that."

He huffed in annoyance.

Julia heaved an unhappy sigh.

"I suppose we'll need to break someone else in now that we're making you a partner of sorts…."

"And good help is so hard to find," Ryu said sarcastically.

I said, "Please, let's eat before it gets cold."

I poured their drinks and my own before resuming my seat.

Julia said, "The mage is the mage to you until we get permission for us to tell the name. It isn't someone we want to anger. I haven't decided yet—we haven't decided yet, if we're even going to tell it we've told you a thing."

I said, "We don't want her to think we're plotting behind her back. I think we should tell her that we're training one human, but we'll leave him unnamed unless she insists."

"And if *she* insists you kill me to keep me quiet?"

"She won't," I said assuredly.

Julia nodded as she stabbed her steak more forcefully than necessary and cut off a hunk.

Ryu eyed her uneasily.

She ate two pieces before pointing the knife at Ryu, saying, "She won't unless she wants a war with us"— she glared at me, tapping my steak with her knife for emphasis as she continued, "But if she asks us to tell him nothing that she tells or shows us, we'll agree!"

"Agreed. I don't wish to fight with her. There's no need for us to fight."

Julia huffed, chewing angrily for a few minutes.

Ryu and I ate quietly.

Julia finally said, "That's a naïve outlook that you need to get over. Just because there's no obvious reason doesn't mean people will act sensibly. We haven't a clue what motivates any of these people, but greed motivates everyone and what we can do is worth more than money. Even good people would be tempted to manipulate us so that we had to work for them. If people learn that you have real affection for Ryu or anyone else, it would put them at risk."

"I suppose you're right," I agreed unhappily.

My eyes burned with unshed tears. I was suddenly no longer hungry.

Julia reached across the table to pat my hand.

"It doesn't mean you can't be friends, Pip. It just means you need to be careful that others perceive it as a business relationship." She pointed her fork at Ryu. "You need to keep looking businesslike when in public. You can be friendly but not familiar and that's for your protection!"

"Yes, ma'am."

She nodded and cut into her steak more calmly.

Ryu cleared his throat, darting me nervous glances while he ate.

I pushed the food around my plate for a few minutes while they ate.

Julia said, "I'm sorry, Pip. I really am, but until you have a large enough group of friends that it would be difficult for someone to single out one in particular then you need to be careful. Ryu doesn't have the skills we do to get himself out of trouble. If Hugh took it into his head to kidnap him, he could seriously hurt him, maybe even kill him before we could find him to get him back. There's a lot of money at stake and people will do awful things for money."

"I ain't helpless," Ryu said angrily.

"Compared to us you are. But it doesn't matter anyway because I'm not worried about you, I'm worried about her. She'll feel horrible if she got you hurt."

He snorted softly. "That's a hard bit to get my head around. I don't know why when I know some other transvestites and shit but… maybe it's because you didn't choose it. I'd fucking hate that! I'd freak if I was suddenly a chick!"

"Me too," Julia said as she patted my hand again. "I'm growing accustomed to the idea, but it isn't something I want right now. Maybe someday though…. It's just such a huge change in how I thought that it's going to take time to really accept it and I'm sure it's the same for you. Then, when you add in all the stuff you were taught was sinful, I'm sure it will take a while to adapt."

"How old are you?" Ryu asked.

"Nineteen or three hundred and thirty-five depending on how you want to look at it.

"Let's not talk about that now," Julia said hurriedly, giving Ryu a glance that said shut up.

I said, "'Tis true that I dislike recalling those years. I wasn't a ghost in the usual sense that I roamed the house. I was trapped in the one room. I knew I was dead. I remember my murder quite vividly…"

"We aren't speaking of it!" Julia glared at Ryu who held up both hands and nodded.

I said, "'Tis natural for him to be curious. But, no, I don't think I'm yet ready to recall the details to another."

"So your memory loss is only partially true. You remember your life but not his?"

Julia nodded. "Correct. Which is why she needs us."

"I'm getting much better at doing for myself."

"You are."

Her smile was real. I could no longer see the anima of anger around her, which eased the tightness in my shoulders and the lump in my throat enough for me to regain my appetite. I began to eat.

She continued, "Pip is a fast learner. She can show you what we've learned about our condition but make no notes on it or anything else we talk about."

"Including any investments?"

"No. Every investment we make will be completely legal. You can keep track of that openly. What you can't keep track of is how we get the information. Which leads me back to the idea that you're really not going to like but just hear me out with an open mind."

I nodded and she took a deep breath.

"I've been thinking about how Reginald planned to get his hands on Fischer's money. When accounts are unclaimed, they go through a process called escheated. The bank sometimes hires lawyers to find the account holders, which is where Reginald comes in. It's his job to ensure that the bank is meeting all legal guidelines in the movement and use of that money. He can recommend it be moved to other banks, invested, or handed over to the account beneficiary. For an account the size of Fischer's, we're talking a lot of money in interest if he can divert it for even a short period of time.

"Which got me thinking, there's probably a lot of these unclaimed funds. If we had someone on the inside telling us who had no beneficiary on the account, we could speak with them and get them to make us their beneficiary just like we did for Fischer."

"By someone you mean Reginald?"

She flushed, nodding as she said, "He obviously has a way to find out the information we need."

Ryu said, "Wait, you mean work with the guy we were going to kill two days ago? The brother who wants to murder you? Are you crazy?"

"What's the risk? We know he's willing to steal and maybe this gets him off my back."

"That's…" Ryu sputtered to a halt obviously at a loss for words. I nodded at him. "'Tis crazy," I agreed.

She said, "In a way, but like I said, what do we have to lose? I'll ask him to recommend another big fish, and we can split the money. I'll get half sent wherever he wants it and the other half to our charity."

"If we do that too often 'twould be suspicious," I said.

"I agree. But I was thinking maybe we've got another avenue. A more modest amount could be left directly to Ryu. Who would question an aunt leaving money to a nephew she never met if he was the only family she had? If we pick carefully, we should be able to find someone with a few hundred grand with no heirs and no one close enough in relationship to contest the will. I can't imagine it would be too difficult to find a lawyer we could use; one we could force to write up any legal document we wanted so that we cover Ryu's ass so he can keep the money even if he's proven not to be a blood relative."

"Information you plan to get from Reginald?"

She nodded.

"No. We don't give him the slightest bit of leverage on us. We'll find another lawyer to ask for any contracts we might need. If we do this, Reginald only knows he supplies us information."

Ryu said, "So he's just going to hand over his marks just like that?" He shook his head. "Man, you broads don't know dick about men, pardon my French, but there ain't no way he's going to forgive that ass whipping we gave him."

"We didn't lay a finger on him," Julia said indignantly.

"You fucking slapped him down hard. He ain't going to just forget it. He'll be looking to even things up and his way of doing that is going to be gloating over your corpse."

"I wouldn't be easy to kill."

Ryu snorted.

"He almost killed Lou without half trying!"

"Don't call me that," I said irritably. "I'm not Lou! Call me Philip if you can't call me Pip."

Julia squeezed my hand, glaring at Ryu. "Don't call him that again. Lou was vile! It sickens me to think I ever said a kind word to him. It'd be like me calling you Hitler!"

"Jeez, fine. Sorry man, but you're losing the thread of this here conversation. Your brother is a no-good piece of shit. He's probably a pedophile himself! But even if he isn't, we know he's a blackmailer, a thief, and an attempted murderer of his own damned sister! It's crazy to do any business with him at all, never mind crooked business."

"I agree."

Julia pulled her hand away to cross her arms.

I continued, "But he does have information we could use. And if we piss him off enough, we might be able to use him without him realizing we are."

"Now you're talking," Julia said happily.

"'Twill need to be done carefully."

She nodded, growing thoughtful. "Ryu, text me everything you know about your family. If we play this right, we can have the money bounced to you through a legitimate connection. Is all we need is a distant relative on death's door. We have our mark leave them the money and they leave it to Ryu."

I said, "That sounds complicated to me, but you're the boss of finance."

"Fischer left his money to you outright. We can do that again but that will take time to set up. Meanwhile, we could use some donations for the work study program. How opposed would you be to giving Reg a spot on that board?"

"Why? 'Tis a needless risk!"

"Because as Ryu said, we know he's a thief. But he's a smart one. He'll know the best way to set it up so the money stays looking squeaky clean."

Ryu said, "It would be dumb to rely on him. He'll stab you in the back the first chance he gets."

"Then we hire a team of lawyers. It will probably take a team of them anyway to get this on its feet."

"Why are you so determined to use him?"

"Because maybe it's a way to reach him."

Her bleak tone made my eyes fill with tears again.

"Oh..."

She continued, "I have no illusions about him. What he did and planned to do is despicable. I don't want to reach him for myself, but my parents love him. If they see the tension between us... I just don't want them to ever know. They don't deserve that! If giving Reg a hand robbing accounts with no owners is what it takes to keep my parents happy then so be it. We need money, he needs money, and it keeps them happy while hopefully changing Reg's mind about killing any of us. I get it's a risk, but we'll be super careful using any information he passes to us."

Ryu said, "You better be super careful about any meeting you have with him."

He slid his empty plate to the side, staring down into his beer as he said, "All of this mumbo jumbo bullshit isn't at all believable unless you see it too many times to discount it. You keep showing him you can do shit, he's going to start looking for answers. And if he does that, he might find out how to really kill your ass, or worse, how to use you. I'm—conflicted, I guess you could say, about working with ya. You seem like nice chicks, not evil or nothing. A little scary, a lot naïve, but for the most part okay. He's an evil fuck. If he had your power... it's just dumb to give him any ideas, and he's going to be getting ideas when he sees what you can pull off."

"'Tis true."

"Yeah. I thought about that and think I have a plan."

Her tone told me that I'd like this plan no better than the last.

Ryu caught my eye, and I knew he thought she was as crazy as I did but we'd both support her anyway, and despite myself, I smiled. It was nice to have a friend.

"Let's hear it," he said, giving me another laughing glance as he sipped his beer.

"It could hardly be worse than the last one," I said, making him snicker and her glare.

But there was no anger in the glare. She was amused. Her small smile at Ryu when she lifted her glass to sip eased my heart. She needed a friend too. We both trusted him despite or maybe because of how he'd lived his life.

She said, "The easiest thing to do is make him think what he'll think anyway, that our work study program is a front to use street thugs to terrorize our marks into signing."

"That could work," Ryu said thoughtfully.

I said, "It doesn't anger you that your friends will be perceived as thugs?"

"Nah, it's good street cred. They wouldn't mind it. It might bring some blowback from others wanting a cut, but that's the game."

Julia said, "We could take care of anyone who tries to pressure you."

He nodded complacently.

I said, "We'll be partners then."

Julia shook her head. "He's a junior partner right now. He still works for us but maybe someday he gets veto power."

Ryu grinned. "Good enough—for now," he said.

Chapter 4

"So, what's the plan?" Ryu asked.

Julia said, "Pip and I will probably be able to sleep tonight but maybe not. We might sleep a few days and you won't be able to wake us. If that happens keep anyone else from entering our room."

"You sleep like vampires?"

I shook my head. "We sleep like normal most of the time, but if we've eaten too much anima we can't sleep and then when we do sleep we can't be woken. We both ate a lot with Reginald. I'm not at all tired so I'll probably stay up studying again."

Julia said, "We try to stagger when we sleep so one of us is awake."

"So is all I need to do is make sure no one sees you?"

Julia said, "That and try to make anyone who's looking for us think we're awake somewhere. I'll send you some sound files that you can use, things like me or Pip saying I can't talk now or tell him to call me back. If you tell someone anything specific then text us so we all tell the same lie if asked."

He nodded.

"You eat food, but do you need to drink blood too?"

"No."

Julia said, "Not so far anyway."

"Seems simple enough," Ryu said, and I could tell he was relieved.

I said, "We wouldn't drink your blood."

"At least not without your permission," Julia agreed. "We need to trust you and you us."

I said more to Julia than Ryu, "We can't always control what we do, but if we *do* accidentally eat your anima, we'll tell you we did."

She nodded.

He eyed her doubtfully but nodded too.

She said, "I'm not sure if we should head to Lourdes now or wait until we've slept."

I said, "Perhaps the morning? Ryu will need sleep even if we don't."

"Our passports should be here by nine a.m., assuming the courier isn't held up. I'll make reservations for a noon flight."

She stood and headed to the bedroom, saying over her shoulder, "I'll call Reg and feel him out too."

Ryu waited for the door of the bedroom to close to say, "He's going to be a problem."

"I know."

"Can you, *um*, nudge her a little?"

I shook my head. "I wouldn't even if I could. She'll listen though if I ask her."

"She's listening but she's only hearing what she wants to."

"Would you not do the same for your brother?"

"I suppose… or maybe not. I mean if he was trying to kill me, I think all bets would be off."

"What bets?"

He laughed, shaking his head as he opened another bottle of beer. "It's just an expression. It means all deals are canceled. So how did you get this Fischer guy to leave you his money, and how much did he leave you?"

"We asked him. He left me a little over eight million."

Ryu whistled softly.

"Honestly, I don't think it would have worked if he really cared who got his money. We didn't have much of a hold on him at all. I think he was a lonely old man who wanted friends. He'd made his fortune by designing a can opener. He called himself a beer and potatoes guy... I think he was amused to help an earl.... I liked him...."

He leaned closer, lowering his voice to ask, "Did she kill him?"

"Of course not! I think Reginald did, or rather, had it done. He has no extra anima."

"If you could find another rich man, one who did have extra anima, you could just order him to change his will..." he said, sounding impressed.

"Yes. She was looking. But having them change it is the easy part. Having it stick would be tricky if they had heirs."

"Couldn't you have him give you the dough while he was still alive?"

"Yes, but Julia assures me large exchanges of money are monitored by the money police."

He snickered. "They aren't really police but she's right, we don't want to draw attention from HMRC. So Reginald would actually be useful—or someone like him. How did you find Fischer?

"By accident. Lou was planning to steal some of his money for some sort of investment scheme he does with a few friends—that Shipley crew, but he stole it all, which, as you can imagine, made them quite angry. We aren't certain what if anything they'll do about it. It wasn't until just a few days ago we learned he'd stolen it for Reginald."

"Lou had his finger in all sorts of pies," Ryu said thoughtfully.

38

I nodded agreement. "It worries me what else he might be involved in. He was a very bad man."

"And you're just a girl…"

"I'm not *just* anything!"

"I didn't mean it like that. I meant you're even more, *um*, inexperienced than I thought. Men treat women differently and you look like a man. A grown man, not a kid. They'll assume you'd know shit and act like a man would."

"It hasn't been difficult to fake."

He snorted. "Because Julia is running interference for you. Have you used a public restroom yet or been told off by a stranger?"

"I… no. I could handle it though."

"If you say so," he said doubtfully.

Chapter 5

Julia had wasted no time setting up a meeting with her brother. He showed up promptly at nine the next morning.

"You summoned me?" Reginald asked angrily when I opened the door.

His anger was visible around him in a light mist of sparkling red motes.

Julia said, "Don't be such a dick. I asked you to come because I think we could help each other."

He snorted and stomped inside, glaring at Julia as he said, "You're a fool to trust him. You know that, right?"

She rolled her eyes. "Like you're one to talk!"

"He doesn't love you. No matter what he says! He's fucking gay!"

Julia shrugged. "Maybe he was but he isn't anymore."

Reginald spun to face me. "So that's it, *huh*? You were lying to me the entire time just like you're lying to her now!"

He slapped me and spun back to face Julia who'd jumped to her feet.

"He doesn't love you! He isn't capable of love! I wish to God I'd never met him! This entire thing was his idea!"

"Would you just shut up about it already!"

"Look at you! Look at what you're willing to do for him! I don't know how he does it, I really don't, but he'll talk you into shit that you didn't think you'd do in a million years. He's poison, Jewels."

"You don't get to call me that anymore!"

He turned away from her.

I was surprised to see tears in his eyes.

Anger flared from him in a cloud of anima when he caught me looking.

"You're such a fucking liar! I should've known better. I really should've! But I thought that despite all your lies that *we* were real, but you were playing me just like you're playing her and everyone else."

"You loved me?" I asked shocked he'd admit such a thing.

He growled a wordless angry sound and stomped to the window.

Julia said softly, "He isn't faking the amnesia, Reg."

I pulled her back when she stepped forward, shaking my head at her. I wasn't convinced this was a real declaration or not, and I didn't really care. I knew he'd kill her and likely me if he had the chance.

He spoke without turning around, "That's such bullshit!"

"I had no idea you were gay," Julia said mildly.

Anima surrounded him so thickly it obscured him for a moment, but his tone and expression were calm when he turned to face us.

"You always win, don't you? It should've been impossible for you to steal him, but you managed it. What I don't get though is why you're with him when you saw the kind of man he was!"

"Why were you!" she yelled, staggering back as her anima collided with his.

He yelled back, "Because I loved him. He told me just like he told you. He asked me for help...begged me! He probably told you the same fucking sob story that he told me about how his dad would abuse him, how his mother ignored his pleas for help and covered up everything. He showed me the room in the basement, said he was fucking forced to do it or be disowned—murdered—and I told him to just leave but he was scared to death of his old man. So we made a plan to kill the fucker!"

"You killed my father?"

He turned from her to sneer at me.

"*We* killed him."

"So why kill Julia? Why involve her at all?"

A dark red flush climbed across his cheeks.

Julia yelled, "Why, you motherfucker!"

I wasn't certain if she'd compelled him or if he was lying when he shouted back, "Because I fucking loved him, and he loves his goddamned house! And, yeah, a big part of me wanted him to prove he loved me too. He could have everything with you and we both knew it. If he was willing to kill you, it would've proved he really loved me!"

His hands clenched into fists as he glared at me.

"But you want it all, right? The house and all of my parents' money! You convince her that it was all my idea and talk her into murdering me? Is that the plan?"

Julia said, "You are so full of shit! You were blackmailing him!"

"Only after he pretended not to know me..."

"So you were going to what, force him to kill me and let him keep on raping little kids? That's fucking pathetic!"

"We had a plan to cover his tracks. And, yeah, I wanted him to fucking kill you! Why should you get everything! I'm so damned tired of you..."

"Not as tired as I am of you! You've always been such a fucking baby. Mum and Dad gave you anything you asked for."

He stepped forward to glare in her face, saying, "You never saw it! You just think you shit rainbows and sunshine because everyone kisses your ass! I've had to work for everything I ever got, including respect from our father! You studied nothing and he was oh so proud. He bought you your fucking apartment, but me—I get top marks in fucking law school and got a fucking lecture on getting married! When am I going to settled down and grow up! When am I going to give him fucking grandkids? How come I can't be more like my sister and get involved with the community, give a little something back. It was always the same damned thing! Nothing I did could ever measure up to wonderful, glorious Julia!"

"You are so deluded..."

"Ha! You never fooled me! Never! I knew all that charity work was a crock of shit! Granted, I didn't know how big of one, but the only deluded were our parents! They'd despise you if they knew what a money grabbing whore you are!"

Julia paled then flushed as red as her brother.

"Enough!" I yelled. "She invited you here in an attempt to make amends. I'm sorry I was such a blackhearted scoundrel with you. I'm sure I was one with her too. I'm trying to do better. She's trying... if you want no part of us, or our work study program—"

He interrupted me with a harsh laugh, saying, "You mean your front for robbing more old men!"

Julia snapped, "It isn't robbery if they agree to it!"

"Stop!" I yelled again. "Let's not quibble over words. He's right that we plan to use him to find potential donors and that isn't strictly legal."

Reginald snorted.

I said, "We're all crooks here but we could be—ethical ones."

He snorted again.

The anima swirling around him dissipated, absorbing back into him.

Julia said, "Just so we're clear, this wasn't Pip's idea."

"Pip…"

The word sparkled with anger.

Julia said, "We aren't giving that money back, not that it was yours to begin with, but we *would* pay a percent for anyone you send our way that we ended up using. I'd be willing to make you an equal partner, on the books at least, for the work study project if you wanted to make our father happy. Or, if you wanted to start your own thing, I'd help with fundraising."

"For a cut," he said snidely.

"For expenses just like I do with all of my other projects."

"You really are a piece of work, aren't you? You've got Mum and Dad eating out of your hand, thinking you're such a goddamned saint when really it's all a front to live large on someone else's tab!"

She sighed tiredly, closing her eyes and pinching the bridge of her nose. "Think whatever you like. I never could change your mind about anything. There's one thing I still want to know though. When did you start to hate me?"

"I…."—He looked confused for a moment before his glare was firmly in place again— "since the moment you were born."

He brushed past me, hesitating the merest second, then slammed out the door.

"Well, that was unexpected," Julia said thoughtfully.

"Did you believe him?"

"I'm not sure."

"I wonder when they met?"

Julia rose an eyebrow and I continued, "Maybe Louis was a seethe and picked Reginald intending to fleece him?"

"You mean he inherited it after they killed his father?"

"If his father was a seethe and had been grooming Louis by putting his anima in him, maybe that was enough to give him some of his father's power despite how far away he was when he died?"

"That's a lot of ifs but it would explain a lot…. Maybe he was making Reg agree to his plans?"

"It's possible," I agreed reluctantly.

She said thoughtfully, "That could explain why you were able to emerge and take him."

She jumped to her feet and began to pace. "He wasn't stupid though. He'd have looked up his symptoms."

I said, "If I hadn't emerged from beyond the veil, I'd think myself quite mad."

She snorted softly, nodding agreement.

"There is that... and he was obviously weaker than you."

"Or less desperate."

"There is that," she repeated sadly.

"And who's to say he didn't look them up? Maybe he knew exactly what he was doing. 'Tis possible his father told him."

She shook her head. "I doubt that, not if he was abusing him, which I think we can safely assume he was. Talk about perpetuating the cycle of abuse!"

"I wonder how many times my father jumped..."

"No offense, Pip, but your father was an evil, evil man."

"I agree."

"Maybe we can help Reg..."

"'Tis likely beyond our power. I believe you to be one of the naturally immune or I'd have consumed you wholly on our first encounter and Lou would have no need to murder you. He could have just ordered you to do whatever he wished."

"Except that he enjoyed it," she muttered.

"Yes, but I meant, if he *was* a seethe, why become involved with you at all? 'Twould be so much simpler to have you leave all of your worldly goods to your brother and then tell you to jump from the roof."

"No, he needed us to marry to be sure he got my money. Gay marriage is legal, but Reg wasn't even out of the closet, if he really even is gay. I never saw any signs of it when we were growing up. Louis was hiding he was gay as well though..."

"Except he didn't marry you..."

She grimaced. "I wish I knew what prompted him to act that night!"

"Marriage would have been unnecessary for a seethe. If Reginald was under his control enough to agree to murder, which we know he did before the father died, then Louis could have easily made him pay for anything he wished. Mayhap he meant to jump into Reginald—or you?"

She said, "Do we know Reginald actually helped plan that murder? I could convince someone that they had."

"We have too few facts. Too much depends on why Reginald is immune to manipulation. There was enough anima present that we should have been able to make him tell us anything we wished."

"Maybe we did..."

"Perhaps... but he lacked the same submissive manner that others display. I think he said what he did by his choice, not our manipulation."

"Then Lou couldn't have forced him!"

"Could he not if he took his time and built up slowly?"

"More like brainwashing, you mean?"

I shrugged but she didn't see me. She hadn't been speaking to me either as she answered herself.

"Yeah, I can see that. Just tiny nudges here and there. Maybe Louis was only capable of small nudges, or maybe not, but if he was careful and only encouraged acts Reg was already contemplating, he could've encouraged him to deeds that my brother wouldn't otherwise have done."

"I understand why you want to believe it, and mayhap 'tis true, but Reginald has been under Louis's influence for years. The damage is done."

"But maybe we could undo it! Slowly and carefully but maybe it could be done."

46

"We'll try."

She barked a harsh laugh. "It's ironic that of all the things he's done, he hasn't actually murdered anyone, the one thing that could help him now."

Her eyes lit and she spun away.

I laid my hand on her shoulder. "'Twould be wrong to encourage him to murder when we know not what doing such would do to a human soul. To damn him to existence in that dark nothingness... that would be the evilest thing you could do to him."

Her shoulders shook with silent sobs.

I held her while she cried.

Chapter 6

Mrs. Roman greeted us at the door when we returned from Rome a week later laden with Holy relics, by saying, "Your mother is upstairs with Mrs. Alder and so excited to show you the study. I must say it's just lovely."

We hurried upstairs.

Mary greeted both Julia and I with a kiss on the cheek and led us down the hall from Julia's room where she waved us inside one of the unfinished guest rooms.

The room had been completely redone in our absence.

Sandra smiled a polite greeting as she finished placing a row of untitled books on a newly installed bookshelf. I was instantly itching to examine them.

She said, "You're mother has been charm itself helping me arrange my wedding gift to you."

Mary looked as excited as a child with a new doll as she showed us around the room, pausing in front of a set of paintings depicting herbs on either side of the on-suite bathroom, then gesturing to new wall-to-ceiling bookcases behind a small writing desk.

The shelves held my writing supplies, paper and inks, stacks of empty notebooks, paints, colored pencils, charcoals, chalks, and an assortment of canvases. The topmost shelves were full of books on botany, mineralogy, natural history and the like, all of them new to me. Plenty of space remained to add more books.

Two comfortable chairs sat in front of the room's window, which had potted plants on either side of it and a decorative metal grill. Directly across from the window was a small side-table that held a brightly lit plastic dome that on closer examination I saw was harboring seedlings. An empty art easel positioned so the painting wasn't visible from the doorway was ready for use beside it.

Mary said, "Sandra has overseen the security for this room. It can be used as a safe room too."

Sandra said, "It's intended to store your more expensive manuscripts." She lay her hand on a stack of leather-bound books on the desk. "These are from my private library. I'm having copies made for you to keep but I thought you'd like to examine the originals. They're insured, but the terms of my insurance are such that they must be housed in a secure location. I'll set the biometric lock on the door for you before I leave."

Mary said happily, "The entire room could be used as a safe."

"'Tis a beautiful room," I said.

We returned downstairs where Mrs. Roman served us lunch while we chatted about our trip and made plans to convert my study downstairs into a reading room. When Mary left, we returned to the new study where Sandra keyed the lock to us then crouched to lay her hand against the carpet.

It was clear she was doing something, but I wasn't certain what it was until the distant sound of construction cut off abruptly a moment later.

She straightened and said, "The number one rule is that my daughter never hears about this."

Julia and I nodded.

Sandra pursed her lips, tapping her manicured nails on my desktop.

"Cassandriel is young in human years but an infant for her kind. She hasn't developed the ability to cope with magic. To expose her would reveal her true form, which would kill her—and maybe us too. It would certainly cause a worldwide panic. She must never see or feel any spells."

"Understood," Julia said.

"All creatures of spirit, fire, air, and water are naturally long lived. They reproduce slowly or sometimes in ways that make the survival of their offspring nearly impossible. Most notably it's predators or the need for specific foods that kill them, but we can get more into that later.

"All such creatures also have their own weaknesses. It can be very difficult to kill one. When such a creature dies, it passes its hamingja to the nearest blood relative. A hamingja isn't a soul, or at least I don't think it is. It's the memory of a life and the natura of the creature. What you know becomes the ability of the inheritor. Your life flashes before *their* eyes. Your natura—which is your natural gifts, become theirs. We can talk more about that later as well. I have many books on the subject that you should read. For those who possess hamingja, they will share it with their true mate. Truly mated pairs die within weeks of each other."

Julia said, "How do you know if it's a true mate?"

"It varies by species. But in some cases, maybe even most cases, sexual intercourse will wed you whether you wish to be wed or not. Sex for a creature from the other realms is a much bigger deal than for a creature of earth."

"Creature of earth...like dwarves?"

"Any creature that turns to earth when it dies is a creature of earth. If you were to murder me or I you, our outer shell would shrivel very quickly or sometimes burst into flame or turn to water or just disintegrate depending on the sort of creature we are. You would become a shadowed version of yourself, what you call a vampire and I call a shadowed seethe. We'll talk more about that later after you've read my books on it.

I said, "Do we become mated if we have sex?"

"I don't believe so. I've never heard of a mated seethe. The body you're wearing is a shell that you can change. Seethe's and inou take lovers, usually many. I've met a few who loved their human spouses and maybe they do become truly mated because both did become shadowed soon after those spouses died..."

"So sex would be bad for us?" Julia asked worriedly.

"The shadowing was their choice. Or not their choice exactly, but if they'd controlled the rage, it wouldn't have happened. I know of one who ceased to exist. I know that because it's hamingja passed to its child, by its own choice. It had lost the will to live or maybe had decided to gift its child with its immortality.

"But for my kind... having sex would likely bond Cassandriel to the human and then she would die when he did. I'd like you to help me make sure that doesn't happen."

I said, "If we can't use our power on her..."

Sandra nodded. "But you could use it on any boy we thought might try to encourage her. You could use it on her guards to ensure they remain diligent. You could even use it on her dog to ensure it would raise a ruckus if someone slipped into her room. And for that help I'll teach you everything I know about seethes."

"I want to learn to cast real spells," Julia said. "What would you take in payment for that?"

"It depends on what you're willing to do. I make my money in the stock market but really, I'm a thief. My spells require materials like gems, precious metals, rare plants, and the like."

"Blood?" I asked.

"Rarely and usually my own. If you're asking if I practice dark magic then the answer is sometimes. All magic can be turned to dark endeavors. I would kill to keep myself and my daughter safe.

I *have* killed for it. My thefts depend on secrecy, so I rarely kill for them, but my wealth sometimes attracts persons with evil intent and those I dispose of at the first opportunity."

"We aren't assassins for hire," I said firmly to Julia.

She nodded at me, saying to Sandra and I, "But we'd kill to protect ourselves too. Or to stop someone else from killing again."

I said to her, "Not killing—murder. 'Tisn't wrong to kill to defend oneself or another."

Julia said, "We won't kill on someone else's say so. We'd investigate—" she huffed a quick laugh— "by just asking who they'd killed and why. They always tell us."

I said, "We've only killed twice."

Julia gave me a quick kiss on the cheek.

She said firmly, "I killed him and he more than deserved it. He'd have killed you, Pip." She turned from me to say worriedly to Sandra, "He was a horrible man. A kidnapper and pedophile who murdered his victims. He was also possessed by a demon."

Sandra's eyes widened and she took a quick step back.

"You defeated a demon?"

"'Twasn't that difficult," I said dryly although the thought of the creature that had emerged from the man made my palms sweat.

Julia said, "I'd shot the man and it emerged. Pip immediately ordered it to go. She said something in Latin, I think..."

"'Twas a prayer."

Sandra said thoughtfully with a hint of humor, "A seethe with true faith... It's dangerous to interact with a demon. They can sense your hidden desires and manipulate your emotions. I'm not certain if they can manufacture an emotion or just amplify it. I *am* certain they can convince you to act in dangerous ways."

"Dangerous how?"

"Mostly with no thought for the consequences, which is why even a seethe is susceptible to one. You could get carried away and start a riot even when you know how dangerous it would be. It's really quite remarkable you banished it so easily, but I wouldn't count on that happening again. It would have returned to its realm and word will spread among them that there's a seethe here with true faith."

"Will they come after us?"

"I doubt it. It's much more likely that it would do it's best to hide from you. It will take it time, how much time I couldn't say, to find a new host with enough power to bridge the gap between realms. I have no idea if a demon can communicate to others of its kind between realms, but I *do* know that communication of that sort is difficult. I think you have some time to prepare."

"How?"

"That depends. Holy objects will work but only if they're placed by someone who believes they'll work. It isn't God exactly that repels the demon but your belief that it'll work. Pip obviously believes. I'm betting it was a common belief in her time. But speaking as we are could lessen the effectiveness of such items for her or maybe it would raise the effectiveness... It depends on what she truly feels, the will she imbues those holy items with when she places them."

"God cannot vanquish such a creature?"

"I'm sure he could. I don't think we should speak of this further until you've had time to read the books. What I think you should do is pray on it." She pointed to the carpet. "The circle of protections I placed on this room will hold one at bay. Nothing that the caster doesn't wish to cross that circle can cross it. Speaking of which, you'll need to ensure that no one enters because the fact that they can't cross will be noticeable. I can teach you how to make a circle so that you can open and close it at will, but it will take you time to learn and even more time to make one of the size and strength of this one."

I examined the rug, which I'd thought was an abstract geometric design until I looked closely and the pentagram in the center became clear.

Julia said, "What if someone moves the rug or burns it or something?"

"The circle isn't really on the rug. That's the visual representation of my will. Because you're both novices, I've made this circle breakable by your will. One of your first lessons will be on how to break this spell in case you ever had to let someone inside this room. Only the two of you can freely enter and exit it. It's meant to be a safe place to practice and speak. No one could hear you while you're standing inside it. If your house were on fire, the fire couldn't touch you here. If you caused a fire while learning a spell the fire couldn't escape the confines of the circle, which is the main purpose. It's meant to keep anything you might do contained."

"So a demon couldn't reach us, but we couldn't hold one either..."

"It's very difficult to hold one. Not only would you need a powerful circle but to know it's true name or else it would just return to its own realm. It's much easier to banish one but when I say easier, I don't mean easy. I think you must have taken it by surprise."

"I was very angry."

"We both were," Julia said.

"And that could do it although normally it would try to make you use that anger against each other."

"'Twould be a useless gesture."

Julia nodded, taking my hand. "I'd not harm Pip for any reason."

"Just be sure if you ever face another that you're in perfect accord. A demon has a way of widening the smallest cracks."

"How common are they?"

"I've never run into one here. Not that I was looking... I've been remiss in keeping up with my magical studies and supplies. There are plenty of materials available, unfortunately most would require travel time to procure and I darn't leave Cassandriel unattended. I was hoping we could work out a deal. You have the manpower at your disposal to acquire what we'd need with no one the wiser as it would be simple for you to send someone and leave them with no recall of what they'd brought back."

"What sorts of things are we talking about, here?" Julia asked.

"Plants, gems, some small bits and bobs. I'd explain their use and teach you how to see the sorts of things that could be useful. Which brings me to my first real lesson, if you agree, of course."

"I'm in," Julia said, giving me an anxious glance.

"I too am intrigued."

"Then let's begin."

Chapter 7

I said to Sandra, "We have a partner of sorts—"

"Our Renfield," Julia interrupted.

I nodded agreement as I said, "A human man who we entrusted with the secret of our existence, which entailed a brief explanation of magic. He needs to know some things to be able to protect us and himself."

Julia said, "He knows we'll be asking him occasionally if he's told anyone else, and his rind is thick enough that he can't resist us.

I said, "It could be that we've eaten his essence so much that we can't resist each other."

Sandra nodded, saying, "That can happen and is something you should learn to guard against. You can show him this room and tell him whatever you wish but it's doubtful he'll be able to perform more than simple alchemy unless he's heavily infused with your anima. Infusing him would have advantages and disadvantages for both of you and isn't something you should rush into."

"Can you make it so he can enter this circle?"

"Yes. I'll need to speak with him and take some hair or saliva."

She eyed me thoughtfully for a moment then nodded decisively. "Call him and we can become acquainted."

I hesitated because I wasn't certain if she meant him harm or not.

Julia obviously had no such compunctions because she immediately left the room.

Sandra said, "You like this person? He's a friend?"

"He could be. He isn't a good man—or not what I'd have considered a good man when I was a girl, but I suppose in *his* world he's a very good man. 'Tis confusing."

She snorted softly.

"No one is all good or all bad. Being trustworthy though—that's what counts."

"He is that."

"I could impose a vow on him."

"'Tisn't needed."

"Don't let sentiment cloud your judgement to practicalities. You want to be friends with this person, and it will feel like a betrayal of that friendship to question his motives. I'm going to insist that you do so though because I darn't take a chance that he turns on me."

"I understand. Julia will have no problem questioning him..."

She laughed an agreement.

I examined the books until Julia returned with Ryu a few minutes later.

I said to Sandra, "This is Martin Poole, my personal assistant."

Sandra offered her hand as she said, "My name is Sandra Alder, and as far as the rest of the world is concerned, I'm just a friend of the Blackwoods. Is that understood?"

She tightened her grasp on his hand. "What happens in this room stays in this room. I'll protect my secrets with deadly force. You're here as an observer at the invitation of Phillipa Blackwood. If she rescinds her invitation, I'll still expect that you'll keep the secrets you've learned here. She's declined my offer to ensure your secrecy by magical means, but I'm insisting that she question you periodically on whom you've told. I'll be questioning you also and I have magical means to tell truth from a lie. This is your only warning."

Ryu nodded nervously.

I said, "You may leave if you like."

"No. I'm in."

Sandra said, "You do understand that most of what we talk about won't be something that you can do?"

He nodded.

"Then let's begin." She crouched, pulling Ryu with her to press both their hands to the floor. A moment later she stood and released him.

I said, "Is he now attuned to the circle? You've no need of hair or blood?"

Ryu gave me an anxious glance.

She snickered. "His hand was sweaty enough."

Julia laughed nervously as she said, "Mine too."

I nodded agreement. He didn't notice because he was grinning at her.

Sandra rested a hip against the desk as she said, "The basic premise of magic is imposing your will on the power that you're trying to manipulate. That power has different names and sources, and we'll get to that later. A mage will focus their concentration in many ways. Some are able to do it quickly while others need longer. Using symbols and incantations is a way to focus, to keep your thoughts firmly on the task at hand. A difficult to remember series of words that you've taught yourself to say while envisioning the effect you want is a very good way to impose your will on magic, but it isn't the only way. The key is to envision what you expect to happen and understand the way the power will respond to pressure. By that I mean, the larger the change, the more the power will react. A mage might say the harder the spell is to cast, but it isn't the spell that's more difficult, it's the process. Some reactions are much more complicated and difficult to envision without interruption.

"Let's take fire for instance."

She snapped her fingers and a spark appeared to float above her pointer finger.

Ryu exclaimed, turning red when I glanced at him.

Sandra ignored the interruption.

The flame flickered and gave off heat when I tentatively ran my hand over it.

She shook her hand and the flame faded.

"When I learned that spell, I knew nothing of the scientific principles of fire. If I were to learn this spell today, those principles would play a part because that's how I perceive fire now. It isn't necessary to know the how of it. It *is* necessary to have a clear vision of what you expect to happen. To learn that spell I stared at a flame until I could perfectly recall the look and feel. Producing the flame requires you to meld your magical power to your vision, and that's the tricky bit. Too much power and your flame will engulf you. Too little and it won't work. Letting your mind wander before the spell has finished will release your magic uncast. And that's were incantations come in.

"Because straight lines are easier to draw than curves, I recommend you start with a simple triangle shape and then the pentagram. Get to know how long it takes you to draw one."

She took a piece of chalk from the desk drawer and drew a line on the top of the desk. "Orange light."

She drew another line.

"Heat."

She drew another line.

"White light."

She drew another line.

"Smokey scent."

She drew another line.

"Fire."

She'd drawn a pentagram.

"I'm envisioning the process as I think the words. In my mind's eye, I see each as a separate action racing down the line of the pentagram culminating in fire—although now I'm so practiced at it that it's just one effect that happens in a snap of my fingers. It's the same series of images that happen so quickly in sequence that it would appear as one image. Condensing the time it takes to cast a spell like that takes time and practice. It can be dangerous because if your mind wanders, you could cause something that you didn't intend to happen, which can be catastrophic if the spell is at all dangerous, which most are."

She began drawing again saying, "Earth. Air. Fire. Water. Spirit. The five corners of the most powerful of spells like transmuting a shape."

She erased the pentagrams and drew five quick lines and said, "I might have drawn a zigzag or any shape or used anything I like to keep my mind and magic focused together. I draw the line while envisioning the process and pushing my magic along that line. It isn't a static image in my mind, it's envisioning the process. I'm showing the magic what I want it to do, so the better I can envision it, the clearer it is to me, the easier it is for me to shape that power. Fire is easy because so much is flammable. It's practically part of everything's nature to burn, which makes it an easy but a dangerous spell to learn.

"Take some time and think about the sort of spells you'd like to cast and then think about the aids you want to use to cast them. The pentagram is a good shape because there's almost no chance that you could accidentally draw it. Magic can, not learn exactly, but wear channels. It will spill out if you grow careless, which is why it's good to train yourself that you don't wish for fire unless you draw or say a specific thing. If I'd envision a large pentagram while saying my spell to myself, the radius of the spell would be large because I've trained my magic. And I can shift my magic quickly because I've trained it."

She snapped her fingers while flicking her wrist and a fireball the size of a basketball bloomed. Another quick wrist flick sent it sailing across the room. She snapped again and it shrank to a tiny pinprick of light. She snapped without making a sound and it disappeared.

I hadn't noticed the different strength of the snaps until then.

She said, "Fire is my birthright, but still I've practiced until I learned to be in perfect accord with it. Anger is yours. Practice until you know what the merest brush of your hand will do on someone who is bored and someone who is furious."

"How do we know?" Julia asked.

"You watch. You study angry people the way I studied fire. You need to know how an angry person reacts, how a person in agreement reacts, how a person who's afraid reacts, and then you can impose *your* will of it over their own."

"There's lots of ways to be angry," I said thoughtfully.

"It'll take you years, centuries even," Sandra agreed.

Julia huffed in annoyance.

I said, "'Tis a skill like any that must be practiced."

Sandra said, "You could bumble about and get things done but yours is a dangerous skill, as dangerous as fire is."

Julia said, "I know. I was just hoping we could learn something practical."

Sandra traced her foot around the edge of the circle on the outer edge of the rug. "The spell of holding. Learn to focus your will. If your will is stronger than the power contained in the pentagram, it will be trapped there. I use this one all the time on guards and guard dogs. It's best to use it sparingly on people as it can frighten them so severely when they realize that they can't move that they have a heart attack. The spell must be crafted with care to let in light and air, or it will withhold all and becomes a solid block. But if you're careful and clever you can use it with none the wiser. No one really thinks twice about stuck doors and windows. You could safely practice this spell by attempting to keep water from spilling out of your pentagram."

"Don't they wonder about the pentagram?" Julia asked.

"Not if they can't see it. It doesn't need to be written. I can envision it. I can draw it in invisible ink or on the underside of a rug or hide it within a larger pattern. I can combine it with the rune of silence—" she tapped the vase beside the door that was decorated with swirled patterns— "and place it on a sleeping guard and he'll sleep right through the alarm and not even know he was unable to move from his chair. The runes can be written well in advance of being activated although that takes practice because magic does like to return to where it came from."

"We have much to think on," I said.

Julia said, "How do we hold the magic?"

"*Ahh*, that depends and isn't something I can answer for another. It varies for us all. Some never learn to store it and must work where they have a fresh source. My advice is to learn to see it and once you can see it, move it."

Julia said in exasperation, "How am I supposed to see something I can't see?"

Sandra's eyes twinkled.

"Can't you?"

Julia huffed.

I said, "She can't see it for us, Jewels. It's *our* magic."

"Very good," Sandra said, clapping lightly in approval. "You are partially a creature of earth, so it's likely that you'll have an affinity for earth magic."

She caressed the cover of one of the books she'd brought.

"Read the book. Everything in it is true but not necessarily true for everyone. It's good to know what others can do though even if it's beyond you."

Julia brightened.

I said, "Only practice here, Jewels, inside this circle."

Sandra nodded emphatically. "Until I say otherwise, stay inside this circle. That means no drawing a potential spell or writing of magic or even imagining it. Discuss your ideas here. If you find that you prefer to work somewhere else, inform me so that I can draw the protections you need.

She handed Julia another book. "Now, let's talk about the magic inherent in plants. This book is by no means the definitive work. There could be many more plants that naturally absorb earth mana. It's a great reference on how it happens and the natural affinities that plants possess although those affinities might be stronger or weaker depending on the type of spell being attempted, where the plant was grown, and how it was harvested and stored."

I was exhausted and overwhelmed when Sandra left.

Julia said, "It will take two lifetimes to learn even half of this, even if that's all we do all day every day!"

"She must be very old."

"I wonder what her ancestry is?"

"There's hundreds of supernatural beings. She could be descended from any of them."

Ryu said, "The power is almost the same for all of them though, earth, fire, water, air, spirit..."

"I wonder if that's fire too? The heat of passion, the heat of rage..."

"Maybe..."

Julia said, "We're obviously a type of inou."

"They don't turn to shadow like a seethe."

"True... but we both feed on emotions."

Ryu said, "A tiger and a puppy both eat meat and they're not much alike at all."

I said to Julia, "Start them building the greenhouses tomorrow. I want our own source of plants. Your mother will be thrilled that I'm going ahead with the formal gardens. They'll be the perfect excuse to cultivate the older plants."

Julia nodded.

"What's troubling you, love?" I asked.

"We know she's been here for at least eighteen years, and according to her, she hadn't seen another from her realm or any other realm until now, and now she's seen five of us and warned there were many more."

Ryu said, "You think she's lying?"

"Why would she bother? It worries me though that the veil between realms is weakening."

I said, "That seems unlikely. She probably saw them now because she was looking. Her daughter kept her home and too busy to do much. Now Cassandriel is ready to leave home, and Sandra is looking for dangers." A new thought struck me.

"Her daughter... 'Tis strange that I should meet someone so like myself. Perhaps 'tis our fate to be the best of companions..."

Julia said worriedly, "And that's another thing. Cass seems so normal..."

"She *is* normal, but take Sandra's warnings to heart. I was just a normal girl until I wasn't. We do nothing that might stir her otherness to waken!"

Julia gave me a quick hug. "I'll call and arrange a visit. She'll need friends like us. And I don't mean because of magic but because we can relate."

"'Tis terrifying to find out that you're not what you thought yourself."

Julia winked at me as she said, "There are more things than are dreamed of in your philosophy."

"The bard had such marvelous insights. Perhaps even now he walks among us, laughing at our admiration..."

"Maybe," Julia said in the tone that meant she didn't agree.

"To be so wise from one lifetime...surely it took many..."

Julia kissed my brow then mussed my hair.

She said, "I'll read the books as soon as I can. You and Sandra can work out the best method for us to proceed with magic, and she and I will work on how to procure the materials we need."

"As ethically as possible," I said firmly. "We don't steal the crown jewels even though we could."

Ryu goggled at me.

Julia giggled, waving over her shoulder as she left.

I eagerly grabbed the books and sifted through them.

Ryu glanced over my shoulder, heaving an aggravated sigh.

"I can't read that... it would take me months to decipher it."

I said, "Neither can Julia. I shall make a transcription. Perhaps your time would be better spent learning the more mundane tasks for now. Julia will surely need help arranging for the gardens and greenhouses. You could likely guide her in the choice of new... servants. And she can begin to teach you how to invest."

"Servants..."

"I know not what else to call them."

"Oh, it's the right fucking word...."

"I truly don't understand why that angers you so..."

"You wouldn't."

"Perhaps you could enlighten me," I said angrily.

"You're entitled and think it's your due."

He was angry too and it occurred to me I might have forced that answer.

I said, "I shall see to acquiring a charm to prevent me from inadvertently forcing your compliance. I'm unsure if I have or not. I *am* entitled and service *is* my due as it is yours when you procure those services... I understand that 'tis my methods of procurement that you find distasteful, or at least I thought it was. But you say entitled like 'tis the foulest thing to be..."

He laughed harshly, shaking his head at me. "You're from a different world. I don't think I can explain it to you in a way you'd understand."

"'Twill be a problem if my mind is closed to new ideas."

"Imagine if instead of being Lou, you'd come back as me. Wouldn't you have tried to get yourself this body? I mean if you couldn't have a female one."

"It wouldn't have been my choice to be born female. No woman would choose such. Not to say that here and now I wouldn't choose it. I'd much prefer it now... I'm uncertain if inhabiting the body of a nobleman is better than inhabiting the body of a commoner or not, being too newly arrived to be certain of my conclusions."

"A commoner," he said bitterly.

"Is not that what you meant?"

"Yes."

"I... is that a rude word now? I meant no offense."

"Calling someone a peasant is offensive, Pip. Even you have to know that."

"But I did not... and how is it offensive unless the person so addressed is, in fact, not a peasant?"

"I give up."

"How will I learn if none will explain? Who shall I ask if not you and Julia..."

"You can't go around labeling people like that."

"What is the correct word?"

"Person or people."

"I shall endeavor to remember that."

He stared at me a moment then laughed as he said, "I forgot what we were arguing about."

"Finding servants. Or should I say finding people?"

"...I think you should speak to Julia about it."

"Finding them or naming them?"

"Naming them. It's probably perfectly correct for a man of your station to call them servants."

"Then I shall inquire."

"It doesn't bother you at all, does it?"

"What?"

"Your station."

He was still angry enough to swirl his anima. His expression reminded me of mine own when I was sent to my room for daring to speak an opinion.

I said, "I quite enjoy being a lord. 'Tis refreshing to be the one doing the ordering." I caressed the book I held. "'Tis an almost sinful delight to read whatever I wish. I too resented being reminded of my station. I'd thought it an obsolete custom now..."

"It's supposed to be."

"*Ahh*, you think me high handed. I assure you, 'twasn't my idea that you be questioned by the mage or myself."

His anger faded.

"That I believe. I'm sorry, Pip. It's hard to remember who you really are."

"I really am Lord Blackwood now."

He smiled ruefully. "I know. I guess I haven't really accepted who I am."

"You're Martin Poole, my most trusted …. assistant. And I hope also Ryu, my friend."

He hesitated then lifted his hand to bump fists with me.

Laughing in relief, I obliged.

He said, "You're right. I should go help your wife. But you *will* show me that transcription, won't you?"

"Of course. You should attempt the spell of holding, but only here in this room."

"I won't be able to do it though unless I'm descended from one of them creatures. And that reminds me, do we know what the types of creatures are?"

"Some. I'll make a list. There *are* human mages, so 'tis possible that you're descended, but 'tis more probable that Julia and I have infected you."

"You're turning me into a seethe?

I couldn't tell by his tone if he was excited or worried about that.

"I'm unsure if such a thing is possible. Sandra warned us that we could infuse you with our anima, which would have advantages and disadvantages, but she didn't say what they were."

"Because she didn't know or didn't want to tell you?"

"She told me to read the books..."

"Then you better get cracking."

He turned back at the door to say, "No infusing me or anything else without talking to me first."

"It shan't be purposeful. I can't promise it wouldn't happen... I shall call Sandra forthwith for charms for your protection."

"Thanks, Pip, you're all right."

I called Sandra as soon as he left, having to leave the room to do it. Her spell was strong enough to block cell phones.

She agreed to make me the charm with the price to be negotiated with Julia.

I returned to the room and chose a book that I began copying onto fresh vellum, using an old-fashioned quill and ink. I intended to make photocopies too, but experience had taught me that I retained knowledge best by writing it, and I loved the idea of having my own handwritten copies.

The book was titled *Myths and History of Ivy*

I copied the first page, drawing a rough sketch of the painting of ivy. I'd do a more detailed painting after I'd read the book.

The first page had a list of words that I realized were all of the names ivy was known by, *Ifig, Efeu, Hedera, Bindwood, Lovestone* and a hundred more.

The next pages were of written and painted descriptions of the plant's complete lifecycle.

Sandra had left a note clipped to the next page that said add sunlight to the affinities.

The list of affinities was already long with sections headed, Climbing, Creeping, Slipping, Spreading, Smothering, and Binding.

I wrote on a new page, *Ask Sandra if a natural affinity means there are equal unnatural affinities that could be manipulated by corrupting the plant.*

The next few pages contained simple spells one could do with just ivy as the base ingredient. They didn't seem that difficult, which worried me a bit. I was glad Julia was leaving this to me because I didn't think she had the patience to learn the basics first. I was almost certain that she'd immediately try one.

I was tempted to try one myself but my long years in that terrible dark had taught me caution.

I forgot I was transcribing and just read.

Ryu knocking on the door startled me. I realized it was morning when I opened the door and the light inside of the room rapidly brightened, which made me realize that Sandra's spell had kept even light and dark from the room, freezing the light from the windows when the spell had been cast and blocking the sounds of construction and yet allowed the sound of a knock.

A shiver of awe rose the hair on my arms.

"Are we riding today?" he asked.

"Yes. Give me ten minutes to change."

"I'll get the horses saddled."

"Bring the gloves. And some towels. We can spar a bit and then swim."

"It's too cold to swim," Ryu said laughingly.

"Is it? I suppose it is... I hadn't noticed that I don't feel the change in temperature much. Remind me to speak with Julia and keep an eye on both of us so we dress appropriately.

"Did you learn anything?"

"Nothing we can speak of here," I said pointedly enough to make him flush.

"Of course... sorry. It won't happen again.

"I think we should adjust our schedule. Perhaps we could lunch or breakfast together in the study? That way we could... chat and catch up."

"The three of us should breakfast there a few days a week at least so Julia can catch us up on anything we need to know, and we can catch her up on anything she needs to know."

"'Tis a solid plan."

A new young man was holding the horses when we arrived.

I disliked him at first sight. His smile was too sly and his eyes too mocking.

"A leg up?" he asked.

Ryu grunted in annoyance.

"No thank you," I said.

I took the reins from him and mounted.

He leaned across my thigh to scratch the horse's right ear. Before I could chastise him for his over familiar manner, Ryu had yanked him back.

He shook him as he said, "Keep your hands to yourself, pal."

"Relax, dude—"

Ryu thrust him away. "Shut up. Not another word. You and I will have a talk later about respect."

The kid blanched then glowered at me a moment before smoothing his expression.

I was tempted to use his anima that was swirling about him to make him respectful, but I had no idea of his status. It reminded me that I needed to speak with Julia about an outward symbol so I'd know which ones were our control group and which she was actively controlling.

Ryu mounted and we rode away, taking the lower path to reach the field where we liked to spar.

When he arrived, we put on the gloves and he said, "That kid is going to be a problem unless you work your mojo."

"I'll speak to Julia," I said absently as I began to do stretches.

When I finished, I jogged in place for a minute while shadow boxing.

Ryu was still stretching, watching me with a worried expression.

I said, "There's much we haven't told you about our plans here. 'Tis truly our desire to reform those who can be reformed and find them useful employment—useful for themselves, I mean. Some will never be... tamed and must be carefully... taught. We have many projects though that can use even such as they, maybe even especially such as they. 'Tis best you speak with her about such things in the study."

"I will, but I meant he's going to be a problem to you personally. I saw that smarmy grin. He's thinks he can seduce you—although maybe you want to be seduced...."

Horror flickered over his eyes. He ducked his head pretending to tighten his gloves.

I said stiffly, "I'd n'er accept favors that weren't freely offered... 'Tis despicable to even consider it! How low you hold me in your esteem that you would think such?"

"Fuck man, I'd be tempted. I'd be more than tempted. You could have any woman you wanted. They'd do anything... anyone would be tempted..."

I said coldly, "If by tempted you mean the thought had occurred... would you truly do such to one who lacked the power to tell you nay?"

"No. You're right. I can imagine it though..."

He grinned at me then flushed, shaking his head, his flush growing as he said, "Man, I forget who you *are*. I shouldn't be saying that shit to you."

"Because of my station or because of what I am or what I was... and I mean no offense. 'Tis an honest inquiry. I'm unsure of what passes for polite conversation or even impolite conversation in polite society, which the discourse of friends *is* no matter if they be born to the gentry or not."

He grinned at me, shaking his head again as if he was boggled by me or maybe himself.

"Both."

He hesitated a moment then said with forced casualness, "Do you consider us equals?"

"Assuredly not. You do many things better than I and I many things better than you." I knew that wasn't what he'd meant but hadn't really considered my place in this society.

I said, "I hadn't really considered if my God-given talents make me superior or inferior... I wonder if I'm perhaps meant to cull the herd as a wolf would... it isn't part of the herd, so cannot be equal or unequal, it just is... I was born of the gentry, but to my eye that means little now. I was born to wealth and that seems much as it was. The wealthy have always been the setters of fashion and the arbiters of law.

"In that respect I'm unequal to you. I pay your wages, which to my mind gives me the right to demand a level of service. I could, if I so wished, arrange to make your life miserable in the way the wealthy always could—to hound you from home and hearth, ruin your business, your reputation. I'm in the enviable position of having no one except Julia to answer to. She and I are equal, although perhaps if pushed to it I would say that I am her master because I believe I could impose my will on her. She might say differently. I wish us to be equal though..."

"You're stronger than her?"

I flexed my arm as I said, "In many ways. 'Tis so unfair...you have no idea the joy of being able to stand up to any man and know I stood at least a chance of holding my own."

Ryu stripped off his gloves and tossed them aside. "Anyone can learn to hold their own. Size helps, of course, but skill helps more. I've seen a small woman kick a big man's ass. Don't rely on the strength of your arms. You got to outthink your opponents. Let's skip the boxing. I think you're ready to learn some throws."

I eagerly removed my gloves and listened intently.

Chapter 8

Two weeks later, Ryu brought our breakfast to the study as was our habit. He'd also brought a stack of newspapers that he handed to me.

My gaze caught on an ad from a local restaurant announcing an American Thanksgiving meal.

"This has to be Julia, Pip. Did you know she was doing it?"

"Doing what?" I asked as I took the papers.

I couldn't imagine why Julia would want American meals served or what the difference might be.

He flipped the stack over.

My heart fluttered as I read the headline. I picked up the next paper and then the next.

I must have paled because Ryu said, "No. I can see you didn't know. What are we going to do?"

"Speak to her, of course. Step out and ask her to pop in for a minute."

"Pip…"

Sweat gathered under my arms as I realized he was afraid to confront her.

I said as assuredly as I could, "She wouldn't have done it on a whim, and she assuredly wouldn't do it to you or anyone else who didn't deserve it!"

He snorted softly but headed to the door.

I read the paper, counting the victims in the gang shootings in growing dismay.

Ryu returned with Julia a few minutes later.

I tapped the paper as I said, "Jewels, whatever is happening?"

"I'm trying to get a handle on it," she said defensively.

"Handle on what?" Ryu asked.

She rolled her eyes at him, crossing her arms.

I said, "Fourteen dead this month..."

She said angrily, "And six the month before, which was when I realized we had a problem. I didn't realize the sort of power vacuum I'd create when I pulled the heavy hitters off the street. So, this time I left a few and told them to take out the dangerous competition but to be very careful no civilians or unarmed people were hurt. It spread a bit farther than I intended..."

"Jesus, Julia!" Ryu yelled.

Her face flushed dark red as she glared at Ryu. "What was I supposed to do? Let them kill whoever the hell they wanted? which is what happened when you guys left!"

"No—but there has to be a better way. Maybe tell them not to let anyone kill anyone at all!"

"Gee, why didn't I think of that? Of course I tried that, dumbass! They were all dead in three days. Three fucking days, Ryu! Not that I give a shit about them as they were all horrible men, but the ones who replaced them were no better. It's a vicious cycle. If I take them away, another just pops up, and they always do something really horrible."

"Of course they do. They got to, don't they if they want to let everyone know that it's their territory now! You can't handle this like you would a club or some shit!"

He gathered the papers as he said to me, "Let me go see what I can do. They'll talk to me, and I can maybe smooth things over or at least find out who needs to be pushed."

"Pushed how?" Julia asked suspiciously.

She yanked the papers from him to shake them at him.

"I'm not helping any of those assholes shake down anyone!"

I said, "We can both accompany Ryu and at least find out what he thinks might help. What normally happens if a gang leader dies or goes to jail?"

Ryu said, "It depends. Usually his second just steps up. If a rival gang murdered him, they'd have to retaliate. If he just did a runner like us, the crew who remained would need to find a new crew to join, which wouldn't take long unless their crew had a bad rep. They'd be low man and might be a bit more aggressive trying to regain their cred. When you're nabbed, you do your time and keep your mouth shut. Most times nothing really changes unless you're doing hard time. This here situation is extreme. You got people poppin' off all over, not just one crew but lots of 'em."

I said, "What would you recommend to quell it?"

"First, call off the hitters. You'll need to send them away."

"No," she said flatly.

Anima showed thickly around her.

I shook my head at Ryu when he opened his mouth to argue.

"And then?" I asked.

"Then you let fucking nature take its course unless you intend to speak to every single person! Once it settles down, *then* you can talk to whoever's in charge and set some ground rules, but if you leave them too weak, you'll be right back where we are now with everyone trying to muscle their way in."

She stomped from the room.

"Give us a minute," I said as I stood to follow her.

I caught up to her in her office.

She said angrily, "If I let them go and they murder some kid or something, it'll be my fault! I'm not doing it!"

I hastily shut the door.

"The don't deserve to be let go! I'm not doing it, Pip."

"Okay. But I think he's right. I'll go handle them, but in future don't go there to recruit. Spread it around. Take only one or two at most. Better yet, go to the jails and browse there. There's probably innocent men and women we could get out; ones who've killed but in self-defense. If we need more, we can get Ryu or another of the former gang members to go find us someone who wouldn't be missed in a way that would make the other members react. What they do isn't our problem. Two people, no matter how strong, can't stop it. There's simply too many people involved."

I took her hand as I said, "What we *can* do is keep this town safe. Maybe in time we could work outward, but first we need to secure this estate."

"...you're right."

She hugged me for a long minute.

When she released me, she headed to the door.

"I'll handle them though. They haven't the will to resist me. I know where to find them and what to do. Besides, there's no need for you to sully your anima with theirs. They're truly disgusting human beings—worse than savages because they know better and enjoy their savagery."

She stomped from the house.

I ran back upstairs but Ryu wasn't in the study.

I called his phone.

"She's going to take care of them."

"Take care of them—take care of them?"

"Permanently, yes. Don't bother try to talk her out of it. Is there anything that can be done to ease the transition?"

"Maybe if we can spread the word that it was a bad cook and that if people are chill, it should go back to normal in a few days."

"A cook?"

"I can't explain now. She just blew past me."

"Where are you?"

"Headed to town."

I began running to the garage.

"Don't get in her way but see if you can follow without her seeing you. I'll catch up."

"Should I be worried, Pip."

"She was furious."

"So… not good then."

"Not good," I agreed.

Asa was in the office inside the garage when I ran in.

I said, "I urgently need a ride. If we can catch up to Ryu…"

"He left ten minutes ago."

"And my wife just minutes ago and she just passed him. I think it shan't be too difficult to catch up!"

"Of course, sir. I'll do my best."

We passed Ryu a few minutes later and both pulled over so I could join him.

"Thank you, Asa."

"No problem, sir. I hope everything is okay."

"Just a small tiff. It will all be worked out soon."

Ryu peeled away.

I said, "She knows where they are. Do you?"

"I have an educated guess."

"She isn't wrong about releasing those men," I said.

He snorted.

I continued, "'Tis one thing to not know or only suspect and do nothing. 'Tis another to knowingly leave a killer free to murder again."

"*Mmhmm.*"

A flush comprised of anger and shame burned my cheeks.

"I am *not* a murderer! I'm not even a man! 'Tisn't the same thing at all!"

He shot me a frazzled glance.

"I know... I agree even, in theory, but I know these men, Pip. They aren't friends but they *are* people!"

"On my soul, I swear she wouldn't have chosen them had they not committed foul crimes!"

"I know."

We drove in silence until we reached his neighborhood.

He parked in a deli's parking lot, turning to me to say, "Wait here. Let me see what I can find out."

"Will you be safe?" I asked.

He walked away without answering.

People passing by gawked at the car and me. Some laughed, some glared, and some had hatred in their eyes. None looked friendly. *'Twas a different world. One I knew not.* He was right that we had no business messing with it.

I turned my gaze to the tall buildings in the distance where Hugh and men like him worked. *Those were the criminals I should be using,* I mused. There my title and wealth would garner respect, not these hostile glances.

He returned two hours later, coming to my open window to say, "Word's already on the street that something big is going down. I started my rumor and already heard a twisted version of It. I think she's trying to gather all the big fish. Word is out and no one is answering their phones."

"Where is she?"

"I don't know. Can you call her?"

"I can, but should I?" I reached to grab the hand resting on my open window. "I don't mean should I stop her. I mean should I risk angering her more?"

Tears blurred my eyes.

"She could get herself killed, Ryu! If she were to cause a riot where innocents were harmed… I think she'd not be able to live with the guilt!"

He pulled his hand away and ran to get into the car.

"We can try by the Brew Club."

My phone rang as he was pulling into a tiny parking lot behind a dingy bar.

She said angrily, "I took care of it and am heading to the apartment. I won't be home tonight."

"Are you angry with me?"

"No. With myself."

"'Tis my thought we should stick to criminals that we understand, like Hugh."

She laughed harshly.

"Shall I come to you, love?"

"No. I need some space—and a shower. I'm okay, Pip. You don't need to worry."

"You *are* my soul, Julia. Please remember that."

"As you're mine. We're fine. I'll call tomorrow, but I might be here a day or so because you're right. We need the real criminals. I have research to do."

"Be careful, beloved."

She disconnected.

I said, "Take us home."

"Where is she?"

"The apartment. And before you ask, she didn't say what she did. Please… I know 'tis much to ask but I'd not have her upset."

"I'm not an idiot, Pip! And I—she's my friend too. I know she didn't mean any harm—just the opposite, in fact. We're all just figuring this shit out, so of course we'll make mistakes. It's just you guys can't go around thinking you can murder anyone you like, even if they deserve it."

"It isn't that at all!"

"For you it isn't."

I pondered that on the drive home with a growing sensation of falling. I was breathless and sweaty by the time we arrived there.

I said, "I know not how to help her or myself."

He exited the car, coming to my side to hold the door for me. He offered his hand, which was warm on my cold one.

I let him pull me out, shivering in sudden cold.

His hug was warmth that I clung to, fighting a sob.

"None of us know how to do this, Pip. She'll be okay. We all will if we help each other. She knows she messed up. We've *all* messed up."

He released me, smiling ruefully. "Now, let's get back to work. Smalls found a promising patch of ivy by the lake."

"Then we should change and gather our tools."

Study would be just the thing, I thought in relief.

Chapter 9

The next day, Ryu handed me a newspaper.

I knew I wouldn't like the contents by his pinched expression.

I read the article with growing dismay.

"We knew there would be…"

"Don't. Just don't. I get she had her reasons, but she can't go around killing—"

I jumped to my feet to glare at him.

"Don't you dare defend those men! She would not have been able to order them at all if they weren't rinded!"

"I'm not defending them! I'm saying Julia can't be allowed to murder whoever she pleases!"

"They were bad men!"

"How do you know? Most of them probably never even shot a gun or pulled a knife."

"How do you know?"

He snatched the paper from me.

"She wiped out three entire gangs! Half of them were just kids!"

"She didn't do it. They did it to themselves!"

"Oh come on, man!"

82

"Did you ask her what command was given?"

"Does it fucking matter what words she used when I can see what happened!"

"How do you know she ordered it? 'Tis it not possible that panic inspired them?"

"That doesn't make it better!"

I grabbed his anima and said, "What do you intend to do about it?"

"Talk to you."

"You wouldn't harm her, would you?"

His eyes widened and he scrambled away from me.

"Stop it! Of course, I wouldn't."

I wasn't sure if I'd compelled a truthful answer or not.

"I'm sorry but I *must* know. I see we're a danger, but I shan't allow her to be harmed, not by your actions nor your words. I shall speak with her."

He ran from the room.

I gathered the paper with shaking hands, drew a pentagram on the desktop, placed the paper on it and wrote upon it the rune of fire.

I debated what to say to her until she joined me there five hours later.

"Still practicing? A fire spell?" she asked.

"We both need more practice."

She said, "I've been thinking on what you said, and I agree, we should leave the criminals we don't understand alone."

"Did you intend…."

"Yes and no. I told them they were a blight on their communities and should be stopped by any means. I was angry and yelled at them for recruiting their own children. I didn't mean for them to kill them. I didn't order it. I only said the recruitment had to stop. I thought if I could remove the major drug dealers… but then I realized that wouldn't be enough. I had to remove the ones who exploit the storekeepers and women. So I went back and asked at a few stores who the real problem people are."

"Are you... done now?"

"Yes. I give up. I've done my best to help them. If someone new moves in, the people there could stop them if they just report it."

"Those police were you as well..."

"It had to be done. By taking those bribes they allowed the entire system of corruption to keep working."

"I think Ryu was right and we should leave it alone. Once things settle down there, we can go back and set some rules."

"No. I won't help them even indirectly."

She stomped way trailed by a red cloud of anima.

I sank weakly to my seat.

Ryu joined me in the dining room where I was eating alone.

"Is she..." he trailed off, looking worried.

"Upset."

"We're all upset," he said dryly.

"I know not what to do... except to give her time to calm down. I shan't order you to leave her in peace. Do or say what you will but know that my loyalty is to her. If I think what you're doing or saying is worsening this situation, I'll be forced to act."

I expected him to leave and never return but he smiled ruefully and sat.

"I appreciate your honesty, Pip. I don't intend to do or say anything that will upset her. I hope you'll forgive me if I do because it wouldn't be intentional."

I shrugged.

He said worriedly, "Don't take this wrong or anything but maybe you should try to make her forget?"

"No. And not because it would be the worst sort of betrayal, but because it would be foolish. This was a lesson we needed to learn—one I've no wish to repeat, which we'd assuredly do if I could make her forget. 'Tis her nature to wish to help. We see now that we lack the knowledge to help as we wish."

"Where is she?"

"She returned to the city. Looking for men in her world who she can stop from committing crimes."

Ryu sighed hard.

I nodded agreement.

"I agree that we've no business looking for such, but she needs this. 'Tis her penance."

"If you go looking for shit, you're going to find it."

I reached to take his hand as I said, "We need this, Ryu, or else why are we here? This power that we are isn't one that can be set aside. We need to partake if we're to live. So shall we eat with no care, using our fodder for our own selfish reasons? I understand that what she's about is dangerous. There'll be casualties but 'tis the lesser evil."

"It *is* evil, Pip."

"Yes. But since we have no intention of allowing ourselves to fade into the mist, 'tis better to learn to feed in ways that benefit others, not just ourselves. I could convince her to hunt the streets at night and feed from the criminals we find—feed until we'd sucked the life from them, but I shan't because doing so would wither her beautiful soul. 'Tis my hope that we can learn quickly enough how to manage our hunger that the damage to her soul will be such that she can recover."

Ryu tightened his grip on my hand, nodding his agreement.

His support was relief enough to let my tense shoulders relax a bit.

He said, "She *is* doing good works here."

"Do what you can to show her that."

He released my hand and stood.

I said, "Stay close."

I had Ollie drive me to the apartment the next day.

Julia was in our small office, which was festooned with piles of newspapers, computer printouts, notebooks, and two whiteboards with messy graphs.

"What's all this? I asked as I leaned to kiss her cheek.

"I'm investigating some things I should've been looking into ages ago."

"Can I help?"

"Not yet. Maybe later."

Ryu said, "What about me?"

She eyed him with narrowed eyes a moment before nodding slowly.

"Yeah, I guess. You could track down some of these leads for me." She rummaged in her messy desk for a moment then handed him a paper. "I want to talk to this guy in person but no one I spoke to on the phone had an address."

"What'd he do?"

"I think he embezzled from one of my charities."

"You think?"

"Someone did. I'm pretty sure it was him."

She headed to our bedroom, saying over her shoulder, "I'm on my way out now to talk to a few of my suspects in person. He's the only one hiding, which makes me think he's the one."

Ryu said, "Do you have anything, an email address, a phone number?"

She turned back in the doorway to say, "Yes. It's all on there. He's still in contact with everyone, but no one knows where his home or office is, which means they're either lying or he's hiding. Word has it he hangs out at the coffee shop, the one I took you to last week. I was planning to go there to see if anyone knew a good time to go see him in person."

"I'm on it," Ryu said.

The anima on her hands faded away and she smiled a real smile.

He smiled back.

I said, "Call if you find him."

Ryu's eyes were full of relief when he turned to me.

He headed out.

I examined her papers while she dressed.

"I'll be back for dinner," she said as she exited our room.

"I'm coming."

Her eyes narrowed.

"You don't need to."

"I do for my peace of mind. I'm not going to pretend I'm not worried about you."

She shrugged.

I knew she was angry even though no anima was showing.

We drove in silence to an office building where she was greeted with hugs, smiles, and invitations.

It took her forty minutes to shake them off and reach the office of Aubert Hawkins.

She knocked once and opened the door.

"Jewels," the man said, sounding delighted, rising and offering his hand as she entered.

"I'm sorry I've been away so long," Julia said as she shook it.

"This is my husband, Louis."

"It's a pleasure, Lord Blackwood," he said as he shook my hand.

Julia said, "I thought we'd drop by and say I haven't forgotten you all."

Aubert shot me a weighing glance from the corner of his eye as he said, "We'd heard you were handling some personal health issues."

"We are. It's been difficult but we're learning to cope. I actually came to ask if you'd heard anything more about the clean water project?"

Aubert's expression darkened.

"Nothing good."

"It's true then, someone scarpered with the funds?"

She leaned across the desk to lay her hand on his arm, saying, "Do you know who's behind it?"

"I have an idea but no proof."

"Tell me everything," she said as she sat on the corner of his desk.

The hand laying on Aubert's shoulder was red.

I wasn't sure if he was answering because she was compelling him or not though. His tone remained normal and was only slightly annoyed.

I knew nothing of the names and places they spoke of.

She stopped in four more offices, and I knew she was growing furious by the brightness of the anima that sparkled on her words.

My phone rang as she was questioning a woman whose name I hadn't gotten.

Ryu said, "I've got his office address."

She turned to me.

"Ryu?"

"Yes."

"He find him?"

I hesitated the merest moment. I was tempted to lie because I knew she'd insist on going now.

"Yes."

"Have Ryu meet us there."

I nodded, turning away to pass on her request.

The woman she was speaking with leaned closer, lowering her voice, saying, "I probably shouldn't say anything when I have no real proof, but I think Odette knows more than she told me. Not that she'd admit anything shady like that to *me*..."

Julia nodded. "I'll drop by and have a chat."

"Jewels, you could ruin us..."

"I don't intend to make a scene, just find out who's behind it."

"If she's working with upper management... we can't afford bad publicity..."

"We can't afford to ignore it either."

Julia gave her a quick hug. "Be a darling and show my husband around while I have a quick chat."

I said to Ryu, "Text my wife the address."

I hung up and grabbed Julia's arm. "I think we should come back later."

"I'm fine."

"You're not. You're angry."

"Damn right I am."

She shook me off and stomped from the room.

The woman followed her.

I grabbed her arm, pushing my anima on her, saying, "Go back to work. We had a nice visit, but you have more important things to do now."

She nodded, smiling in agreement, continued down the hallway a few steps after Julia before pausing and turning back for her office.

Her hesitations were making me really nervous. Julia was using too much of herself on these people.

I hurried after Julia but was thwarted by a locked door.

"We'll be out in a minute," Julia said when I knocked.

"Please come back later."

"I just need a minute.

"Can I help you?" a passing man asked.

"No thank you. I'm just waiting for my wife."

He eyed me as if debating if he needed to call security.

I didn't blame him. I *was* acting oddly.

I took out my phone and pretended to make a call.

He hesitated another moment then walked away.

I debated banging on the door again, but it seemed pointless. They only thing I'd do was make a bigger scene. My anxiety grew the longer I waited. I was just about to bang again when Julia exited in a cloud of swirling anima.

I followed her to the car.

We drove in silence across town to a shabby office building.

Julia walked directly to the desk to say imperiously to the woman there, "I want to speak with the owner."

"You'll need to make an appointment."

Julia leaned closer. "Now!"

She laughed when she straightened.

The woman reached for her phone.

Ryu rose from his seat in the waiting room to say worriedly, "Jewels?

Julia said angrily, "Which office?"

"The one at the end of the hall."

I followed Julia.

The woman at the desk held the phone, staring after us looking unsure if she should stop us.

I whispered, "She wasn't angry enough."

Julia shrugged.

She didn't knock at the door.

The man sitting at the desk glanced up, sighing hard and reaching for his phone.

He said, "I told her to make you an appointment."

Julia marched up to his desk to lean over it and say, "I know you stole the money from the Clean Wells project."

His eyes narrowed and he set down his phone.

"I don't know what you're talking about."

"You and probably all of your partners here are dirty. You used that fundraiser to pad your own pockets!"

"Get out or I'll call the police!"

"How much money did you take?"

Her anima expanded to engulf him.

"Two million but I only got to keep three hundred thousand."

She laughed, sitting on the edge of his desk.

"Where did the money go?"

He listed names and companies answering all of her questions.

She stumbled when she stood.

I said, "'Tis enough for now, love."

"Hell, no, it isn't! He's going to send every penny he took back! Call them all! Every person involved and get them here! They should all send it back!"

I grabbed her arm to pull her toward the door, saying to him, "Forget we were here."

"He stole it, Pip!"

"Come with me, please. We should discuss how to make him return the money unless you mean to have him arrested and the money to remain lost."

"He *should* be arrested!"

"I think he doesn't have it all now. Please, Jewels. Come home and we can talk about it. The plan called for finding out what he'd done with it. We know that now. Now we need a new plan. They aren't going to come when he calls unless we have a good reason."

She jerked away from me to glare at him, "You can get them here, can't you?"

"I can get them here," he agreed.

She giggled as she turned to me, saying triumphantly, "See!"

She reached across the desk to pat his cheek, miscalculating and falling across the desk herself.

"Come with me now!" I said forcefully.

I was more frightened then angry.

91

I continued, "You're going to cause a scene, and even if it doesn't escalate, it will be spoken of. Please, beloved, come with me."

"Not until I get the money back."

"He said he put it back."

"He did?"

"Come with me."

Laughing and staggering she took my arm.

We left.

The secretary gaped at us.

"Get back to work," I snapped.

Julia giggled all the way to the car.

"Take us home," I said to Ryu, shaking my head at him.

She complained about the man stealing from the charity all the way home and was still angry enough that I could see her anima when we arrived.

I sent Ryu for tea, and we headed to the study.

"Jewels, darling, we need more practice before we attempt that again. And a better plan. I agree he should be made to pay it all back, but we need to make him do it in a way that doesn't lead to us. Too many people saw us go in. Word could get to one of his confederates. It must be done slowly and with care. Or we have the man turn himself in and let the authorities sort it out."

"They'd never get the money then."

"We must decide which is preferable—that the man is exposed as a fraud or that the charity receive the stolen money."

"Both! I want him to pay. That smarmy asshole was too damned smug when I confronted him!"

"I think we should discuss it again when you're calmer."

She snorted angrily. A red flush climbed her cheeks as she paced the small room.

"You're right. I get a bit... carried away when I use my own essence."

"Tomorrow we'll begin some experiments—here where we can retreat to this room if we miscalculate and there would be no witnesses. I shall speak to Asa and have him send all of the hired staff away for the day and take himself and his wife elsewhere. 'Tis past time we learned our limits."

Chapter 10

"Thank god," Ryu murmured.

I held a finger to my lips and tiptoed from the room.

"She'll likely sleep a day or more," I said as I closed the door.

I was a bit worried by how quickly sleep had claimed her but more worried about what she might do when she woke.

"Should we bring her to the bedroom?" he asked.

"No. I don't want to take the slightest chance she wakes. Call Asa and have him tell the contractors that work is to stop here by the house for three days. Make sure he tells everyone to keep quiet."

Ryu nodded as he said, "I'll tell him that Lady Blackwood is suffering from a migraine and you don't want her disturbed."

"Very good. Give the house staff the days off too."

"Will she be... calmer when she wakes?"

"I hope so."

"We should handle that asshole for her."

"I would if I knew what to do."

"I know you said that we shouldn't tell Sandra you're having any issues, and I agree, but maybe she'd know how best to handle him?"

"'Tis a marvelous idea. I shall call her forthwith."

"Maybe I should call her."

I lifted an eyebrow and he continued, "It isn't exactly a magical problem. And since we don't want her to know that it's a problem for Jewels, maybe I just ask her like it's no big deal? Like it's the sort of thing your secretary deals with?"

"*Hmm*... I think not. 'Twould be rude of me to have a servant call her as if my time is worth more than hers."

"Except I'm not really a servant—I'm a partner."

"*Ahh*... I see. Yes. Call her. But be very polite. I don't wish to offend when we aren't really her equals. Don't grovel but don't be pushy either."

"I've got this, Pip."

I wanted to listen in, but he was correct that I should be treating him as a partner, one that I trusted. So I went out to continue my training with the animals, which was teaching me so much about what I was capable of.

The animals were easier to read than the humans were. Their responses were clear without leaving me wondering if I'd influenced them or if they'd chosen to respond like people did.

I hoped I'd have some real progress to report by the time she woke.

I hoped we'd learn to control this gift of ours before it controlled us.

Chapter 11

I was excited to welcome Sandra to the estate. In the weeks since our last meeting I'd practiced long and hard, spending innumerable hours just staring at the anima of our tenants as they went about their day, beginning to see what my merest touch did to them. Learning to guide the wisps as I willed them.

Julia had been practicing as well and we now knew that she became drunk much quicker than I if she wasn't careful about absorbing the anger. She tended to become careless about absorbing anima when angry herself. She was getting better at it, which was reassuring, and she was very adept at manipulating the rinded, which she'd begun doing in larger numbers as per Sandra's request for staff.

Julia, Ryu, and I greeted Sandra at the door.

"The house is coming along marvelously," she said as she kissed Julia's cheek.

She offered me her hand, which I kissed, then shook Ryu's hand, handing him a pin made to resemble her logo, which was a red question mark inside a white triangle with the words Query Inc running along the curve.

She said, "I thought you might appreciate this. It doesn't look like much but it's actually quite valuable, there being few like it. It should also facilitate your admittance to any of my offices as only my most trusted employees receive such."

"Thank you," he said.

I took his hand and said, "Tell Sandra what you had for breakfast."

A smile full of relief lit his face when he said, "It's nothing she'd want to know."

He carefully pinned the charm to his collar.

Julia said, "Our Mrs. Roman has prepared a lovely lunch and then I thought you might like to see the gardens?"

"I'd be delighted."

We headed to the dining room.

Sandra stopped to pet Oliver, laughing lightly when she straightened, saying, "I've yet to meet anyone of worth who didn't love cats. I've been meaning to study on that but somehow never found the time."

We took our seats at the table and Mrs. Roman began to serve.

Sandra continued, "Speaking of time, I'd hoped that you'd spend the holidays with Cassandriel and myself at my home in Minnesota. Her friend Andre will be there. It's truly beautiful there in winter, and I thought as my Christmas gift to you, Pip, that you'd enjoy picking your own volumes to borrow."

"We'd be delighted," I said.

Julia said to Ryu, "Will you be able to manage alone here for a few weeks?"

"Yes. I've got a handle on them."

"Then we accept," she said to Sandra.

"Splendid. As a present to myself, I've purchased a jet. We can leave whenever it's convenient with no pesky bag restrictions."

By which I deduced she intended us to make custom agents look the other way.

Julia nodded happily.

Five fascinating hours later, we waved from the front step as Sandra drove away, then we returned to the upstairs study.

I sat at the small desk, sliding the notes I'd taken aside. I wished Sandra had more time to devote to lessons. She knew so much. Her insights on the books that she'd lent me gave me an entirely new appreciation for them.

I'd need to find the time to read them all again with her newest advice in mind. I much appreciated her teaching style. 'Twas so helpful to have such a large volume of reference material and the freedom to experiment as I wished. Sandra encouraged me to find my own answers, giving advice and encouraging me to try different methods.

I was learning so much from my mistakes.

Julia flopped into her usual chair, saying, "We need to devise a way or place for Ryu to hold anyone who acts up until we can return and force obedience."

Ryu said, "It won't be necessary."

"It might be seeing as how I don't want you to call the police. I normally keep a close eye on them and question them if I think they're going to do anything like sneak away to buy drugs, or if I see them displaying any strong emotion—and not just them. I ask all of the project managers if they think anyone is contemplating a crime." She gave me an exasperated glance as she added, "and I don't need to use anima to do that although I sometimes do if I think they're hesitating." She turned back to Ryu to say, "But I doubt they'd answer you as directly."

Ryu said, "I can handle them. My boys will know what's what and they'll tell me."

"Keep a very close eye on Bent and Smalls. I believe they're firmly under my control, but it isn't a chance I can take. I've caught them twice now trying to recruit a new arrival—although recruit is the wrong word. Influence might be closer. Both young men thought it a joke. Bent was serious though when he was encouraging them to lay in wait in her room. I'm going to be more than angry if we come back to find one of the women here has been raped in my absence."

I said, "Did you not tell them saying such things were forbidden?"

"Sure, when I found out about it. But what if there are other loopholes that I missed?"

Ryu said, "You can't just make them not want to rape?"

"I thought I had. I told them they didn't want to rape anyone, and they both agreed. It didn't occur to me to tell them that they didn't want anyone else to rape anyone. I've told them now. I told Smalls that he's not interested in sex at all. I try to keep him busy because I think he could become mentally unstable in a different way seeing as he has no outlets for his rage. Bent is my control. If Smalls seems stable in a few months, I'll give Bent the same command."

"Man..." Ryu shook his head as he jumped to his feet to pace. "That's a harsh sentence. I know they deserve it but..."

I said, "The women they murdered would think it a lenient sentence. 'Tis entirely too good for them!"

"My head knows that, and I believe you when you say they murdered those women, but I've known them since they were just kids. It's hard to see them as anything but the friends I knew..."

"You never once suspected?" Julia asked doubtfully.

"No. In hindsight I should've, not because I saw anything, but they were hanging with Birdie an awful lot and the three of them would get all quiet when I came in or smirk and laugh. I thought they were just planning some job they knew I'd be pissed about."

I said, "You never worried they'd murder you?"

"*Nah*. Why would they? They'd have had to do it on the sly and that's the sort of shit that gets found out. And when it did, no crew would've taken them in. They might have tried to do it boldly by baiting me or picking me a fight with someone, but it'd have to be someone who could beat me, and I ain't no dummy. If I thought they were doing that shit, I'd have called them out and the crew would've backed me or at least not interfered if me and Birdie threw down."

"Threw down what?"

His shoulders relaxed and he laughed as he resumed his seat.

"It means if we fought each other."

"*Ahh,* threw punches."

Julia said, "If you need us, call. The police are the absolute last resort."

"No *duh*."

She rolled her eyes at him.

She said, "Pip and I need to go to London this week. We'll do the first meetings that Sandra requested together and once Pip sees how it's done, you can escort her to the meetings when I go to Paris."

"I should go with you," Ryu said gruffly with a hint of angry sparkle on the words.

She flushed as she shook her head.

I said, "I can leave off studying if you need him to guard your sleep."

She said, "If I overeat, I'll call, and he can come then."

They were both clearly unhappy and avoiding my gaze.

I said, "Are my long sleeps a difficulty for either of you?"

She stood to kiss my forehead, saying, "No. It's fine, Pip. We don't mind at all." She hurried from the room.

He said, "It's fine. She's just worried you'll ask her to study as much as you do. She sleeps like a normal person. A regular guard is all that's needed."

I said, "Find a trustworthy one. Someone ethical without us ensuring it, but someone we *could* ensure if needs must. A retired soldier perhaps?"

"She's already hired some. I'll talk to her again before she goes."

He headed to the door but hesitated and finally turned back to say, "It isn't any of my business but… she told me the two of you aren't really man and wife. Birdie is too dangerous for her, Pip. He beats his women as a regular thing. He could hurt her before she could react."

"Julia and I are married in every sense of the word, but one, and that one is by my choice. She's truly my spouse in a way that human law can't mimic. 'I love her utterly. 'Tis her choice who she shares her affections with. 'Twill always be her choice! It would never be with a man like Birdie though."

"I don't think she'd choose him unless she was drunk on her power."

"I'll speak to her. She really is much more in control now though. We both are."

He nodded but looked unhappy.

"She needs to know we trust her," I said.

He nodded again, avoiding my gaze.

I said, "She won't take chances with him, but accidents do happen, which is why you'll accompany her. Use the pills if needs must but only as a last resort."

"She wouldn't take them if she's drunk."

"Which is why you'll need to pay attention."

"I don't think I could get her to eat or drink anything because she'd know why I was doing it."

"Then you'd need to force her."

"I'm not sure I could."

"That pin will make her powerless against you. I'm not saying she wouldn't fight you, but if you were fast enough you could force her to drink before she could fight you off or call for help."

"She'd never forgive me..."

"Of course she would. She'd be grateful once she regained her calm, but even if she didn't wouldn't it be worth it to save her from him?"

"Yes. I hate the idea of it though, Pip."

"I too... but I hate the idea of her losing control more."

"We need an injectable sedative," he said.

"Speak with Doreen."

He grimaced at me.

I made a face back that made him laugh.

I said, "You have a week before we go. Make sure you have your boys in order. I know you don't want to lock any of them up, and I hope it isn't necessary either, but prepare for it anyway. It really is very important that everything run smoothly in our absence. Not only for my peace of mind but we need to show Sandra that you can handle things here, and we don't want any bad publicity at all. So make absolutely sure that no one is planning anything. If you have any doubts at all, tell me and I'll speak to them myself before I go."

He nodded agreement. "I'll arrange a place to hold anyone who causes trouble, and I'll make sure that none of the hired help will run across it."

"Keep in mind that we won't be here to keep the kids from complaining either. We don't want them talking about holding cells or anything while in town."

"I'm not an idiot, Pip."

"I didn't mean to imply that you were. 'Tis just that I already take my skills for granted. This small break will be good for all of us. 'Twill be good to see how things go on here in our absence and good to go where we've no control of anyone. To my mind it could be dangerous if we begin to believe that we'll automatically receive the respect that we get here."

"You guys could both use a vacation."

"I enjoy the research."

"Does Julia?"

I said, "She enjoys the work she does with Sandra. I'm not certain how she truly feels about the work she does with the boys. She doesn't enjoy the work we do in the study at all..."

"I don't think she dislikes it," he said, "I think she's just busy doing things she enjoys more. Once you've got the books all translated, we'll like it better too."

"Do you dislike it?"

"Hell no! It's fascinating."

I smiled in relief.

His answering smile made my pulse flutter.

I hastily turned away, heading for the door, saying over my shoulder, "Get some sleep yourself. We can go out tomorrow night and retrieve more ivy."

Chapter 12

Two days later, Ryu and I followed Julia into a plushy appointed office. She'd woken in a good mood; one I hoped this visit wouldn't ruin.

She said, "Andrew, so nice of you to take my meeting on such short notice." She kissed the air by his cheek. "My husband, Lord Blackwood, and our assistant, Martin Poole."

We all shook hands and Andrew waved us to seats.

Julia said, "Such a shame about your son. You must be quite distraught."

Andrew's smile remained firmly in place, but angry anima lit the air by his mouth as he said, "I'll have it sorted in no time, seeing as he's completely innocent."

"No doubt," Julia said smugly.

Anima grew visible on his exposed skin.

I watched anxiously as Julia reached across his desk to take his hand.

She said, "You should sell your shares in Gaber Tech immediately. Friday, when Blanch Unlimited goes on the market, you should invest five million."

His smile relaxed.

I relaxed. She was controlling her anima nicely, merging just the smallest bit with his.

She grabbed his hand in both of hers and said, "Sell Gaber and buy Blanch."

She released it and stood, "It's been lovely catching up. I hope I can count on you to attend my next fundraiser."

She headed to the door, and we followed—even Andrew.

She rolled her eyes at me, and I had to bite back my laugh.

Our testing had shown that people who liked us or thought us sexually attractive could become infatuated when we used our anima on them even when it was just small amounts, but it usually wore off quickly. Rinded people remained infatuated even or maybe especially when we disliked them.

His secretary stood when we exited.

Julia said to Andrew, "I'm sure you have important work to do, calls to make. I'll call about that fundraiser. Ta."

He returned to his desk.

His secretary escorted us out.

Julia burst into giggles when we reached the sidewalk.

"Oh, his face! I despise that man! It might be harder to gain admittance at the next stop seeing as I don't know the man."

She rummaged in her purse to pull out a small notebook.

"Sandra said he's a gambler and gets mad when he loses. She thinks his wife, Lisa, is having an affair—or at least he thinks that. She didn't bother to check, but we can probably leverage it. Ryu, if the secretary won't let me in, get her angry. In fact, you go in first and ask if I can have a quick word with him. Tell her it's a personal matter and drop Pip's title."

"Your title too," I said.

She waved dismissively.

I said, "I shall accompany him. You shall be backup."

She nodded in agreement.

Ryu and I headed inside.

The girl at the desk was already angry. Dark red flickered on her fingers as she banged her computer keys.

I grabbed Ryu's arm, shaking my head as I pulled him back and stepped to the desk.

"Tell Mr. Quincy that Lord Blackwood desires an immediate conference—regarding Lisa."

She smirked at me as she banged on his door, opening it without waiting for an invitation and saying triumphantly, "There's a man here about your wife!"

Quincy was already angry as well.

He snapped, "Let him in and close the door. In fact, go to lunch! Now, Leslie! I'm in no mood."

"*Hmph!*" She stomped to her desk, grabbed her purse and coat and stormed out.

"What's this about my wife? And who are you?"

I grabbed his hand as I said, "You should sell your shares in Gaber Tech immediately. Friday, when Blanch Unlimited goes on the market, you should invest five million. Sell Gaber and buy Blanch. I've never met your wife. I just dropped in to say my wife will be calling on yours in the near future to invite her to a fundraiser. Have a lovely day."

We left while he was nodding agreement.

Julia said, "Well?"

I held up my hand for a fist bump, which Ryu laughingly obliged.

He withdrew his phone from his pocket as we headed to the car.

At the car he was still scrolling on his phone.

Julia said impatiently, "What are you doing?"

"There's a stock I need to sell."

"*Uh oh...*" I took his hand and said, "You don't need to buy or sell stock right now. That advice wasn't intended for you."

I released him to ask, "Where's your charm?"

"I left it in the car."

"Put it on. In the future, don't take it off when I'm working unless I tell you to."

"You enchanted him?" Julia asked in dismay.

"I was holding his arm. It wasn't purposeful. I'd meant to warn him the woman was already angry."

"We need some sort of signal," Ryu said.

"If I clear my throat and step back, you should approach them with the intent of angering them. Wear the charm unless I take your arm."

Julia said, "I'll do the next one but don't wear the charm and I'll see if I can use your anima as you shake their hand."

He sighed hard but nodded.

"'Tis just a stock sale—of stock you don't own," I said as reassuringly as I could.

He snickered and got into the driver seat.

I watched closely as Ryu and the secretary shook hands.

"Send us to the boss's office," Julia said.

The anima brightened.

A bead of sweat trickled down Julia's cheek. I thought it more from nerves than effort.

She tired much faster than I when spending her own anima on those who weren't rinded or angry, but it would take more than one simple command.

The secretary led us directly to a door down the carpeted hall and knocked once on an office door.

"Come!" a man called impatiently.

She opened the door and walked back to her desk.

"Yes," he said, glaring at her retreating back.

Julia cleared her throat and stepped back.

Ryu hurried forward, offering his hand to the man who took it by reflex.

She said, "You should sell your shares in Gaber Tech immediately. Friday, when Blanch Unlimited goes on the market, you should invest five million. Sell Gaber and buy Blanch."

She staggered hard.

I caught her arm to steady her.

"What in the world? Who are you people."

I released Julia to hurry closer.

"Hold his hand," I ordered and grabbed both their hands and said, "You should sell your shares in Gaber Tech immediately. Friday, when Blanch Unlimited goes on the market, you should invest five million. Sell Gaber and buy Blanch.

He stopped trying to pull his hand away as soon as I'd started speaking.

"I'll sell Gaber and buy Blanch," he agreed.

"We were never here."

He stood as I turned away.

"Go back to work."

He gave me a woebegone smile but sat and began typing.

We left.

In the corridor, I gave Julia a quick hug. "You were too far. I could see the strands reaching. I think if you'd been angry, it might have worked better."

Ryu said, "Don't try that again. You look sick. How bad did that hurt you?"

"I'm fine just a bit shaken. It felt like hitting a wall. I'll be careful."

I said, "Test your limits slowly and pick people who are alone in the room else they could escape your reach before you could manipulate them."

"I'll be careful," she repeated. "I should've made sure he wasn't immune to me first. From now on, do that first thing by telling them to do something completely unrelated to the task we mean to set them on."

I nodded agreement.

Ryu said, "Are we buying this Garber stock?"

"Yes. It'll skyrocket on Friday when Blanch goes up for sale."

I said to her, "I don't like the idea of you trying this alone in Paris."

"I won't be alone. I'll take Frankie and Jacob."

Ryu said, "Jacob... he's from Newport? Right? I don't recall what gang he belonged to."

"Because he didn't belong to one. I found him by accident. He's a lawyer. Other than his penchant for murdering criminals, he's a nice guy."

"Oh my..."

She shrugged at me.

Ryu frowned at her.

I said, "Let's go. We can stop for lunch and then make our next stops."

We headed to the car.

Julia got into the back with me.

I thought she was feeling better but wasn't certain.

I said, "Are you recovered?"

"Yeah. Just thinking. I'll need to train us some helpers. Ones who will just do as their told." She wrinkled her nose at me as she said, "You don't need to worry about it. He isn't my type at all."

It hadn't occurred to me that she'd been romantically interested in this Jacob person until she mentioned it.

I said, "Your affairs are your own. I'd not wish a criminal on you though... although, I suppose, *I* am a criminal. My worry was that you'll be traveling with two dangerous men, and as Bent has shown us, there are loopholes."

"I'll be fine. Neither is the type to hurt someone for the hell of it. They had their reasons, and they were good reasons. I won't adopt a gangbanger unless I'm certain I'm in control."

She handed me her little notebook.

"Now, let's see how many of these we can get to today."

Ryu was angry.

We both pretended not to notice it.

I flipped through the pages. There was a long list of stock transactions that would keep us busy until we left to visit Sandra at Christmas.

I said, "I shall require my own list as I have no earthly inkling of what any of these products are or do."

"We don't need to know. It doesn't even matter if we buy or not although I intended to invest exactly as Sandra advises me to. She's paying us for this and most of it is for long-range plans of hers. She warned me that we won't notice much difference in the market itself. Her accountants will be watching for those share prices to drop as our marks sell because once it's noticed that they're selling, others will join in. Then we swoop in and buy. There's still a chance that the company tanks though."

"Goes bankrupt," Ryu interjected.

Julia nodded agreement, continuing, "But it's more likely to recover and even flourish when Blanch goes big because Blanch needs the parts Gaber makes—or so I've been told."

"'Tis complicated."

"It is, it's interesting though. I'm enjoying learning the ins and outs, and I have some investment ideas of my own that we can talk about after the holidays when things slow down again for us. This is our safety net, Pip. I *need* to learn how to do it!"

"I can hardly wait to see her library!" I said, realizing as I said it that to Julia managing money in this modern way meant safety to her as the books did to me.

Julia and Ryu laughed.

The tension in the car eased or mayhap it was just my lingering unease. She had a boldness I lacked. One I must strive to attain if I wished to be a modern woman—man.

I snorted with laughter, earning inquiring glances from both of them.

"'Tis nothing. I just sometimes forget who I am now."

Julia laughed too, squeezing my knee. "You're Lord Blackwood. No one would dare turn you away. You're sure to breeze right into their inner sanctums."

"We shall get every person on the list to do our bidding."

She laughed in delight.

I resigned myself to a long week.

Chapter 13

December 23

Julia leaned closer to whisper, "I'd have thought her house would be grander."

"*Shh.*"

Sandra hadn't appeared to notice the exchange.

She and Drew were speaking to an old man who Cassandriel had greeted with a quick hug.

I'd met Drew numerous times with Cass but hadn't realized until that moment that he was one of Sandra's confidants.

The golden anima of love flashed between the two—or at least that's what I believed the thin golden filaments meant. I only ever saw it briefly when people were greeting each other fondly. It sometimes took on a dark hue that I thought represented lust.

It occurred to me that Drew was more than just Sandra's assistant or Cassandriel's guard. I'd always thought they had a strong family resemblance, now I was certain of it.

Three men began removing our luggage from the car and bringing it into the house.

Cassandriel and the old man hurried to the barn.

Sandra and Drew escorted us to the house where Ms. Hargrove, Sandra's top assistant, was holding open the door. We'd spoken often and met a few times.

I quite liked her.

I'd have thought Sandra's home would be grander too, I mused as we stepped inside. It was large but nowhere near as large as her English one. The outside was misleading as to the elegance of the inside, which I thought purposeful on her part.

I stopped to admire the elegant foyer.

Drew said, "I'll take your bags up."

Julia handed him her carryon.

I followed Drew.

At the head of the stairs, he gestured with his chin to the left.

"Sandra's room is down this corridor. Andre will be staying in the room beside hers. You'll be in the room right beside Cass. If you need anything, don't hesitate to ask Ms. Hargrove. I expect Cassandriel and I will be taking an early morning ride. You're welcome to join us."

He opened a door as he was speaking and set Julia's bag on a dresser right inside the doorway.

"The bathroom is through the door there."

We stepped to the side to let the men carry in our luggage.

"Ms. Hargrove will have this sorted in no time. If you need anything cleaned or pressed just leave it in the bathroom or tell her."

A white cat wandered in.

I crouched to pet it.

"Fluff," Drew said. "She's a favorite. There are more of them around. If they bother you, just tell Ms. Hargrove and she'll corral them.

"I quite like cats. She's a beauty."

"I'll leave you to settle in. Have a nice evening, Lord Blackwood."

"Please, call me Philip or Pip."

He smiled as he nodded, saying, "Pip, then. Have a nice evening," as he left the room.

I picked up Fluff, cuddling her a moment before setting her on the bed then unpacked my carryon into the bedside table before returning downstairs.

Hargrove was waiting in the foyer and said, "Sandra is in her study with your wife. She thought you might like to browse her personal library."

I followed her to a large room lined with bookcases and glass fronted cabinets. A narrow table in the center of the room held the same sort of tools I was used to using in the museum library.

Hargrove unlocked leaded glass doors of a case in the back of the room and handed me a pair of white gloves.

"Feel free to browse the shelves just keep in mind the age and delicacy of the books. There's a card at the front of the book that will tell you if there's a transcription available here in the library.

"Dinner is at eight. Would you like me to send the maid to remind you to dress?"

"That would be lovely, thank you."

She left and I reached eagerly for the first book.

In our room later that night as we dressed for dinner, I said to Julia, "We need to buy copies of her books."

"You should see the ones she has in her basement."

I held a finger to my lips and whispered, "My rune of silence might not be strong enough to please her."

It had taken me a maddeningly long time to write the rune. It was a simple spell, or appeared to be, but getting my anima to infuse it took multiple passes where my least inattention let the anima escape. Tracing it multiple times could strengthen it when it didn't destroy it completely. My inexperience with managing the timing of the cast coupled with my inability to hold the necessary anima was keeping my spells weak. It worked, but not well.

Julia kissed my cheek as she headed to the bathroom.

I dressed in an evening suit—one of Lou's that I despised.

We went down to dinner together.

Sandra escorted us to the table where Cassandriel was waiting.

She said, "I hope you're planning on joining Drew and me in the morning. I'd love to show you my babies and take you around my favorite ride."

Sandra said, "Darling, maybe Pip could borrow a few? He'll need some gentle beasts for his guests until he finds the time to shop for himself."

Cassandriel nodded.

Two maids began serving dinner.

I said, "Drew won't be joining us?"

Sandra laughed as she said, "I hadn't considered that you'd have no masculine company. I'll ask him for tomorrow evening."

Cassandriel said, "We should invite him for Christmas Eve and day, Mom, since he doesn't have family to visit."

"Will Andre be joining us for Christmas Eve?" I asked.

"He'll be here around noon Christmas Day."

Sandra said, "Hargrove has arranged a special treat for us. She won't be here herself as she's visiting family. We'll have to take plenty of pictures because she's very excited about it."

She turned to me and said, "We wanted to do something to help the town heal after some dreadful happenings this summer, and this seemed the perfect opportunity. She found the most charming carriage company so that snow or not we can enjoy horse drawn carriage rides and a winter fair that will run for three days with all sorts of fun horseback events, musical performances, magicians, jugglers, clowns, games, and free food. Speaking of which, I thought it'd be fun to play roulette this evening.

"Hargrove had considered using the wheel at the fair, but on second thought decided gambling, even if it was for treats or trinkets, wasn't the best idea. It's a beautiful antique... I think I might keep it."

Cassandriel snickered.

Sandra grinned at her as she said, "I'll send it to the estate as it's rather large... so how was Abda?"

"Beautiful. I might move him and his brides to the estate." She heaved an unhappy sigh. "Next fall. I won't have time for him now..."

Sandra said, "You'll have plenty of time to enjoy him."

It struck me how differently she and I saw our immortality. She hadn't grown up with the expectation of outliving her friends and family. Nor had I. It shaded all of my decisions now because I knew I'd outlive any friend I might make. Cassandriel wouldn't adjust as blithely as I because nothing I'd loved had survived. I hadn't had to watch them all die while I lived. She'd have to leave them behind— *unless she could change the human shape she wore or had friends—like me— who could keep her pets for her if she had to hide.*

I said, "Would you be interested in selling us one of his foals?"

"I'd love one of the white mare's foals," Julia said enthusiastically. "The pictures you showed us were absolutely gorgeous! Will you show her to me tomorrow, Cass? And don't forget I want one of little misses kittens."

"Sure. Mischief won't be ready to have kittens until next fall. You're first on the list though."

Julia said, "While I was looking at property for a business idea we had, I came across a lovely old estate on the outskirts of Oxford.

It's close enough to town to be easily accessible and I thought of you immediately because of the large barns. There's a gorgeous new indoor ring. The grounds are a mess but they're large enough for parking and maybe even a small track. It could be exactly the sort of place you could fix up to house your horses and hold events."

We chatted about the possibilities there all through dinner.

As soon as dinner finished, we headed to the living room where Sandra taught Cassandriel and I how to play roulette.

"'Tis a fools game," I said laughingly as I slid my last chips onto the board.

"You're right." Sandra winked at Cassandriel. "It's played at a lot of charity events. It's important to know all the rules for all the common gambling games because you'll be playing them or hosting the game at some time or another. Learning to spot tells and bluffs is always helpful. I go to casinos occasionally to see who's playing and how desperate they are."

"Sounds fun," Cassandriel said sarcastically.

"It *is* fun. I can have fun and still learn something."

Julia said, "I host some sort of gambling party at least once a year and can vouch for the loosening effects of alcohol on your wallet."

Sandra said, "Will you be doing any fundraising this year?"

"Yes. We'll have a ball at the house in the fall. I think we'll do an auction or maybe a blind dinner date raffle. I'm not sure if I'll do any others. Organizing the house and Pip's finances is my priority."

"You spoil me," I said as I took her hand to kiss it.

Cassandriel said, "I don't know about you guys, but I'm beat. I'll see you in the morning. Night all."

"Good night, darling," Sandra said as she kissed her daughter's cheek.

Sandra took out her phone, fussed with it for a moment, then set it on an end table.

"One moment," she murmured and a second later the curtains fluttered.

"There. No one can hear us now until the door opens. How are your studies progressing?"

"I can hold water inside my pentagram," I said.

"And you, Julia?"

"Not as well as Pip."

In truth she couldn't do it at all. She hadn't the patience to practice as was needed to form the spell quickly enough to stop all of the water from leaking away.

Sandra returned to the roulette wheel.

"The spell of holding can help in some games of chance. You never know when you might find yourself penniless or needing fast cash or maybe you might need to launder money in a hurry.

"No one will question money that you claim you've gotten from gambling if you occasionally gamble. Save cheating for when you have to win. Avoid huge wins as a regular thing, but roulette lends itself to a huge win, especially if you can afford to dump some large chunks of cash on double zero. You need to be fast and precise. Casinos have security cameras, so mistakes will be recorded. If you make a mistake, you need to be prepared to take drastic action to get to the security tapes, although in your case, you could probably manipulate any security guard who apprehends you. Go along quietly to keep as few people as possible alarmed and work your way up to whoever controls the recordings. Make sure you've erased them all but it's best not to get caught. So practice!"

She handed the roulette ball to Julia.

"Roll it and watch how it stops."

We all leaned over the wheel as Julia spun it.

"There," I said, pointing to the edge of the cup. "A hesitation wouldn't be noticed as the ball drops in."

"Very good. You can sometimes catch it on the bounce but that's tricky. Don't try that unless it's life or death."

Julia frowned.

I said, "She means we could apply this same spell to any small thing moving at speed."

Sandra nodded. "If a man were to point a gun at your head, you could place the holding spell on the bullet or the barrel. It's likely to be noticed, which could be a problem or not depending on who's doing the noticing. The barrel could explode from the force, which could be dangerous to people nearby, so it could be best to put a weak hold that the bullet can push through. We'll practice that too. I'll teach you all of my survival spells that you have the skill to learn."

She drew a circle with her finger while jumping and then was standing a foot off the ground.

"I'm holding myself."

She did it again. In four hops, her hands were against the ceiling.

"That is a holding. This is levitation."

She took something from her pocket and ate it. A second later she began to sink to the ground.

"The spell I used was weak. A strong enough spell would keep me afloat but without something to push against or pull on I'd be stuck. There's ways around that which don't require magic like portable fans, bellows, cloth wings, and such. You aren't ready to learn this spell yet, but I thought I'd show you so you don't get confused on what holding can do. It's important to understand how the holding spell works. You're holding the air beneath your feet or the air the object will hit. Holding air is difficult. It's much easier to hold things you can see. Throwing a handful of sand into the air for instance can help immensely. You can hold solid things in place like doors and windows but things that move like bullets, balls, people and animals require walls of air. Putting the spell on the person could kill them if done incorrectly. It's difficult to use that spell that way because of the energy people have. You have to hold that energy. That's a lesson for another day though.

"What's important for this lesson is you learn the size and timing of your spell so that if you ever did find yourself falling from a roof you could hold yourself without cutting off an arm or leg.

Your spell to hold that little roulette ball needs to be the right size and strength, or you could clip a piece from the ball. Not that we need to worry too much about that. Anyone seeing it in this realm would just think the ball shattered, but you need to learn how much your spell will hold and how quickly so that you don't break things or people using it.

"Tomorrow, when Cassandriel is at Anne's, we'll go to my lab and practice. Speaking of which, I'd like you to download an app to your phone so that we can coordinate who's interrupting them. I don't want she and Andre alone together for more than minutes."

Julia said, "I've been practicing with the animals and can make a horse lay down or act up if we need to fake one is ill."

Sandra nodded approval but said, "That's a last resort as it would seriously upset her."

She reached into a side table drawer and handed me a bottle of pills.

"These can calm her. I plan to teach you this recipe. They might work on you but use caution when trying it because grie can have weird effects on creatures of spirit."

"How would I get her to ingest one?"

"You can put it in a drink or food. It will dissolve quickly. This batch was made to look like aspirin, so you could just offer it to her as that. It would help with aches and pains if she had them. Speaking of which, if she's injured, under no circumstances let anyone operate. Remove any foreign objects but don't use anything—no stitches, no staples, because she'll heal much quicker than normal. It would be noticed. The few times she cut herself badly on branches, I just tell her it's just a scratch and cover it with gauze and then when she looks, it *is* just a scratch."

She sat on the arm of the chair as she said, "This goes for you two as well as her. Never leave blood or hair clippings behind. Burn it if you can.

"I always arrange for the hairdresser to come to me although now with your help, you could find us an angry one who won't remember sweeping up the clippings and giving it to us."

"I'll look for one when we go home," Julia said.

"There's no rush. I have a project I'd like to get started. It would require one of you, preferably Pip, to be in Dubai for a month or more."

"Doing what?" Julia asked.

"Making tile."

"Is tile something different now than it was?" I asked.

Sandra grinned as she shook her head.

Julia said slowly, "Pip and I want nothing to do with drugs."

"It *is* smuggling but not drugs. It's a complicated project that I'll explain more fully once I see if we can get it off the ground. The tile factory doesn't need to make money although that would be a bonus. I could own it, but I thought it'd be easier for Pip to boss everyone around if he *was* the boss.

"I'd like to build a hidden lab there like the one there. I think all of us could do business there and the lab would be useful for all of us. We'd need a construction crew under your control and the factory workers. If you're able to shift anima you could use your mules to make the existing workers train the people who you pick to replace them without needing to use your own anger."

"Our mules?" Julia asked.

"It's what the seethes I knew called the people they controlled. Some seethes can shift that anima around. They'd place it on a few men who followed them around to be food if they were injured or energy if they needed it. The more anima, the better they can be controlled."

"Our boys," I said.

Sandra shook her head. "Not really. Your boys aren't nearly as deeply under control as a mule is. You're just nudging them. A mule requires a firm grasp on the reins, as it were. You ride them to your destination; you don't point them at it. Small nudges done over time will train someone, but it would require hard shoves more often if you were trying to make someone do something they didn't want to do. I'm talking about when you leave them. When you're right there, grabbing their anima, you're imposing your will on them, so they'll do just about anything, especially if you're angry. But in a few weeks or so it's going to occur to them that they don't want to do it unless what they're doing is something they'd normally do. You'd need to reinforce it over time until they believed it was their idea."

I said, "What happens if we nudge them too often?"

"It depends, some grow to resent it, some to crave it, and some never seem to notice."

"And a mule?"

"Is animated with your anima. I'm uncertain how it's done but I've seen it. Always on violent men with hard tempers. A mule will love a seethe beyond its own self. Or maybe it just lacks any will at all to disagree? The ones I've seen all seemed to be obsessed though, only showing any emotion at all when their seethe's regard was on them."

She stood to toss Julia the roulette ball.

"Let's practice."

Chapter 14

The next afternoon Julia and I were in the stable yard with Cassandriel when Drew approached with a handsome young man.

Cassandriel's anima swirled in excitement, sparkling on his name as she exclaimed happily, "Andre!"

"Cass! he said in an equally emotion laden voice, but not a speck of anima appeared.

The two embraced.

I was close and staring hard and still almost missed the exchange of anima. A thin thread of gold wound across her cheek to his, and when it connected, two glittering lines appeared for the merest moment, trailing from him to her.

One was a brilliant white as if the gold were pure light and the other the more normal tone of gold shaded with the darker color of lust.

His hold on her tightened when he caught my stare, which he did immediately.

Drew said, "This is our friend, Lord Blackwood, from England."

Andre offered his hand.

I shook it saying, "Please, call me Pip. I count Cass as one of my dearest friends. She's spoken so often and so highly of you I feel like we're friends already."

Cassandriel said, "Where's Julia? I want you to meet her too."

Drew said laughingly, "She's with your mother talking over some investment scheme or another. There'll be plenty of time for them to meet. I was going to stop by Anne's to say hello and drop my present. Did you guys want to come?"

Again Andre's grip tightened on her for a moment. He smiled ruefully when he released her, kissing her on the lips quickly.

Another small thread of gold went from her to him.

He said, "Sure. It'd be nice to see her and say hello."

Cassandriel heaved a sigh but nodded, making a face at Drew. "Why didn't you give her your gift yesterday or when we got here? We've seen her every day...."

"It wasn't done yet. I needed Sandra's workshop here to finish it."

We headed to Cassandriel's car.

Andre said, "I can't wait to give you your Christmas gift. Are we exchanging after dinner?"

Cassandriel frowned at him, putting her hands on her hips.

"I thought we agreed that gifts need to be handmade."

"It is," he said laughingly.

Her eyes narrowed. "By you?"

Drew said, "I can't read his aura, but I know he didn't make it," which made Andre flush and her giggle.

She linked her arm in his, beaming up at him.

I exchanged quick worried glances with Drew.

Sandra joined me beside the temporary paddock on the town green that evening.

We were alone. The rest of our party was inside the paddock admiring the horses with a group of young adults who Anne was introducing to Cassandriel, Andre, and Drew.

Most of the crowd was on the far side of the green, enjoying the fair. A few couples strolled the street behind us, but it was private enough for me to say to Sandra, "He has no thread to grasp. I tried when he was angry at that boy who was rude to Anne. I'd swear it was real anger, not feigned, and yet I couldn't force a connection. My anger just flows into him. He's dense somehow... I believe he truly loves her though. For the merest moment I saw his anima when they first spoke. 'Tis clear she loves him... shall I try to anger him directly?"

Sandra said, "No. I want the four of you to be friends—and not just to keep her safe from forming an attachment with a human male but because you and she are so much alike. You could be real friends for many years. Both of you are more human in your thinking than not. I think you'll have very much in common. The three of you could help each other remain hidden, which she'll need to do once it becomes clear that she isn't aging as she should.

"Hopefully, I'll have been able to tell her what she is by then and help her learn the spell to change her shape. It worries me so that she'll lose this shape completely..."

"Julia and I will do all in our power to assist—for her sake."

"I'd like to ask you for a favor," Sandra said. "It would put me into your debt completely. If ever she had need and I couldn't help her...I wish you to be her guardian, Pip, in this form or another. To look after her to the best of your ability even if she never knows what you truly are."

I nodded as I said, "I envied her him for a moment, but they're doomed to tragedy, aren't they? He'll die and leave her alone here in this realm where she has little chance of meeting another of her kind."

It occurred to me as I said it that maybe Sandra meant for Cassandriel and I to fall in love.

I said, "I could grow to love her as I do Julia. Already I cherish her as a dear friend. 'Twould be many years, many many years before I could see a woman, any woman, as a potential mate. I wish it weren't so because my Julia would gladly be all to me but in my heart, I am a woman."

Sandra clasped my arm, giving it a reassuring squeeze.

"I too am female in my thoughts. Nature formed me to want a male mate. It never once occurred to me to search out a female. But now that I *have* mated, it wouldn't matter to me what form he has. I think it would be the same with you. Your human values are different than my daughter's. Here and now the line between the sexes is very much blurred. I think in time you'll be more comfortable with the idea of a same sex mate—although you're not really either sex. I promise you, Pip, once you feel your true mate's hamingja, their outward shape will mean nothing."

"I don't think I'll ever feel that. Julia and I... she's a part of me. If seethes were meant to share themselves that way I think 'twould have happened 'ere now."

"...just don't give up on love, Pip. The richness of friendships is to be treasured because none of us truly know how long we have. My daughter will lose all of the humans she loves, and it does worry me, but what a cold empty life it would be for her without them."

"Was it fate that we met?"

"Did I plan it, you mean?" she asked tartly.

She linked her arm in mine and began walking to the pasture gate.

"It was pure chance—although it's more likely than not that any others who've crossed the realms will also be interested in the same things we are. They too will be using their magic to better their lives here, so it's likely you'll run into more of us. Be wary when that happens, Pip. Prepare places where you can retreat to should it become necessary."

"None ever approached you?"

"No. But I was keeping as low of a profile as I could. Once Cassandriel finishes school and has matured a bit I plan to tell her everything, and then we can decide if we want to hide or not. I prefer hiding. I'd be quite content in my la—lab studying, but she needs these human accouterments, the security guards, the comfortable human dwellings."

"I prefer that too."

She laughed lightly as she said, "I've grown to appreciate human comforts."

Anne called, "Lord Blackwood, Pip, come see my Sahara!"

She ran over to us to take my arm, grinning up at me.

For a moment I was transported to a similar gathering with Violet and our friends. It might have saddened me, except when I accompanied Anne all of her friends gazed at me with respect or admiration, which was a heady feeling and much of a change from the weighing or pitying glances I'd gotten when accompanying my sister.

I much preferred being the lord to the spinster lady.

The young people chatted and flirted exactly as they had in my day.

Two boys were standing with their arms entwined like the other couples were and no one seemed at all concerned.

Perhaps Sandra was right, and it was time to shuck off some of the human morals that I'd learned in my youth.

Chapter 15

"Looking forward to getting home?" Drew asked as he leaned against the fence beside me.

"...I'm not sure. I love it there, but that estate is already engraved in my memory. I find travel very interesting. It's nice to make new memories. All of these new thoughts when for so long I had none..."

To my surprise, he gave me a quick hug.

"I'm glad we met, Pip. Cass needs friends like you. It's hard to embrace the inner self and you do it so gracefully."

He hugged me again. I returned his embrace, wishing I'd had a father like him.

The thought was so unfathomable that it made me laugh.

Drew pulled back, giving me a worried look.

"Pip!" Julia called and we both turned.

"The car is here."

"Have a safe trip," Drew said as he smoothed my collar.

The small gesture touched me. I wished I knew what to say to acknowledge I saw his kindness and real worry for Phillipa the girl I was, not the man I looked like.

I kissed his cheek and went to make my goodbyes.

Ryu greeted us at the front door, taking Julia's carryon and offering his hand to shake.

"How was the trip?"

"Most informative," I said.

Julia kissed the air by his cheek.

I wished I dared do the same.

She glanced pointedly around, saying loudly, "Did you have a nice visit with your family?"

He laughed as he said, "My brothers were thrilled to see me—or at least the gifts I brought them."

He ushered us inside and we all headed upstairs.

"And your mother?" I asked. "Has she agreed to accept a job here and relocate?"

"She's sure I'm up to something... she was surprisingly pleasant though. When she spoke to me, that is."

Julia frowned at him.

His anima surged, showing his anger.

"It ain't nothing I done! She's always hated me—always! She never had no time for me. When I look back now, I'm amazed she didn't just leave me on a street corner somewhere or sell my ass. I guess I should be grateful she let me stay as long as she did..."

"Did she abuse you?"

"*Nah.* Nothing like that. I mean, sure she'd smack me if I didn't hop to but mostly she just didn't give a shit."

"Was she doing drugs or *um....*" Julia flushed, shrugging apologetically.

"Turning tricks?" he asked with amused anger.

He shrugged.

"I have no idea. Maybe… it isn't something I can ask."

I said, "If it troubles you, I would ask…"

His eyes widened then grew thoughtful.

"Maybe. Someday… it don't matter none. She said she'd think about moving. If she won't, then yeah, I want to make her. My brothers would be a lot safer growing up here."

Julia said, "What about your brothers' father? Is he still in the picture?"

"He's in jail, which is lucky for those boys *and* her. He's a mean one. Although it never seemed to bother her none. She'd be throwing shit too…"

We dropped the larger bags inside my bedroom door and headed to the study with my carryon, which was practically bursting at the seams.

I said, "And what of your father?"

Julia gave me an exasperated glance, shaking her head.

Ryu said, "I have no idea who he is. Which reminds me, I got that list of names. But really, it don't matter none who we pick cause only she can refute it and why would she?"

We settled into the seats in the study, them in the chairs by the window and me at the desk.

Julia said, "True, but we don't want her to take you to court for her share either."

"Can't you just magic her to leave it alone?"

I said, "Yes. But as I understand it, we need to pick our marks carefully because they'll be subject to outside influences who will be encouraging them to sue, or who might be able to sue on their behalf."

Julia nodded in agreement. "Ideally, we'd pick a relative of your actual father and she would be supportive of it without needing to do anything to her. We could convince any number of people to drop a lawsuit, but if we do it too often people are going to notice. But there are options. Show him, Pip."

I removed a small white ball from my coat pocket and set it on my desk.

Ryu stood to watch closely.

Julia said, "Sandra warned us about using this too often. But it's probably something we could do to get your stake."

I rolled the ball across the desk, stopping it dead on the edge by activating the spell of holding I'd placed there.

"She's really good at that," Julia said approvingly as she stood to flick the ball.

It didn't budge.

I released it by canceling the spell, which I did by pulling the anima from the rune.

She flicked it again and it rolled off the desk coming to a stop in midair—caught in the spell I'd hurriedly placed.

"I'm too slow. It has to be done perfectly," Julia said.

"Holy shit!"

Julia laughed as she said, "You're going to take your Christmas bonus to the casino."

"Hot damn!"

I said, "I shall place the rune on the board, which could take me some time as I need to be close to do it. The wheel must come to rest positioned correctly. Once I've placed the rune, I shall signal you and you'll begin betting on zero. Hopefully, in a few rolls, the ball slows enough that I can stop it without anyone noticing."

"We should practice," Ryu said eagerly.

"We have..." Julia said in a tone that made me laugh.

I said, "My lady finds the practice quite tedious... Sandra has agreed that I may try it unsupervised."

Julia muttered, "You'd find casting one rune over and over while standing in flour dust thick enough to choke you tedious too."

I said, "'Twas a brilliant way to see the spell and quite useful to learn to gauge the needful size."

I took a simple white paper napkin with smeared writing in runny ink across the corner from my pocket to hand him.

"'Tis your job to place this and pick it up again."

Julia said, "Don't let anyone walk off with it."

"What's it do?" he asked.

"'Tis a spell that will cause whoever it's touching to throw his or her drink. 'Tis meant to be a distraction in case I miscalculate."

Julia said, "It's a spell Sandra and Pip made together. They don't always throw the drink, but they always yell and jump up, which should be good enough."

Ryu frowned worriedly. "It'll be caught on camera, man. Even if you could activate it really fast, if you stopped a ball too sudden, it's going to be noticed."

"'Tisn't for the roulette table," I said. "We're going to rob one of the patrons."

Julia said, "Pip can fill you in later. She can draw a really good rune of silence now. You'll be able to talk in the car on the way there and in your hotel rooms. Speaking of which, you need to pick her a driver."

"Two drivers," I interjected.

Julia nodded absently.

She said to Ryu, "I have a list of positions that I need to fill. You and I can go over it later, but we need that driver for tomorrow. I was thinking Ollie, but I'm not sure if his driving skill is up to it."

I said, "'Twill be a boring job waiting in the car, but 'twas my thought he'd be quite content if given a laptop to play on while we were occupied."

"Are we talking a getaway driver?" Ryu asked.

Julia snickered. "No. Pip needs someone to drive for her when you're busy elsewhere and that person needs to have enough anima to use in an emergency. He needs to do whatever Pip says to do without argument, without her needing to enforce it each time even if it makes no sense. Ollie doesn't mind wearing a uniform or carrying bags and doesn't seem to care what he's sent to do."

I said, "He's actually quite a cheerful companion."

Julia nodded as she said, "So we were thinking of offering him a full-time position, but it wouldn't be just Pip he was driving. He'd be sent to pick up guests or whatever else we needed picked up. So it needs to be someone who *wants* the job. Someone who can use their common sense if they have a problem because some of the things he'll be sent to pick up might be...troublesome."

I said, "'Tis my plan to speak with the custom agents and such but 'tis possible that he runs into a problem."

Ryu said, "Ollie won't be able to handle a real cop or anything, but he does follow direction. If you tell him what to do if things go sideways, he'd do it."

Julia said, "He's bound to seriously dislike a lot of the people he's sent to pick up, and while I can magic him into being polite..."

"I'll talk to him."

She said, "Be careful in what you say. He's your friend but when he sees that you're our right-hand man, he might try to use what he knows about you and us to leverage—"

"I can handle Ollie. Shit, I can handle all of them, except Birdie maybe. Birdie ain't going to go the cops or no shit like that but he might try to make me disappear."

Julia said, "Birdie will be busy in Paris on another project."

"Still... he wants you, and it's going to be eating him up that I'm here and he's there."

I realized as he said it that Ryu wanted her too. It was in the heat of his gaze, which darkened when she smiled at him.

Her response surprised me, which in hindsight was naïve of me. It was clear Julia enjoyed sex and Ryu was a beautiful man.

A hot flush scalded my cheeks.

I hastily turned my attention to the contents of my pocket, laying the rest of the napkins on the table.

I said, "'Tis beyond my ability to make such yet. The blue will hold with a sense of calmness, mayhap even put a relaxed person to sleep. It may only be used one time, and the cost is great to make one, so we must use care when using them. The red will combust, burning anything it's placed upon to ash within minutes, even metals. The green will cast a ring of invisibility in a four-foot-circle and the yellow will levitate an object."

Julia said, "If you jumped, you'd still fall but slowly. It doesn't make you fly; it just makes things light."

"Can you fly?" he asked in awe.

I said, "Not yet. Someday maybe."

Julia heaved a hard sigh. "Pip will master it decades before me."

"If you chose to study more..."

She laughed as she headed to the small bar we'd added to the room to pour herself a glass of wine. She poured me a lemon seltzer and handed Ryu a beer before resuming her seat.

I carefully folded the napkins and tucked them into my jacket pocket as I said, "'Twill be our job to decide the best use. I can activate the spells at a distance, but it requires that I can see it."

Julia said, "I'm counting on your street smarts, Ryu, to keep the plan practical. She can place small holding spells, but they'll lack the strength to hold long. A determined person could break it in a few minutes or so, maybe much quicker if their will was strong, so don't count on it holding doors or windows closed for long."

I said, "I shall be cautious."

Her eyebrows rose and I realized I'd said it angrily.

"I don't require a nursemaid but I'm quite aware I require a knowledgeable opinion. I shall listen most respectfully to his advice."

"You're the boss," Ryu agreed in a too jovial tone.

Julia stood and headed to the door.

"I'll leave you two to catch up. Ryu, meet me here after dinner and we'll go over the employee list."

I said to Ryu, "Have you made any progress on a holding spell?"

"Nope it doesn't do a thing when I draw it."

"I have in my bag some… potions. Sandra believes that you will likely have enough of my anima that you'll be able to replicate them as they're alchemistic, needing just a tiny bit of earth magic to activate. Some of the potions anyone may use once they are activated. I'm unsure if you wish to learn it though…"

"Damn straight I do!"

"Then I shall teach you. If we find you cannot activate them, we can discuss then our options. But first you need to make your tools. 'Tis a critical step. You'll require funds to purchase the base elements. Sandra was quite clear that you must believe that you are the owner of your implements, so she recommended that we never use stolen materials to make our tools unless the tool itself would benefit."

"How could it benefit?"

"A lock pick forged from metals stolen from a very secure safe would have inherent abilities that metal taken straight from the ground lack. The principles of attraction are quite fascinating. Inanimate objects all have chi. An innate energy. Like with living things, that chi can change and be manipulated by external forces. Pixies can see the chi like we see auras. 'Tis a fact such things are real. But pixies, like most beings, don't share their knowledge much. Or maybe they don't understand how they do what they do any more than I understand what I can do…. But I digress.

"Sandra has lent me her books on the subject but most of it is supposition gained by observation, and trial and error. So while she knows how a lock pick forged from different sources will work, the exact what and how of it eludes her other than the knowledge that 'tis the chi of the object itself."

"If she thinks the metal is from a strong safe, would it work as if it was?"

"No. Forgeries can be exposed that way. But the fascinating bit is that she can manipulate the chi by training the pick to work."

"She probably just gets better at using it."

"Of course, but she can lend it and it would be easier to use than an identical one, even if the person to whom she lent it to had no idea. I myself have tested it. 'Tis true."

"I believe you."

I wasn't sure he did, but I didn't think it mattered much as long as he acquired the right tools.

I said, "Good. Then you'll understand why we need to make the purchases that she recommends, despite the expense."

I opened my carryon and withdrew my notes that I handed him.

He whistled a low whistle as he read.

While he was reading, I laid my tools that Sandra had helped me make in the desk drawers and placed the bottles that she'd given me on the shelves behind me.

I said, "She gave me samples of everything that she had but she had few potions made. We made these here together."

I nudged three bottles containing the ivy mixtures to the side.

"They're simple recipes. The gathering and preparing is the complex part."

He set the list down to pick up one of the bottles.

I said, "Use care because it needs nothing to activate."

I set the bottles containing the base elements on the next shelf.

"These bottles contain the ingredients to make the binding potion and the unbinding potion. They can be handled as you would handle any herb or metal."

I tapped the skull and crossbones on the front of a bottle of liquid mercury.

"'Tis a poison. She gave me many such things and warned I should study on their safe use, which is doubly true for you. These small bottles could kill. We'll need a lab. She recommends it be secret so that we can label our materials and leave projects out without worrying that they'd been seen. Julia will have one built for us. Sandra sent her recommendations on what it should contain. Read the notes, and if you have any ideas, tell Julia."

I set the rest of the bottles on the shelves as I said, "Sandra also warned us not to leave the slightest clue that we were using magic because it would attract predators that we won't be equipped to face. She told us quite clearly that if our actions brought attention to her or magic itself that she'd have to act."

"She'll kill us?"

"Not on a whim, but yes."

"And if you become too powerful for her peace of mind..."

"'Twas Julia's thought as well. I imagine Sandra is much more powerful than she appears if she's willing to teach us these things..."

He said worriedly, "She'll be looking to see if you're faking how good you can make this shit. Be careful if you try to bullshit her, Pip. And if she's teaching you, it's because it's helping her. She must need you able to do this binding shit."

He waggled the vial containing the binding potion at me.

"She does. We've worked out an agreement that should help both of us. Speaking of which, the central part of that agreement is that her daughter Cassandriel remain unaware of the existence of magic. Our jobs for Sandra all revolve around keeping her daughter safe. Julia will be telling you about that because we need to pick men to guard her—ones who wouldn't be at all tempted to touch her. We can't take the slightest chance that anyone lay one finger on her."

While I was speaking, he'd dipped his pinky into the bottle.

I snickered when his finger stuck to the shelf as he set the bottle down.

He yanked for a second while I laughed.

"I thought the pin protects me?"

I rolled my eyes at him as I said, "From spells that affect your anima. It would take much more than a charm to protect you from all spells. 'Tis meant to stop the alteration of your thoughts; to keep your anima purely your own. Roll your finger up slowly."

He gave me an exasperated glance then examined his freed finger a moment before picking up the bottle again, which made me laugh.

"It's still there," I said sweetly, laughing harder as he tried to shake the bottle off.

I ripped a page from a notebook and sprinkled a pinch of anti-binding potion on it.

"Careful. Just roll your finger off like before then roll it in this. But don't get it on anything else or anything bound on you like buttons and zippers will unfasten."

He did as I said then tentatively touched the desk.

"It feels slippery."

"It'll wear off in a few hours. Sandra says you can use it if you're constipated or have imbibed some poisons but to be really careful."

"Is that what she uses it for?"

"I don't think so. She showed me how to apply the binding powder to my shoes. You can climb a vertical wall with it—or at least she can. I need more practice."

I carefully poured the powder back into the bottle.

"As part of our education, we're supposed to devise our own ways to use it. But first we need to make more. So the tools..."

He retrieved the list.

I said, "She wasn't sure if using my anima to steal will affect the chi, which is why we're going to use distraction. But once we have the watches we need, I can use my anima to get us away if needed. The safe will be the most difficult thing for us to get."

"Shouldn't Julia come with us?"

"She and I are connected. What's mine *is* hers. But if we find that's an issue, we'll just steal another."

He snorted with laughter. "When do we go?"

"In two days. We'll have dinner with Julia's parents in London tomorrow night and then you and I will begin, assuming of course Julia has things handled on her end."

"Begin... how long will it take?"

I said, "At least a month. We'll get your stake in London and then the main haul in Monte Carlo, but then we're going to Dubai to handle some business for Sandra. We can only hit twice on the roulette table, so make it count."

"I wonder how'd you do with craps?" he said thoughtfully.

A hot flush rose to my cheeks.

"I... have no need of anti-binding potion."

He laughed like that was the funniest thing he'd ever heard.

"Oh man," he finally gasped out. "It's a game, Pip. Your face was just priceless. I can see we need to do some studying though."

"I haven't time for more lessons today."

He looked worried for a moment then his normal smile was firmly in place as he turned to go.

"I'll teach you all the casino games. It'll be fun. Maybe we could stay a few days just to play for fun?"

"Perhaps. We have until the tenth of January to be in Dubai but sooner is better. Julia thought you could win here and then double it in Monte Carlo. She warned me I'd need to play and lose some money, which I assuredly can do as it seems simple enough to play the game."

He turned back to say, "It *is* easy to learn it and fun to play."

"I haven't time to play..."

"Sure you have. What's the point if you ain't having fun," he called back over his shoulder as he left the room.

What is the point? I thought as I gathered the notebook.

We'd been so worried about Hugh that we'd started this plan in motion without really considering any goal other than survival. We had the animals and even people to feed off of if it ever became necessary. And we knew enough now to keep ourselves safe.

I left the room and was immediately inundated with the sounds of construction.

I headed to my room and the small balcony there that overlooked the new barn that was going up where mine had once stood.

I want this, I thought as I surveyed the progress.

I wanted this house to once more be the grand estate it had been. I wanted the money and power that only the truly wealthy had, but more than that I wanted the knowledge that had been denied me my entire life.

I wanted to rule as I had been ruled.

"But not in fear," I said to my reflection in the glass doors of the balcony as I returned inside. I had no wish to become like my father.

I wanted true admiration. I was growing to despise the pity or condescending smiles that greeted me.

I returned to the study where I read until Julia entered to remind me of dinner.

"Set a timer, Pip, so you don't miss meals."

I nodded, following her from the room.

She continued, "Mrs. Roman has recommended two of the girls to stay on as permanent helpers and I agree if they meet with your approval as well."

"Whatever you think best is fine with me."

"Now that Ryu is working with us, you'll need a new valet."

"Let Ryu choose since it'll be his job to make sure whoever he picks does it right."

"Would you prefer a man or a woman?"

"...I hadn't considered. Would it be proper for a woman to enter my bedchamber or handle my clothing?"

We took our seats in the sitting room where we preferred to eat when it was just us two.

The space had once been servant rooms in the back hall, but we'd torn out all of the walls and merged it into what had been the sewing room, creating one very large room.

I quite liked the new décor. It was cheerful with bright yellow couches, white walls, and glass doors that opened into the inner courtyard.

New wood floors had replaced the brown tiles. Rugs in varied shades of green were scattered about. The same shades of green and the yellow of the couches were in the curtains that bracketed the French doors.

The original deep shelving that had held supplies in the sewing room had been torn out and been replaced with narrower shelves that held a few of her knickknacks, an enormous television, a bar, the stereo system, and a small wet sink.

There were two small seating areas and this table that sat four comfortably.

She said, "Call it a bedroom, not a bed chamber, and I suppose not. We wouldn't want her to get the wrong idea if you asked how to wear something. Speaking of which, you should go shopping more. You're able to pick your own clothes now. You don't need to keep using his."

"I suppose..."

"Stop worrying about it. Just be yourself. Look at Drew. No one turns a hair when he wears purple pants or a velvet vest and he wears more jewelry than I do. Just stay away from dresses, skirts, and high heels."

Mrs. Roman delivered our meal while a girl I didn't know poured wine for Julia and chocolate milk for me.

She had no rind and hard wary eyes.

I waited until we were alone again to say, "'Twould be enjoyable to shop. Can we afford a new wardrobe?"

"Yes. Money isn't an issue. We have plenty and can get more. Sandra will be showing you some properties in Dubai. We need to buy one. We're buying another property in Scotland. I'll send you pictures of my top choices, and we can visit and decide which one when you get back."

"Are you happy, Julia?"

She laughed, standing to lean over the table and gave me a smacking kiss on the cheek.

"I love our life, Pip. We're going to have so much fun!"

"'Tis the sticking point. Mayhap we need to have that fun now? I'd not have you work all hours doing distasteful tasks against some future that might never be."

"I'm enjoying it. I just meant once we get the ball really rolling, we'll have more time for travel and indulging our hobbies. I can hardly wait until we can have balls here. Speaking of which, Baron Fardenay has made good on his invitation, and you should be back in time. We can attend his ball on the sixth of March while we look over our property options.

"Will we have time to explore the flora there?"

"Absolutely. By the time we get back here by the end of March, the cellars under the barn will be done. We'll have that project done by April."

I laughed in giddy excitement that made her laugh too.

She said, "Just be careful. Has Ryu agreed to it?"

"He didn't say?" I asked in surprise.

She flushed guiltily as she said, "We only spoke for a few minutes and most of that was about potential new tenants. Speaking of which, I've decided all future tenants will be housed in one of houses that we just bought bordering the estate. Only our personal help will live here and maybe a very few others."

I nodded my agreement. It made no difference to me where they stayed.

I said, "This house was built to house a large staff. I quite like having people around. 'Tis...homey. 'Twill be a relief when the construction here is done though."

"It shouldn't be too much longer until they're done in the main halls and our wing... I could have them only work while you're on your morning rides or away, but it would take them much longer to finish."

"No. I can retire to the study for peace and quiet."

"Speaking of which..."

"Tomorrow I shall layout the needful things to place a rune of silence in your office."

She nodded happily.

We finished our dinner then watched the late news together before separating for the night; she returning to her office and me to my room.

I stared at the ceiling wondering if I should attempt to learn to manage the estate and our finances or if we were better as we were, with me doing the mystical and her the mundane.

Chapter 16

"You're distracted," Ryu said as he tapped my knee with his notebook.

I'd been distracted for the last two days. We were on our way to the casino, and I still wasn't certain if I was being foolish or selfish by spending my time studying the arcane arts instead of practical matters.

"'Tis true. Think you that I should endeavor to learn how to manage the running of the house and business to allow Julia more time for study?"

"Shouldn't you ask her?"

"I did and she claims to be quite content. I think she speaks truly, but is it wise?"

"Probably not in the long run but I think it makes sense now. You can get much more done this way."

"'Tis my thought that Julia will never wish to pursue the study of botany... nor I the inner workings of Lombard Street... and yet, both have equal worth."

"Would it matter if you aren't as adept as her or her as you?"

I shrugged. "How can I say?"

"I think you should learn to manage money, but you could always hire investors if you had too... it's the process you need to know, not the details. Unless... you wanted to do it yourself..."

"Heaven forfend!"

He laughed although a hint of unease lurked in his eyes.

I said, "'Tis a worry for another day. She is safe with her mundane ways...I suppose 'tis just my lingering prejudices which make me worry to leave her defenseless."

The unease faded from his face, and he smiled more naturally.

"She can handle herself," he agreed.

I took the notebook from him.

He said, "Don't try to manipulate the dice until we've had time to practice."

"I shan't. 'Twill be long before I can move them so naturally, although perhaps a spell could be made to roll them in an exact pattern. We shall need to record such a roll from all angles."

He took the notebook back and wrote, *buy a craps table and six motion stop cameras. Find someone who knows how to operate the equipment and can teach us.*

He said, "We should learn how to ruin someone's roll too."

"Show me again the winning cards in poker."

By the time we arrived I was certain that I understood the rules of poker, blackjack, roulette, and bingo. I was a bit fuzzy on baccarat and craps.

We separated the stacks of money. Both of us putting a hundred grand in our pockets, leaving the rest in the briefcase.

"Man... this is a lot of dough to lose," he said worriedly.

"I shan't lose it. And if I do, 'tis no loss of yours."

I lowered the partition between us and the driver.

Ollie glanced at me in the rearview.

"We're almost there, sir."

We exited the car a few minutes later.

Ryu said to Ollie, "We'll be at least four hours. Make sure you check your messages after that. I'm going to be pissed as shit if you make his lordship wait."

"No problem, boss."

He grinned cockily at Ryu and drove away.

"He better not scratch that car," Ryu muttered.

I said, "Shall we?"

"Let's take a walk through so you can see what's what."

I knew enough now to open the door for myself, so was surprised—and flattered—when he reached past me to open it. Which I knew was silly when he'd meant nothing by it.

Stepping inside was an assault on the senses. Lights, noise, motion, and the hectic roil of excited anima.

"Oh my," I said breathlessly, making Ryu laugh.

We walked through slowly and then sat at a bar overlooking the casino floor.

Ryu said to the bartender, "I'll have a scotch on the rocks, and he'll have a G and T."

I said, "'Twould be easy to become drunk here."

"Should we go?" he asked worriedly.

"'Twas just an observation. I have no intent to partake."

The bartender handed me my drink. I made a face when I sipped it that made Ryu laugh.

"Try a Pimm's or how about a beer? They have light ones."

"Tonic and lime, please," I said to the bartender, which made Ryu laugh again.

"'Twould be well to keep my wits about me. Shall we play?"

He followed me to the roulette wheels.

I laid my money on the table and the dealer said, "I can't cash that much as once, sir. I have a five-thousand-pound limit."

Ryu said laughingly, "This might not be the place for you, sir."

The dealer said, "The last three tables have a higher stake limit."

I handed her five thousand pounds.

"'Tis well to smart small, I suppose."

Ryu said, "Max bet is five hundred pounds, sir."

He dropped a stack of hundred-pound notes beside mine and accepted his chips.

The other patrons at the table stirred with an excitement I could see on their anima.

I picked a number at random.

We played until we ran out of money, which we did in ten hands.

I said, "'Tisn't our lucky table."

We headed to the higher limit tables, and I watched a few minutes at each.

He said, "If you're not feeling lucky, we can play cards a while."

"As Julia would say, the cash is burning a hole in my pocket."

I stepped close enough that I could mentally draw the rune of holding on the wheel, not in the cup but on the edge. The ball would stop dead and hopefully slide in when I released it, which is how it worked nine times out of ten on Sandra's practice wheel. Of the hundreds of times I'd practiced, the ball had stayed in place three times and a few times had bounced out after rolling in.

I said, "I predict that it will be the number twelve," which was my warning to Ryu that I'd placed the rune.

The plan called for us to win a small roll first just to see how everyone reacted.

The woman sitting closest to me laughed and set a stack of chips on number twelve.

We all stared intently at the ball, but I didn't dare stop it because it was going much too fast when it passed the twelve.

"Next time," I said.

The woman didn't place her chips on twelve.

I was able to stop and release it on the next roll. It plunked into the little cup as neat as you please.

"This *is* our lucky table," I said to Ryu who'd begun laughing.

The woman said, "I should've believed you..."

I again set fifty thousand pounds down.

"Hundreds?" the dealer asked.

"Thousands."

Again the anima of the watchers swirled in excitement. It happened quickly and was centered on their chests, not their mouths or hands, which is where the anima of anger usually appeared. It was much more visible on the women than the men, but I thought that was because the women had more exposed skin on their chests.

The numbers had come to rest with the green zero in the perfect position for me to reach it. I carefully drew my rune of holding.

The dealer spun before I could get chips in place, but the rune would hold for hours.

I said to Ryu, "I'm feeling very lucky. 'Tis certain to be my anniversary number."

He traded his cash for chips too.

I said, "Five thousand on twelve."

"Green for me," Ryu said, as he leaned passed the woman to make our bets.

I think everyone at the table was holding their breaths, hoping it would hit green despite the bets they themselves had placed because I could see the excitement of sparkling anima in my peripheral vision as the ball slowed. I was worried it was going too slow and would fall before it reached the square.

"Come on, come on!" Ryu chanted softly.

I stopped it and released it, and it plunked into the little box. The entire table jumped up and began cheering and yelling congratulations.

"Holy fuck! I won! I fucking won!" Ryu said as he gave me a quick hug.

"Sir," a man said a minute later. "If you'll come with me, I'll settle your account."

Ryu said, to me, "Will you be okay here alone, Lord Blackwood?"

"Assuredly. I shall continue to play. Perhaps I too will have some luck."

Ryu went with the man.

I placed another five-thousand-pound bet on twelve. Everyone at the table followed along.

We, of course, all lost.

A waitress approached and took orders. I ordered another tonic water and lime, missing the next bet to do it.

My drink arrived at the same time as another casino employee who said, "We're opening another table if you'd like a seat?"

"I'm fine here."

The people at the table all exclaimed, two in excitement and the rest in aggravation.

I turned to see twelve had come in.

"It seems I missed my luck..."

The man flushed and scurried off.

I placed a one-thousand-pound bet on twelve and spread another thousand randomly.

I won on one of my smaller bets, which generated excitement at the table. And again they all followed my next bet.

Ryu returned two bets later, looking smug.

He said, "We've been invited to the high rollers' room."

I said, "I'm famished. Shall we eat first?"

I tipped the dealer as Julia had instructed me too and followed Ryu.

I was surprised when the strangers at the table all wished us luck.

I said, "It appears that seeing a win is almost as exciting as winning yourself."

"Not even close," he said laughingly.

"I'm looking forward to trying my luck at cards."

We stayed eight hours. I was up sixty grand, poker being easy to win when I could see their anger when dealt bad cards.

Ryu had lost thirty at the poker table. We both received dinner vouchers and tickets to the show.

In the car again, I said, "Did you remember to pay the taxes?"

"Yep. It's clean as a whistle."

"Are whistles particularly clean?"

He rolled his eyes at me, which made me laugh.

I said, "That was close. I wasn't sure it would reach the square."

"I have three shots at it next time."

"Two. I doubt anyone will notice or report your losses, but they will wonder why you tried three times with such a large bet. I noticed most only try twice before placing smaller bets again. If I miss twice in a row, we'll go to a new casino where they won't know you tried it."

"Then we'd really be down two hundred grand."

"It means nothing. 'Tis the tax man we must cozen. Your five-thousand-pound bonus becomes a million, which you let your boss invest. All perfectly reasonable, or so Julia assures me.

"So, after this next win we must stay and make similar bets for the evening. I think we should start off with cards, have a meal, and then play roulette. Bet ten thousand a hand until I signal I've marked the board. Then we can quit immediately for celebratory drinks.

"We'll return the next night and do the same thing but this time I shall endeavor to lose at cards and after your big loss, we'll leave."

"Man... a fifty-k bet I know I'm gonna lose... maybe you could give me a sign at the poker table?"

"'Twould surely be noticed, would it not? And I don't always see their anger or excitement over the cards they get, and I have no way to judge whether you should stay in or fold."

"True…. Maybe you could just scratch your nose or something if you think they all have crap?"

"I shall try…'Tis possible you can lose a great deal that way…"

"Fifty-k on green to win will be more than enough to pay my stake back."

"'Tisn't necessary to pay it back. 'Tis money we ourselves stole…"

Chapter 17

Two days later Ollie drove us to the airport right after breakfast. I was tired of casinos already but looking forward to the shopping in Monte Carlo.

I said to Ryu, "Will he be able to find his way to his plane with the luggage or should we wait?"

"He's got this. He'll pick up the car and then bring the bags to the hotel."

We both grabbed our carry-ons, leaving the luggage for Ollie, except for one bag that Ryu took that held our tuxedos, sweat suits, and clean undergarments.

Ryu checked us in.

I'd been in enough airports that I was able to find the flight information and departure gate.

"I think I could manage this on my own."

"It's not hard," he agreed absently.

I managed the security check-in with no help or undue confusion.

I stopped to buy a tea for myself and coffee for Ryu and we settled into seats to wait for the plane to board.

"Thanks," Ryu said.

I nodded absently as I looked through my carryon for the book I'd brought—a text on the evolution of the Germanic language that Drew had recommended. It was a fascinating insight into the changes that had accompanied the use of local plants.

He was frowning at me when I glanced up and immediately flushed and looked away.

"Is aught amiss?"

When he looked back his flush had faded but small lines had appeared by his eyes.

"Is Ollie... am I more to you than he is?"

I realized I was gaping like a halfwit and snapped my mouth closed.

He added hurriedly, "I mean, are you grooming him to take my place?"

"Yes. I have need of a good valet... as do you."

He mulled that over for a moment before saying, "Would you let me... retire if I wanted too? I don't want to; I'm just wondering if you would."

"You mean with the money?" I asked dryly, or at least I hoped it sounded disinterested and not hurt. I hated to think that he stayed out of fear or obligation to his friends, *which was probably naïve...*

I continued, "Yes. 'Twas simple enough that I could do it again if needful, not that it *would* be needful. We weren't looking for a partner..."

"*Hmm....*"

I said, "If such is your intention, 'tis best to do it soon else Julia might be concerned that a simple request might not be enough to ensure your silence."

"Ha! I'm no fool, man. I know there ain't no going back."

The reminder of what Julia would do to clean up loose ends made my stomach roil.

I said, "I'd been considering how I would feel if I were to meet me—to be thrust into this... strangeness that is my life. I think I would be terrified. I would certainly be mistrustful. I doubt anything you said or did could reassure me because I'd know that even were your intentions honorable that you were what you were.

"I cannot speak to Julia's intentions—but for mine own, my hope was that the money would provide a sense of security. That you could build a life far from us, mayhap with no knowledge of why you'd quit such a lucrative position or how you'd gotten such a position in the first place; but 'tis the only security I can offer."

He said, "It would really be mine? Not just a front to pad your own accounts?"

"It's yours right now.... when I said earlier that the money would be invested by your boss, I meant under her guidance, but you're free to invest or not however you wish. I expect that you will do all in your power to protect what's yours from us."

"I don't think that's possible."

"'Tis not as difficult as all that. A will filed in multiple places; witnesses told often what you intend. Multiple accounts spread through different banks. 'Twould be much more trouble than it would be worth to circumvent."

"And I'd change it all on her whims..."

His tone had been wistful. I wasn't certain he meant her power. It made a lump grow in my throat.

"'Tis true that you began as Ollie is now but you're much more to both of us. I think it fate that we met. But if you hadn't been the man you are, we'd not have offered a partnership. 'Twill be an uneven one because no matter how we wish things might be, they are what they are. I am a lord and she a lady."

"And I'm nothing at all...."

"Not so! You shall be a gentleman of refinement as adept as myself—more so really—at mixing in polite society. We shall—all three of us—choose our own destiny, follow our own dreams, and hopefully remain friends for a good many years. I like to think our goal, Julia's plan, will not only benefit *us* but allow us to benefit others."

I frowned as I considered our earlier conversations.

"I see that my views on what is proper are old fashioned. Julia's approach might be more pragmatic or maybe less pragmatic... 'tis certain we all see the problems *and* solutions differently but 'tisn't that a good thing?"

He smiled a rakish smile at me, smoothing the Query Inc pin he wore on his baseball cap.

I said, "*Ha*! 'Tis a ridiculous place to wear it! I might knock it off with one hit and then where would you be? 'Twould be better to attach it to the inside of your clothing."

He laughed in delight. "I don't wear it for you."

"*Ha*," I said again softly and opened my book.

We didn't speak again until they called for the first-class passengers to board.

"Aisle or window," he asked.

"Aisle. I can see better."

I settled into my seat, donning my sunglasses to hide the direction of my gaze.

I spent the short flight watching the other passengers and trying to ignore Ryu's constant staring.

"What are you looking for," he finally whispered. "I thought we were getting the watches in Monte Carlo?"

"We are. I'll tell you later."

I was glad I hadn't attempted the trip alone when we landed. The exit ramp disgorged us into a crowded concourse.

I followed Ryu who acted as if he knew exactly where to go.

I said, "Explain to me how you're finding our car."

"I'm not. We're just getting out of this crush. There'll be cabs outside. We'll just get one. It'll be quicker than calling for a ride."

"With all these people?"

"Trust me. There'll be cabs."

He was correct. Within minutes of exiting we were on our way.

"So the plane?" he asked.

"I watch and see how people of my... I'm not sure of the correct word. How people who also ride in first class dress and behave. How they speak to each other and the help. What they do to pass the time. 'Tis difficult to pick them from crowds in most cases. I'm beginning to recognize clothing that's considered fashionable. But even that is sometimes no real indication of real wealth or breeding. Not to say that genealogy makes a gentleman. I suppose I should say upbringing and not breeding. In my day 'twas simple to tell who the gentlemen were. You knew what to expect when making discourse with one. Now, I'm unsure when I should take offense or act amused... 'tis very confusing."

"If you're offended, call them out on it."

"Nay. 'Tis most times not their intent. Or at least I believe that to be true... besides, I've no notion of the proper response to offense. My options appear limited to immediate violence or vulgar threats, neither of which appeal. I simply cannot imagine my father behaving thusly. Not to say he wouldn't immediately draw on any man who dared insult him or demand satisfaction... but fisticuffs... So, I watch and learn. "

Ryu snorted with laughter, which was slightly insulting when I hadn't said anything humorous, but I smiled back politely and called Julia to tell her we'd arrived.

Our beautiful hotel was on a street lined with small shops that I was dying to explore.

Ryu checked us in and handed me my keycard, saying to the man at the desk. "Can we get our tuxes pressed for tonight?"

"Of course, sir. Just dial housekeeping and someone will be right up to collect it.

I said, "I think I'll go explore a bit. You can nap or do whatever you like."

"I'd like to look around too if you wouldn't mind the company."

"You're welcome to attend."

The man at the desk said, "You can request laundry to be left in your room if you aren't in. If you'd like to access the safe in your room or rent a box in our vault that can be arranged."

I shrugged at Ryu.

He said, "I think one room safe is enough."

We dropped off our bag in his room and headed out.

Ryu stopped to gaze into the window of the first store we reached.

I'd have walked by it as I already owned a pair of sunglasses, but it was clear he was interested.

He said, "Man, look at this place! The prices are sick."

I knew by his tone that he meant that in a good way or perhaps not good but that he was impressed.

I said, "Let's see if they have anything we want."

I entered the store and approached the desk where I asked the girl there, "What pair would look good on me?"

"Any," she said.

I exaggerated my annoyed sigh.

"Have you no fashion sense?"

Anger sparkled on her words when she offered me a pair that she took from the glass case and said, "These are one of most popular models... for those who can afford them. They'd suit the shape of your face quite well."

"*Hmm*... not quite Paris fashion, are they?"

I swiped my hand through the anima of anger that the statement produced and said, "What's the cheapest price you ever sell them for?"

"Two hundred euros, which is cost. The boss only did that once."

"What happens to you if you misplace a pair?"

"I'd get fired."

"Are you allowed to offer discounts?"

"No."

I left her to browse the display Ryu was looking at.

"Find any you like?"

He leaned closer to whisper, "You can't. She'll lose her job."

I plucked the pair he was eyeing from the display, rolling my eyes at him as I did so, and handed them to the girl. "We'll take these and those."

"Very good, sir."

She was all smiles as she packaged them.

I handed her Hugh's credit card and Ryu laughed, quickly stifling it.

We continued down the street. A flash of red caught my eye, and I changed direction, catching up to the man in moments.

He was well dressed, wearing expensive clothing, and yelling on his cell phone in French.

His rind was thick enough that I knew he'd murdered more than one person.

I grabbed his arm—and his anima—and said, "How many people have you murdered?"

"Two."

"Who were they?"

"Franco Lavigne my business partner, and his wife."

"Why did you do it?"

"He wouldn't sell to me."

"Give me your credit card. You won't notice it's missing for three days and when you do notice, you won't be alarmed. You'll just cancel and get another one. When you get the bill, you're not going to worry at all about any charges on it. You were feeling so guilty for murdering your partner that you bought a stranger who reminded you of him some things, but you don't like to think about it. You'll just pay the bill and forget about it."

While I was speaking, he handed me the card.

"What are you going to do when you get the bill?"

"Pay it and forget about it. I don't like thinking about it."

"Don't kill anyone else."

I walked away.

He followed me for a few feet then stopped, looking puzzled for a moment then shrugged and pulled out his cell phone.

Ryu whispered, "Holy shit...."

He followed me into the next store. We spent the next two hours shopping in the different boutiques. I bought five-thousand dollars in clothes for myself and Ryu on the man's card.

We returned to the hotel to drop our packages.

Ryu admired a new shirt he'd picked for himself as he said, "What if he wakes up and calls the police or reports his card stolen?"

"He won't but even if he did, do you think he's going to press charges if I mention Franco's name?"

I put his credit card into my carryon.

"Shouldn't you throw it out?"

"I haven't yet decided if I'm done with him. 'Tis possible the pair of them had it coming but 'tis more likely he was just greedy. Julia and I are testing to see how long our commands will hold. I shall speak with her and see if she thinks more must be done about him."

I began hanging my new clothing beside my freshly pressed tuxedo.

"Part of your job will be helping to decide such things. 'Twould be impossible for us to question everyone we see with that rind—and unwise. But when we *know* that evil men such as that are walking freely about, 'tis our duty to act—what must be done is something we're still unsure of. For this man though... I quite like the thought of leaving him penniless."

"And you want me to tell you what to do?"

"Not as such. 'Tis more a desire for a fresh perspective. What would you do to a man like that?"

"I'm good with stealing his dough. I'm going to grab a quick shower."

I took one myself and then put on my tuxedo.

Ryu joined me in my room an hour later.

"I've been thinking, and I guess you're right. We should do something about him but maybe he did have his reasons. Maybe we should track him down and ask him?"

"His reason could be true to him but not *the* truth. He might have believed a lie or thought it was true or even be deluded."

"So... what... we have a trial?"

"I don't know. What would his punishment be if a trial were held and he found guilty of the crime? Does it matter *why* he did it or just *that* he did? 'Tis why Julia dislikes when I speak to them. 'Tis why I prefer to bring them home. I should hate to release a villain who then commits more villainy. 'Tis easier to watch them there to better judge if they should be released from our control."

"How many did you see tonight?"

"Four men so far."

I didn't mention the rinded women I'd seen because all of them had the pale rinds of unborn children. Julia and I disagreed on what should be done about them. 'Twas her opinion that we leave them be unless needs must. I couldn't get over the coldness of the act of murdering your unborn child, but I was willing to concede this was a different time with different morals and humans hadn't the ability to see the remains of the soul like we could—if it was a soul. And some might've lost their child through natural means. I contented myself with prayers for the child's soul and ignored them as best I could.

"Four..." he laughed a rueful huff of laughter. "I don't know why that seems like so many to me. I guess it's because I know what we did was murder, but we *had* to do it. It's kill or be killed. They all had it coming. But I'm sure they'd say the same thing..."

"'Tis possible they were soldiers or doctors. 'Tis possible they were the vilest of people... 'tis possible I am the vilest of creatures because I see and do nothing or mayhap because I see and then act..."

"You aren't vile, Pip.

"I am what I am."

I headed to the door.

We caught a cab to the casino.

Ryu led us to a cashier and handed over four hundred thousand dollars.

She slid two credit cards across and said, "The standard withdrawal when you offer a high stakes card to a dealer is ten thousand in chips. If you want more or less just tell the dealer. You can cash in chips under a hundred thousand right at the table and have that applied to the card. Have a nice evening.

"I can't believe I'm doing this," he muttered as he tucked his new card into his jacket pocket.

"Let's find a game."

Before we reached the casino floor a woman in a silver gown approached. She had the merest blush of rind.

I wished I dared give her my sincere condolences. I knew better than to ask her because more often than not the women who had such a rind had purposefully killed their children. But still I felt sorry for her and the child.

She said, "Lord Blackwood, Mr. Poole, my name is Lena and I'd be delighted to be of assistance."

Ryu said, "His lordship is looking for a poker game, five card stud."

I said, "Or maybe blackjack. We haven't yet tried that."

"Right this way, sirs."

She told us of available services and games as we walked to a smaller quieter room off of the main one guarded by a man who undid a velvet rope to let us pass. The room had four tables dedicated to blackjack, six for card games, two roulette wheels and three bars.

Two of the card tables were full of intense looking players with a small crowd observing them.

Ryu stopped to watch, so I did too.

Lena whispered, "It's a high stakes tournament with a fifty thousand euro buy in."

Ryu began walking again.

"How often are they held?"

"Almost nightly. The buy ins differ. I could arrange a place at the next one if you like?"

I said, "We're only here a few days."

"There might be another tonight. Shall I inquire?"

Ryu said, "Sure, why not. Want a lime and soda, Philip?"

She said, "What would you like, Mr. Poole? Francois makes an amazing whisky sour."

"Sounds good."

I said, "Just tonic water and lime for me, please."

Blackjack was fun. Reading the anima was only a slight advantage. Our dealer was a charming gentleman who was honestly amused by my intent stare. He joked with everyone at the table, noticing all of our foibles and commenting on them until it felt like we'd all been friends forever. We were all laughing and teasing each other. Everyone except myself was a bit drunk.

Ryu and I both spent more than we'd meant to and had taken three times longer than we'd intended. We'd have probably stayed longer but the dealer went off duty.

We both tipped him and stood. Ryu staggering just a bit.

I hoped 'twas for show.

I said, "I think it's time to change our luck. Shall we try roulette?"

Lena appeared like magic, which made me snicker to myself.

She said, "The no limit table has a minimum bet of a thousand."

Ryu said, "Sounds good. I'm feeling lucky."

"Another whisky sour, sir?"

I said, "He'll have water with lemon. I'm not carrying him to his room."

"Spoil sport," he said as he slung an arm around me.

Lena led us to the roulette table then went to fetch fresh drinks.

I watched the ball until Ryu released me and sat. He asked for a hundred grand in ten-thousand-dollar chips. I handed the dealer my card and said, "Same for me. My friend can watch them until I get back."

I went to find a restroom.

When I returned, Ryu had another whisky sour in front of him, was down about forty grand and had a beautiful blond hanging over his shoulder. I hoped his drunken spending was just an act, but it was making me nervous.

I watched the ball a few more times while I placed my rune then sat beside Ryu.

He slid me my chips.

"Here's to the luck of the first-time gamblers!"

He clinked his glass to my untouched one, almost knocking it over. Then drank his in one long gulp.

"Let's get 'um. We got this, Pip. I'm feeling lucky!"

"You're looking drunk."

I slid ten grand onto number twelve.

He slid fifty onto zero.

I knew the spin was a dud when the ball slipped into the squares and began bouncing.

One of the people at the table hit and said smugly to Ryu, "Tough luck man. Winners and losers."

Ryu ordered another drink.

The heat of his anger felt like a caress. I realized I'd leaned into his shoulder when the blond said in my ear, "Good luck."

Ryu bet fifty thousand on zero again. I bet ten on twelve.

"Damn," he muttered when the ball slowed and we could see it wouldn't come close.

I lay my hand on his and said, "Slow down a bit."

He slapped down ten thousand on fifteen.

I spread ten thousand in ten bets and won on one.

We played for an hour winning a few but losing way more than we won.

He said, "You ready to try poker or get something to eat?"

"One more. I'm feeling lucky."

I put ten on twelve.

He laughed and pushed his remaining chips to zero.

"My that's a big one," the girl said.

I wanted to smack her.

Ryu stood, leaning forward to stare hopefully at the ball.

"Fuck!" He said when it began bouncing.

I caught it in my rune, releasing it almost before it had caught, and it rolled hard into the zero box but didn't bounce out.

"Hot damn! We did it! I could kiss you."

He flushed when he caught my eye and hurriedly grabbed the girl, having to turn awkwardly in the chair to do it.

"Go ahead," she giggled, and he gave her a long kiss.

"You sure did bring me luck." He turned to the dealer, "Can I get twenty k? She deserves a tip. So do you! Take ten for yourself! I can't believe that fucking hit!"

He grabbed me in a headlock and mussed my hair, which was annoying because I had no idea if that had been an actual display of affection, drunken exuberance, or an act for the onlookers.

The table congratulated him while the dealer called for a pit boss.

I didn't at all like the look of the man who approached. He was rinded in stolen anima. Anger sparkled on his words despite his polite smile when he said, "If you'd come with me, sir?"

I said, "One minute, please."

I grabbed Ryu's arm and slid my chips to the dealer to cash in.

Ryu halted, looking a bit puzzled. The man looked annoyed and the girl pouty.

I released him, stepping to the side to make room for new patrons to sit.

The girl had gone to the bar by the time I got my card back.

I wasn't sure if she'd gone because Ryu had sent her away or because the man had come.

Ryu and I followed the man who said, "That was some lucky roll."

"It's my number."

I said, "It is. Next time, I'm following you."

The man said, "Are you here long?"

"One more day."

Ryu said, "If we finish our business in Dubai early, we might stop back on the way home."

"If my wife permits it," I muttered, making Ryu laugh.

He said, "You were doing okay at blackjack and there's always that poker tournament. Speaking of which, did Lena say when the next one was and the buy in?"

"Tomorrow at eight and it's a half a million buy in."

I said, "'Tis too much for a novice like me."

"Yeah... beginners luck only goes so far. I'd do it for fifty-k though."

"As would I."

"I can send you the schedule."

I nodded.

Ryu said, "I'm in."

We reached a locked door that he opened and held for us. A man in the corridor shrugged at our escort.

A chill traveled through me. I broke out in a cold sweat.

I knew him. Had thought he was dead.

Our escort opened another door and said to the woman sitting there, "Table five. Forty-eight thousand on green."

"My, that's a nice win. Our biggest so far this year. Can I see your card, please? Will this be cash, check, or direct deposit?"

I said, "Is there a restroom I can use?"

"Right down the hall on the left."

I straighten his lapel pin, which was the enchanted Query Inc pin as I said, "Wait here for me."

He nodded, looking a bit worried again.

"Direct deposit," he said to the woman.

I stepped into the hallway and made my way into the bathroom while looking for the man who'd shrugged. I didn't see him. I headed back out to the table and said to the dealer, "Excuse me, did anyone see a hotel key?"

Pete was removing Ryu's seat.

I wanted to run but instead I lingered pretending to watch the roll while I erased the rune—at least I hoped I did. I had no way to tell, except by touching the spot or trying to use it again. The lights above the wheel were too bright for me to see the faint sparkle of magic that rune left.

I headed back to the locked door, glancing back to see Pete had handed off Ryu's chair and had taken mine.

I knocked on the door and was let inside a minute later by the man who'd escorted us.

I trailed my hand through the edges of his anima, saying, "How often does a win like that happen?"

"No idea. One in a million maybe?"

"Have you seen it before?"

"Lots of times for much smaller amounts."

"Was that the biggest win on a single play that you've ever seen here?"

"No. There was another a few years ago."

The door opened behind us and Pete entered.

"Everything okay, Bob?" our escort asked.

"Looks like it." Bob approached smiling, offering his hand, saying, "Congratulations on your win."

I crossed my arms, turning to the closed door of the room Ryu was in.

"It wasn't my win."

I hope they took it as an angry sulk, but there was no way I was shaking Pete's hand.

My escort knocked once and opened the door.

"I lost my hotel key," I said to Ryu. "You almost done here?"

The woman at the desk said, "Yes. He just needs to log in and verify the transfer went through. He can use my terminal."

"He can use his phone."

Ryu's eyes widened at my tone.

He verified the transfer on his phone and followed me out.

"We leaving?" he asked as I headed to the main door.

"Yeah. I want to make sure no one used that damned key."

"Did you cash out?"

"I can do it later."

Little worry lines by his eyes deepened.

He flagged us down a cab.

"The hotel?" he asked me.

"Yeah."

I held my finger to my lips.

We didn't speak until we were inside my room and I'd placed a rune of silence on my suitcase that I then leaned on the door.

I called Julia, putting her on speaker phone.

"Having fun?" she asked.

"Pete is here."

"What!"

"Pete is working here. The guy called him Bob, but it was him. He had no rind at all and didn't look like he recognized me, but I recognized him."

"It can't be Pete. He's dead.

"He isn't dead. He was standing right there! What do I do?"

Ryu's eyes widened.

She said, "Stay the hell way from him!"

Ryu said, Who's Pete and how can you see him and he be dead? Is he a vampire?"

She said, "You didn't see him, Ryu?"

"He never saw him."

She said, "It must just be someone who looks like him—but stay away from him anyway. Do you have your holy items?"

"Pete the demon Pete?" Ryu asked. "Holy shit! Was he the guy who escorted us to the teller?"

"No the guy in the hall."

"Him? He looked harmless."

"See, Jewels?"

"But it *can't* be him!"

"Call Sandra. Ask her what we should do. We're going out to find a grocery store."

We returned from shopping laden with bags of fresh herbs, flowers, salt, ointments, candles, a glass bowl, and jewelry picked for the quality of the metal.

Ryu fell asleep on my bed watching me mix the ingredients, which took me six hours since I said prayers over every single one of them. I was still praying when he woke and tiptoed from the room.

He returned wearing the jeans he'd worn on the plane.

I stood, saying, "It should sit in the sun a few hours. We can go buy ourselves some crosses and get something to eat."

"Did it work?"

"I have no idea."

He eyed the runny goo in the bowl doubtfully.

"What's it supposed to do?"

"Protect from possession and hopefully repel evil spirits."

"Hopefully...."

"'Tis the best I can do... 'Twould work better if I could harvest fresh herbs and make the tinctures myself."

Julia called while we were eating.

"Sandra says she'll check the guy's background and that we should avoid him for now, but she thinks it's just coincidence because only mages and pixies change their shapes, and neither would want to be recognized as Pete."

"'Tis a lot of assumptions to my mind."

"What do you want to do about it, darling? I can come there..."

"Nay. 'Tis nothing *to* be done. 'Twould be foolish of me to confront such a creature so ignorant of their and mine own abilities."

"Did you get Ryu's stake?"

"Yes."

"Then stay and gamble one more day but choose a different casino. And make sure he repeats the bet and loses. Let me talk to him a minute."

I handed Ryu my phone.

"Jewels," he said worriedly.

He listened for a few minutes, agreeing occasionally, giving me worried and thoughtful sidelong glances, then said, "I'll keep an eye out. Stay out of casinos yourself. I think it'd be hard to resist getting—drunk. Take care of yourself."

He handed me back my phone.

I said, "I don't believe I imbibed too freely."

"You're still up, ain't you?"

"True... but fear is a powerful motivator."

He said, "Julia wants to get me started investing. I'll need to fly back to sign some paperwork once we're settled in Dubai. Will you be okay with just Ollie for a few days?"

"I believe so."

"She can courier it over..."

"If I cannot manage, I shall inform you."

"I'm worried you might fall asleep."

"*Ahh*...perhaps. I shall be most careful. Now, shall we shop?"

We headed directly to a jewelry store.

I said, "Pay with money that you earned, so in your heart you know 'tis a righteous piece. The chi should be made as pure as we can make it."

I browsed the displays while Ryu asked the clerk to show him crosses.

I rejoined him as they were discussing the karats to say, "I'll take four of the silver ones if you have it in stock and two of the gold. Also, I saw you had signet rings and custom designed pieces, and it occurs to me I have none. I should like to order one with my family crest.

Three hours later we left the store with the necklaces and two fancy silver letter openers with crosses embossed on the hilts.

I'd ordered signets for Julia and myself, a pen and ink set with a matching stamp, and matching watches for Julia and me with our names and crest. The designer was going to be sending me some pin designs meant for our staff that I intended to ask Sandra to enchant for us.

Ryu had bought a Rolex, eight silver crosses on thick silver chains, and two smaller ones.

We returned to the hotel room.

"Would you bless them?" he asked me as he handed me the bag with the crosses. "I want to send them to my crew and my brothers."

"Of course. This will take me a few hours and 'tis best if I'm not interrupted. You don't need to wait." I handed him the credit card I'd stolen. "Go out and have some fun."

He hesitated at the door, gazing at me worriedly, then let himself out of the room.

I set about laying out the crosses in the glass bowl. The sun had warmed the contents, perfuming the air with a strong scent of sage with an undertone of peppermint and metal.

"Dominus vobiscum sicut in caelo, et in terra libera nos a malo."

Peace filled me as I prayed. I knew He heard.

"Ego sum servus tuus, ego sum servus tuus, ego sum servus tuus."

I am your servant, Lord.

I'd just finished cleaning everything when Ryu returned.

We dressed in our tuxedos, and new jewelry, and brought our packages to the desk to be posted.

I said, "I'd intended this one for Ollie, but since you've supplied him one, perhaps I should send it to Birdie?"

"He won't wear it if it's from you…. For Julia though, have her send it to him."

I sent it to Julia with a note.

In the cab to the casino, Ryu said, "I found a great store I think you'll really like. I bought you this—with my own money."

He handed me a small box that contained a silver silk ascot with flowers embroidered in a shade lighter, metallic-silver thread that glittered in the light of the streetlamps.

"'Tis beautiful!"

I began removing my tie, fumbling a bit with the small buttons of my collar.

"Let me," he said gruffly and unbuttoned my collar, replacing my tie with the silk ascot and fastening it with an antique silver tie clip.

"It suits you perfectly... Pip."

I dropped my gaze to the empty box so he wouldn't see my tears.

"Thank you. 'Twas very thoughtful."

He patted my knee, the heat of his hand shooting directly to my cock.

Our cab pulled to a stop, and he stepped out.

"Look at this place! And these folks... you can do some serious people watching here, Pip. These dudes are the real deal."

Elegantly gowned women, escorted by equally elegantly dressed men, filled the foyer, laughing brightly, sipping drinks, chatting... I wished I could be one, but I was a shadow, unseen, hidden in this human shell.

Chapter 18

Ryu leaned close to whisper in my ear, "He's drunk as a lord. Introduce yourself and just slide it off his wrist. I'll jostle him and he won't notice a thing. Lean over his hand to block any cameras. Turn so that your hand is hidden by the chair and your legs and just slip the watch into your pocket. I'll storm off and you follow me."

I nodded that I understood. The man Ryu had spotted playing at the poker table was the ideal mark to acquire the time piece we needed, him being well to do and the watch an expensive one that would work perfectly for spells that required the timing of a theft be exact.

Ryu eyed me doubtfully for a moment before snickering, turning away muttering, "I'm corrupting a minor," which in my nervous state I found hysterical.

I burst into giggles. He glanced over his shoulder to laugh with me, gesturing with his head at our mark.

I straightened and marched over, extending my hand as I said, "I'm Lord Blackwood. 'Twas a beautiful play."

"Garret—" he cut off abruptly when Ryu bumped him hard. Garret continued shaking my hand by reflex.

I had his watch and turned to drop it into my pocket.

Reginald smiled sardonically at me.

"Having fun?"

Behind me, Ryu and the man were arguing.

Ryu saying laughingly, "Chill. I said excuse me!"

He stomped off.

I hurried after him.

Reginald caught up to me, grabbing my arm to yank me to a stop.

"What the hell are you up to?"

From behind us, Bob said, "Is there a problem here?"

Sweat broke out on my brow. I grabbed Reginald's arm and yanked him a step back.

"No!" I yelled at Ryu as he stepped closer.

Bob rose an eyebrow, peering at Reginald as he said, "Sir?

Were they together, I thought with a shiver of horror. Julia would be undone.

Reginald glanced from me to Bob, his eyes narrowing, a small triumphant smile building.

"Are you casino authority?" he asked Bob.

"Yes."

The way Bob was examining Reginald was reassuring that the two hadn't met before—but still the coincidence that both were here was alarming.

Ryu said, "Everything's fine. It's nice to see you, Reg. Your sister didn't say you'd be here."

I pulled Reginald another step back.

Bob looked perfectly ordinary, not at all dangerous, but every hair on my body remained standing.

I said, "Bob, isn't it? I thought you worked at the other casino?"

"Same company owns them both... how's the luck tonight?"

"Shitty—for them," Reginald said.

I cast Ryu a desperate glance that he didn't see. He was gaping at Bob.

I wanted to walk away but was afraid Reginald would stay and speak with Bob.

I said to Ryu, "His sister would be quite discomposed if we left him here."

Ryu turned a frazzled glance at me.

My mouth was dry, and my legs shook as I turned, putting my back between Bob and Reginald to mouth, "Come with me, please."

I said to Ryu, "Have the car brought around—now!"

"Yes, sir."

He hesitated, wiping his hands on his trousers. I bet they were as sweaty as mine own, which made me laugh nervously.

"I can't leave you with him," Ryu said in an anguished tone.

"He's hardly going to shoot me here."

Reginald said, "Oh please, like I ever even threatened you."

"I didn't mean you." I rolled my eyes, hoping he'd see I meant Bob, but he snickered a mean laugh as he said, "You did just steal the fuckers Rolex."

Bob said, "Sir?"

Reginald jerked a thumb at the man at the card table.

"Ask him." His smile at me was full of malice. "It's in his pocket."

I pulled Reginald with me back to the table where I grabbed the drunk man's arm. Ryu had a tight grip on my shoulder, which likely looked ridiculous, but I was glad of the support even though I didn't need his anima to sway Garret.

"Hey," Garret sputtered indignantly.

"Tell these gentlemen that you weren't wearing a watch here."

"Lord Blackwood... I wasn't wearing a watch... what's this about?"

"Nothing."

175

"I saw him take your watch!" Reginald said.

"Don't be ridiculous. Why would I? This Rolex is mine," I said while grasping the man's anima.

I had to release Reginald to remove the watch from my pocket.

Bob said to the drunk, "Is it his?"

"If he says so. I wasn't wearing a watch."

Bob shrugged at Reginald, saying, "I think you were mistaken, sir."

I tugged Reginald with me as I backed away.

Bob followed us.

Reginald shrugged from my grasp, glaring hotly at Ryu, appearing completely oblivious to the weighing gaze of Bob.

Ryu didn't seem to notice Reginald's glare. He was staring at Bob in a mix of horror and bewilderment.

"Do you have a brother?" he asked.

The *non sequitur* confused everyone except me.

Bob stared for a moment before saying mildly, "I have no idea... why?"

"I met someone who looks just like you. He could've been your twin."

"Really? Where?"

"Paris."

Amusement danced in Bob's eyes.

I grabbed Ryu's arm.

We both took a step back.

Bob laughed as he said, "Never been there. Well, that ain't strictly true. I was born there. Maybe I should go check my birth records and see if I have a long-lost brother?"

"Hey, Bob?" a man yelled from down the hallway. He waved a radio at us. "They want you in the head office."

"Have a nice evening," Bob said as he headed to the man with the radio.

We trailed slowly.

As Bob approached, radio guy said, "You did it this time. Celine was pissed as shit! When the hell are you going to learn! These jokes of yours are going to get you fired!"

The two men walked off together.

"Did you see?" I asked breathlessly.

"See what?" Reginald asked.

"He was as amused as fuck," Ryu said uneasily.

I turned to Reginald who looked honestly perplexed.

I said, "Stay away from that guy. He's dangerous."

"Pip..." Ryu said warningly.

Reginald gazed after Bob. "Him... how do you know?"

His question was asked so sincerely that I thought he honestly hadn't recognized him, which meant he'd never met Pete.

Julia will be relieved, I thought.

"I just do. Don't go near him, Reg. In fact, don't come here again."

"He's the guy who's going to shoot?" he asked disbelievingly.

"Pip," Ryu said again.

"I can't just leave him here!"

"You don't know that Bob is dangerous."

"Like hell I don't! There's no way I'm letting him do whatever..."

I stopped talking to wipe my sweating brow and let my heart stop pounding.

Reginald said, "If I didn't know better, which I do, I'd say that you were honestly scared of that man."

I hated his thoughtful tone.

He gazed back at the drunk, pursing his lips then smirked at me as he said, "I wonder what Dankworth will say tomorrow about that watch when he sobers up?"

He swaggered away, joining the drunk with a casual slap on the shoulder.

"Fuck," Ryu muttered.

"Never mind him. I can handle him."

I dragged Ryu away.

Out on the street I said, "Reg is going to look Bob up. Julia will be undone! Despite all, she loves him. I cannot let that... thing infect him."

"He might've been telling the truth."

"I know that!"

I turned away to take a few deep breaths.

"Can you make Reg forget he was ever here?"

"I... I know not. Reg is a mystery to me. We'd thought that Lou had been manipulating him, but if so, then why cannot I do it? It takes such effort and does so little... Julia and I can't move the other much, but it doesn't leave the tiredness that trying to alter his anima does."

"Because you love each other. You aren't fighting, it simply doesn't work."

"It *should* work. I see her anima."

"Do you see mine?"

"Sometimes," I said absently.

"I meant with the charm on."

"A charm...you think he has a charm?"

He grabbed my arm, yanking me to a stop.

"Calm down a minute, Pip."

He pulled his phone out and called Ollie.

"We're going back to the hotel."

To my shock—and delight, which I knew was wrong to feel when he meant only comfort—he hugged me for a few minutes.

"He scared me too," he said when he released me. "We shouldn't go back in without a plan."

Ollie pulled up and Ryu leaned in his window to say, "There's a drunk guy called Dankworth at a poker table in there. He's blond with a shitty beard, about six-foot, overweight, wearing a black suit with a pink tie. He might be with Julia's brother. See if you can find out where he's staying, and if you can, keep an eye on Reginald, but don't let him catch on that you're watching him."

He handed over his wad of cash.

"It's important, so don't fuck it up. We need to find that guy when he leaves here. Call me when you think he's on the way out."

I removed my cross and draped it over Ollie's head.

"Keep it on. It'll bring you luck."

His eyes lit.

"Pay attention and don't talk to any balding men or any security."

Ryu got into the driver seat.

Ollie held the back door open for me.

I got into the back.

"Where to?" Ryu asked.

"I have no idea... just find a place close by to park."

"You can't confront him. You know that, right?"

"I'll have too...."

"Like hell you do! Look, Pip, he's either a human or he isn't. If he isn't, he's hardly going to tell you that. You'd have to force him to say it somehow and who knows if you could? And it doesn't matter anyway because that doesn't mean he's evil like Pete was. Maybe that demon picked Pete because he wasn't human to begin with? But who cares about that anyway. As I see it, we have one choice. We either whack the guy, doing it quick before he has time to gather his mojo, or we leave him the hell alone. My vote is we leave him alone. He hasn't done a damned thing to us or anyone else or he'd have a rind."

I called Julia, putting her on speaker.

"We ran into Bob again," I said as soon as she answered. "Reginald was there."

"With him!"

"No but Reg saw that Bob scared me. He might try to go talk to him. Ryu thinks we should just leave Bob alone because he has no rind. I think Bob is dangerous but Ryu's right. I have no way to prove it or stop him if he isn't susceptible to me. It's really worrying me that Bob could tell I'm not human. What if he tries to infect Reg to get to us?"

"How would Bob know what we are?"

"He saw me ordering a man."

Ryu said, "It was smoothly done though, Julia. The guy was drunk."

I said, "If he can see anima like we can, he'd have seen me do it."

"You think he's a seethe?"

"I have no idea what he is."

Ryu said, "He's probably a pixie. You heard that other guy. He said Bob was in trouble for his bad jokes. And he claimed he was born in Paris. He didn't come right out and say he was adopted but he said he didn't know if he had a brother and maybe he should look."

I said, "I warned Reg he was dangerous, which in hindsight..."

Julia heaved an exasperated sigh.

She said, "It's probably nothing. And we can't be worried about others finding us because we know the vampires and God knows what else already know about us. I'll put some of the boys on looking into Bob's background and tell Sandra. Maybe I'll move Birdie there for a while to follow him? It might cool him off about Ryu when he hears..."

I said, "We're going to need to do something about him too. He's too dangerous, Julia."

"I know. He's so damned useful though."

"Just don't ever go near him alone," Ryu said. "I don't know what he could do if he got his hands on some meth. You might not be able to hold him then."

"I'll be careful."

Ryu said, "So we're leaving Bob alone, right?"

"For now," Julia said.

"And Reg?" I asked.

"Is a big boy. He was warned."

"'Tis worse than a death sentence. If he were to become infected by a demon, I know not how we'd stop him except by murdering his body to excise the demon—sending him straight to hell."

"Let's not worry about it. He isn't infected, and frankly, I'm amazed that he isn't... I think he's too strong willed to let himself become a host. If we see any sign that Bob or anything else is trying, we'll talk about it again."

Ryu said, "I'd say get him a charm like mine but..."

I said, "'Tis a good idea. I shall ask Sandra to make one and infuse it with all of the spells that she knows to repel such things."

"I'll call her," Julia said. "Keep me in the loop."

She disconnected.

I said, "My nerves are too disrupted to attempt to steal the safe."

"*Meh*, we can find another easy enough in Dubai. One more watch and you're done with that too." He gestured to the people entering a nearby bar.

"We can find one while we wait for Ollie to call. Just walk up and ask the time. When they look at their watch, I'll distract them."

"I'd prefer to wait.... how are you so calm? Does the idea of a demon not terrify you?"

"Sure it does. I believe you saw one, but until I see it myself, I *can't* believe it—if you know what I mean. I mean, you're so normal, what you can do is spooky as shit but not crazy scary. I seen people do similar stuff on stage with hypnotism. Your friends place was scary..." his eyes grew uneasy for a moment before his normal 'nothing bothers me' expression returned. "And Pete's house was a nightmare, but in a human sort of way."

He laughed a soft deprecating huff of sound as he said, "Maybe I'm just getting used to the idea. The magic stuff seems almost normal now. Almost as if I always knew about it—you didn't do that to me, did you?"

"What? Make you believe in magic?"

"Yeah. You didn't make me okay with all of this, right?"

"No. It hadn't occurred to me."

"Don't do it. Even if something really scares me. I don't want you messing with my head."

"I won't—on purpose at least. 'Tis my thought that my power is addictive."

He nodded, saying, "I seen how they fawn on you. It doesn't do that to me though. I like you an all but..."

You love Julia, I didn't say because I could see by his face that he was already thinking it and didn't like the idea.

I said, "See if you can get us an earlier flight. There's no sense in hanging about if we aren't going to gamble."

He nodded and took out his phone.

He was on the phone speaking with the airlines when he said to me, "Ollie is calling."

"Drive by the casino and drop me off."

I called Ollie as he pulled out.

Ollie said, "Your mark is leaving now with a woman. I think she's a working girl. Reginald is still at the table."

"Stay with Reginald." I disconnected and said to Ryu, "Drop me here."

A few minutes later, Garret stumbled outside, shaking a woman off his arm to hail a taxi.

'Twas simple to grab his arm and say, "Don't forget that you lost that watch on a bet, not that you care when you got the girl."

The woman with him laughed and kissed his cheek.

She said, "He's drunk as shit. I doubt he'll remember his own name tomorrow never mind mine."

Garret said angrily, "I'm fine and remember perfectly! Was a hand of poker, wasn't it..."

"Have a nice night."

He and the girl got into a cab.

I was debating going in to retrieve Ollie or maybe take another look at Bob when Reginald exited right as my phone rang.

We stared at each other a moment before he said, "Looking for me?"

I turned and walked away, getting into the car with Ryu.

Ryu said, "He's just standing there..."

I glanced back in time to see Ollie exit. He looked startled to see Reginald standing there.

"Come on, fool," Ryu mumbled.

I think we were both holding our breath that Ollie wouldn't approach the car.

Ryu pulled away as Ollie took his phone out.

He walked in the opposite direction before Ryu said anything.

I said, "Tell him to get a cab back to the hotel. He can have that cash. I'll reimburse you. But tell him to go to a different casino if he's going to gamble."

Ryu said, "Ollie, man, we got another flight. You're still on for the day after tomorrow. Pack our things and check us out. The boss says do whatever you like with that cash."

He listened a minute and then said, "Yeah. The rooms and shit on the credit card and you can use that for food and shit. Save the receipts and don't be an ass. Make sure you return that car in good condition. And good job. Oh, and don't go back to that casino. Pick one of the smaller places and watch your back. Don't be a dummy and flash all that cash."

He put his phone into his pocket.

I'd need to do something about Ollie. Ryu was right, he needed someone to watch his back.

Chapter 19

I hadn't felt the need to sleep, which was worrying when I hadn't consciously absorbed the anima, but I must have ingested it to be so wakeful.

I spent the flight to Dubai rereading my instructions from Sandra.

A stranger was waiting at the airport for us with a rented limousine. He drove us directly to a meeting that Sandra had arranged, which told me she was really anxious to get started on this project.

The building was huge, the biggest I'd ever seen, surrounded by even larger buildings. Despite the heat, they were all cold and imposing without a spec of charm.

"'Tis much too modern," I said, which made Ryu laugh.

There wasn't a taxi in sight of the portico just expensive looking cars dropping off and picking up well dressed men.

The foyer was gaudy in its lavishness. Huge potted plants did nothing to soften the marble. To me they appeared chosen for the size and impracticality. The building screamed new money.

Ryu went to speak with a woman at the desk while I gawked.

The entire place was unwelcoming in the extreme—mostly because of the people. Everyone within sight, except for the women at the desk, sported a red rind.

"There's so many," I said in dismay.

I hated to see them all and leave them to commit more villainy, but we already had a ridiculous amount of mules to house and feed.

Julia was trying to find work they could do and still be under our eye. I'd known this project was meant to employee quite a few of them and hoped now it wasn't meant to gather more.

"So many what? People?" Ryu asked.

I grabbed Ryu's arm and pulled him back toward the main doors.

"Lord Blackwood!" the woman at the desk called after us.

I ignored her, pulling Ryu after me.

On the sidewalk I said, "We need some signal—some way for me to warn you when you confront a killer. They reek of anger. 'Tis my thought they will be quick to violence."

"Who? The men getting into the elevator?"

"All of them have the glow of stolen anima. The two you speak of were evenly matched. 'Twas something about them…" I wasn't certain if it had been something I'd sensed or seen, but I was certain the two were cold blooded killers. "It matters not," I continued. "To me they can do no harm. To you…. Perhaps you should return to the hotel?"

"Hell, no! I might not be as, *err*, gifted as you, but I ain't afraid of those douche bags."

"If violence does break out, stay behind me."

His expression told me I'd insulted him.

I grabbed him by both arms and shook him hard.

"Stay behind me!"

He immediately walked behind me.

"Damn it! 'Twasn't my intent! Why aren't you wearing your charm?"

"I didn't think I'd need it."

I wasn't sure if I was still compelling him or not.

I said, "*I* am bullet proof. *You* are not!"

I stomped back inside.

The girl at the desk said, "Floor thirty-two. Conference room Two."

Ryu joined me in the elevator, and we rode up in silence.

Jane Conroy, a lawyer supplied by Sandra, was waiting. I shook her hand, introduced Ryu as my assistant, and we took our seats. The two men with the matching rinds were the men I'd come to meet. Sandra had arranged the sale. They were extremely polite and more than happy to sell because the equipment would all need updating soon.

I still had no idea why Sandra wanted a tile factory.

Three hours later, I owned the tile fabrication plant at a discounted price, compliments of their stolen anima. The two men left with their cashier's check. The check lessened their anger appreciably, but it worried me that they'd eventually grow angry over the deal and act on that anger.

I said to Ryu, "Set someone on following them. I don't want to lose track of them. I don't need any information, except on their whereabouts. I want to be able to find them again in a week or so."

Jane looked confused.

Ryu nodded, making a note in his notebook. He left the room to make a phone call.

Jane said, "Sandra has given me her power of attorney to sign a contract ordering tile to be delivered next month to her home in England.

I signed the papers she handed me.

"Has she spoken with you about being her daughter's guardian in the event that Sandra is incapacitated?"

I was surprised she'd told her lawyer but said, "Yes."

She slid another stack of papers to me.

"This gives you legal guardianship and a limited power of attorney to act on Sandra's behalf."

I signed and initialed a huge stack of documents.

"I'll drop off copies of everything you've signed here at the hotel tomorrow. Copies will be filed in England and America. As a thank you, I've been authorized to pay half of the cost of any of the properties that you chose from the list that we've been considering."

"I haven't had a chance to inspect any yet."

"There's no rush. I'll be here for another month tying up loose ends at the library. If needed, I can return, or maybe by then we'll have permanent staff here. Sandra will be faxing me her final choices on office space, which I've been directed to forward to you for your inspection and recommendation. She's also considering purchasing an apartment building but hasn't yet begun looking. I think she wanted your input on that as well?"

"Yes. I'll be looking over the neighborhoods while I'm here. I intend to purchase housing for my employees and have an appointment with a realtor tomorrow to look at a few properties."

"If you require assistance, I'm available day or night. Oh, I almost forgot. Sandra asked me to give you this." She handed me a small, wrapped box. "Happy Birthday. She told me to tell you she made it herself and to warn you that the tack is pointy so use care when donning it."

"Thank you."

We shook hands and she left with her two boxes of files.

I opened the box and removed two simple leather necklaces with a single pearl. I understood the runes inscribed on the underside and her cryptic message.

I went to find Ryu.

He was in the hall by the far window still on his phone. He held up a finger when he saw me.

I went to the elevator, and he caught up with me in the lobby.

"Julia says to talk to the management here to see about renting office space because rind is good for us."

"I wish to see the other properties first and we should visit the tile factory so I can get started there."

"It's too late to get much done tonight. Let's just check in and call it an early night."

That reminded me that he must be exhausted after only a few hours of sleep on the plane.

I nodded agreement and Ryu called for our car.

The driver pulled up a few minutes later.

"It requires a pinch of blood," I whispered as I handed Ryu one of the necklaces. "It's an amulet to speak Arabic. Don't get it wet."

I put mine on then used my silver letter opener that I took from my carryon to cut my thumb. I rubbed my bloody thumb across the pearl.

Ryu said, "You sure that's what it does?"

"I'm sure that's the intent. If it actually works.... we'll see."

"Can I borrow your knife? I left mine in my bag and you shouldn't bring one in your carryon. It's against flight regulations. No weapons."

I rolled my eyes at him, making him snicker.

'Twas a simple thing to make an inspector not notice my bags.

We went to check in and then walked to a restaurant.

I spent the night examining maps online.

Ollie had arrived by the time we had to leave for our first meeting the next day.

The two men bumped fists.

I myself was surprisingly happy to see him.

He laughed when I held out my fist to him.

Ryu laughed too, rolling his eyes at me and cuffing Ollie lightly.

He said, "It should take about an hour or so to get to the factory. You okay to drive after that flight?"

"Sure thing. I slept on the flight. Man you should've seen the casino I found."

"Tell me later. The boss needs to concentrate now."

Ollie nodded agreeably. Ryu and I got into the back.

I took out my book on Germanic languages. Ryu dozed until we reached the factory.

I said to Ollie, "Drive around and see what's available for housing. Take some pictures."

Ryu stepped from the car and leaned in the window to say, "You're looking for a place some of our crew can live when they're here. It needs to be close by so they can keep an eye on things."

"Who'd want to live here," Ollie muttered.

He saluted Ryu with his habitual sarcastic salute and drove off.

I said, "We'll be sending a full construction team, so we can fix up the housing if necessary. Now, let's see what we have to work with."

The tile factory was small and already contained the equipment to produce handmade, custom shaped tile, which was why she'd picked it. My job was to ensure the workers wouldn't mention anything.

The manager spoke heavily accented English. I wasn't sure how much he actually understood of what I said.

Ryu and I understood his Arabic just fine thanks to the amulets supplied by Sandra, but neither of us mentioned we could because I thought they'd be more likely to speak freely amongst themselves if they thought we couldn't understand them.

We spent the morning and afternoon touring the small factory, taking notes on what was needed to upgrade the machinery to produce the tiles we needed and which employees needed to be under my control.

The manager followed us anxiously the entire time.

Ollie was waiting, sleeping in the front seat when we left the factory.

I said to Ryu, "Let's take a walk. I want to see the desert."

"It's all desert," he muttered.

"See if you can find out who owns the land behind the building. Julia will be sending me a crew any day now. Send some of the boys to the neighbors on either side. I'll want to know who owns it and what they do there."

"That building on the right looked abandoned to me."

I nodded agreement.

"If it is abandoned, tell the boys to walk through and aggravate any squatters. I'll want pictures and names if they can get them. And remind them no physical stuff!"

"I don't know what you're planning in there, but I don't see a way to keep the employees from seeing what's going on. You're going to need to replace all of them."

"Or move end-stage painting."

"You're not going to tell me?"

"Because I don't know either."

He glanced back worriedly.

"What if it's drugs, Pip?"

"'Tisn't. Julia and I were quite clear about the types of endeavors we'd lend our talents to. 'Tis certain Sandra will tell us when needs must. 'Tis wise of her to see if I can handle a project of this size before committing her secrets to it."

"I guess... I just don't want it to be us left holding the bag."

I must have looked as confused as I was because he laughingly added, "getting the blame."

I nodded as I said, "We'll see if we can find someone qualified to begin making the necessary repairs tomorrow. We'll hire a translator so we can get started with the employees. Tell Julia to send us the crew. Now, let's go get something to eat and then meet the realtor.

Julia called me as I was sitting at the realtor's desk.

"My wife. Excuse me, please."

I stepped into the hall to answer.

She said, "I'm coming tomorrow with your new footmen and a few mules. I've already spoken to Ollie and he's arranging temporary accommodations for them. When you speak to the realtor, find another apartment building or a house large enough for the twelve of you."

"Mules?"

"I'll explain when I see you."

"Are you well?"

"Perfectly." She laughed a quick giddy laugh that relieved me as she added, "This is fun! Stay safe, darling."

She disconnected.

I returned to the meeting and Ryu glanced worriedly at me.

"Lady Blackwood is arriving tomorrow with new staff. Ensure that Ollie has made proper arrangements to retrieve her."

I turned to the realtor, "Now, where were we?"

"I've lined up ten properties that I think will meet your criteria."

I placed my hand on Ryu's knee and leaned forward, guiding his stolen anima like I'd been practicing onto the realtor.

"I require temporary office space in the Maamoun tower. Arrange for a suite with two offices, a reception room, and a private bathroom. I also need a small apartment building or hotel. What's the best one available?"

"I'd have to check."

"Find out by our next meeting in two days, and I want the real rate with no hidden commissions or fees. Every price you give me will be the best possible one."

I released Ryu and sat back in my chair.

"Warn me next time," Ryu muttered.

He was a bit sweaty, which worried me.

I said to the realtor, "The printouts with the owner's details?"

He handed me a thick folder.

"We'll take my car and meet you there," I said to the realtor and then to Ryu, "I'm sorry. Is this too... taxing?"

"Nah, I got this."

"I've no wish to harm you."

"I said I got this, Pip."

The realtor listened with a puzzled expression.

I let it go until we were in our hotel room later that evening.

"Did I hurt you?" I asked as we took seats at the small table in my room, laying my hand on his as he began to demur.

"'Tis important that I know truthfully so that I can better gauge mine own actions.

"It didn't hurt exactly. It was more unbalanced. As if I was suddenly dizzy or was in an elevator that dropped too quickly."

"I did yank it quite aggressively. I shall try to be more delicate."

He snickered a moment but then his levity faded into a worried expression as he asked with forced casualness, "How does it feel to you?"

"It depends on whom I'm using it on. I barely felt it on the realtor; I think because he makes no commission on the sale but gets a flat fee, so 'twasn't much of a push at all."

"No, I meant, it doesn't hurt you at all... or feel good?"

"In this instance it felt—satisfying. It sometimes tires me or makes me feel giddy as if I'd taken strong drink. For Julia 'tis always like that, which is why she's better suited to work with those who already possess a rind to manipulate. She can shift the excess anima to others but 'tis a noticeable change in the recipient and herself. I dislike being so heavy handed."

"Can it kill us?"

"Yes. But 'tisn't something we could do lightly."

I stood to retrieve one of Sandra's books I'd brought with me and handed it to him."

"I can't read this," he said dryly.

"'Tis the pictures I wished you to see. The text speaks of a seethes power to withdraw the life force from a man and says that is when we are the most vulnerable. Absorbing it, assuming the man was a healthy one, would leave us engorged with the anima as a man would be should they drink a cask of brandy. We would be giddy and pray to falling in a stupor as if drink taken unless we immediately spent it. We could easily be baited into a rage in such a condition. 'Twould also heal us though, so physical damage would need to be extreme.

"A practiced seethe can use that stolen anima to increase his own strength, giving himself the strength of ten men. 'Twas common for a seethe to suck the anima from his opponents, weakening them and strengthening himself. A smart opponent would kill the seethe's victim, causing the seethe to swallow the excess anima all in one gulp as it were, which if the man was still very much alive could cause the seethe to become drunk if they couldn't withdraw quickly enough. But, if I had need of the anima, I could drain it all, leaving my victim a corpse."

"...I see."

"Taking small sips would be best, except then the seethe runs the risk of becoming addicted as a man does to drink. I'm speaking of a man's own anima, you understand, not anima stolen from others. That stolen anima lacks the potency and 'tis much easier to manipulate. 'Tis strongly connected to the man it encapsulates but lacks the will of the man. It isn't a part of him exactly but more a— blanket that he wears.

"What happens if you use all of that up?"

"I suppose it depends on how one used it. I could use it to deeply embed my commands on the man."

"Make them a zombie..." he asked.

"Of a sort, I suppose. 'Twould depend on the commands given. Take Birdie, we regularly order him to obey us but in no other way limit him. He can think and feel as he likes."

"You could make him think and feel whatever you wanted to though..."

"Yes."

"Why are you telling me all this, Pip?"

"If it were me facing a creature like mine self, I'd wish to know. There are no other living seethes to my knowledge in this realm. Telling you harms no one but myself. The shadowed seethes are more limited in their actions than we. Their strengths and weaknesses are different than mine. For the most part they seem content enough in their shadows.

"I, on the other hand, live firmly in the realm of man. 'Tis my thought that there should be humans who know of and could combat us should the need arise."

Ryu said doubtfully, "I'm just one man and you could swat me like a fly..."

"My hope is that you'll learn as we do—that we won't remain as unequal as we are now."

"I appreciate the thought, Pip, but I don't think it's realistic. No human man could best you."

"Perhaps not. But mayhap if that man were cunning and surrounded himself with men of even temperament, ones who'd naturally abhor evil."

I tapped the drawing of the five knights in the picture.

"They went forth, not in anger, but in love. 'Twas with true regret they slayed the creature—their prayers, their state of mind made possible what two thousand men failed to do. If you hate me, you shall be powerless against me."

"I've never hated you, Pip."

"'Tis my hope that you can learn to love me enough to never let me become an evil creature."

"You won't."

"'Tis good the laws of this age keep me in check. If I hadn't the need to hide my income... but 'tis necessary, so 'twas my thought that on the morrow we shall visit the men whose property we wish to purchase and see if any have a rind that I can manipulate."

"You can use mine. In fact, I'd rather you used it up. It gives me the willies to think of dying and having it weigh my soul down."

"'Tis possible..."

He said worriedly, "Of course, if you use it all, I'd be a crappy assistant..."

"If 'tis in my power, I shall ensure that no excess anima encumbers you on the moment of your death. But 'tis my thought that in time I could learn to use it to prolong your life."

His eyes widened.

"You can do that?"

"So the books claim. That seethe had four human companions. One is the knight there kneeling beside the dead body. He spoke of the hundreds of years they'd fought together with their seethe who at one time had been a good king. But he'd become corrupt, prone to vicious fits of rage, thinking nothing of murdering his human subjects. Two of his companions became as corrupt as he. One became a hermit and died a hundred years before the seethe's death—two hundred and fifty years after the man's birth. So it can obviously be done. How 'tis done without making a zombie, I know not."

"Two hundred and fifty years," Ryu said in awe.

"That knight was six hundred years old...."

"Six hundred years! Imagine that?"

"I truly cannot. The world has changed so much err I was born. I could n'er have imagined such wondrous things as now exist. I surely cannot imagine what may lie ahead. My Julia is consumed with planning for that unknown future. To her, wealth will see us safe. I agree, but 'tis my thought 'tis knowledge that will truly see us safe."

"You're both right. I think all three of us should hone our skills on the smaller scams, the turn of the dice, getting people to give us gifts and money, because those are the skills that we'll need if we ever do need to go into hiding."

"I agree, but there's also creatures like Pete. 'Tis my thought that such a creature would strive to ingratiate itself with us. We must prepare as best we may to fight such."

I stood to grab another book that I handed to him.

"Read it and consider the words."

He heaved a discontented sigh but took the Bible I offered.

I said, "I've left notes and highlighted passages that I thought might be of particular use."

"I'll read it," he said.

I opened my appointment book. "Now—Julia's arrival."

"I'll pick her up. Ollie can take you around to the sites."

We discussed the pros and cons of the different properties until he began yawning.

Chapter 20

The next day, Ollie and I went to visit all of the owners, finding two with their own rinds who could be manipulated.

We returned for an early dinner and found Julia had rented a conference room at the hotel. The man at the front desk directed us to it, handing me a note from her that just said, *'Come down and meet the crew when you're ready.'*

"Pip!" Julia said happily when I entered.

She jumped up from the table to greet me. Immediately ten men and six women seated there who I didn't know also stood.

She kissed my cheek.

"Yusuf," Ollie said to one of the young men, but he didn't look at all pleased to see him.

Yusuf didn't respond to Ollie other than a brief glance. His rapt gaze returned to Julia.

Only a few of them looked as deeply enthralled as he was. I hoped she'd done it purposefully.

Julia said, "Meet your new footmen. Jacob West is a lawyer and vigilante specializing in corporate law."

Jacob offered me his hand to shake. I could tell by his rind that he'd murdered or been present at the death of at least three people. Everyone in the room had a rind of varying thickness, except one girl. Her rind was very light. She looked unassuming, neither beautiful nor ugly. A born spinster as my mother would've said. There was something about the hardness in her eyes that I disliked.

Julia followed my gaze, "Emma Eades. She murdered her stepsister. You'll need to keep an eye on her. She's to be one of your secretaries."

Emma lowered her angry gaze to her hands that were clasped on the table. A human might have thought her embarrassed or even repentant, but I could see from her anima that Julia had angered her.

Julia said, "Frankie Bidwell is your other secretary. Frankie burned his home down, killing his entire family."

"They had it coming," he muttered.

Julia rose an eyebrow at him, and he flushed, mumbling, "Excuse me, sir."

No angry anima appeared. His eyes had a haunted look that belied his tone. I thought he regretted his actions and wished he didn't.

She said, "He's my newest acquisition and not as well trained as the others, but he's a hard worker—and his parents did have it coming. His brothers on the other hand..."

"Were as bad as them—or they would've been if given the chance!"

"Talk about that on your own time. Lord Blackwood isn't interested. What he *is* interested in is the smooth operation of his business and home. You've been chosen for your positions because of your—pragmatic attitudes. You've all agreed to the stipulations of the job, namely that you work as a team. No one acts outside the law without express permission from Mr. Poole,

Lord Blackwood, or myself. Anyone who causes a problem in the group will be find themselves terminated."

Ollie's eyes widened.

I didn't think she meant fired either.

She continued, "Personnel problems are to be directed to Mr. Poole. If you have reason to believe that your past crimes have come to the attention of the police, or anyone else, inform me immediately. There won't be a second chance here. So no trying to handle any illegal situations on your own. If you find yourself being questioned by the police, what do you say?"

As one they said, "I request counsel and say no comment until my lawyer arrives."

She nodded approval. "Jacob, I mean you too. If questioned by police, remain polite and speak calmly. No smart-ass comments or attitude. Just politely ask for your lawyer. If questioned by anyone at all, you only confirm your name and public job description. We only ever speak about official business to others."

They all nodded or said, yes ma'am.

She introduced the rest of them to me. All had committed at least one murder.

One of lighter rinded, Vicky Atkinson, had committed thirteen murders. Like Jacob, she was a vigilante, except where he targeted people who used the law to escape justice, she went out looking for them, walking the streets at night or hunting down rapists, who were her target of choice. She'd been too far from most of her victims to absorb much or had fled the scene before they died.

Most of them looked bored by Julia's recitation. They all obviously knew of each other's crimes.

When they'd all been introduced, Julia said, "Gather around, children."

The formed a tight circle around her, allowing her to touch all of their anima at once.

I watched anxiously as she said, "If taken and forcibly questioned by a rival gang, you can confirm you work for us but only give your official information. You can tell them that Lord Blackwood has taken abduction insurance out on you, but the policy doesn't pay if you're harmed.

"Now, what's you're unofficial job?"

As one they all said, "Anything you tell us to do."

"Yusuf, Frankie, Roy, Patrick and Jean, please stay. The rest of you can go. Check the app for your assignments."

Everyone except the five people she'd mentioned, us, and Ryu left the room.

The five who remained, except for Frankie, had deep dense rinds. Roy was older in his fifties or sixties. Jean and Yusuf were in their late twenties or so and Patrick was in his thirties, wearing the same suit I was. None of them looked like the hardened killers they were except for Yusuf. He had scars on his hands and face and tattooed knuckles.

She said, "Frankie is your day-to-day secretary. He'll be accompanying you to meetings to take notes and whatnot and he can drive you as well. He isn't a mule. Ryu, you'll be training him and Ollie how to handle the mules."

She jerked her thumb at Yusuf. "Bring one of these lunks with you. There's no rehabilitating them. Their sole purpose is as a battery and grunt work. They can drive but they lack any initiative at all. Keep them locked down because if you give them an inch, they'll be homicidal."

Frankie's eyebrows rose and he scootched away from Jean who sat closest to him. The rest of them kept smiling at Julia.

Ryu said, "Are we training them as muscle?"

"They already are. If you tell them to do anything, they're going to follow your literal order, so be careful around them."

She turned to me to say, "You'll need to nudge them to follow anyone else's order. So if you're out somewhere and you need them to answer someone else, you have to tell them. I picked Patrick because he has the same build as you. With a wig and one of your suits, he could pass as you, which will be useful if you need to appear to be somewhere else. I'm training another mule at home to be me. Bonnie is an awful woman. I'm having to train her in short bursts because she won't be released for another few months. I'll speak with the parole board to be sure she is because she's the ideal stand-in for me."

She pointed at Jean and then to the floor by her side.

Jean stood and walked to stand behind and to the side of Julia.

Julia pointed to the door and Jean headed to the door.

Julia twirled her finger and Jean spun to face the wall.

"She'll stand there until she collapses from fatigue, so don't forget to collect them when you're done."

"Jesus... do we need to be so..." Ryu shrugged uncomfortably.

"For these guys we do. You can leave them in their room if you won't need them. It's harsh but better them than losing Frankie or one of the others. Four is probably too many, but since I wasn't sure how many you might need, I figured better too many than too few."

"Losing Frankie how?" Frankie asked.

"Lord Blackwood will be dealing with some dangerous people. People like you who hide what they are behind a charming smile."

He grinned at her. If I couldn't see his stolen anima or didn't know he'd murdered his family, I'd have thought him a completely normal handsome young man.

"*Awe*, you think I'm charming," he said, giving her a flirtatious smile.

"I know exactly what you are."

His smile hardened.

Ryu said, "No flirting with the boss—either of them."

Julia took Frankie's hand, "No flirting with anyone except fellow footmen."

I was staring intently so saw the briefest flickers in the anima.

I said, "I really wish I could record that. It happens so quickly..."

"Have you told the others that?" Ryu asked.

"Yes. Multiple times. Frankie is new though. Pip will need to remind him of his job for a week or so."

"Shit, I don't need no reminders, lady."

I grabbed his hand and said, "Always speak respectfully to Lady Blackwood, Ryu, and myself. Even in your thoughts. You respect us and want to please us."

Frankie's anima brightened as it condensed, but again it happened almost too quickly to see. I thought the brighter bits were flowing from our clasped hand to his heart then eyes.

I released him.

Ryu said wistfully, "I wish I could do that."

I said, "I need to do it while one is naked so I can see where it goes better."

Julia said, "You can't hurt Jean. So use her. Just try not to mix your anima with hers more than you need to though. She's a disgusting person who murdered her own children."

Ryu said, "Did she say why she murdered them?"

"She was tired of the first one. If she'd stopped there, I'd have been inclined to believe it was just because she was so young herself.

"Fifteen is much too young to care for a baby. Not that I think that justifies murdering a baby, but it's at least a bit understandable. But she didn't even try to get herself help. She was just tired of being a mom, like her son was a doll she could toss out when she was done playing with it. She didn't even try to hide the murder really. She was honestly surprised no one ever said or did anything.

"The police only questioned her once. She got pregnant again right away—on purpose. The second baby she tortured first... you really don't want the details. Her daughter only lived nine months.

Nine months! It makes my blood run cold to think people believed her bullshit and felt sorry for her. Three kids dead in five years and no one questioned it..."

"She's so young...."

"What, you think she can grow out of being a homicidal maniac? That third child she kept for another year she was having so much fun making it scream. She was getting off on annoying her neighbors and all the sympathy from her friends and the doctors. And don't get me started on them! How could they not see what she was doing to that child? It makes me sick! I'd make her drown herself, but Pip might need an expendable woman. But if she doesn't..."

"She really murdered her own kids?" Frankie asked. "How do you know?"

"She told me."

She took his hand, saying, "You don't like Jean, Yusuf, Roy or Patrick. You know they're all cold-blooded murderers, but you'd never mention that to anyone. Ignore them as long as they're doing what they're told."

She released him and continued, "Yusuf, Roy, Jean, and Patrick are temporary help too stupid to get permanent positions. They stay in their room playing video games when not working."

"I don't like any of them," he said.

"Me either," Ryu said.

Julia wrinkled her nose at him.

"You're not supposed to like them."

I said, "Frankie, we leave at six. Speak with Ollie and he'll inform you on the appropriate clothing to wear. You're dismissed."

Julia snapped her fingers twice and all four of them, including Jean, gathered close enough she could touch their anima.

It gave me the shivers to see their eager smiles.

They loved her.

It relieved me that she despised them.

She said, "When Lord Blackwood says you're done for the day, go to your room and shower and change into sweat clothes. Share the food delivered to the room. You can watch tv or play video games until eleven and then go to bed. You get up at five thirty and make coffee and have breakfast, sharing the cereal and fruit in the room, then dress for the day in a clean suit or whatever Mr. Poole tells you to wear. You can watch tv, use the exercise equipment, or play games until he calls you to report for work."

I said, "You're done for the day."

They all left the room.

Julia said, "I wouldn't bother teaching any of them how to ride or box but the others could do it. They should always tell you the truth so you could ask them first if they have any interest—or force them…"

Ryu said, "You picked them all because of the sort of crimes they did?"

"Yes. I think we could rehabilitate them. Not cure them but keep them under control and they'd be happy enough doing it. Honestly, I'd have probably done the same damned thing Frankie did. He's screwed up as shit because of it, but I think we can help with that. They all have their reasons for taking the law into their own hands. They all have issues. We're doing the community a service by watching them. Emma is the only one besides the mules who's what I'd call evil. She murdered her stepsister because she was jealous. It's only luck that she hasn't murdered again. She was planning to murder a girl in her college. I never told her she couldn't murder because I want to see if given the chance to repent and taught coping skills if she *would* repent of her own freewill. Just ask her occasionally if she's planning a murder."

Ryu huffed.

Julia patted his shoulder. "Sorry to saddle you with them but we need them. Sandra has given me a list of items she needs and requested our help for an unspecified job. Speaking of which, Ryu,

I have a list of items we need to do the job. One of the things we need is a place to meet where you can build a model."

I said, "I found a condominium complex this afternoon that would work to house all of them, assuming they can share rooms. We could give them one of the blocks and rent the others for triple the going rate. I vow it'd take me less than a day to find us all new tenants. There are so many rinded people about 'twill be simple to order them to move in."

Ryu snickered.

Julia said, "Have the agent send Jacob the details. Go to a local bank and choose the angriest manager you can find, assuming you can't find a rinded one. Then take one of the mules and demand the lowest interest rate and see if they can take off any fees. Once the paperwork is signed, Frankie or Emma can handle setting up the accounts and all the paperwork. I've already told Jacob to brush up on local laws. He'll be looking for ways for us to write things off, so you can discuss with him the best way to proceed with purchases."

"Could we not buy it outright?"

"We could but we shouldn't. Our capital is limited. We need to show we have some liquidity to get a loan, I mean if the bank itself is ever audited. We could make them give us a loan, but it's best if it looks good on paper. So we keep as much of our money in the accounts as we can and buy on credit. As long as we can make the minimum payments, we keep buying. In fact, find us another hotel or maybe a condo we can make a time share. I can send marks from home here on vacation. So find something with suites so we can make them really expensive. It only needs to be breaking even now."

She turned to Ryu, "Speak with Frankie or Emma. One of them will need to act as our travel agent. I'll need to know who's made reservations in the suites so I can nudge them again if necessary."

He said, "It should have a conference center too because you could nudge a few corporate heads to hold conventions here and book out all the rooms."

"Brilliant. In fact, I'll look for more in other places as well."

She pulled out a notebook and wrote busily for a minute.

"I'm sending construction crews here, but you need a native to head the operation. If you need any specialists not on the list that I send, let me know."

She rummaged in her briefcase for a minute then pulled out a thick folder that she handed to me.

"Destroy this file after you both read it. It has all of the information on the men on the construction crew, including their crimes. The head man, Efren Bass, is a total piece of shit but he's really good at his job. You'll need to keep a close eye on him. The support people I'm sending are listed in a separate file. They aren't mules so you need to check up on them like you would any employee."

She grasped Ryu's hand quickly. "That's a job you have to do yourself because their job is taking care of the mules. Make sure they're delivering food on time, keeping their accommodations clean, paying the bills and anything else's the mules need done for them, and most importantly not mentioning anything off that they notice about the men. We can go tomorrow, and I'll introduce you."

She released him, sitting back in her chair as she said, "I'll be ordering them to follow your orders just like we did at home, but don't count on that until it's been tested more."

Ryu nodded.

She continued, "Sandra supplied us with a list of accountants and lawyers. I need to go in person to speak with all of them, so I'll be away for at least a week, maybe as many as three. We need these people to want this job, but I'd like to meet them to see if I could nudge them if we needed to before hiring any."

She placed a thick stack of folders on the table.

"Now, these are the businesses I'm considering at home."

Chapter 21

By three a.m. Ryu was yawning continuously.

I said, "Go get some sleep. You can sleep in. Ollie and one of the mules can accompany me to the realtor."

"You can't call them that," he said laughingly. "At least not in public. Call them guards."

I nodded.

Julia shook her head. "I'm training guards. Good decent men, mostly retired service men and police. We'll need quite a few of them for our different business ventures. Call the mules the chauffeurs. But don't rely on them as drivers. I've trained them not to remember what they did the previous day, which means they won't remember how to get anywhere without being told specifically and they're all easily distracted when I speak. If one is driving you, put the privacy screen up and remind them to follow all traffic laws."

Ryu said, "What about my crew? Tate and the others?"

"I'm using some as messengers and spies and some keep an eye on the place—those who haven't gone to work with Birdie that is."

"What's he doing?"

"Working for Sandra although he doesn't know that. She gives him direction by phone. She has him doing something in Paris."

"But you don't know what it is?"

"I know it involves breaking and entering, watching a few houses to see who's coming and going, searching public records, and tailing people. The why of it I don't know."

"I don't like this," Ryu said.

Julia shrugged. "It's not much different than what we do for ourselves. I asked your crew before assigning them there. We don't plan on doing it for anyone else...."

"Except perhaps Delphine," I said.

Julia gave me an exasperated glance but nodded her agreement.

"Just be careful, Julia," Ryu said. "Birdie's going to be pissed if he finds out he's working for someone else as your hire out. If he thinks you're stringing him along..."

"I can handle Birdie."

He stood, hesitating as if he'd like to say something but then leaving without further warnings.

Julia said, "I wish I could stay longer to visit. How are you really, darling, with all this Pete nonsense?"

"Would that it *was* nonsense."

"His story checks. Sandra went to see him herself and says he had no active magic about him."

I said tartly, "We have none either unless we're carrying spells."

She winced then brightened. "I have news that will cheer you up. Sandra will be arriving with a spellbook for you to use here. She's promised to show you how to make your own."

"Do you know what we're planning to rob?"

"I have an idea... an educated guess based off what she'd like us to do. I think we're robbing a gold refinery."

"Goodness!"

"You haven't got to do much except set our people out as a distraction."

"Is it bad that I'm disappointed?

She laughed.

I hadn't been jesting.

Chapter 22

My mules followed me into the warehouse I'd just rented.

I hadn't seen the interior, except for pictures. It was a bit dirtier than the pictures I'd seen but otherwise the same empty space.

I'd chosen it because it had a narrow driveway that led to a small back parking lot with a large garage door and a small loading ramp to accept deliveries.

We'd be able to park inside to hide vehicles or back a truck up without anyone seeing what we were unloading.

I said to my mules, "Look around for a broom and sweep the walls and floors. I'll have cleaning supplies brought.

"Ollie! Where you at?" Ryu yelled.

"Here, boss!" Ollie yelled from a loft above us.

The loft was about fifteen feet wide and ran the length of the building, reachable by a metal staircase at each end.

The rest of the interior was wide open. Three small rooms were along the left wall. One had a glass window that looked into an office that held two metal desks and a dented filing cabinet. One room was marked bathroom, and the other door was closed. I knew from the listing that it was a utility room. A few empty barrels were in front of a rolling door that opened onto the street in front.

Ryu tapped Yusuf on the shoulder, pointing to the utility room as he said, "Check in there for a broom and cleaning supplies."

The four mules headed to the closed room.

Ollie thundered down the stairs, jumping the last few and running over. The rest of the footmen were standing in small clumps and had obviously been talking together until we'd arrived—except for Emma who sat in the only visible chair, an old rolling chair that I assumed she'd taken from the office.

Ryu handed Ollie a wad of cash. "For contingencies."

He clapped his hands.

"All right, children, gather around!" Ryu said loudly as he laid his briefcase down to drag an empty metal barrel closer.

He tipped it over to use as a table.

My footmen gathered around it.

He withdrew a paper from a folder and handed it to Ollie. saying, "Make sure you get the right kind of spray paint. It needs to be the metal shit so the magnets stick. Hold this a sec."

He handed the folder to Ollie, revealing stacks of money beneath it.

All of them stirred in excitement.

He began handing the blocks out.

I said, "All of your purchases made for unofficial business are to be paid in cash—no exceptions. Most of you will only be making unofficial purchases."

Ryu took the folder back from Ollie and withdrew another sheet of paper that he handed to Jacob as he said, "Jacob will be picking up burner phones for all of you. When you arrive here in the morning, you leave your real cell phone here and take a burner with you. You never call anyone's real cell phone from a burner. Do it one time and you're out! It's burner to burner. Real cells are for work, calling home, or ordering food delivered here and shit. If the job you're sent on is listed as official business, take your real cell phone along too. If not, leave it here."

Jacob looked up from his list to say, "When in doubt leave it here. They'll be able to track your movements by your cell really good here."

They all nodded.

Ryu began handing out the papers from the folder.

"Vicky, Nick, Emma."

He handed everyone a list of supplies they needed to get, stopping when he said Frankie, holding out the last sheet to him.

"Your list has some bigger items. You'll need to rent a truck. Do that with the business credit card. Get with Vicky before you go because her list has some bigger items too and she can use the business credit card. Your budget is on your list."

Vicky said, "Did you want new or used furniture?"

"Either. You can pick it. Just make sure your budget will cover it. We don't need anything fancy. Jacob will be picking up the office supplies. Your stuff is meant to be used by you guys when you're hanging out here. If anyone has a problem filling their list with the money provided, report it to Frankie on a damned burner phone. If you have an idea or see a problem, report it to me."

He pointed to the floor then gestured around him.

"This is your new hangout. When you ain't out working, you're here waiting to go to work."

I said, "Or working from here."

They nodded.

Ryu said, "This ain't no nine-to-five gig. If you need time off, talk to Jacob or Frankie. If a job is going south, call me—on the damned burner phone."

I said, "Some jobs are extremely time sensitive."

Ryu frowned thoughtfully.

"We don't mind if you stop for lunch and shit but there'll be times when we need shit done pronto. If I or Lord Blackwood tell you to go do something, assume we mean pronto unless we specifically say there's no rush."

A loud clang made us all look.

Yusuf had knocked a metal grill from a window with his vigorous sweeping.

Ryu said, "Ollie, add black window tint to your list. Help each other out. We all know we plan on doing some criminal shit. So don't be dumb asses! Use your common sense. If you see a problem, say something."

I said, "No one brings anyone here without my permission. If civilians do stop in act polite like the professional people you are. You only ever speak freely about official business, but when I say freely, I mean as any professional person would. It isn't something you talk to a casual acquaintance about, except in polite generalities."

I consciously gathered their anima as I said, "You never speak about unofficial business!"

"We never speak about unofficial business," they all agreed.

Ryu said, "Frankie, you can go with Ollie to the hardware store and the two of you can help Vicky pick up the furniture. I don't care how you all arrange who does what. We only have the three cars though until Nick fills his list, so you need to cooperate."

I said, "I expect everyone except Nick to have your list done by this time tomorrow. Dismissed.

Ryu and I left them conferring, heading out to meet the realtor.

"We need a few new suckers," he said.

"Sucker?"

"Marks, chumps, assholes, people we intend to fleece—rob, scam."

"There's a plethora of likely suspects at the office building."

"Yeah. Those will be some big fish. We need a few minnows for some fast cash."

"Nay. I have a plan. Take me back to the office."

C.M. CONNEY

Chapter 23

      Ryu followed me to the desk in the main hall.

I said to one of the women working at it, "Excuse me, I've recently rented office space here. Is there an office directory available?"

She handed me a thin binder.

I offered her a fifty-euro bill.

"Might I buy yon yellow marker?"

She giggled as she traded me the bill for the highlighter.

"Thank you so much."

I opened the binder, which listed the renter for each suite by corporate name. Some of the listings included a short description of the business or I could infer what it was by the name while others, like my own, could be anything.

I flipped through the entire thing then headed to the elevator and pressed for the top floor.

"What are we doing?" Ryu asked.

"Fishing."

The top floor was rented by a company calling itself Worthy Shipping. The elevator disgorged us into a lobby very similar to the one on the main floor, including a desk that sat three women. Offices lined two corridors, one to the right of the elevator and one to the left. A sitting area with couches, chairs, a fireplace, a coffee bar, and large table were directly behind the women's desk.

People who were obviously waiting sat on the chairs and at the table. One of the four doors leading from that larger room was open and I could see a woman sitting at another desk with two closed doors to her right and one behind her.

"Can I help you, sir," one of the women at the main desk asked in Arabic.

"I hope so," I said in English. "I'm in need of a shipping company, and since I've just recently rented space here, I thought why not inquire?"

The woman who was sitting beside the woman I'd addressed said in English, "I can arrange a consultation with one of our agents if I can just have your name?"

"Louis Philip Blackwood, the Earl of Horsham, at your service."

She stood to escort us to the open door and the woman at the desk there.

"Ms. Zaman can assist you. Please, have a seat. Can I get you coffee or anything?"

We sat in front of Zaman's desk.

"No thank you."

Zaman gave our escort an irritated glance but said pleasantly, "And what can I do for you today, Mr...."

"Lord Blackwood," Ryu said haughtily.

I said, "I require fast secure transport for quite heavy products."

She slid a brochure across her desk.

Ryu said, "We'll be moving millions of dollars in inventory."

"I see..."

I flipped through the brochure then laid it on her desk.

"It appears you have adequate facilities. I'd need to examine them myself." I stood, saying, "I, of course, cannot do business with men I haven't personally met. Mr. Poole, my card, sir."

Ryu laid one of my business cards on the desk.

"Good day, madam."

I swaggered out.

Ryu followed me saying, "Sir, we really do need to settle on a shipper if we're to make the deliveries on time for his majesty."

I waved airily.

We went down five floors and visited Xion exports, which was a much smaller office more like my own with a timid looking man at the front desk in the reception area, two offices, and a bathroom.

We gave him the same spiel and were immediately admitted to an office where I was pleasantly surprised to find a woman behind the desk.

The art on her walls appeared to be original pieces and she wore designer clothing a bit above what the typical secretary wore.

"How may I help you?" she asked.

Her English was heavily French accented.

I answered in French, "I'm shopping for international transport, specifically for tiles, but not the typical fare. These are handmade and embellished with precious metals and gems, so will require discrete secure shipping."

"That isn't my usual line at all, but I could arrange for security to accompany a shipment."

"You are the owner, madame?"

"Yes. Madame Marion Bélanger."

"Lord Philip Blackwood. 'Tis a pleasure to make your acquaintance."

We shook hands.

I said, "Forgive me for asking, but are you new to this area?"

"Newish. We've been here two years now. Our main branch, as you've probably deduced, is in Paris. We typically move household goods although we do have a few merchant contracts as well."

Ryu said in English, "What's your service area?"

I wasn't sure how much of the conversation he'd been following.

She replied in English, "We have no set route. Most of our business is in Europe, but we've sent shipments to the Americas and even to Russia and the orient."

"Mr. Poole, my card."

He laid my business card on her desk.

"My man will be in touch with the particulars of my requirements. If a suitable price could be arranged, we'd need to tour the facilities."

Ryu said, "We have our own security who could accompany the shipments. Speaking of which, they'd want to run background checks on all of the drivers."

"That wouldn't be a problem at all. We run thorough checks on all of our employees.

I said, "It was a pleasure to meet you, madam."

I bowed over the hand she held out to me.

Her smile appeared genuine as she said, "I hope we can reach an accommodation."

We let ourselves out.

A rinded man exited the elevator we were waiting at. I followed him to an office in a small law firm on the same floor.

He walked past the receptionist to enter the office directly behind the desk. She heaved a sigh and set down her coat and purse to resume her seat.

I said to her, "Excuse me, but was that Mr. Asgard esquire?"

"Mr. Asgard junior, sir. Do you have an appointment?"

"No. I'd thought I recognized him. What sort of law does he practice?"

"Corporate tax law."

"Then I should like to make an appointment for the first available time. Mr. Poole, my card if you'd be so kind. Please make arrangements."

I exited, leaving Ryu to settle the details.

She'd given me an idea. I headed directly to the cafeteria, phoning Ollie as I did so.

"I'm in need of immediate assistance. It shall probably take the remainder of the day. Give your list to one of the others, Frankie, perhaps, and join me at once in the cafeteria at the office building."

"Yes, sir. Is everything okay, sir? Should I call Ryu?"

"Ryu is engaged with business at the moment. "'Tis nothing dire. I just need someone to help me take some unobtrusive photographs and my subjects might not remain long."

"I'll be there in fifteen minutes."

"If anyone else is available, bring them along. Be sure they're dressed appropriately."

I disconnected, texted Ryu to tell him where I was, and got into line to buy myself a coffee and danish then sat by the main entrance of the cafeteria to eat it.

Ryu joined me ten minutes later.

"What are we doing?"

"May I borrow your phone, please?"

He handed me his and I handed him mine.

I said, "I noticed that the brochure we were given at Xion contained portrait shots. There was a picture directory on the wall by the door at Asgard at Law. I believe the man whose picture I just snapped works there. See if we can find the same sort of directory—or make one ourselves for the building."

"Which picture? There's three men here."

"The one with the pink tie. All have a rind I can use. I shall sit here and take pictures and we shall see which companies we can take."

220

"Was the lady at Xion rinded?" he asked in surprise.

"No. I quite liked her. 'Tis a shame we can't do business together although perhaps we can..."

Ryu said, "If you're trying to see everyone who works in this building, we should come here at opening and closing."

I nodded agreement as I said, "Follow that group there and see where they go."

Ryu followed my gaze to the coffee dispensers, nodding as he stood to follow the group of men.

"Which one?" he whispered.

"All of them."

"Good grief... I'm on it."

I took a picture as they walked past.

Ollie and Vicky joined me a few minutes later.

I said, "That group at the far table by the window all appear to be wearing ID tags. See if you can find out for which company they work."

They both headed to the group.

My attention was caught by an older man with a very deep rind who was speaking to a young woman right outside the doorway. He looked a lot like his son.

I opened the brochure and highlighted Asgard at Law.

Ollie returned to the table carrying a tray with three cups and an assortment of pastry.

"They work for a cleaning company."

"Interesting. Visit the offices and see if you can find out what services they offer." I grabbed his hand as he went to stand.

"And be careful. They're all killers."

His eyes widened and he cast a dubious glance over his shoulder at Vicky who was laughing with two of the men.

"How do you know?"

"Go."

He went.

I beckoned to Vicky when she glanced at me.

She said something to one of the men that made him laugh with her.

As soon as she turned and started back to me his smile died, replaced by a weighing glance at me.

His cold gaze followed her all the way back to my table.

She said, "The man in charge is John Doweled, and he's a cold one, boss."

I lifted my cup to block my lips as I murmured, "He's murdered at least two people. Everyone at that table is a killer."

"How do you know?"

"Does it matter?"

"No. So now what?"

"See if you can find out who the lady with the blue hijab is—but be careful. Give her no reason to be wary of you."

"Her too?" she asked and by the tone I knew she doubted my assessment.

I waved her away and continued taking my pictures.

Vicky accompanied the woman from the room.

I debated following. The woman had an extremely thick rind. But Vicky had been warned and the woman was unlikely to do anything in such a crowded setting even if Vicky had walked right up and asked her if she was a murderer.

I was relieved though when Vicky returned five minutes later.

"She's a doctor," she said as she sat.

"*Ahh*, what kind?"

"I didn't ask."

"Find out. It isn't urgent though. The man there adding the beans to the buffet, go read his name tag and make a note of it."

Ollie returned while Vicky was chatting up another group of women, two of which had light rinds and one who had a thick one.

He said, "They have garbage trucks and rent dumpsters. I got a picture of the office directory hanging on their wall."

I said, "Go back tomorrow morning and set up an appointment for me. Ask if they have a crew who'll come and remove bulk items."

I texted Julia, *'Have we need for a cleaning service? There's one here I could buy for a steal.'*

I pointed to an older man arguing with a younger one. "Follow him—discreetly."

By the time Ryu returned I had a long list of potential businesses that I could manipulate.

He sat beside Vicky to hand me a brochure.

"That's the guy who built this place. Abd al-Ra'uf Maamoun. The secretary at the desk says almost everyone here works for him in one way or another. I think she's scared to death of him."

"Is she..." I said thoughtfully. "I'd like to chat with her direct boss. Vicky, see if you can find out who hires and fires the building staff."

Ryu said, "See if you can find out if there's people who work here all night. Don't ask her directly because something is sketchy. If you hit number thirteen in the elevator, you get to floor twelve and fourteen gets you fifteen. I only tried it once, so it could've been a fluke but..."

"We need a map of the building," Vicky said.

"Don't ask for one here. Pip and I will try the city planning commission if we decide we need one."

I said, "I need to see the building security personnel. How can such be arranged?"

Ryu said, "We can ask about renting some storage space here for the gems and metals?"

"Yes. Do that. Tell them I might require an escort to and from my car occasionally and I'd like to hire their in-house security for that. Make me an appointment and get a complete list of employees if possible. If not, find me one and we shall work on giving him a very bad day."

Ryu snorted with laughter.

Vicky looked confused.

He said, "Text Frankie your pictures and we'll start building a list. That girl at the desk could probably identify most of them, if not by name at least by which office they go to."

"Find out her name and address. I'd like to find out why she's so afraid..."

"Damn it, I shouldn't have said anything. It has nothing to do with us!"

"I'm making it my business. I will be *damned* if I see such and turn a blind eye—*damned*!"

"Fuckers got to pay," Vicky said approvingly.

I grinned my approval at her, lifting my hand for a fist bump that she laughingly obliged.

"Jesus," Ryu said in aggravation. "Don't encourage her—him! Each other!

Shaking his head, he stood and headed to the door, saying over his shoulder, "Don't sit in here all day. Lunch will be over soon and it's a beautiful day outside."

"Yes, I suppose the front door would make a fine vantage point."

Vicky followed me outside.

There were few parking spaces that had a clear view of the main doors.

I pointed to a small, landscaped divider across from the main exit with a sorry looking palm shading a bus stop. A row of two-story boutiques and restaurants lined the road for two blocks on both sides of the street followed by a long line of skyscrapers.

There were just a few parking spaces on the street in front of the stores, all of which were filled with expensive cars. I headed to the only bench in sight, which was at the bus stop as I said, "Arrange for us to get that parking spot tomorrow. Rent a few cars so we can switch them as needed. Tell Jacob that I want everyone to come to do some shopping. I mean no offense, but you'll need a better-quality suit, and those stores appear to be just the sort of shop that would have it."

"Lady Julia picked my clothing."

"And it's very nice, quite appropriate for work, but I think you need the sort of thing that lady there is wearing."

I nodded at one of the women exiting the shops who wore a long purple silk skirt with a diagonal white stripe with a matching silk scarf draped partially over her head and four-inch stiletto-heeled leather boots. Her sunglasses alone would've cost more than Vicky's entire outfit.

"If you say so."

I sat on the bench.

She sat beside me.

I said, "Jacob shall supply the necessary funds. You may pick whatever style you prefer as long as it looks like something a woman like that would expect her companion to be wearing were they to take tea."

"I never know if you're putting me on or not."

"I never am..."

She laughed, which made me laugh too.

She said, "Lady Julia told us you had some odd idiosyncrasies, but she never mentioned that you thought you were psychic."

"I'm not."

She nodded as she said, "I can sometimes tell just by talking to a bloke that he's a no-good asshole. If I follow them for a day or so I usually get all the proof I need. You're jumping straight to a conclusion on a glance."

"Not so. I shan't be convinced that they're evil men until they tell me so. I'll admit I assume it until then..."

She laughed as she said, "Have you ever been wrong?"

"Never. Not one single time. 'Tis possible I miss many murderers. Not all stand out as such. You, for instance. I'd have said you'd murdered three people. By your demeanor, I'd have thought you a doctor or nurse or mayhap a soldier and likely not have bothered to question you. Or maybe I would've because there are fewer woman killers than men."

"Julia said the same thing—almost exactly. I thought she was crazy at first just asking me and then telling me her plan like that…"

"She told you her plan?"

"Does that worry you? You don't look worried. Only surprised. You're very hard to read…"

"Worried—no. 'Tis surprising. She must have liked you. What is her plan?"

She bit her lip, clearly debating if she should tell me or not.

I lay my hand on her arm, consciously manipulating her anima the tiniest amount as I said, "Of course you can always speak freely to me. Julia and I have no secrets."

"She told me she was looking for people who weren't afraid to do whatever needed to be done to right large wrongs. That you and she had decided to use your position to track down the people behind the scenes who get rich from the misery of others. She offered me a job—this job. It pays well but that isn't why I agreed. I liked what she was doing, and she was having amazing success— I saw that for myself.

"She can read people at a glance just like you can. She spotted me right off. And my girls all love her—or most of them do anyway; the good ones who just needed a break. I get you two are getting rich from your schemes but you're also trying to make a difference. I'd like to be a part of that."

"Your girls?"

"I'm a social worker, or I was at least. When Julia came to the woman's prison to talk with the potential parolees, she saw right through the liars and picked the same exact women to help that I'd have picked, which to this day amazes me. I mean, I was there often enough to see them and hear the rumors. She was there just a few hours—unless... did she do what you're doing now?"

"I have no real idea how she conducts her investigations, not because it's a secret but because we're both so busy. My injury left her in charge of the finances. Neither of us had much experience with that. Luckily, we have a good friend who's generously giving us advice. But even an ignorant person can see that investments are risky. Stocks, bonds, it's all a bit too modern for me. What's needed is businesses that we control—ones with real tangible assets. It seems like simple good sense to me that we can offer training, supply a fair wage, and man these businesses, giving people who deserve it a second chance."

She nodded happily, saying, "And stopping the fuckers who don't deserve it from stealing those chances!"

"There are many such here—many."

She followed my gaze to an Arab man walking toward the entrance.

"He does have a vibe," she said as the man stopped by the door to speak with three men who exited.

"He's killed many times—how can he be so free? I've seen those like him before, but most appear dangerous. They've served time for some of their crimes and been released. The most casual of observers would know they were bad men and stand clear. Yet he looks no different than him or him or him, except in the way they fawn—how do they not know? They must know... why do they allow it?"

"Fear, probably."

"I suppose."

"I'll see where he goes."

She crossed the street and entered the building.

I took photos for a few minutes, sending the rinded images to Jacob and the un-rinded to Emma.

Vicky returned and said, "I think your hunch was correct. He keeps muscled goons in the outer office. No one does that who isn't trouble."

"The sheer amount of them is staggering. We have offices in London and never have I seen this many gathered."

"All Arabs?"

"No. Or at least I don't think so. I'm not very good at determining ethnicity. I miss wardrobe cues that Julia notices. I do better when I can hear them speak."

"Maybe it's just this building?"

"Perhaps."

She said, "If you'll excuse me a moment, I need a lady's room."

I waved her away.

I thought it likely that Sandra would've sent me to a building where I could use my gifts but thought it unlikely she could know there were so many here, *but she had access to information that I didn't. It was possible a spell would reveal that. Or she knew of these men from past misdeeds.*

That thought distracted me until Ollie joined me.

I said, "Find a greenhouse where you can buy herbs and flowers. The bigger the plant, the better. I'm going to text you a list. I'll also need some small shatterproof vials. I'll send you a link. If you can't find them locally, have Mrs. Roman ship them."

"Yes, sir."

"Ryu has a list of materials I need, things like glass-coil condensation tubes and Bunsen burners. Set me up a space in the loft. Include a hot plate, tea kettle, and cups. I'll need some paper packets. The lined kind that keep herbs fresh."

"Herbs, sir?"

"Teas and such. I find the mixing and grinding soothing. It can get a bit pungent though so needs a more private place than a hotel room. The loft will do nicely for now. I shall also want a comfortable chair and a safe for my books. It needn't be too large as I have few valuable ones with me—say two-foot square. Gather Vicky and you can return to whatever I pulled you away from-and thank you for your prompt response."

I called Ryu when Ollie left.

"It occurs to me that this building was chosen by Sandra precisely because it harbors such men, which means I needn't track them at all as they're most likely all part of the same gang but simply take one and demand answers."

"I've got the head of security's name."

"Lovely."

We returned to the office.

Chapter 24

The next morning, I met Ryu for breakfast in the hotel restaurant.

He said, "Jane Conroy called and requested an appointment."

"Grant it at once."

"It wasn't for her exactly. She's couriering over some files from Sandra meant for your eyes only. They need to be signed for by you. I told her you'd be in the office in the morning from nine to ten."

"Call her back and tell her I shall be there daily at that time. Sandra can then courier directly to me."

"You still don't know…"

"She's requested we build a model, so I assume that whatever she has planned will happen within those confines."

We headed to the office directly after breakfast.

Ian was there already, parked in the spot directly across from the main entrance.

I said, "Take a break. Go have breakfast or sightsee. You shan't be needed until 'tis time to switch the car."

Ryu and I got into the front seat.

He laid a camera on the dashboard, having to lean awkwardly to view the screen as he said, "I thought we could just record. It's recording sound so you just have to say find him or not him as they enter, and we can set the team on finding out who they are."

"Is it ready now?"

"Yeah. See the light there in the corner?"

I nodded and he continued, "That light means it's on. Most electronics have some sort of light that indicate it's working."

"I shall wish to take a class on modern surveillance. See if you can arrange such."

"We should all take that class."

"See to it. That man there with the brown briefcase. The woman in blue. The young man. The older man behind him. The woman there who's walking with her head down. Everyone in that big clump."

"Jesus..." Ryu breathed.

"'Twould almost be simpler to find the innocents," I agreed.

I continued to call out descriptions for another fifteen minutes. The influx of rinded was slowly dwindling. For the next hour 'twas mostly innocent men and women who entered.

Emma arrived. She stopped by the entrance to look around, which she did for a good ten minutes before heading inside.

I said, "I think she was looking for me—or at least to see why I wanted a car parked here."

Ryu said, "I'll talk to her about being discreet."

We watched for another thirty minutes, seeing ten more heavily rinded men arrive in a large bunch.

Ryu said, "You need to get to the office to meet the courier."

"Tell the crew to do some shopping here and supply them with cash. Use the remainder of the casino cash. I shall replenish it shortly.

"What do you want them to get?"

"The sort of clothing that would blend into that last casino and that those people would wear to take tea."

"Okay."

I picked up the camera to turn it off so I could say, "Find a good place to make handoffs or perhaps the office would do? Arrange for everyone on staff to acquire a briefcase. Have a few such available from the sort a very wealthy person would use to one a poor one would. Yours and mine should be identical and large and we'll need a few of them."

"What are you planning?"

"I shall tell the rinded here to bring me cash and forget they have. We'll collect it in the cases. You bring in an empty case and leave the full one in the car, taking an empty. We'll need a place to hide it, perhaps at the tile works? Somewhere no one would wonder why we visit, where we can then remove the cash from the cases in the car."

"How much can you take from them before they notice it?"

"It depends. I shall ask them."

He laughed for a moment before looking worried.

"This is obviously an organized crime ring. They'll be heavy hitters, Pip. You can see for yourself they ain't afraid to whack a rival."

"'Tis my exact thought. My hope is that they have a lot of cash they hide from the tax police."

"Just be careful."

"I shall. Have the crew record here for the next week. I saw a few people who maybe we could help as they appeared distressed. They had no rind for me to grasp but 'tis my thought that I could simply speak to whomever is distressing them if I could ascertain whom that is."

"There's probably lots of lower henchmen working here who the men at the top blackmail or scare into their jobs, and there's probably a lot more who voluntarily work here hoping to step up.

Just because they look scared doesn't make them good people, Pip."

"I know."

I exited the car and went to my office.

I said to Emma, "I'm expecting a courier from Jane Conroy's office. Send them in directly."

Ryu said to her, "Speak to the manager at the tile factory. He still hasn't sent his employee records. I need that and the position and hours each employee there works on my desk by tomorrow. Find copies of the original building plans for that building."

I left Ryu giving her directions, closing my office door so I could work on my own projects, which was making a list of the men I'd need to have and where I thought I might be able to find them to complete my assignment.

Thirty minutes later Emma knocked on my door, escorting a man about my age wearing bike shorts and a helmet into the office.

"Lord Blackwood?"

"Yes."

"From Ms. Conroy."

I signed his clipboard, and he handed me a thick envelope.

The inner envelope was protected by cleverly designed runes worked into what appeared to be a decorative embellishment. I recognized the runes from study so knew to press my thumb against the metal closure hard enough to draw blood.

I was careful to keep my blood from dripping onto the envelope as I slid the contents onto my desk.

I read it all then called for Ryu.

"She's planning a robbery here," I said as I slid the contents of the envelope to him. "She wants me to break into the fourteenth floor where she believes there's a safe holding raw gold bars."

He scanned the pages.

"A portal?" he asked uneasily.

"'Twill be simple to place. It only requires we prepare a flat surface large enough to spread the spelled paper."

"A safe for raw gold will have serious security, Pip. We won't be able to get passed electronic time locks—unless we can find whoever programs it, I guess."

"Which is why she recommends we go through a window. She sent us binding powder to practice with, which we'll do daily at the warehouse. Arrange for us to have the use of it alone for at least one hour every day. Once we're inside the office building, I could order any people in there to do what I wish, like assure the guards in the hall that all is well."

"The windows and doors are bound to be alarmed."

I tapped the stack of papers. "She warned me. I shall find out. Maamoun, the man who owns this building runs this section of town. He's tried to shake her down in the past—what is shake her down?"

Ryu snorted with laughter. "It means to threaten someone to get them to give you money. It's usually a payoff to do business. Sometimes it's a weekly payoff."

"What happens if you refuse to pay it?"

"It depends, but it's usually things like you get beat up or the business suffers from accidents. Anything from delayed deliveries, the help scared away, to fires, or even murder."

I took the papers back from him to re-examine them then handed him one.

"She intends to purchase a building owned by Maamoun. Since I doubt she intends to pay him his tribute, I assume the plan will call for his removal at some time."

"Then she must be planning to step into his place."

"Perhaps.

"I know you like her, Pip. That you respect her and want to learn from her, but Julia is right to urge caution. What do you really know about her? If you set her up here, she could end up being a bigger asshole than the men in place!"

"True, but unlikely. 'Tis not naïveté that I speak thusly, nor a willful ignorance. I have met her employees, have seen how she does business. There are few rinded working for her."

"Don't assume that means they're good people or that she is. She knows how a seethe could bend such people to their will."

"If I give her this town, then I could take it back. She would know it. She would know 'twould be a war between us. Why would she risk that? Nay! She will rule here but not as a tyrant who murders the innocent. You yourself pointed out that removing the people in charge requires the installment of another. She treats her human staff well. I've no reason to think it shall be otherwise here. I shall offer my assistance as needed to assure the smoothest transition possible."

"I guess."

"What is your fear?"

"That she'll get you involved with organized crime."

I stared at him perplexed.

"Am I not already fully embroiled with the task of organizing crime?"

"I meant for her. As her stooge. She could be setting you up, Pip."

"To what end?"

"Your incarceration! Your murder!"

"Neither of which any mortal *could* do. To destroy me would take magic else I should simply re-emerge."

".... true."

"I'm not making light of the danger. I have no wish to lose the place I have now. I have people who depend upon me and friends I'd not see harmed. I'm simply pointing out that she has no need to use human methods against me. But I trust that you and Julia will be keeping a close watch."

Emma knocked on the door to the office.

"Come in," I said as I gathered the papers and carefully replaced them into the envelope.

"A Mr. Raymond Hall from Worthy Shipping is here requesting to speak with you."

"Send him in."

I placed the envelope in the bottom drawer of my desk.

"'Tis keyed to me. If you desire to view it, ask. To open it yourself would cause it to burst into flames."

"Right," he muttered, shooting me an exasperated glance.

I shrugged at him, making him laugh.

"Safes being much too mundane," he continued, which made me laugh.

From the doorway, Emma said, "Mr. Hall to see you, Lord Blackwood.

I said, "Please take a seat. This is my assistant, Mr. Poole."

Hall remained standing, saying snidely, "Mr. Tussaud will be expecting you today at three."

Ryu's eyes narrowed, "And if we can't make it?"

"If you want to do business in this town, you'll make it."

I stood, intending to grab his arm.

Hall's smirk deepened.

He said, "I wouldn't try it, if I were you. I'll leave when I'm good and ready to leave." He leaned forward over the desk to glare nose-to-nose with me.

"No one throws me out."

I placed my hand in the heat of his anima and said pleasantly, "I wasn't intending to. We're having a nice chat. Do you visit everyone in the building like this?"

His breath left him in a long sigh and his eyes brightened as his stance relaxed.

"Most know their place."

"So what prompted this visit?"

"Orders."

"From?"

"My boss."

"Who is?"

"Francois Tussaud."

"And he intends to do what?"

"Make sure that you know what's what."

"What is what?"

"He gets his cut or maybe the whole shebang. He told me you thought you were trying to make a move, hiring your own crew, recruiting from the slums like you can make those assholes anything. Pussies like that don't know how to play the real game. Crackheads and ho's is all they know.

Ryu's anger was warmth I wanted to snuggle into.

I turned to say to him, "Please assure you've worn your pin."

I gestured him back, saying, "He's quite enough. I've no need of you."

Ryu frowned, crossing his arms and stomping away, stopping at the door.

I said, "Too much is distracting is all. I meant no offense."

Hall looked puzzled.

"Too much what?"

"Who will be at this meeting at three?"

"Me and Sid."

Ryu said, "Make him shoot the fucker if Tussaud tries anything."

Hall turned to glare at him.

I waved my hand through the trailing edges of his anima, and he turned back to me with an eager smile.

I said, "You want to be friends with me, don't you?"

He nodded.

"If anyone were to point at weapon at my assistant, you'd do whatever Mr. Poole told you to do."

I grasped his hand, pressing my own anima on him. "You'll do whatever I or Mr. Poole tell you to do."

I released him, taking a step away.

"Tell your boss we'll be there. This was the usual sort of meeting that you have. There's nothing out of the ordinary that you need to report or even think about. Go."

He went.

Ryu said, "That goddamned motherfucker!"

"Your anger distracts me. I can use it, but when 'tisn't needed, I fear it will intoxicate me."

"Sorry. He's just such an ass! All my life there's always a dick like that who thinks he can muscle in and take whatever he wants!"

"Well, he's about to find out I have a bigger dick."

Ryu snorted with laughter.

"Oh man... sorry, Pip. I shouldn't use words like that with you. Dick isn't a gun. It's slang for penis."

"I know."

Ryu looked confused.

I said primly, "I was using it as the appropriate colloquial expression."

"You were... never mind. It doesn't matter. You never cease to surprise me... What will we do about him?"

"Do? Go to the meeting of course. 'Tis certain his boss is just the man I was looking for—to fuck over."

Ryu snorted with laughter again.

"Oh man. Julia is sure to think I'm corrupting you."

Warmth spread from my groin to my cheeks as I imagined explaining to Julia that I'd encouraged Ryu to corrupt me—and not with slang words.

I said, "My wife teaches me appropriate slang and encourages my use of such."

"Those aren't the sort of words a gentleman uses."

"Not even between friends?"

"I've no idea. They probably do. You should just be yourself with me."

By which I deduced I'd made him uncomfortable.

It made me laugh with excitement because I thought it meant he was seeing me as the girl I was.

"You find it disconcerting to hear me say such..."

"Yeah... I guess I do."

Emma knocked on the partially open door.

"Frankie texted me to remind you that you have a meeting with the realtor at eleven. He sent you the address in case you forgot. Can we get an intercom for the office? And why not have him text you directly?"

Ryu said, "You can use an intercom. He texts you because Pip sometimes forgets to turn his phone on. It's your job to be sure Lord Blackwood gets where he needs to be, so make sure you're checking the app all the time for updates in the schedule. If you see one, call me to confirm that he's aware if he isn't in the office. If I can't be reached, then call whoever is assigned as his driver. Call him directly as a last resort."

I said, "You'll need to reschedule me this afternoon. I have a meeting here at three and I expect it to take a few hours. So anything else scheduled for this afternoon needs to be rescheduled."

"Yes, sir."

Ryu and I headed out to meet with the realtor.

There were a great many choices available, which gave me an idea.

I excused myself and called Julia.

"Jewels, are there laws on what you can charge for rental fees on homes and rented rooms?"

"Sometimes, why?"

"It occurs to me that the simplest way to make money is to collect rents. There are many buildings here with no tenants at all.

It would be a simple thing to ask people to move. And even simpler to tell those with the means to pay whatever we wanted."

"I agree. The trick is we need the capitol to buy them, and I'd rather buy them here where we can oversee it."

"We can't pay in cash?"

"We could update properties with cash. For the best return on our money, we'd need to raise the rent, but there are laws about doing that for buildings that already have tenants and we can't raise them suspiciously high."

Ryu said, "Let me talk to her a sec."

I said, "You're on speakerphone with us."

He said, "We just visited a completely empty apartment building. They aren't asking that much in comparison to some of the places we visited. The apartments were a lot smaller. The rents here vary a lot. The exteriors of the buildings are pretty similar though. I think you could buy that place and charge on the high side. Have the mark fix up the inside themselves. If you told them they loved the place..."

"That could work," she said eagerly. "Buy one place like that, Pip. Make sure it has good parking and access to the tube. See if we can buy or lease the closest shops too. We'll make them shop and eat there and turn it into a trendy spot."

Ryu said, "I can help him with that. I know just the sort of thing we need."

"We'll still need another condo or a hotel. Somewhere with a cleaning service and food delivery where people don't live for long stretches."

"Send me the budget," Ryu said. "I think we can work a deal if we buy both places from the same company."

I said, "We should buy in this area else we have more shaking down to contend with."

"Have you been approached?" Julia asked.

"I have a meeting with a local thug at three."

"Call me after."

"I shall. Stay safe, my darling."

"Love you. Ta."

I pocketed my phone, and we went to speak with the realtor again.

"I've spoken with my wife about increasing the budget. My man will be in contact tomorrow. I found that last apartment building an interesting option. Can you find out who owns the eateries and grocery stores closest to the building?"

Ryu said, "We want a list of all the stores on that street and all of the commercial spaces available to buy or lease."

"Are you looking for anything in particular?"

"An affordable apartment building with shopping located conveniently or that could be put in. Not retail shopping but food and drink, coffee shops, groceries, dinners, the sorts of places people go daily. It needs to have good parking and access to public transportation and the buildings themselves need to be attractive or at least have the potential to be with minor cosmetic work."

"Then that last place is probably exactly what you're looking for. There's two small delis within walking distance and plenty of empty storefronts that could be purchased to put in a grocery store or anything else you wanted."

"Why are they all empty?"

"This entire city was built with the prospect of expansion. People like you are moving In and buying now while the prices are cheap. Eventually, they'll all rise, and these properties will triple in price."

"Or the entire thing will fail."

The realtor shrugged.

I said, "We'll be in touch."

We returned to the car where Ollie said, "Where to, boss?"

"The warehouse and then back to the office."

I closed the privacy barrier to say, "It's a suckers game. They lure us in and then once we buy, they shake us down."

"It seems likely."

"Good. Then it should be easy to convince them to sell me all of the properties I need at a price I can afford."

I began making notes.

Ryu took out his phone and called Jacob.

The two of them discussed the sorts of business licenses that would be needed until we arrived at the warehouse.

"Very nice," I said in approval on entering the warehouse.

It had been cleaned and painted white. Yusuf was removing tape and plastic from the windows while Pat and Jean were applying black plastic film to the windows that had already been cleaned of the tape.

A large table made of four pieces of plywood painted white sat in the middle of the space.

There were four seating areas, one in each corner of the room. One was a grouping of chairs and old sofas facing a television on the wall.

The corner closest to the front entrance held six desks and a few extra rolling chairs. The corner by the loading dock held an exercise machine. A punching bag lay on the floor by a box that said Table Tennis. Tape outlined a section of flooring.

I said, "What does the tape signify?"

Vicky said, "I bought some old lockers, but we can't get them until Friday."

"We'll done! Ryu, arrange for a bonus!"

I headed to the corner that had a dining table and rolling office chairs with a few smaller upholstered chairs. A scuffed buffet table held a microwave and coffee pot. Shelves above it held mismatched plates and glasses. Jean was plugging in a refrigerator. Ian and Claudia were putting together a shelving unit beside bags of what I assumed were groceries that were waiting to be unpacked.

"Whose idea was this?"

"Mine," Vicky said.

Emma turned to smirk at her. By her expression I thought she assumed I was annoyed although why I'd be annoyed eluded me.

I handed Vicky all of the cash I had on me. "Brilliant! 'Tis a bonus to use however you wish."

Emma flushed.

I didn't think Vicky noticed because she was stuffing the money into her pockets as she headed to Ian, saying, "You have that going the wrong way. Flip it over."

I headed upstairs to examine the loft.

A tangle of extension cords and an assortment of lights had been left by the head of the stairs. Only one area to the left of the stairs appeared finished.

It held another old buffet table with my requested supplies. A reading lamp was lit behind a comfortable-looking armchair with a small table directly beside it and a closed folding screen on wheels rolled against the wall.

Boxed bookcases that required assembly were leaning against the wall. Nick was assembling another small table. He nodded a greeting.

In the center of the loft by the railing a table that sat four was piled with bags and an assortment of tools.

At the other end of the loft, two screens separated a small sleeping area with two twin beds on frames that still required assembly from a desk with a computer that Jacob was working at.

Ryu said to him, "I'll call you later and send you links to the places the boss was most interested in."

"I'll have those comparisons ready in a day or so."

I'd no idea what he meant but assumed Ryu did by the way he nodded.

"See if you can find out who's in charge of licensing."

I returned downstairs to say, "Whose idea was the beds?"

Vicky grinned at me as she held her hand up while Ian laughingly said, "Vick. She picked almost everything."

Vicky said, "I've been in enough shelters that housed small groups to know the sorts of things they need."

"Ryu, double that bonus and get Vicky her own company credit card. Vicky, you're in charge here. What Vicky says goes. Jean, you'll come in every day at seven and keep the place tidy. Clean whatever Vicky tells you to."

Emma glared down at the groceries she was unpacking.

I said to her, "Why aren't you at the office?"

"Vicky ordered me to come. Frankie is there."

Her lip curled the slightest bit as she said to Vicky, "He can finish this. I better get back."

She stomped out.

"What crawled up her butt?" Ryu asked.

Vicky laughed as she said, "She's pissed I made her go grocery shopping. I didn't want to order in until I cleared it with the boss. Can we have food delivered here?"

"Yes. Just be sure no one comes inside."

"What do we do if someone does?" Ian asked.

"Get their name."

Ryu said, "Follow them if you can do it discreetly. We'd want to know who they go see and speak with. But don't let any assholes force their way in. No repairmen, no gas guys, nothing. It better be people with honest to God warrants!"

I said, "If an official person such as a police officer or city assessor requests admittance, let them in."

Ryu said, "Vick, get some cameras up that show if anyone stops so you have some warning. Someone will be here around the clock. If someone stops, rearrange the model."

"What model?" Vicky asked.

I said, "The one you're going to build of the street where my official office is and four blocks to either side of it. Nick is in charge of that. It needs to be to scale. And it needs to include all doors and windows. I don't think it will matter if that model is seen. Leave off the names of the buildings for now though. I shall confer with my wife on what should be labeled."

Which was a lie. But I assumed Sandra would give me clearer instructions on what the model was intended for once it was built.

Ryu said, "Get us another big table. One sheet of plywood should do it, and some clamps to hold maps on. We'll need some heavy-duty magnets to hold the drawings and construction plans and some whiteboards."

"I'm on it," Vicky said.

I said, "I've been hired to act as a general contractor for a friend. We're building a small private housing community—a joint venture. Official Business. I expect to have some large drawings that will need to be displayed. I also have some private unofficial business that I think we could hide under those maps and drawings."

They eagerly gathered around me.

I continued, "Maamoun runs a large crime syndicate. We need to map the people, who reports to whom and what each does. I'll want pictures of them and a place to write my thoughts."

Ryu said, "He needs a tree graph, Vick. And a dry erase board. Take stills from the camera footage from the car and get them labeled. Get us a bunch of colored magnets. How many colors will we need, Pip?"

"Red, orange, yellow, green, and blue for unknown."

"Fifty or so of each color, Vick."

I said, "I'm very pleased with the progress. Assist Ian with the model. I'd like it done as soon as possible."

Ryu and I headed back to the car.

"Vicky's on top of things," Ryu said musingly.

"It worries you?"

"She's smart. Are you sure she's working for you?"

"Yes."

"I like her."

"But?"

"She's clearly the type who acts. If she thinks something is going down, she's going to act—maybe before you notice and tell her not to."

"You mean if she believes I'm a bad man?"

"That too. You never asked me if I planned to betray you, Pip. Or did you?"

"No. *I* never did."

"Julia?"

"We never discussed it. But I'd think so. If you don't remember it, it's likely she didn't wish you to remember. I *will* ask her if you wish."

"You never discussed it...."

"She never demurred. I wouldn't have told her no if she'd asked me to question you—then."

"And she never asked? Why didn't you just ask?"

"I suppose I should have."

"But why didn't you?"

"It never occurred to me any more than it occurred to me to try to question her. I believe her. I believe *in* her. To attempt to force her in any way would be a breach of trust that we could never recover from. 'Tisn't what friends do."

"You can ask me," he said gruffly.

"There's no need."

"You're right. There isn't any need. I think we're real friends too, Pip. But it makes me feel like a hypocrite that I want you to ask Vicky."

"Then I shall ask her. I like her too, but she isn't a friend as you are—she isn't you."

Chapter 25

Patrik accompanied Ryu and me to the meeting at three.

In the elevator on the way there, I said, "Your sole purpose is to protect Ryu. Do whatever he tells you to do. Be prepared to stop anyone or anything from touching him, except me."

Ryu said, "I don't need a babysitter and be careful what you say in here. The cameras in the corner there can transmit sound."

"It matters not. I shall make my feelings known quite clearly."

We were ushered directly to a large office with its own reception area and left to wait for an hour.

I spent the time going over the prospective apartment buildings for sale. Pat spent it gazing adoringly at me. Ryu fumed while checking his phone.

I finally said, "Not that I don't appreciate your anger over this ploy, which is obviously done for just such effect, but does it not amuse you how they play right into my hands?"

He burst into laughter.

"You shouldn't have said that, Pip! Now I'm not mad at all!"

"'Tisn't *your* anger I crave."

Moments later the secretary ushered us inside.

Tussaud was an older man in his sixties, sitting behind a large desk. Two upholstered chairs faced the desk. A couch with end tables on either end were along one wall with shelves and a closed door opposite it. Hall and a man who I assumed was Sid stood beside the doorway we'd come in.

Tussaud said, "So, Lord Blackwood. A real honest to God earl. Ray tells me you're a sensible man."

"I've never been called such before."

Ryu snorted with laughter.

Tussaud gaze traveled him and Pat.

"Frisk them."

I grabbed Sid's arm, saying, "I think not."

I released his arm and pointed to the floor while directing Pat's anima and a smidgeon of my own.

"Sit."

Both Sid and Hall sat on the floor.

Tussaud's eyes narrowed. He stood as I stepped closer.

"Who the fuck do you think you are! I don't know what you promised them, but I'm protected!"

"By what?"

He gaped a moment then lunged for his desk drawer as I walked closer.

If I hadn't been so angry, I'd have laughed at his expression.

He yanked a gun from the drawer, backing away as I approached.

"If I fire this gun, there'll be twenty men in here."

"Good."

Sweat trickled down his cheek.

"You can't have paid them all off!"

"I've paid none. They just like me better."

Ryu laughed again.

"I'll blow his fucking head off!"

248

I wasn't certain if he was talking to me or Ryu. It angered me enough to make my anima appear to me. I sent it to Tussaud with a thought.

"Sit. And put the gun down. We're having a nice chat."

He frowned, sitting slowly.

Ryu ran forward to grab the gun.

"Ask him if he has another weapon or if anyone is listening."

"Is anyone listening to us?"

"They better not be," he said uncertainly.

I rounded his desk to lay my hand on his shoulder.

"You like me and want to impress me. You think you can use my connections. This meeting is going exactly as you planned."

He nodded his agreement.

I released him and perched on the edge of his desk.

"Do you have more weapons in this room?"

"They have their guns. I can get you any sort of weapon you'd want," he added eagerly.

"Write me out a list with the going rate. Put in all the details you know of, where they come from, and who else is involved. Don't tell anyone about that though. This is just a normal meeting.

He reached for a pen.

I touched his hand with my fingertip.

"Write it after I leave and drop it in my office with Mr. Poole on your way out tonight. Don't let anyone see you write it and make up a believable excuse if anyone asks why you stopped by. Now, let's chat about why you wanted to meet with me."

"To tell you to use my company as your shipper."

"Does Xion work for you?"

"No. We use them as a cover sometimes, but she doesn't know it. We send some of our shit through her to keep it all squeaky clean."

"So I'm supposed to ship with you... Was that your idea?"

"Yes."

"Explain to me how it works."

"We get a percent of whatever you ship, and you get protection."

"Protection from what?"

"Us. Your cargos go through with no problems and when you want to smuggle shit, we make that happen, for a price, of course."

"What sorts of things do you smuggle?"

"Anything."

"I'll want details, but I think I'll stop by again in a day or so for that. You'll want to see me, won't you?"

"Yeah. Sure. We can do some deals."

"Maybe we can."

I placed both my hands into his anima, not touching him, but I could feel the heat from his body.

"I could use some cash. How much could you get me without anyone noticing?"

"Right now?

"Yes."

"I keep a hundred grand in the office safe."

"Get it for me. But no one can know."

He nodded as he jumped to his feet.

Ryu and I watched him open the safe.

I said, "What's all the files in there?"

"Bearer bonds, deeds, IOU's."

"Will anyone notice if it's missing a few days?"

"No."

"Can I borrow it?"

"...sure."

"I'll give it back in a few days. I just want to see how a man like you does business."

His shoulders eased and his smile brightened.

He helped me put everything into our briefcases.

I said, "It's really important that no one knows this meeting was anything out of the ordinary. You and I can be the best of friends, but no one can know yet. You're my secret mentor. Everyone you know will be so impressed with you. I can get you anything you ever wanted but it all depends on everyone thinking it's just business as usual. So tell whatever lies you need to tell."

Ryu whispered, "Ask him if there's anything we need to do."

Tussaud frowned at Ryu, "I'm not hard of hearing..."

My friend just meant that he and I should appear as one expect servants of yours to appear. When you have a new client like me, is that client expected to make payments or anything else?"

"Not until we sign the contract."

"Then write that contract just like you would for anyone else. If I'm supposed to bring cash, you bring it for me."

"That isn't how it normally works."

I guided anima from Pat and myself over Tussaud as I said, "But you and I aren't normal friends. We're the best of friends. I'm going to make your dreams come true, remember?"

"Right. I'll bring the cash."

"When do we sign?" Ryu asked.

"I give you a week."

"A week it is," I said cheerfully. "Nothing at all unusual happened."

I crouched to take Sid and Hall by the hand, pressing my anima on them. "Nothing at all unusual happened. You remember a normal meeting like you've seen hundreds of times in the past. Escort us out and go back to work.

I released them.

The three of us left.

In the hallway I said to Pat, "Go home."

Ryu and I headed directly to the car where we both burst into nervous laughter.

"He was resisting you."

"No he wasn't. I was trying to be subtle. If he thinks it's his idea, he'll work with me. I didn't want to make him a mule or at least not a mule like Pat."

"He's going to realize we took that money eventually.

"He'll realize it's gone but I'll tell him someone else stole it. At our next meeting, I'll ask for a lot more."

"A hundred grand *is* a lot."

"What else is in there?"

He flipped on the interior light so we could see the contents.

Ryu whistled softly as he flipped through a stack of papers.

"Bearer bonds for a bank in Panama. There's a few million here, Pip."

"Call Jacob and tell him we're bringing some USB's we need to make copies of." I held out what I thought was a hard drive. "And this."

"It'll be password protected."

I snorted, making him laugh.

Jacob was on the computer in the small office when we arrived. Four of my footwomen were sitting at the table working on laptops.

Vicky was loading paper into an industrial size printer.

I stopped to examine the wall that already held over a hundred photos, most of them with names, addresses, phone numbers and job titles written on white cards beneath them.

She said, "Social media, baby. Your magnets, my lord."

She bowed extravagantly over five colored plastic containers.

Francois Tussaud's image was in the top row. I plopped a red magnet onto it. I meant to kill him before I left here.

She said, "The colored buckets were Claudia's idea. We're lining them up by the floor they work on for now."

I nodded my appreciation to Claudia as I said, "I'll need to sit outside and watch again because I won't remember what color most are."

"Will it matter?" Ryu asked.

"Not urgently. My thought was to supply my partner with a full report. Knowing what they're all capable of would be a big help in dealing with them."

Ryu said, "Vick, print this out into a catalogue. Keep it organized by floor and business just like you are but leave space for Pip to write some notes. He can just mark them off as he sees them."

"Do you still want the portrait shots printed?"

I handed her my briefcase.

"Copy everything in here. Save the pictures you already did but hold on printing the rest of them for now unless it's helping you organize it."

Ryu said, "Can we take them off the wall for now?"

"I suppose."

I turned from the wall to say to them, "Those men and women are very dangerous. Take a good hard look at them."

"*Ahh*," Ryu said, shaking his head at me. "You're worried about them. Don't be. We all know that it's the headquarters for the local mafia."

"We do?" Ian asked.

Nick hip bumped him, shaking his head and turning back to the table where he'd been drawing out lines when we'd arrived.

"Pay attention," Vicky said impatiently. "We've been talking about it for the last few hours."

"I thought it was all hypothetical... for real? That's where the head guy lives."

Nick turned to slap him on the back of the head.

"No one lives there, fool! It's an office building."

"You know what I mean."

"Just get back to work," Vicky said.

I said, "Split the cash evenly between you, except for the chauffeurs. Use it to buy clothing. Make sure it's well fitting."

Ryu said, "No knock off stuff. The boss will supply accessories, except for shoes. It should be enough for two outfits each. Maybe three for the men. Buy classy stuff, nothing too out there."

"We going to visit the king?" Nick asked laughingly.

I said, "You never know. So buy something appropriate."

They gaped at me.

I said, "Uniforms might be occasionally appropriate when accompanying my lady or myself. I shall speak with a tailor."

"You better leave that to me," Ryu said hurriedly.

I shrugged as I continued, "Think of this as another uniform. Unless directed otherwise, the business attire you normally wear is adequate."

"Dress to blend," Ryu said. "After business hours wear what you like unless your assignment is directly with the boss. It's always a suit and tie with him unless the planned activity calls for something else."

I said, "Shoes can be quite expensive. I'll arrange for further funds."

Ryu rolled his eyes at me as he said, "Don't go getting any ideas. The boss is generous and maybe a bit too trusting. I'm not. Use the money for clothes like you're told. You'll be getting your normal pay to spend how you want."

"And part of the take?" Nick asked.

"The take...what I take from the marks?"

Ryu nodded, saying, "Yeah. He means a cut from what we make on illegal activities."

"*Ahh*, of course. I hadn't considered. I shall talk it over with my wife. 'Tis a reasonable request. Arrangements will be made for suitable compensation."

Vicky frowned at me, quickly smoothing her expression when she saw me notice.

Ryu said, "It's nothing to worry about, Vick. Julia handles the finances. He never thinks about money.

Her expression eased, but it was a practiced smoothing, not a real one.

He caught my eye, and I knew he wanted me to shut up, so I said, "Let's see what Jacob can do with the computer devices."

Chapter 26

"Pip!" Ryu yelled followed immediately by Emma screaming.

We'd only just come in. I hadn't even removed my jacket yet.

I jumped to my feet and was halfway to the door when two men barged into my office.

One was dragging Emma by her hair. The other held a gun on Ryu.

I was instantly furious.

"Release her! And give him the gun!"

Emma gaped at me as the men fell back, pushed by the anger powering my command.

Ryu plucked the gun from the man's lax hand and tucked it into his waistband.

"What's the meaning of this intrusion?"

"You want to do business here, you pay us!"

"Who is us?"

"Me and Ahmed."

Ryu smacked him on the side of the head. "Who do you work for, dumbass?"

"Answer him!" I yelled as I stomped forward to smack him too. I hit him twice and would've hit him again, but Ryu pulled me away.

"Easy, Pip. We need to find out who sent them and what they were meant to do.

"Who sent you!"

"Maamoun."

"To do what?"

"Murder your bitch here in front of you so you know to pay up promptly."

Emma said, "Jesus—they were going to kill me!"

She ran forward and began hitting Ahmed.

Ryu huffed in exasperation.

"Stop!"

He thrust her toward the door. "Go finish whatever you were doing."

"Go!" I barked when she hesitated.

She ran from the room.

I pointed to the couch. "Sit. Answer him as you would me." I leaned close enough my lips almost brushed his cheek. The heat from his body was a caress along my angry anima that I saw as a shimmer that flowed to me and back to him.

It wasn't really sexual, except that I had no other frame of reference for the pleasure it brought me. Pleasure I knew he felt too by the way his eyes darkened.

Pleasuring him angered me more—and made my skin crawl in revulsion.

He moaned as if he was on the edge of orgasm.

I stepped away, urging my anima away from him. It retreated until I could no longer see my own just his that wound toward me in streamers that thinned out the farther they had to reach until I could no longer see it. I could feel it though.

I whispered with intent, "Tell me everything I want to know."

He moaned again, staggering back, kept upright by Ryu's grip on his arm. His partner fell then crawled to the couch.

I stepped back and Ahmed shrieked, "Please!" falling to his knees.

Ryu snatched a pen and paper from my desk and thrust it into Ahmed's hand.

"Write down where he lives, where he works, and the names of every man or woman who works for him."

"Do it!" I yelled.

Ahmed sobbed as if his heart were breaking, nodding frantically and trying to say forgive me but he was crying too hard.

"Pip, I think you should take a walk and cool off.

"And leave you alone with them? I think not!"

I leaned to yell in the other's face, "Don't move an inch! You dare come here and threaten me! You dare to touch her! You dare!"

I slapped him as hard as I could, rocking his head back with the force of my blow.

He'd have murdered anyone it pleased him too.

It so infuriated me that I punched him.

Ryu pulled me away.

"Emma! Get Lord Blackwood a cold wet cloth for his hand. Come out here a minute, Pip. They piss me off too, but we can handle it. We don't want to stain the carpet or have to explain to the neighbors."

I let him lead me into the reception room.

Emma ran from the restroom clutching a handful of wet paper towels.

"Should I call the police?"

Ryu said, "Don't be ridiculous. We can handle this. Find me something to tie them with, not that they'd dare move," he said to me, winking his cocky grin.

I could see it was forced, which infuriated me more.

He took the towels from her to dab at my hands.

She said, "Should I call Frankie? He's our medic."

"It isn't Pip's blood," Ryu said dryly.

I glanced down at my bloody jacket.

"Call and have a clean suit delivered. Two clean suits. No four. Two for Mr. Poole and two for myself."

She gaped at me.

Ryu said, "Pip, stay here and we'll go tie them just so you feel better about leaving me with them."

"Nay! She shalt not go near them! Swine! Unfit loathsome toads!"

Emma giggled.

Ryu frowned fiercely at her, shaking his head.

I forced myself to speak calmly.

"Ryu, have an alarm installed here that will summon me should anyone else attempt to harm Emma—or yourself. Find out all that you may. I've no wish to see them again. I've no wish to let them free to pray upon others as they please…. Emma, call for Yusuf to accompany me. We shall pay a visit to Abd al-Ra'uf Maamoun.

It took an hour for my clean suit to arrive and me to make myself presentable—most of that time I spent taming my own anima.

Ahmed and his partner Yasin spent that hour telling Ryu anything he asked. They were in a car behind us with Yusuf and Emma driven by Ollie.

I rode with Ryu, Jean, and Vicky. I'd picked her to accompany me figuring Maamoun wouldn't think her a security risk, not that I thought we'd need to actually fight them. I was still so angry I could see my own anima when I relaxed my grip on it. The mental effort to keep it contained was making my back and neck ache.

Maamoun's estate was right outside the city set in a landscaped housing development with other such large estates. Each had a six-foot wall and gated drive and was far enough from its neighbor to be private.

Ryu followed me from the car saying, "This is a bad idea, Pip. You shouldn't go in there while you're so angry."

Vicky said, "I have to agree with Ryu. It's crazy to come here to confront him."

I said to Ryu, "Wait in the car. My footmen can attend me."

I tapped on the window of the second car and Yusuf stepped out followed by Ahmed, Yasin, and Emma.

Vicky whispered, "Look at them, Lord Blackwood. They all have guns."

"I see them."

Ryu said, "You're going to get yourself shot."

"Perhaps. 'Tis more likely he'll allow me inside—within reach of him. After all, what threat am I accompanied by women as I am?"

"Just....be careful."

"Yusuf, Guard Ryu."

"I don't think I should be here," Emma said.

"The insult was to you and to you they will make amends. Come!"

We marched up to the door, which was being held open by a man carrying a semi-automatic rifle.

Other armed men stood by a closed garage door.

They'd started toward us when I'd exited the car but stopped when Ahmed exited the car.

I walked up to the man at the door and said loudly, "Abd al-Ra'uf Maamoun wished to speak with me."

"If you think your whores are going to be payment, think again."

I itched to slap his smug face.

"Take me to him."

My anger collided with his stolen anima.

He smiled as he bowed, waving me forward.

Emma giggled nervously. Vicky looked perplexed and frightened. Jean wore her usual smile.

A man further down the hall yelled in Arabic, "Aren't you going to frisk them?"

I walked up to him. "There's no need. I have no gun."

A man spoke from a small intercom I hadn't noticed.

"Frisk them, Omar."

I lifted my hands and let him frisk me.

"Take no liberties," I said.

Sweat beaded his brow.

He politely frisked the rest of my party.

I thought he was likely naturally immune to me. If he hadn't had that stolen anima, I might not have been able to sway him.

We were allowed through a locked door that led into an inner courtyard.

Omar led us through a tiled hall and then into an office where an older man waited. He was lightly rinded in comparison to the men he'd sent to me and the one standing on his left. The man at his right was old with a deep rind and dead eyes.

I said, "Turn off all of your security. All surveillance and recording devices."

Anima flowed as I willed it from Jean, Ahmed, and Yasin in a wave that shimmered the air like heat across the desert.

Maamoun's hands stilled on his desk.

His breath left him in a hard sigh.

"Who are you," he whispered as if to a lover.

"Lord Blackwood—your master."

Maamoun and his men made calls, tapped their phones and computers, called a few orders to men outside the door then Maamoun said, "It has been done."

I said, "Your men have insulted me. They've grievously insulted these women. How will you make amends?"

Maamoun stood to bow over Vicky's hand.

He lifted Emma's hand to press it to his forehead.

He bowed deeply to Jean who stood so closely behind me her breasts pressed against my back.

"If you have been wronged, then all shall be done to make it right." He snapped his fingers and the man who'd been standing at his left stopped gawking at me to peer in bewilderment at Maamoun.

"Dispose of these two so that no man thinks to do what they have done." I gestured at Omar saying, "And Omar. I dislike him."

He bowed over Vicky's hand again then kissed Emma's. "Their worldly goods shall be yours."

They gaped at him.

He snapped again, saying angrily to his man, "Now!"

Ahmed and Yasin went willingly. Omar began yelling in Arabic.

I released my anima, letting it collide with the dense cloud from the others and yanked Omar into it.

"Go! 'Tis nothing more than you deserve! Pray to your God for forgiveness. Truly repent by freely admitting who you have wronged!"

He began babbling prayers.

The two men who'd been in the office with Maamoun led the three of them out.

I took my cellphone from my pocket, called Ryu, putting it on speaker phone and setting it on the desk as I said, "Tell me about your business. How many do you employee? Who do you report to? Let Emma sit at your desk. Emma, take notes. Vicky, you can go if you wish."

She said, "What's happening here?"

He said to her, "I've no wish to insult Lord Blackwood. If I'd have known—but of course, I didn't. I didn't," he said again urgently to me. "They shall be an example!"

On the phone Ryu said, "Find out if there's others we need to worry about, Pip."

Maamoun said, "Worry—never. This is my territory—yours now. None shall dare insult you!"

"Why did you send them to me?"

"I was told that you'd put in an offer on three properties—all of them in my territory. I wanted it clear that you could do business here only with my permission. No one was supposed to hurt you. Never think that. We'd have shown you how valuable an alliance would be!"

"And the murder of Emma?"

"...I thought her just a secretary. No one of importance to you! At most a whore. You'd have been offered a beautiful woman to take her place. I can arrange for one—two—a hundred!"

Vicky growled a low angry sound.

"I'm not a whore!" Emma said indignantly.

Vicky's anger was much hotter than Emma's. I drew it to me and thrust it at Maamoun along with my own.

I said, "Tell me of your rivals."

He eagerly began talking. After forty minutes or so I said, "Stop. Come to my office tomorrow and tell Emma there."

He bowed to Emma.

"What is on the thirteenth floor?" I asked.

"Our safe."

"Why not use a real bank?"

"The money needs to be laundered first."

I want a complete list of every cent, every bar of gold or gem, every item of worth. I want to know who pays you and who you pay. You have two days to drop it off to me in my office. Tell no one. Show no one. What is on the fourteenth floor?"

"My private office."

"I want a list of who works there and what they do."

I laughed when he nodded eagerly.

I said, "You are Vicky's to command. Her words are mine own until I tell you differently."

"All will be as you wish! Will you stay and take dinner with us?"

"No. Tell no one that we've met. If your men would think it odd that I don't pay you tribute, then you pay it in my name. If you even suspect that anyone is thinking badly about me or mine—"

"I shall cut off their heads!"

"No. You'll call me and do nothing unless the threat is immediate. Every man in your employee will treat every woman they come across with respect, or you will act. If I hear of one being assaulted or even insulted I shall be greatly displeased. Greatly!"

"It will be as you say. We shall treat them with kindness even those we dislike as the prophet abjures."

He followed us down the hall wringing his hands.

"Will you not stay and—visit?"

"Not today. Another day perhaps."

His men by the garage eyed me or maybe him in amazement.

He yelled in Arabic, "Cast down your eyes from these good women!"

I pointed Jean to the car driven by Ollie.

We got into the car with Ryu.

Maamoun stared at me longingly. His man gaped at him. I glanced back as we drove away to see Maamoun looked angry. He began shouting at his men, taking that anger out on them, I supposed.

He was a man unused to bowing to others. I'd need to reinforce my control soon.

I looked forward to it. I wanted to hurt him. I hated him with the same passion that he loved me.

Ryu said, "Oh man, what did you do? Are you okay?"

"I think I should like to walk on the beach."

"I think that's a good idea. Vicky, Emma, you okay?"

"What the hell just happened?" Vicky asked angrily.

Ryu said, "That fucker learned he was messing with the wrong man!"

"He was scared as shit—and Lord Blackwood just said his name! What the actual hell! Who are you really? I'm not working for some drug lord!"

I began laughing.

Ryu started laughing too *more in relief then levity*, I thought.

I said, "'Tis not drugs I peddle."

Ryu winked in the rearview at me as he said, "Pip's more a Robin Hood."

"Is an apt description, I suppose. I'd not have labeled myself a hood as I rarely burgle from such neighborhoods."

"Not a *robbing* hood. Robin, like the name." He began laughing real laughter, which eased the heat of my anger.

I was loath to let that warmth go.

I said, "I think I'd like to shower before my walk. Drop me at the hotel and see the women safely home, please."

"So you're a thief," Vicky said musingly.

Ryu said, "It isn't anything you should ever speculate about. Lord Blackwood is always a gentleman. Tell her, Pip."

"Vicky has her own secrets to protect. She shan't share mine."

Emma said, "That guy is going to kill those men, isn't he?"

"'Tis my hope. 'Twould save me the trouble."

She grinned at me.

"So we're your merry men," Vicky said musingly. "The lord's footmen..."

I said, "Not the Lords. Blackwood's. Never confuse the two. 'Twas the Lord who gave me this gift of anger but the use of it is mine own."

Maamoun was at my office door at nine the next morning with all of the lists and information I'd requested.

Seeing him infuriated me all over again.

I didn't like Emma. She was a horrible human being, but he'd have murdered her even if she'd been a saint.

I said, "How many people have you had killed?"

"I never counted. Hundreds, maybe thousands."

"And no one ever noticed?"

He grinned smugly at me.

"Everyone knows that to cross me is to die."

"The police work for you or ignore you?"

"Both. Some from fear and some I pay. The city is safe. I see to that. Property prices are rising. Jobs are plentiful. Everything is good."

"A hundred people though... I just can't imagine how the federal authorities here don't notice."

"Why would they? Thousands of people die every day. Few of the people who die in this city die by my order. But we have to be firm when dealing with the Russians, Israel, Iran, even the French. We sink their ships, burn their buildings."

He shrugged like it didn't matter.

"They die. It's as Allah wills."

"So the money you extort and steal is here in this building?"

"Some."

"How much cash is here right now?"

"Eighty million or so."

"Is it all yours?"

"No. I keep my cash hidden."

"Where?"

"I have a place in the desert and another in Egypt. I have twelve million at the house in London and another ten in Paris. My biggest stockpile is in Africa."

"How much is there?"

"Two hundred million or so in various currencies."

"Then why don't you retire?"

He frowned in puzzlement then shrugged.

"So most of the money here isn't yours?"

"The money here is being cleaned. We funnel it through our legitimate businesses."

"How's that work?"

"Each member pays in, and we take ten percent off the top. Then we take up to another sixty percent depending on how quickly they need the cash back. Most of the members have more than enough of their own money squirreled away that they aren't in any hurry. We turn over about two hundred million a month on average except for December and June. We do ten times that in those months."

"How many members do you have?"

"Three hundred or so."

"Do they all live here?"

"No."

"How many have offices in this building?"

"Twenty or thirty."

"How much cash do you have here in the banks and otherwise?"

"I'm not really sure. I'd have to check with my accountants. I invest most of it but there's always some cash reserve. I'd say a few hundred grand in the bank and then there's my escrow account. It has a few million in cash in it. I keep a few million in cash at all of my homes. The cash I get from the bank here gets sent out to one of my hiding places, so if we've had a large deposit, I'll have a few million waiting to be sent out. I also have large sums if I'm in the middle of moving someone else's cash."

I said, "Imagine you wanted to steal every member's money. How would you do it?"

"I don't think it could be done. They'd know it was me. It'd be easy to take some out but not everything."

"Pretend you don't care if they know."

"I'd tell each one I had an opportunity to launder a hundred million but that it needed to be done quickly and had to be kept quiet from the rest of the members, but I'd tell them I had already lined up two others for the deal that way they'd keep their mouths shut because they wouldn't know which two. I'd have them drop off their cash in secret, giving them ten percent of the cleaned money to hold as collateral with the stipulation that I get five percent of the cleaned money. Once they'd all dropped it off, I'd either have to kill them all or disappear, but neither would work for long."

"Could they come up with a hundred million on short notice?"

"Yes, if they called in their markers. Most of them would offer their junior partners a buy in at ten percent. You figure a man like Francois Tussaud has ten or fifteen sub lieutenants that could each come up with ten to twenty million of their own, and probably another twenty from their twenty subs. He could probably bring in two hundred million all on his own."

"Write me a list of who in this building has that kind of dirty money. And then think of a scam that could clean that sort of money. I bet I could clean a billion dollars in a month."

He chuckled happily.

I pressed my anima on him.

"Tell me exactly where you keep the cash you hide, who knows about it, and how it's guarded. I want to learn everything I can from you. You're teaching me so much! You're an inspiration. My mentor!"

He happily complied.

The more he wrote, the angrier I became.

He had so much—could do so much, and yet he continued to steal just for the pure joy of stealing. And he was willing to murder uncounted hundreds to do it—for no reason at all. He was burying it with no intent to ever spend it. He had almost three hundred million dollars hidden away—every penny of it stolen.

I was going to steal it all back.

Chapter 27

By the end of the week I owned the buildings on either side of the tile factory, one of which I'd gotten for almost nothing, had bought the condo complex, which we closed on in a few weeks, and an apartment building to house my crews that Julia would be sending. We'd also begun refurbishing the tile works, which was being expanded.

It would now be three separate buildings, production, painting and shipping, with the third building holding the raw materials.

The manager was thrilled, cooperating fully with training his new staff without the need for me to nudge him. The existing staff wasn't happy. They could see they were on the way to being replaced, which gave them enough angry anima for me to manipulate, so they were cooperating.

I hadn't decided yet if I'd use their anger to keep them working there or find them new employment. There was more than enough work available on our construction projects to keep them employed elsewhere.

Sandra was working with Julia, deciding how best to launder the money I was planning on making every company in the Maamoun building give me. Ten of them were my mules already. I planned to make them all my mules—for a short time.

We stopped at a busy construction site on the way back to the hotel so I could speak with the foreman on the job.

Ryu removed the charm Sandra had made him when I signaled him.

The foreman was annoyed to be interrupted, which made it easier for me.

I grabbed his arm as I said, "Which construction company is the shadiest in the business? The sort with dangerous men."

"Seiner and Sons. They're a bunch of thieves though, you don't want them. You'd be better off hiring guards if you're worried about looters."

His answer confirmed information I'd gotten from Maamoun's men. They knew all of the criminals in the city and most of the major players kept offices in that building.

Ryu said, "Ask him who's the best architect around. One who knows what palms to grease to get things done."

"I'm standing right here. What's this ask him bullshit? You want Mifsud but good luck getting him. He has a waiting list a mile long."

We went directly to Mifsud's office, barging past his receptionist.

Ryu began yelling at the girl for losing our appointment. Within minutes Mifsud was angry enough to agree to design a luxury apartment complex with stables, riding rings, pools, tennis courts, and underground parking all built as a front to hide our lab underground, which was going to be a huge space per Sandra's newest request.

I got him to sign a contract with a bonus for early completion.

I shook his hand at the door while placing my other hand on Ryu's arm.

I'd learned the knack of using just enough to avoid the backlash. It seldom made me giddy at all anymore.

I said, "We'll talk again in a few days. You're looking forward to it because I don't care if we build a copy of something you already built. This is going to be a lucrative, easy, fast job."

Mifsud's tense expression faded, and he nodded happily.

In the car again, I handed Ryu's charm back to him.

"Any I'll affects? Are you tired or hungry or anything?"

"No. I didn't even notice...how do you know it worked?"

"They always like me when I use my anger on them. They just stare blankly when I just use theirs. You need to pay better attention so you can tell if something is off."

"Like what?"

"'Tis possible a naturally immune person could pretend to be under my thrall. Or one on drugs could recover quickly or grow very angry too fast for me to handle." I shrugged at him as I added, "Or maybe I could be careless and tell them to do something that would be harmful to us or others. I could get distracted or misjudge. And what if there is another seethe out there? Wouldn't you want to be able to recognize one if you saw it chatting?"

His eyes widened.

"Holy shit, you're right! There could be lots of you ass...guys."

I pretended not to notice he'd been about to call me an asshole and he pretended not to notice that I'd noticed.

I said, "Now we need a project manager and I know just where to look."

I didn't want to return to the office building though. Or face the decisions I knew I should make.

"We'll go in the morning," I said.

The office hadn't grown more appealing when we arrived the next day. If anything, I resented it more as I'd much rather have continued my studies then face another roomful of these vicious men who hated us all—until I spoke to them that is.

Their fawning was worse than their hatred. I knew I'd return to the hotel to masturbate or maybe the bathroom here... because despite how I despised them, touching their anima with my own still felt good.

"Well?" Ryu asked impatiently.

"'Tis an important decision."

I sat as far from them as the room allowed.

"You're... stalling. Any of them could do it."

He gestured to the five men who stared with eager expressions waiting for my next command.

"'Tis true... and none *deserve* to do it."

"You could make him come home after work and stay in."

"'Twould be odd—a noticeable oddness. The man I leave in charge must appear as he ought. He must do all of the things that a man of his station *would* do. He must do it naturally. Behaving oddly could raise suspicion. Perhaps not of what he is doing now, but what he *has* done in the past. Any investigation would be bad for us."

"Okay... so tell him not to kill again."

I rolled my eyes at him.

He crouched beside me, surprising me by taking my hand.

"I get it, Pip. It sucks that he gets to live a normal life, but we can make sure he never marries again or even dates. Those others... killing unarmed villagers—they're own people, is vile but they're hardly likely to do it again."

"'Tis unfair that he gets moments of happiness when she has no moments at all!"

I jumped to my feet to pace.

Their eyes followed me with an eager intensity that rose the hair on my arms.

"Stop looking at me!" I snapped, and they immediately shifted their gazes.

Ryu said, "I think you need a break, Pip."

"I'm fine. Which one would you pick?"

"Him. Reid fits the bill perfectly. He's English but has been here ten years so speaks the language and knows the ins and outs. He can handle the project and if he really murdered three people, then he'll have enough anima that you can control him for a few years at least."

"You didn't believe him—or me?"

"I can't see the anima, Pip. I meant if he'd murdered them in such a way that his rind was thick enough."

"'Tis."

"Then choose him. Tell him what you want done and make him spend his money on charitable works. In a year or so you can make him sell his house and devote more time to charity. Do it slowly enough so his acquaintances think it's his idea, that he's a changed man, and who knows, Pip, maybe he *could* feel real remorse..."

"Ha!"

Ryu winced.

"He's full of hate," I turned to Simon Reid, saying, "Tell me what you would do to your secretary if you knew you could get away with it."

"I'd beat her until she bled. I'd beat her and beat her and beat her until her skin was purple and soft and then—"

"Stop! Why would you beat her?"

He said wistfully as if speaking of buying her ribbons for her hair, "She'd be so beautiful... she *is* beautiful... her husband doesn't deserve her."

"That's enough," Ryu said to me while Reid continued to tell me his reasons for wanting to hurt her.

I'd known the moment I'd seen how he eyed her, how she'd ducked away from his gaze, that he had evil in his heart for her.

"Stop," I said tiredly to Reid who immediately snapped his mouth closed, grinning eagerly at me.

Ryu said, "He's a sick fuck. There's no doubt about that."

"I should make him jump. I should make them all jump. Instead I profit from his sickness—on the murders of those poor innocents..."

"That had nothing to do with you. You have to stop thinking like that, Pip. What they did is on them! What you're doing is good! You're keeping dangerous people busy doing stuff that helps others, and if you're one of the others it helps, so what! It's disgusting hard work that you do. You deserve to be paid for it!"

I'd said the same or near enough to him. It was true but not the truth entire, and yet there was no other good option.

I grabbed the arm and the anima of the man beside Reid and said, "When Darron Caldwell from Query Inc or Vicky Atkinson from Encore Enterprises calls you, you'll immediately agree to invest in anything that they recommend. You'll sell and buy when they tell you to. You'll tell anyone who asks that it's your idea. You will *never* lift a hand in violence against anyone. If you begin to fantasize about murdering anyone, you'll feel so badly that death would be the only escape. You'd end your own life before taking another one. When I call to arrange another meeting, you'll agree at once. Now go back to work and forget this meeting ever happened."

I gave the same instructions to all four of the men.

They all eagerly agreed.

When it was just the three of us least, I turned to Reid. "I want you to work for me."

He nodded eagerly. The heat of his anger mixed with mine. It was more intimate than an embrace. Keeping my hand in it made my skin crawl and my cock throb.

"You'll resign from your position tomorrow and call and arrange a meeting with my current manager. You're excited about this opportunity. You've been wanting to make some changes. Managing a complex building project with a small crew using local resources is your way of relaxing. You really enjoy it. So much so that you spend most of your time working on the project. You really respect the people at Query Inc and want to please them, so you always try really hard to make their requests happen."

I spent an hour giving him directions and another hour repeating them, which was probably unnecessary because I was furious.

I finally said, "I'll see you Monday at the meeting with the manager for my tile factory. You look forward to it."

He leaned forward to clasp my hand, saying, "I do look forward to it. I've always wanted to try my hand at real art. These artisan tiles are truly beautiful. I'm excited to design some myself."

We shook hands and I left.

He followed me to the elevator and probably would've followed me down in it, but Ryu held up his arm to block him.

"Don't you have work to do?"

"Yes... of course. See you Monday, Lord Blackwood."

In the car I said to Ryu, "We need someone watching all of them. Have them call if my commands seem to be weakening or if they begin showing signs of stress."

"We could have Reid watch them."

"I don't think that's a good idea. I don't want him thinking about the meeting. I could find a local but it's a simple job. One anyone at all could do. We must have someone who could check to see if they keep themselves and their house up like usual?"

"I'll talk to Julia."

"You do that."

I turned to glare out the window.

Back at the hotel, I relieved myself which felt physically good but left me feeling mentally dirty. I took a long shower then soaked in the bath. Tomorrow would be another long day.

"You should've woken me," Ryu said irritably when he arrived at the factory.

I'd been there since dawn.

"I hardly need an escort when I've been here daily for a week."

"I had to take a taxi. Do you know how expensive that is?"

"You should've called for the car."

"And leave you stranded out here?"

I snorted.

"Any of them would gladly give me a ride. And why not call me first to see if I needed help? Which I do not, or I *would've* woken you. But seeing as you're here, you might as well check to be sure that the housing is adequate."

I headed back into the factory and was surprised when he pulled me to a stop.

"You need a break, Pip. You haven't slept in almost two weeks."

I shook his hand off my arm.

"I need no nursemaid. There's much to be done. Tomorrow things should be handled enough to move along without me while I nap. You can make excuses and handle any problems while lining up next week's purchases, the trucks, the suppliers, the drivers, and then get started on the shipping."

"Are you mad at me personally or just having a bad day?"

"'Tis my *job* to have a bad day."

I stomped away followed by his worried gaze and the helps adoring one's.

Their regard was like walking through sewage. It clung and stunk of sickness and things long rotted.

I headed directly to the mixing barrels where a group of men were arguing hotly over the practicalities of reusing the old equipment.

The group was composed of the factory manager, Reid, a few of the carpenters Julia had sent, the foreman of the construction company that I'd chosen, and three of his men.

My factory manager greeted me with a triumphant smile.

"Lord Blackwood. Mr. Reid wants to take apart the machine. I tell him that isn't possible that all new machine is needed."

I grabbed Reid's arm and his anima.

"Can you build another one?"

"Yes."

"How long will it take?"

"A month maybe two."

"Can it be done faster if you had more helpers?"

"It's an old machine, outdated. Every part will need to be fabricated."

I said to the factory manager, "Is there a better newer machine that can do the job? I need to be able to adjust the thickness of the tile using up to four layers each with a different material."

"Yes. It's a larger machine and much more expensive."

"Why wasn't this machine replaced with that one ages ago?"

"The cost, I assume."

"How quickly can you install a new one?"

"I'd need to check to see if it's in stock. It would take two weeks or so to install and that doesn't include the time to move this machine. It might not fit here."

I said to Reid, "Order whatever parts are needed to keep this machine going and get them fabricated as quickly as you can. Find out about getting a new machine. If one isn't available, find out who has one."

He nodded his agreement, taking out his phone.

"Come with me."

The entire group of them followed me, which was fine. I needed my manager to know the plan.

By noon I had the men working together to rebuild the building next door to house the new machine. I'd have to travel to France to make the supplier send it immediately. Or perhaps Julia could do that or maybe Sandra could offer a cash bonus... I sent a memo to Ryu for him to see to it while I napped.

By eight p.m. Seiner, the construction boss had a rough sketch of all the work that needed to be done.

I said, "I want the plans finished within a week and permits applied for as soon as possible. Let me or my assistant know if a clerk is dragging their feet."

"Yes sir."

"You can go. Thank you for staying late. You're doing a good job."

"Thank you, sir!"

"Mr. Poole will be in charge here for a few days. Treat him as you would myself."

"Of course, sir!"

They loved me. Their adoring gazes followed me, and they hung on my every word.

I hated them all.

I said, "Have a nice evening. Sleep well."

Ollie wasn't about when I reached the car. I called him to say I was ready to leave. And then Ryu.

I said, "Seiner should have the plans drawn up and be able to get the permits. If you need to bribe the clerks, do it, and I'll get the money back after my nap."

"Are you heading back to the hotel now?"

"Yes, but it will be a day or more before I can sleep. I plan to stay in and do some studying. Just have meals delivered to the room. Or maybe your room... My thought was I can have an extra table set up in my suite and complain to the management that the maids are disrupting my paperwork and arrange for them to come in when called. If I eat in your room as a regular thing, you just need to order extra food. If I sleep longer than three days, you can just drag me into your room to let them clean."

"Okay. I'll be back in an hour or so if you want to get dinner."

"I shan't require food for another day at least. Have a nice evening."

I disconnected before he could offer further company—I didn't want his pity or his impatience.

"Drop me at the church complex," I said to Ollie. "You can have the rest of the evening off unless Ryu needs you."

"Yes sir."

"How are the rest of your crew settling in?"

"They ain't my crew but they doing all right."

"And you? Are you finding this job satisfactory?"

"I guess... it's boring as shit though, begging your pardon," he added sarcastically.

"Is there something you'd prefer to be doing?"

"I... don't know. All my boys be gone from our crib. Man, when I think about it, it be just wild we up and walked away like this."

"Would you go back?"

"We can't go back, not without some serious hassle. It be tough as shit to work ourselves back up to the sort of respect we need...it'd be better to take over new territory."

"What would happen to you if you went back without them?"

"I could find another crew, but that shit be the shit. I'd be low man for sure. No one be trusting a bitch who skates out like we did."

"...you miss your friends."

"You be trippin man?"

"I'm fine. I'll speak with Ryu about getting more of your crew here."

"*Nah*... this place sucks. They be pissed as shit to be sent here."

"I could get another driver?"

"Man, I ain't no idiot. This be a sweet gig most of the time. Sides, Ryu needs a mate he can rely on. He be all minted now but he's still one of us. How much longer we gonna be here though?"

"A few more weeks."

He sighed hard but nodded, flashing me his crooked grin in the rearview.

I said, "Tomorrow, find a stationary store and pick me up some more notebooks and writing implements. Then buy me a full-size computer and a comfortable computer chair and install them all in my hotel room. If the hotel can't supply a larger table to work on, buy one and install that too. In the future, when we're traveling anywhere for an extended stay, bring a computer and arrange for a chair, a desk and a a few small filing cabinets and a printer. Speak with Ryu and see if he requires one. You can arrange to store and ship our traveling office. You can ship your own with ours."

"Yes, sir," he said happily. "Should I see if I can rent another room to use as your office or see if they have a suite available?"

"Speak with Ryu. One of our apartments might be ready soon enough."

"I doubt it...not unless you be okay with cracked walls and loud neighbors."

"Tell Ryu to make a list of all of the people who need to be evicted and remind him that I want those spaces finished ASAP."

"Yes, sir."

He left me off in front of Saint Francis.

The few parishioners who came in and out that evening left me alone.

The priest looked startled to see me still sitting there when he arrived in the morning but said nothing other than welcome.

He was old and thickly rinded but with a kind patient air I was unused to seeing especially on anyone as rinded as he was.

I sat through the morning service, which as far as I could tell he'd said with sincere respect.

When the church emptied after the service, the priest returned in simpler street clothes and began to neaten up.

An older woman entered, saying loudly and in distress, "Father you must come at once. Mother has fallen and I fear…Please, Father!"

The two hurried away.

I strolled the square briefly, visiting all of the churches before returning to Saint Francis.

The priest had returned in my absence and joined me when I rose from my prayers.

He looked exhausted, not sad exactly, more grim or as if he'd completed an arduous task, which I supposed he had. His rind had gained a dark sparkle.

I said, "So the woman has passed on…"

"God will welcome her," he said assuredly, sitting beside me with a heavy sigh.

I said, "But the weight of those souls that you usher to God lingers…"

"It's my service to Him and His flock."

"But still, a heavy price… although 'tis probably made lighter by your certainty that you've done all that can be done."

"What troubles you, my son."

"Naught that any man may assist me with."

"God is always there. His words can guide you if you let them."

I said bitterly, "Thou shalt not lie. Thou shalt not steal. Thou shalt not murder, nor commit adultery, nor even covet another man's wife…thou shalt have no other gods before Him or take His name in vain…his commandments to man. But what then when man breaks them?"

"You forgive."

I snorted with anger.

"What say He on the treatment of dangerous men? Even if one forgives, is it not our duty to ensure such men be constrained from further evil action? Shall we turn the other cheek and be done to death or let others be so done by? I vow only one who has never felt their life slipping away on another's whim would espouse that."

"Jesus forgave even as he was so grievously wounded."

"Have we no duty to our fellows to protect from the wolves that masquerade as men? What would you council your flock to do should they know of a man who has murdered?"

"To turn him in to the authorities."

"'Tis a cowards way—or maybe just the easy way. A phone call and your conscience is clear. What befalls the wolf or his victims no longer of concern—unless, of course, the wolf comes to your door. And who is the authority? Law often protects the misdeeds, through ignorance, laziness, and greed. 'Tis a simple thing to escape the law's notice or at least it appears so..."

"The wheels of justice can sometimes turn slowly, but they *do* turn. And no one escapes God's judgement."

"And how does that truly help? What use is God's judgement to the living?"

"How are you any better than the criminal if you take the law into your own hands? Judgement *must* be God's will."

"So say you, and yet the church has murdered uncounted souls in the name of God. And it too bows to the authority of the state. Men chosen, not by God, but by circumstance—by men who *seek* to be judges. Rules that change on the whims of man—this murderer may go free and this one hang and this one shall be locked away for his lifetime, and some are innocent and some repent, and some dream of the day of unleashing their hatred again."

The priest said, "Only God knows the true heart of man. Only He can judge those things. We must act with mercy and kindness but also wisdom. Through prayer and good works we can help guide our fellows."

"And those who have no wish to be guided but instead hunger for violence? Who murder and revel in it... who hide what they are..."

"God will see."

"*I* see."

"Then you must do what's right."

"What is right?"

"God will speak if you listen."

He clasped my hands and began to pray.

His sincerity was warmth I could feel. It stirred the anima coating him, tiny sparks drifting away—to Heaven I hoped. I hoped he felt lighter for his prayers.

Ryu entered, hanging back by the door until the priest stood.

I said to Ryu, "His burden was freely accepted and lays lightly on him. Another could shoulder it if they would."

The priest said, "It's no burden to administer to my flock. The sadness of their passing is eased by the knowledge that they go to a better place—prayer *will* comfort you if you let it."

"Still. I can see it weighs on you and perhaps that weight might aid another?"

Ryu gaped for a moment, pursing his lips before nodding.

I spread my hands, directing my own anima to that of the priest as I intoned in Latin, "Loosest those things which are bound and art the hope of the despairing. Yea, O Lord who lovest mankind, give thou command, and he shall be released from the bonds of the lingering soul of his dearly departed brother in Christ—" I turned to Ryu— "Receive thou in peace the soul of this thy servant. Give it rest in peace with all thy Saints; through thine Only-begotten Son, with whom thou art blessed, together with thine all-holy, and good, and life-giving—to us your servants that we might turn evil to good. Amen."

The anima flared, winding about my outstretched hands and then settled about Ryu, who staggered back a step but then stood firmly.

The priest stared in consternation as if unsure whether he should protest the prayer, which wasn't an official version, but parts stolen for one of mine own making, say a prayer of his own, or simply leave the madman to his mumbling.

"Join me in prayer, Ryu, for the safe deliverance from evil of all who shelter with us."

He knelt beside me at the altar.

The priest prayed the Psalms with me. He crossed himself and left when I began saying the Litany of Matins that I'd learned when I was a child.

I don't remember falling asleep. The litany was still fresh in my mind when I opened my eyes. I was shocked to find myself in my hotel room and even more shocked to see Drew sitting beside my bed.

He laid his book aside and stood to pour me water.

"How long?" I asked.

"Four days."

"Were you here the entire time?" I asked worriedly. "Is everything here—and at home—as it should be?"

"Yes. Sandra is thrilled but I'm worried. Ryu is worried..."

"'Tis nothing. A lesson learned. I'm sorry if I alarmed you and pulled you away from your family.

His hand stilled then he resumed pouring.

"So you know..."

I accepted the water and drank the entire thing in one long gulp. He took it to refill.

I said. "Know what? That you're a mage or that you love them both? Aye, 'tis clear. A simpleton can see that you're her father. Although, I admit that seeing the lines that bind you confirmed it."

"The lines?"

"We see hatred and anger, but we also see love although those golden lines are soft and fleeting. 'Tis clear you love Sandra and she you. Your love for Cassandriel is always a fierce surge of gold when you greet her. She loves you too, you know..."

His eyes grew shiny, and he turned away to say gruffly, "That pleases me greatly."

He handed me the glass of water.

"When Ryu called to say that you'd collapsed in the church, it occurred to me that you're probably confused and conflicted. I've been thinking on this. Cassandriel too will face this same realization that she is other than she thought herself. Like you, she must be taught—must believe the truth of what she *is*. You're not a mis-made man; you're a different species completely and can't hold yourself to their rules. Their morality, their laws, their gods, none of that applies to you."

"God still sees me. 'Tis certain."

"I don't mean that he doesn't see you, or love you even, but he isn't judging you as he does man."

"I know it."

"You know—but do you believe?"

"I believe in many things."

Drew sighed hard.

I said, "I understand what you're saying. I wasn't created to be a woman or a man but to be other. You're afraid I'll adopt man's laws and think myself a creature of evil. I think I could become such a creature—or I could choose to serve God in my own way, which can't be as man does because I *see*."

He said, "God is man's deity. They endow him with man-like attributes. There's no place in their theology for creatures like us— for pixies, trolls, imps, inou. All are hated by man—hunted to extinction. Everywhere, every realm that man has entered it's been so. They overwhelm us with sheer numbers and then it's war between us—a war that always starts by making laws that we *cannot* keep else we would die. War that is always in the name of *their* gods. I've lived long enough to see the rise and fall of their gods—gods they believed in as devotedly as any Christian. Gods they attribute *their* law too, *their* morality.

"When I was young, I'd helped man make war because I'd believed—and still believe—that demons should remain in their own realm. I fought to keep the species unmixed, but then I realized that not only was that a losing battle when almost all of the mixing was being done by choice, but it was wrong of me to take their choices from them as much as it was for them to take mine from me."

He laughed a quick huff of laughter.

"I hide among men, but their law means less than nothing to me because I know in my heart that I am not a man. When I die, my hamingja will go to my child, not God, exactly as nature intends for me.

"My needs and gifts differ from a man's needs. I was born knowing what I was, so never doubted my right to take what I needed to survive. Cassandriel will likely feel guilt for her needs, which is as ridiculous as a cat feeling guilty for pouncing on a mouse."

He headed to the door where he turned back to say, "We owe man nothing."

I showered and dressed then called Ryu.

"You're awake," he said in relief. "Julia was so worried. I wanted to hide you, but she told me to let Drew sit with you. Are you hungry? I can be back in an hour, or you can order room service."

"I'll want to meet at your earliest convenience to discuss what needs to be done next. But I do mean when it's convenient. Finish whatever you're about. I can find my own meals. You don't need to worry about that."

"Julia was insistent that I make you eat real food, and she wants you to keep up with your exercising. I found a stable where we can rent horses and a gym where we can rent a mat. I'm sure she'll call and have some words. She was really worried, Pip."

"I'll call and reassure her."

"I'm supposed to make you sleep more regular hours, but I don't see how I can do that..."

"I believe 'twas the transfer of anima that tired me. Have you felt any ill effects?"

"No, just the opposite. I was up two straight days myself. I slept the third night, but it was a pretty normal sleep."

"And the priest?"

He was silent long enough that I knew that he hadn't thought to check and was debating lying.

"Send someone there or call and inquire."

"I will. I'll be back in an hour or so. I'll text you the name of the stable. Ollie is with me, so you'll need to wait for the car, but the man at the front desk can arrange a ride there if you want."

"I'll be back by four."

I disconnected and went to buy myself lunch.

Afterward, I went to a Buddhist temple.

Drew was correct that God's laws for man couldn't apply to me. It simply didn't make sense that I'd be given this power if I shouldn't use it—but Drew was also correct that I was hiding amongst men.

I might not owe man anything, but I owed myself. I wished to do good but could see that I could easily become evil. What I needed was my own law. One that my God, the God who'd sent me here with this power, given me this second chance, would approve of. Laws that fulfilled my purpose *and* my obligations to Julia and the people we'd taken in.

Chapter 28

Over the next two weeks I visited every temple and spoke with every sort of clergy whenever I got the chance. I'd found a routine that let me sleep for twelve hours every seventy-two or so. Two days of anima usage followed by a day with none while I studied or shopped while looking for my next marks and visited the churches, then a long sleep followed by a day where I ate normally while setting up my next two days of usage.

Ryu and I went riding every morning followed by an hour in the gym then back to the hotel for showers and breakfast where we talked over the plan of the day.

I dressed after my morning shower after my latest nap and let myself into his room, finding him on the phone.

"And I'm telling you, it's becoming a problem. Good, I miss you too."

He put his phone into his pocket and turned, jumping a foot and exclaiming when he saw me.

"Excuse my interruption," I said.

"You startled me is all. The usual?"

"Tea and waffles for me, please."

He nodded and pulled out his phone again to place the order.

I debated calling him out on that phone call but didn't want to hear another lecture about attending the churches—or anything else.

We both sat at the small table in front of the window.

He handed me his notebook, keeping his hand on it to hold it closed as he said, "I know this is supposed to be an off day for you, but there's a guy on the second floor who'd be perfect for the hotel bill. We can move into the penthouse condominium tomorrow, which will have much more room. Ollie can have your computer all set up in a real office, one where we don't need to worry about cleaning ladies."

"What's the scam?"

"He's married but has a different woman there every night, and by the look of them he's doing some kinky shit. You tell him that he rented our room for his favorite mistress who then walked out on him. You speak to the night desk guy tonight after he's had his nightly hit and tell him to put Ollie's room bill with ours and send the bill to our mark at the discounted price and he pockets ten percent, which we leave as a tip in cash. The mark isn't going to talk even if he throws off your compulsion, not when his wife might find out. He'll lie to cover it up. The clerk isn't going to talk when he's getting a cut."

"Fine."

"And seeing as you're using today, we can swing by the car dealership and buy the van we need for Sandra and then the pool place and sign that contract so we lock in those water rates. I can use the credit card we got last week to pay that bill off but then I better dump that one."

"Have you found a good safe for us to steal?"

"Yeah. I've stolen all the watches I need already too and picked up everything else on the list that I could. We'll have an extra bedroom in the penthouse that we can use as a lab while we're here until the real one is ready, which won't be for at least three months."

"I should ask Sandra to come and seal it."

"She'll be here next week for three days. If you're sleeping, I'll ask her."

"I'd like to be awake for that, so let's see if we can move some appointments."

He flipped through the notebook, frowning thoughtfully.

"The store opening could be postponed."

"No. 'Tis critical else I have to return to ensure the necessary orders. Make sure the samples are ready and the advertisements placed."

He glanced at the notebook and said, "Wine, cheese, the fancy display lighting, all of it is ready to go."

"Who's on duty?"

"Me and Ollie. We don't want to overdo it. I've been coaching him. He won't annoy anyone for the hell of it and he'll be subtle." He snickered as he added, "He's really good at pissing people off."

"Mayhap 'tis time to promote him? You need an assistant. 'Twould be well to have one you like and trust. His rind could be strengthened by a priest's if needed."

"Yeah. Okay. You might need to nudge him a bit just to be sure he takes guard duty seriously if I leave him watching your door."

"Pick one of the footmen as a new driver; someone Ollie can oversee, and make sure his wardrobe is adequate to attend meetings. I care not what he wears when not working but 'tis always a suit and tie when accompanying either of us unless we specifically state otherwise."

"I'll make sure."

"If you intend to take Ollie riding, he'll need to be properly fitted out. I'll pick up a new credit card today, but I think for now that he has no need to know 'tis a stolen card."

Ryu said, "Speaking of that, I think we should ask for cash next time. It should be simple enough to tell your mark to withdraw half of their savings and deliver it to Ollie."

"'Twill be handled by Monday, assuming the apartment complex is ready for occupancy. I was just waiting for Julia's newest recruit to arrive. Every day my footman will arrive at the office where they'll drop off their empty briefcase in exchange for one full of cash. I shall text you the schedule so that we don't have a pile of briefcases waiting for pickup. Sometime after their pickup, they drop by the apartment complex where they hand over their briefcase and get an empty one from the man there.

"Every day..." he said in surprise.

"I shall instruct them not to notice the case is empty or even that they're dropping off and delivering. Is all that is needful is that they arrive here in a timely manner, which shouldn't be too difficult to arrange. The apartment door is locked so they only need to place the briefcase on the right in the foyer when checking their mail in the mail room and taking the case on the left when they leave the room."

"I meant that we should ask for bigger bills or wait or something."

"They might need to come more often than once a day. I'm working on devising an alternate method of dropping off the cash.

He googled at me.

"How much cash are we talking about here?"

"Almost a billion dollars."

"Jesus Christ, Pip!"

"My Julia is thrilled."

"... I bet."

"No one else knows. Not even Sandra although she probably has her suspicions."

"Where the hell are we getting it all from?"

"The men in the office building. They're gladly giving me everything they've squirreled away. I shall take everything they stole. Some I intend to return to the rightful owners but most we're keeping. It shall take us our lifetimes to use it all and years to move it. Julia is purchasing us safe houses. I shall give you your share to do what you like with but please find yourself somewhere to hide some too if only to ease her heart."

"...okay..."

"Hide some from us as well to ease your own heart. I swear on my soul that I shall never ask you."

"I don't know what to say, Pip."

"Say you'll do all that may be done to keep Julia safe. When we return home, she'll know in her soul that there is safety for us and that she needn't strive so hard. She can let them all go, except those she chooses to help. I shall rid us of the mules, and she shan't worry over it or be subjected to their loathsome presence."

"It's bad then when you touch them?"

"The bad is that 'tisn't bad at all...."

"You're right. We should do whatever we can to keep her away from it. A billion fucking dollars..."

I said, "We need plastic to wrap it in. Drop that directly at the apartment wrapped in a rug or something. Go buy us enough matching briefcases too."

He nodded, heading to the door where he paused to glance back at me.

"I'm sorry you need to do this, Pip."

"I want to do it. And you're right to be worried about that."

His worried expression deepened.

I pretended absorption with my notes.

He left and I began checking my notes to see who I still needed to speak with.

My lists grew at an alarming rate. Every one of the men I took knew at least ten others at least as evil as they were.

I was amazed—and suspicious—that I hadn't run into a demon yet.

I flipped to my other notebook, which thankfully was much thinner. There were only a few people left in it who needed to be warned away.

Now to close down the street.

I mused on ways to do that until it was time to leave for my first appointment.

Sandra arrived in time for the tile store's grand opening. She'd brought a cadre of her acquaintances with her.

"Pip, darling," she said as she stood on tiptoe to kiss my cheek. "Whatever are you doing here?"

"Shopping. When my lady wife got the brochure you sent, she insisted that I be here to get my order in first thing. She hasn't any patience at all when it comes to decorating."

"And have you decided on a pattern?"

"She sent a pattern that Mary designed that we'll have custom made. I fell in love with a lovely blue tile with a raised seal in gold leaf that I just had to have. And the brown with the copper swirl will be perfect for the barn. I've gone a bit over budget but there's simply nothing like it at home. How about you? Have you come to admire the art or buy?"

"Buy, of course. And if you'll excuse me, I want to get my order in before they sell out."

She hurried away followed by her friends.

I headed to a man who was frowning at the tile that the woman with him was admiring.

Ryu offered the man a glass of wine.

I grabbed the man's arm—and his anima—as he grabbed the glass and said, "Stunning isn't it. It'd be just perfect for your project. You better get an order in before they run out."

"Darling, it is perfect, isn't it?" the woman asked hopefully.

He said, "Let's order before they run out."

She squealed in excitement.

I stepped up to a woman with her arms crossed, sneering at the tile.

"I could do better on my kiln at home," she said dismissively.

Ryu leaned close, brushing her shoulder with his, gesturing dismissively with his wine glass as he said, "Your home must be ugly as shit."

I laid my hand on hers as she inhaled to retort and said, "Your friends would be so impressed with this in your kitchen. And don't you deserve the best? Why not have someone else make it for you? Order and enjoy it!"

Her angry anima flowed to Ryu, then me, then back to her. It faded in seconds.

Ryu laughed as she headed to the desk.

I leaned close to whisper, "If you begin to feel tired..."

"I'm good. Look at that ass over there yelling at his girl. Why bring her here if you don't mean to buy?"

We headed over and sent the man to buy her a gift certificate for the tile of her choice.

She looked excited and confused.

Ryu said, "We'll fill all the orders we need tonight at this rate."

I said, "Some might cancel in a few weeks."

"Will it matter?"

"I'm not sure. Have Ollie mingle a bit and point out people who like the tile just not the price. I think they'd be more likely to believe they love it for the long run."

Sandra joined me two hours later and murmured approvingly, "Good job, Pip. I think we can let them sell themselves on it now. I have another small proposition for you along these same lines, if you're interested."

"Of course."

She wrinkled her nose at me, leaning closer to say, "You can say no. I won't be offended or angry. If the job is urgent, I'd tell you. This one is more in the way of an opportunity."

She stepped away as two of the couples that she'd entered with approached.

"I'd be delighted," I said.

She said to the nearest man, "I was just telling Lord Blackwood about a local artist I discovered quite by chance. She does simply amazing landscapes. I'd like to become her patron and Lord Blackwood has graciously agreed to lend me a hand finding a suitable studio."

"I know just the place," I said.

"Then I'll call tomorrow at noon? We can have lunch and catch up."

"That would be lovely."

I bowed over her hand to kiss it.

Ryu and Ollie followed me outside.

In the car, Ryu said, "I'll look for a place."

"She might have one in mind, but find us one anyway, somewhere downtown. Talk to your crew and see if any have artistic talents."

"Leandro can tag," Ollie said.

Ryu laughed in delight. "Perfect. Call him and get him here pronto. Then call the tile works and get them making us some walls, say six-by-nine."

I said, "Tell them we want some rough pieces too as if taken from a broken wall. Better yet, find us some real broken wall, nothing too thick; we want them to be able to hang it."

Ryu said, "Get some chunky pieces too. They can lean them or use 'um as sculpture or tables."

Ollie said, "We should bring his whole crew here then."

I said, "Do it. Find a trendy fancy spot to put them up. Ryu, take them shopping."

He said, "We want to keep it real."

"Clean them up so they don't scare the ladies. And warn them about their language. I'll have Julia buy us another studio closer to home where they can be more themselves."

Ollie nodded as he said, "We for sure don't want no shit with the natives. They be some uptight assholes."

"They're rich as fuck though," Ryu said, and he and Ollie bumped fists.

He laughed a low eager laugh that made my cock jump.

I pulled my briefcase into my lap, saying, "Let's go over the plan one more time."

He said to Ollie, "Keep the radio down," and rose the privacy barrier, sliding closer to read my notes.

I wished I dared lay my hand on his knee. I wished I knew if he thought of me as a man or a woman or anyway at all other than the shadow that made things happen.

I hoped we were real friends, but I wanted more.

I said hastily, "Put your charm back on so that we can speak as equals."

I didn't dare even wish for more when his unprotected anima was touching mine.

Chapter 29

I set down my newspaper, leaving the headline showing, signaling the waiter to refresh my tea. I was certain that Sandra had been behind the refinery robbery. Four tons of unprocessed gold had been reported stolen. The paper mentioned that the processed gold had been moved to an unspecified site for safe keeping while police investigated. I had my suspicions on where that site was.

She said, "How are you liking it here?"

"Not at all. That isn't a complaint, just an observation. 'Tis possible I'd like it more in a more secluded area. I find this city ugly in the extreme. The sea and desert are beautiful though. I imagine short visits would be enjoyable."

She picked up the paper, her eyes sparkling with mirth as she said, "With so many refineries it's surprising it doesn't happen more often."

"So many thieves... I imagine the vault in the Maamoun is chock full of stolen money, they go to such lengths to hide its existence."

Her smile gained a sharp edge.

"How foolish of them with so many criminals about."

"'Tis true. So many blatant criminal types terrorizing that building. They could all fall off the face of the earth and 'twould be a blessing to the city. I'm glad I have only a short-term lease as I imagine such a building wouldn't stand up to that sort of assault."

I opened the paper to examine the destroyed refinery again.

She said, "Most thefts go unnoticed."

"Some should make a statement."

I folded the paper again to let the waiter pour us fresh tea.

"I'd like to make a statement while I'm here, leave my mark, do what I may in the spirt of civil works."

Her eyes widened and she tapped the tabletop with her manicured nails a moment before nodding.

"So, tell me, have you and Julia decided to invest in more businesses here?"

"Oh yes, we'll be buying a garbage company, a cleaning service, and our shipping line. We have a partner already lined up for that."

She snickered.

I said, "As with any investments, timing is critical. I shall require a few weeks to ensure I don't scare off possible investors by moving too aggressively. Perhaps you'd like to visit the warehouse where I keep the models of the apartment complex we're building?"

I was dying to observe her cast the spells on the model. The books she'd lent me on the process of sympathetic magic were just fascinating.

"I'd like that," she said. "I have more business here in a few weeks myself."

We clinked glasses.

Chapter 30

When I woke from my next nap, Julia was sitting beside my bed.

"Jewels!" I said in delight.

Laughing, she jumped onto the bed to hug me. We laughed and hugged for a long minute until that traitorous piece of male anatomy began to stir. Abusing myself as I did after dealing with Maamoun's men had made my male anatomy more active or perhaps lessened my self-control. I found myself masturbating most mornings now and my cock was ready for its daily massage.

I said, "I must shower and then we can talk."

I kissed her flushed cheek, noting her worried eyes and paused.

"Is aught amiss? Why are you here?"

"I missed you guys. So I decided I'd come see you. I'm only here a few days." She leaned closer, putting her hand on my thigh.

Embarrassment turned me as red as she. My aroused condition was blatantly apparent.

"I could help you with that..." she offered.

"I prefer to help myself," I said as I hurried for the bathroom.

Her light laugh sounded relieved to me or maybe I was relieved that she'd laughed.

I turned back at the bathroom doorway.

She'd flopped back onto my bed, smiling her beautiful smile when I caught her eye.

I said, "'Tisn't you. I love you with all of my heart. You're a beautiful woman, Julia. 'Tis just I want no woman. 'Twould be... untrue."

"It's fine, Pip. I love you too."

She jumped from the bed and began undressing.

I entered my bathroom, closing the door.

She said loudly, "You can show me around and take me to lunch."

"I'd like that!" I called back.

It was a relief to drop my sleep pants and grasp my cock, which throbbed eagerly.

"You're such a stupid thing," I muttered. It didn't care whose hand was on it. My manly one and firm grip were just as arousing as her feminine one was, more so even because I could easily imagine it wasn't myself but a handsome man and just give myself to the physical pleasure of the body.

I hastily put a stranger's face over Ryu's, not wanting to think even in my secret heart about him this way because I knew he had no interest in me. We'd both be embarrassed if I made my infatuation known.

And I darn't let myself contemplate him as a lover least I inadvertently use his anima for my own pleasure, which would be the ruination of our friendship and myself.

Knowing I could have him if I gave up my morals was maddening, but to do such would be to succumb to evil, which I was determined I would *not* do.

I stepped from the shower, relieved of my dirty thoughts as well as the grime of such a long sleep.

Julia was just slipping a skirt on.

I wondered if she had relieved herself too—*or maybe Ryu had...*

She could have come here the moment I fell asleep and spent the last day and a half —and night—with him.

Contemplating it upset me, which upset me even more.

I had no right to be jealous.

I didn't ask when she'd arrived.

She said, "Ryu left your notebook but says there's nothing urgent in it. So we can take this day for fun. I missed you so much, Pip!"

She hugged me again and I was reminded of what a small woman she was.

I returned her embrace saying, "Any problems at home? Are the boys behaving?"

"Everything is right on plan. Did Drew tell you Sandra would like us both available when Andre comes for his visit in February?"

"Then I shall return home."

"She's working on an excuse for us but warns that Cassandriel can see auras and will know if we lie. So don't tell her you wanted to come home unless you really do."

"Of course I do... think you I wish to be parted? 'Tisn't so! I dislike this place immensely!"

"You can come home whenever you want. You're doing a great job here. Sandra is really pleased. But if you've had enough and want to quit or just take a break, then come home."

"Ryu has you worried?"

She stepped back to peer into my face.

"He's right to be worried. You're obviously troubled, Pip, if you're spending all of your free hours in the churches."

"I am but perhaps not as you imagine." My stomach rumbled and we both laughed.

I released her to dress." Let's go eat, I'm starving."

She slipped on her shoes, waggling her foot to show me.

I said enviously, "Brilliant! The color is called?"

"Nude. They cost a fortune, but I couldn't resist them."

I said, "There are many nice stores here. I've chosen all of mine own clothing. Have Mrs. Roman clear out my closet at home."

I tensed, worried the reminder would upset her, but she didn't react.

She looked through my closet, flashing me a happy grin over her shoulder that loosened the tightness in my neck that asking her to rid us of Lou's clothing had produced.

"It's all lovely, Pip, and perfectly you. I brought two of your tailored suits with me that I'd ordered. They *finally* came in. You need to try them so that I can have them altered if necessary.

She removed the garments from a bag hanging on the back of the door.

"In case you need to be the lord," she said laughingly as I admired gold stitching of the family crest on the left breast.

She drew her hand down the sleeve of the other. It was dark blue, cut in a style similar to the one that women in my day had worn when riding.

"This one is more you. I left the black version at home."

I tried both on and we agreed that the fit was perfect.

I put on a gray suit that I'd picked for myself with the silver ascot that Ryu had bought me.

"Beautiful, Pip!"

She covered her head with a silk scarf in light blue with gray flowers on the ends.

I said, "We match perfectly," which made her laugh as she stood on tiptoe to kiss my cheek.

We left together arm-in-arm.

Our new driver, one of my footmen, Ian Grehan, drove us downtown to one of my favorite restaurants.

The man at the door said, "Your usual table, Lord Blackwood?"

"My wife would prefer the patio if it isn't too crowded."

"Right this way, sir, ma'am."

He led us to a glass enclosed garden in the back and seated us in the shade of an enormous palm tree.

"This would be my usual table," Julia said in approval.

I said, "'Tis a pleasant view but too distracting to get work done. I find myself watching the people, not reading the reports like I should."

The *maître d'* said, "Tea?"

I nodded as Julia said, "Coffee for me, please."

"My usual for two," I added.

"Very good, sir."

He hurried away.

I said, "Look! you can see the tower of the mosque. 'Tis a beautiful building. I'd like to show you."

Small lines appeared by her eyes and her smile dimmed.

I took her hand and kissed it.

"Worry not. I know I'm not meant to worship as man does. There is a God though, Julia, and he *does* welcome me. I feel that in my heart. I *saw* His power. I go to the churches to see how they... I suppose 'tis to see what they think a fair punishment when they transgress. I've seen rinded men and women enter and pray, to all appearances as devoutly as I do. 'Tis my thought they feel their rinds."

"Maybe," she said doubtfully.

"I'm certain that some feel it and revel in the weight of it..."

"You question them?" she asked in dismay.

"Some. I must if I'm to learn to read the anima, and I *am* getting better at gauging what the thickness, position, and tones signify."

"We can't stop *all* of them!"

"I know it. 'Twould be an impossible never-ending task that would surely lead to our deaths. I have no desire to live as a hunted despised thing. I ignore them when I have no use for them, which is no more than they themselves do."

She smiled in relief.

I took her hand again to say, "But when one tells me that they intend to do harm... then I *will* act."

"Ryu tells me that you order them not to..."

"Of course. But sometimes that isn't enough. Not for God, but for me. So many that I've encountered have been previously apprehended and released. The law now boggles me. It purely *boggles* me. Law in my youth was harsh, swift, and clear—and I despised *it* as well because 'twas inherently unfair. I had less rights then a criminal today. I was nothing with no power, no voice, no say. Now I can be whatever I wish. And what I wish is to be a law unto myself."

Her lips pursed, her eyes narrowing as she examined me, but a moment later her expression lightened.

I clasped her hand as I said, "I am what I am. I cannot—will not—obey any law but God's own as He has revealed it to me through mine prayers and the gifts He has bestowed on me."

The waiter arrived with our drinks followed a minute later by our meals.

We ate in companionable silence.

When she laid her fork down, she said, "As long as we don't let ourselves crave that action... I like to give the worst ones the worst jobs, which is nothing more than what they deserve, but the ones who piss me off, I try to stay away from. I don't like the idea of you working daily with men you hate."

I changed my mind about explaining my plan, *which wasn't a lie,* I told my guilty conscience. She had no need to know or worry.

"'Tis of no consequence."

I paid in cash, tipping lavishly.

"Let's shop, my beloved. Tomorrow I'll show you the business."

She laughingly complied and we spent a fabulously fun day in the stores.

Ryu joined us for dinner, and it felt to me as if our family was complete. Julia's smile dimmed when I stood and said, "'Tis time for me to retire." I kissed her cheek. "If you prefer to go out, than do so. I shan't be offended. Ryu or Ollie can take you to the clubs. Don't go alone! A woman alone here at night..."

Ryu said, "I'll keep an eye on her."

She flushed as she said, "I came to see you. Not the bars."

"I shall be sleeping. You know I don't enjoy the bars, Jewels, but that's no reason you need to stay in. Go! Have fun! Just be careful. Don't go anywhere too crowded with exuberant people. Ryu, keep a careful eye on the crowd, and if you think there's too much high emotion get her out."

She laughed, shaking her head at me.

"I can take care of myself."

"It can happen unnoticed. The casino kept me wakeful for days and I didn't consciously imbibe once."

"I'll be careful," she said again as she stood to hug me.

I hugged her back, giving Ryu a speaking glance over her head.

He nodded, looking a bit embarrassed and uncomfortable.

I retired to my room to read the itinerary for the next day, which was boring enough that I fell asleep easily.

I woke when they returned and knew they'd been drinking by the laughter they were trying to muffle.

I expected her to join me and lay awake debating joining them before drifting to sleep again.

When I woke in the morning, they were both up and dressed, breakfasting on the small patio.

"Did you have a nice time or we're you too intoxicated to remember?" I asked teasingly but with a bit of censor as I poured myself a cup of tea.

I laughed when they flushed.

"I heard you come in. There's no point denying you were both inebriated." I kissed the top of her head and sat. "'Tis just I worry that you'll lose control when drink taken."

I could tell by her flush and the way she was avoiding my eyes that I'd embarrassed her more than I'd meant to and maybe hurt her feelings.

"But we need speak no more of it. 'Tis my worry. You're clearly able to manage. Now, did you wish to see the offices here or go directly to the factory?"

"Factory first. I'd like to see our shops too. Ryu told me of your plan to sell art and I think it a good one, except I'm not certain how we get our cut. Not that I'm against giving Ryu's crew most of the profits, but the entire point is to make us legitimate money."

Ryu said, "He can rent the space from you and pay agent fees and sales commissions. He's no dummy. If I explain that your friends will be laundering cash through the art, he won't raise a stink about cash sales disappearing."

She said, "Don't tell him that unless we have to. Give me a week or so to look up what the standard commission is. We can sign a partnership agreement to legally give us a percentage for overhead. And I can nudge him to invest his profits when needed. We need a few more businesses like that."

Ryu said, "What about Pip's book? It would take you like two seconds to tell every rinded person you run into to buy it."

"Genus! I'll hire a photographer or artist the instant I get home and we'll put together a book on our ghost."

I said, "I shan't have time to write much for the next few weeks."

"You can layout the detail and I can hire a ghost writer—or nudge one. Don't worry about that."

Ryu said, "You could buy a brewery and go to places where there's plenty of anima like the casinos and tell them to buy your beer."

Julia laughed in delight.

I said, "We could sink ships like Hugh planned to. We could buy scads of some cheap knick-knacks and resell them at exorbitant prices," all of which I was already planning.

Ryu said, "A high end boutique."

I said, "A jewelry store. 'Twould be simple to order our marks to go make a purchase. We'll fence our stolen jewels ourselves, Jewels!"

She giggled and we toasted each other.

She said, "I'll ask Sandra about businesses we could buy that we could make serious profits on if the business had investors."

"'Twould be a fitting use of the rinded who have served their prison time yet still retain their funds. 'Twould be my wish that any profit they reap from their investments with us be spent on charitable works or in our stores."

She stood to lean over the table and kiss me.

"Mine too."

I reached to lay my hand on Ryu's arm.

"How about you? What would you have us do with the profits?"

"Buy another estate and help some other kids. Young ones who'd have a chance if they had a safe place to live."

"Then we shall do it!"

His grin lit his eyes as he turned to Julia.

"We could fix up my old neighborhood. Put in parks for the kids and hire more teachers. Maybe fund some clubs or something to keep them busy after school? Shit, we could make the shops there give them jobs and pay them a decent wage!"

"Sounds good," she agreed. "I'd like to fund my charities. Maybe we can work out something with that? The kids might like to go to the missions to help out? We could offer them jobs there. Not full-time stuff just a week or two on their school breaks to let them see the world and encourage them to become doctors themselves?"

"I love that idea," he said eagerly.

He took her hand.

I laid my hand on theirs.

"I vow 'twould be simple to convince the doctors to look after the children when so many doctors are rinded..."

I released them and stood.

"Now, off to the tile factory."

Julia whispered, "It's real gold."

I nodded.

"The stolen gold!"

"It seems likely."

"We'll be so fucked if we're caught."

"I'm very careful."

"What on earth are they going to do with this much gold?"

"'Tisn't our concern, is it?"

"I suppose not."

She set the tile back amongst it fellows and turned to examine the packed pallets.

"How much weight difference between these and regular tiles?"

"None. There's less than half the amount of tile in Sandra's boxes. The packaging makes up the difference in the space."

"If they open one...."

"The top row is normal tiles. If they dig down, they'd see that the raised seal on the tiles is delicate and it's covered with real gold filigree. Anyone would expect something like that to be packaged well. A cursory search won't notice our packing materials are flimsy, and even if they did, they'd need to break the tile to reveal the gold center."

"Still..."

One of us could be close by when the ship reaches port. Our man there will call immediately if there's a problem."

"Someone could see us making the tile."

"I don't see how. Our people won't talk, and strangers aren't getting in. We have very good security, which shouldn't worry anyone when we use so many precious metals and gems. And if they did see, we could claim it was an order. We buy quite a bit of gold openly and use two different shipping methods—one of which is completely off the books."

"Put in an order on the books for some solid gold tiles. If Sandra's tiles are found, we can just claim it was that order and there was a clerical error."

I showed her the tiles our artisans were currently painting, which were a legitimate order. Each was hand painted with flowers with real silver and copper details.

"'Tis beautiful tile," I said, and she snickered.

I led her to the storage building. The guard at the door let us in. Two armed men, both chosen by Julia and sent here from England, worked inside readying the paints and supplies for the next day's projects.

I said, "They'll size the diamonds and weigh out the gold to be sure each tile has the same amount. Then they personally inspect the finished product before sending it to be packaged. The small silver squares there are part of that same order. We have quite a bit of capitol tied up here in supplies—not our capital, but still..."

"This is all real orders?"

"Eighty percent of it. Our manager makes sure that there's always a real order ready to go to packaging and one on the belt. That way Sandra's stuff can be out in plain sight. Not that we've ever had anyone demand access to the building. We have normal people coming in but it's all by appointment and most times we can just leave her stuff out."

"Where do we store her gold?"

"Sandra's supplies are under this building and only accessible by her and Drew. She brought me down. 'Tis a huge space and very hot. The floor is solid gold, not bars like one would expect..."

"I wonder how they stole it all and got it here?"

"'Tis probably best if we don't ask."

Julia said, "Will we have enough orders to finish her job?"

"More than enough. I plan to keep this factory open. When sales drop off, we'll hold a showing for new designs. 'Tis amazing how much people will spend on such things. I swear, the more ridiculous the price and materials, the more they want it."

"Ryu is worried you're making too many mules—of powerful men."

"'Tis a complicated undertaking to shift so much wealth around."

"Still, when you go..."

"Then they shall go to. Worry not, my love. All is going to plan. I'm fully aware of the consequences of my actions—and theirs. Stick to the plan that Sandra has laid out. Make all purchases exactly as she recommends. Not a farthing more nor less."

"It's going to take all of our capitol, Pip."

"And we shall recoup it a hundred-fold—besides, 'twould be a simple thing to begin again."

"Not so simple...." She huffed a laugh, hugging me quickly. "It's nice to see you truly happy."

"And you. I'd see you have everything you want—the repose that comes from knowing we shall be safe come what may."

She relaxed against me.

I kissed the top of her head.

Chapter 31

Ryu and I accompanied Julia to the airport to see her off.

"To the office," I said when we returned to the car.

Small lines appeared by his eyes.

I said, "My lady worries greatly—more than she admits even to herself that she and I will end up as shadowed things with no safe place to rest. If vast sums of money will ease her mind, then she shall have them—and the quicker the better so that she may have more time to study the arts that will surely help her evade that fate."

"I'd never thought about how scary it'd be to know that could happen to you..."

"It *shan't* happen to her!"

All of my footmen joined me within minutes of my entering the warehouse.

I headed directly to an enormous map of the city hanging on the side wall.

Only two new pins had been placed.

"That's it?"

Frankie said, "I think we've got them all, boss. There just isn't anymore."

"*Hmm.*"

"Pictures?" Ryu said as he held out his hand,

Frankie slapped a folder into it.

Vicky said, "These guys are new. The girls that were working there have moved on. At least I hope they have and they aren't buried in the desert somewhere..."

"Drugs?" Ryu asked.

She shrugged. "Muscle for sure."

Frankie said, "When I asked at the bakery there who'd moved in next door, the clerk just said trouble. One of the other patrons said Maamoun would take care of it, and he and his pal started trash talking Russians in general."

"They're Russians?"

Vicky shrugged again. "Maybe. The dude at the door is but that doesn't mean they all are. And he's a cold one, Pip. I don't need psychic power to know he'd slit my throat as soon as kiss me."

"Stay away from him."

I headed to the other side of the room and the lists there.

"Where's the progress on this?"

No one answered me.

I turned to glare at them. "You have until I return from England to get me every last name and address of every single person working on that entire block. Am I clear?"

"Yes, boss," they chorused.

"Do we have the van yet?" I asked Nick.

"Yes. I can get it any time. And the vests and hats."

"And the barricades?"

"They're already in the storeroom."

"Good. Get the model finished for my return. Make certain that you don't make any changes at all to the existing parts of the model. Don't move it by a hair. Don't touch it! Am I clear?"

"Yes, sir," they all said.

I glanced at Vicky and she nodded, giving Ian a pointed glance that almost made me laugh.

I said, "Ian can make the buildings and you can place them as needed, Vick. I need this entire thing to run like clockwork. Ollie, you can take me to pick up Jean and Yusuf. We'll pay our new neighbors a little visit."

"You're not taking me?" Ryu asked anxiously.

"No need."

"Don't get cocky."

I headed to the car without answering.

He followed me, waiting until we were outside to say, "When do you plan on telling me the plan, Pip?"

"When you have need to know it."

"You don't trust me?" he asked in a hurt tone.

"Don't be ridiculous. I'm being cautious. What you don't know, you can't tell. I know there's more men out there that I haven't had a chance to speak to and any one of them could notice that their boss is acting off. If one were to take you, you're not knowing could save your life."

"...oh."

"Keep the spells on you. I'm certain Sandra could find them if I couldn't. And maybe carry some binding powder and unbinding powder. If you were taken and one was so foolish as to sniff it...."

"I'll be careful."

"Tell everyone to watch their backs. It's just a few more weeks. Sandra is making me a spellbook—" I broke off as the door opened and Ollie approached— "I shall explain more later."

Ryu's worried gaze lingered on Ollie.

I said, "Yusuf will drive me. He's just picking them up."

"Thanks."

"Ollie is my friend. I'd not risk him."

Ollie smiled uncertainly. His gaze skipped from Ryu to me.

He said, "I ain't afraid if you need some muscle."

Ryu snickered.

It made me laugh.

The elevator in the underground garage opened to a wide carpeted hallway. A man standing in front of closed double doors glanced over and said, "This is a private club, and it don't open until twelve."

Jean followed me to the door. Yusuf walked one step ahead of me. Their stolen anima was warm against my skin. It drew the heat of the man at the door's anima from ten feet away.

He was a stone-cold killer.

I laughed in giddy excitement.

The man we were approaching said, "Beat it, shithead."

I was practiced enough now that it took little effort to roll the anima over him, which I did, not caring that it would make him a mule. I wanted him to be as deeply enthralled with me as I could make him.

"Let us in."

He opened the door.

"Come with us."

He jostled Jean aside to follow me so closely I could feel his breath on my neck.

"Who's this?" a man polishing a bar to my right said in Russian— or at least I thought that was what he said.

Three other men were sitting at a round table in front of a low stage with a metal pole. I ignored the bartender to walk to the table, thrusting the anima at the men there.

"Who's the boss here?"

"Sergei."

"Speak English when speaking to me. Where can I find Sergei?"

"The office in the back."

"How many men does he have?"

"Twenty-four."

"Are all of them killers like you?"

"Who the hell are you?" the bartender asked again, this time in accented English, sounding really agitated now.

When I turned to look, I saw he had a hand on a gun laying on the bar.

I said, "If he lifts that gun, kill him."

All three men who'd been sitting at the table stood and pulled their weapons.

The bartender gaped at them.

I said, "Are all of Sergei's men killers like you?"

"No. Dominick never killed no one."

The man I'd taken at the door said, "Cheslav's son got his head in the clouds."

"He's a queer," one of the men at the table said. "He's only one of us cause of who his father is. I think his dad lied about him making his bones."

I pointed at the man who'd spoke first. "What's your name?"

"Vidal."

"Take me to Sergei, Vidal. You and you stay here. The rest of you come with me."

The gathered anima was hot enough to make me sweat.

The bartender stared at me in horror and at them in confusion. I found his rapid changes in expression hilarious and knew I was treading dangerously.

The anima engulfed him when I was still ten feet away from the bar.

"Watch the door. No civilians are allowed in. Just your crew."

He nodded, dropping a hand to his zipper.

"No masturbating!"

"What the hell's going on out here?" a man yelled angrily in Russian. "Why aren't you on the fucking door!"

My certainty that that's what he said confused me.

I yelled back, "Speak English, asshole!" which made me and then them all laugh.

"Are you fucking drunk?"

He stomped up.

Vidal said, "Sergei."

I pushed Yusuf aside to hug him.

For a moment he was tense and then he relaxed so much we fell to the floor, which I found hysterical.

We all laughed again, with them trying to help us up and falling too as I reached for them.

I finally gave up trying to stand and just lay there catching my breath and gathering my wits.

I said, "On February twenty-six at ten in the evening you and all of your men except for Dominick and Cheslav's son will go to the Maamoun building and take the stairs to the thirteenth floor where you'll kill everyone you see there because you hate them all and want to take over their territory."

"We hate them," they agreed.

I giggled.

"Why are you here, Sergei?"

"To take over this territory."

I wasn't certain if he'd said that because of my prompting or not.

I pushed myself to my feet by pulling myself up on Yusuf's leg.

"You speak Russian, don't you, Yusuf?"

"A little."

"Sergei, you just hired Yusuf. You'll do whatever he says. Yusuf, stay with Sergei and wait for my call. I think I better go now. Next time I come, one of you will escort me right to Sergei."

I patted his cheek, and he grabbed my hand to press it to his face.

"You love me," I said.

"I love you."

"We'll talk later. I'll want to know all about your business."

"Stay."

I tried to pull my hand away and he tightened his grasp.

"Stay."

"Release me."

I staggered back, losing my balance when he did.

"Excuse me," a girl said, and we all turned to look. She was mostly naked as were the other four women with her.

"Are we opening?"

"Business as normal," I said. "Just don't break any laws."

They all laughed as if that was the funniest thing they'd ever heard.

The four women approached laughing and teasing flirtatiously.

The men's anima heated with lust.

I headed to the door, staggering drunkenly.

I remembered Jean when I reached it and heard a woman laugh.

When I turned back, I saw Jean was pulling her shirt over her head.

Loud music made me jump.

"Jean!"

She didn't turn, not hearing me over the loud music and too intent on removing her clothes.

I'd have to go back to get her, which I didn't dare do.

I staggered out the door and to the car where I sat leaning against it for a good twenty minutes before it occurred to me that I could call for help.

I called Ryu. "I need a ride. Send one of them here."

"Are you okay? You sound …. off."

"I think I started an orgy."

"Jesus Christ, Pip!"

"I left Jean behind, or I'd have gotten caught in it."

My sudden erection was painful in its intensity. I badly wanted to return to that bar. Instead I undid my pants and grabbed my cock and realized I'd moaned loudly when Ryu said urgently, "Are you okay? Don't try to drive. I'm coming to get you."

"No! Stay away from here. Have everyone stay away!"

Heat built, my pulse thudding in time to my frantic tugs.

I disconnected, shouting with my release, falling back against the car and giggling. Headlights blinded me and I realized I was standing out in a public garage with my pants down and cock swinging in the wind.

I hastily yanked up my pants, my embarrassment killing my buoyant mood.

Two cars pulled into parking spaces beside mine a minute later.

The four men who got out gave me sneering glances and stomped for the elevator.

It occurred to me that I could call Jean and Yusuf.

I called him.

"What's going on in there?"

"They're all fucking."

"Who?"

"Everyone."

"Get Jean and come outside. Tell them to all stay in there."

He didn't answer.

I said, "Did you hear me?"

"Yeah. They don't want to let her go."

"Put me on speaker phone."

Feeling like a fool, I yelled, "Let Jean go and stay in there and stop fucking. Get drunk instead and sleep it off. It was just a booze dream!"

I had no idea if it would work.

Yusuf and Jean didn't exit.

I waited a few minutes and then said, "You still there?"

"Yes."

"What are you doing."

"Getting drunk."

"Good. I'll call tomorrow. Tell Jean to call a cab to the hotel before she passes out."

"She's already passed out."

A hot wave of shame flushed my body.

"How badly is she hurt?"

"I don't think she is."

"...oh."

"I'd like to fuck her again."

"No."

"She liked it."

"No."

"She said she did."

"I meant no you cannot."

He said nothing.

I felt like an even bigger fool.

I hung up.

Ian arrived thirty minutes later.

I said, "Take me home. To my room—alone!"

My pants felt painfully tight. I wished this car had a privacy glass.

I practically ran to my room to kick off my pants. My thumb barely grazed the head of my cock, and I came in hard waves that left me gasping.

I went to soak in the tub, giggling as I soaped myself. I wished Julia were there and then felt bad to even think of using her for my own pleasure as if she were no more than a receptacle for my lust—but I knew she'd enjoy it too. Except neither of us would enjoy it the next day, not when it had been brought on by contact with such evil men.

But I didn't release myself, instead watching closely as I stroked myself slowly, giggling as I imagined making a spell that would do this. *I bet there were hundreds, no thousands of spells that did this,* I thought as my breath grew ragged and my hand sped up.

By morning I was feeling more normal and very ashamed of myself.

I had been cocky. That thought made me laugh in grim amusement.

I bet they'd be thrilled to see me again.

Chapter 32

I wasn't wrong. The next night, the man at the door greeted me eagerly and followed me to Sergei's office.

I'd prepared for this visit, donning three crosses all of them steeped in demon repellant. My true preparation had been hours of prayer—heartfelt prayers to God that I'd escaped the demon's clutches so easily. I was certain there'd been a demon present. 'Twas only luck that had let me escape. My certainty of mine own power, my hubris, had almost led to my downfall. To partake would've been the first step to me ruination.

Self pleasuring myself as I'd been had lessened my self-control, fortunately enough for me, not to the point to be comfortable with sex in this form, but 'twas close.

I imagined I'd have made excuses if I'd partaken, perhaps even returned to partake again. The demon had been clever—so clever I hadn't even realized it was present until I'd regained my wits enough to contemplate why I'd become so intoxicated so quickly.

The only answer was the men hadn't been resisting me but had given me their anima—themselves. It knew what I was, mayhap had even deduced what I planned and wanted those men dead for its own reasons. Or perhaps was willing to see them dead to corrupt a seethe. Or perhaps hoped I'd rethink my plan if I believed the demon wished them all dead too.

"Any idea can be both good and bad."

"What?"

"Nothing," I said.

"Send for Natasha," Sergei said to my escort as he stood to clasp my hand.

His grip was firm, neither tightening, lingering, nor jerking away, which I thought meant the demon wasn't currently inhabiting him as I didn't think one could withstand the ointments I'd bathed in.

I said, "Tell me about your business."

"We have girls. I can get you any type you like. Old, young, blond, brunette, you name it. You name her and I'll have her delivered to your door or keep her for you in one of our houses."

"Whether she wants to come or not?"

He shrugged.

It made me angry enough for my anima to appear.

His smile gained depth as my anima engulfed him.

"What about weapons?"

He nodded eagerly.

"Are there more of you somewhere else?

He waggled his hand side-to-side.

"We have contacts—friends. It's good to have friends. You and I could be great friends!"

"What are your plans for February twenty-sixth?"

"We're going to the Maamoun building to kill everyone on the thirteenth floor."

I took out my phone and showed him a picture.

"Go there or send someone to take your own pictures. Enter through this doorway. It'll be unlocked. Then take the elevator at the hall. This one."

I showed him pictures, walking him through the entire plan.

"They'll be armed at the door, and you'll have to break it in."

"We can do that."

"I have no doubt you can. What will happen to your girls here if you don't come back?"

"Orlei will take over."

"Is he one of your twenty-four men here?"

"Yes."

"What if none of you come back?"

"Then I guess some of our girls die and some get away."

"From now until I tell you differently, no one visits any of your girls, except to bring them food or medicine. Treat them nicely. Before you leave on February twenty-sixth, give them all ten thousand dollars and let them go. Don't leave any locked up. Can you do that for me?"

"...yes."

"You don't sound sure."

"I don't know why I would."

"Because I have a plan that's going to get you everything you deserve. You'll never want another thing! And it would make me so happy. As happy as I was last night. Happier even."

"I was too drunk to remember last night."

I took his hand, pressing my anima on him.

His eyes darkened and his breath grew ragged.

I sensed nothing untoward. To my senses he was a mule like any other.

"You're really looking forward to killing everyone on that thirteenth floor."

I withdrew my hand as he nodded eagerly.

"I really am."

"Don't go early. It has to be then."

"You have a plan."

"I do but you can't tell anyone. Don't mention we met."

He nodded.

"I'll call."

Someone knocked on the door and Omar opened it, stepping inside followed by a beautiful woman with a hard smile, cold eyes, and a thick rind. Her smile became puzzled as she sniffed the air, looking confused and a bit worried.

She made my skin crawl. Her anima roiled and then stilled and I knew her demon had fled or retreated or whatever it is one did when it didn't wish to be noticed. I thought it was gone though although I couldn't pin down why I thought it.

I said to her, "Are you here of your own free will?"

"Yes." She sauntered closer to put her finger under my chin.

"My, aren't you yummy."

Sergei laughed.

I grabbed her finger. "Don't do anything you don't want to and don't break any laws."

"That's no fun. Everything's against the law here."

"How many people have you murdered?"

"None."

"Who died near you?"

She giggled.

Sergei said, "She don't like getting her hands dirty, but if that's your thing, we can accommodate it. She does like watching."

He leaned across his desk to slide his hand up her thigh.

Lust colored anima swirled around her.

"Got any candy, lover?"

Omar dropped his hand to his crotch.

I said, "I'll call you."

I left, leaving them to do whatever depraved thing they wanted.

I returned to my office where I greeted a steady stream of visitors as pleasantly as I could, pressing my anima on them to reinforce my commands—the same commands I gave every day to every visitor.

By closing I was exhausted, more from worry over the demon than my commands. Their rinds were thick and my anger hot. That the demon would be gleeful over my inner turmoil, I had no doubt.

I repeatedly had to remind myself that these were terribly evil me who's deaths would be justice and necessary for the welfare of the innocent who lived here. I would *not* cower, not from this distasteful duty or from fear.

Ryu joined me in my office as he did nightly at closing to discuss who needed a visit from me.

"Is everything okay, Pip? You seem worried."

"I *am* worried. Those Russians have some women captives."

"Can't you make them let them go?"

"That's just it. I can—I did, but now I'm thinking that maybe that isn't good enough. How are they going to survive here when they can't even speak the language?"

"How many women are we talking about?"

"I have no idea...does that matter? I wouldn't wish it on one girl."

"No. Me either. I meant if you sent them all to the apartment or tile company could they just work there?"

"They can't come work for us at least not unless I can make them all forget."

"That might be a blessing."

"But then how do they go back home?"

"What we need is a woman's shelter."

I called Vicky. "Can you get away?"

"Sure. What's up?"

"I'll tell you when you get here."

Ryu said, "You going to leave her here to run it?"

"Maybe. She'll probably know better than we do what they'll need."

"I'll start looking for shelters."

"And a way to ship them home."

"Maybe they could just go to their embassy here?"

"Ask Jacob to find out but warn him that it can't lead back to us."

He left.

I'd have to go see Sergei again. I didn't want to because I wanted to. The heat of his lust was enticing enough to stir my cock just thinking about it.

I was angry by the time Vicky arrived.

"Have a seat," I said briskly, sliding a Query Inc pin across my desk.

"Put that on."

She frowned but pinned it to her lapel.

"There's some women being held by those Russians. I can get them out, but then what do I do with them?"

"You'd have to hide them, or they'd just take them back and likely murder them for running away."

"I plan to kill them all—the Russians I mean, not the women. So those women can't be employed by me. There can't be any connection between us."

"If you just kick them out, someone else is going to take them."

"I know. Ryu went to look for a shelter and Jacob will be asking at their embassy, neither of which I know a thing about. Will they be able to just walk into a shelter?"

"It depends on the shelter."

"I arranged for them to get cash. I could arrange for them to be dropped somewhere, but where?"

"Maybe we could smuggle them out or back to their home? How many women are we talking about here?"

"I don't know. It could be girls too..."

"Then call the police, Pip."

"I can't."

"You can't or you won't?"

"I can't. Besides, the police wouldn't be able to do anything. They'd just take more girls. My plan is better."

"Not if little girls are getting raped it isn't!"

"They aren't. I told them to leave them alone."

"... And if they don't listen?"

"I want to help them. I really do, but I want to stop those men permanently more. I need another week to do that."

"You want me to what—absolve you for waiting that week?"

"I want you to help me think of way to help those women in a way that doesn't involve me!"

"You could always call the police anonymously and have them picked up."

"What will happen to them?"

"I have no earthly idea. I guess it depends on who they are. They're really strict here about drugs and sex. It's possible they charge the women."

"So the police are out then. It isn't a chance I can take."

"What we need is a place for them to stay, a way to get home if they want it, or jobs to live on."

"Find me that. But don't say or do anything that will lead anyone back to me."

"How the hell am I supposed to do that?"

"Find me someone like you who we can leave them with! There must be someone else in this city who would care what happens to them!"

"There are probably lots of someones, but caring and being able to do a thing about it are two separate things. If it was easy for those women to escape, they wouldn't wait, Pip!"

"Damnation!"

I forced myself to take slow breaths. *She was right—about everything.* I did want her to absolve me and it to be someone else's problem—which gave me an idea."

I said, "Never mind. I know what to do. Dismissed."

She examined me for a long minute before heading for the door.

I called after her, "Don't lose that pin. They're very expensive!"

She didn't answer.

I headed upstairs to Worthy Shipping to borrow a cellphone from Francois Tussaud to call Sergei.

He, of course, eagerly handed it to me.

"Can you meet me to discuss some details?" I asked.

"Yes. Where?"

"There's an apartment building for sale in Al-Nahda. I'll text you the address. Can you be there in an hour?"

"Yes."

"See you there."

He hung up without the usual enthusiasm that others displayed when I agreed to meet with them.

My hold on him wasn't as deep as I wished it to be. He loved me and would agree, but he was able to question me in a way that told me he thought about my commands when he wasn't with me. I thought in time he could break free of them, which shouldn't be possible with his rind. I thought he was likely possessed of a demon or perhaps truly insane, or mayhap both.

I thought, given time, his demon might be able to wrest him away from me. It hadn't tried to entice me again with sex, which I believe was because it realized I was aware of it.

It would be plotting.

That thought made me laugh harshly. I sobered quickly as I wondered if it thought it had already won.

I entered the address into Francois's phone, saying, "Meet me here in one hour. Don't tell anyone where you're going. If anyone asks, lie."

"Of course," he said happily.

"Don't be early or conspicuous. One hour!"

I handed him back his phone and headed to the fourth-floor realtor's office.

He gave me the key I needed.

I said, "Will anyone notice if there are people living there for the next ten days?"

"I can postpone the showings."

"Do that. Make the excuses believable. If anyone presses too hard, come to my office and leave a note. Don't call me about this."

"Can I call about our other projects?" he asked eagerly.

"Yes. Have you heard back on my offer?"

"Not yet. They said tomorrow."

"Put an offer in on my second choice just in case but put a clause in that I can back out tomorrow."

"I will."

"You're doing a great job. Keep up the good work."

I let him clasp my hand for a few seconds.

I wasn't trying very hard at all to keep him under control seeing as almost everything he was doing for me was perfectly up-front, but he was deeply under my control. He had no rind so 'twas only my own anger that was swaying him, or perhaps he too was possessed by a demon, one that was laying low or one too weak for me to sense.

I mulled that over as I headed to the meeting.

Sergei and Francois arrived right on time. By the anger that flickered across their faces and showed in their anima they knew of and disliked each other.

I said to Sergei, "Francois is going to help us move your women."

"What for?"

"A better place, much more convenient for me, and others, to visit. It's my gift to you."

His eyes brightened and the tenseness left his shoulders.

I said, "Are you on any medications?"

He listed a few.

I said, "Text Yusuf the list."

"What for?"

I clasped his shoulder, urging my anima to him as I said, "I wish to be sure you're receiving the best care available."

He stepped close enough I could feel the heat from his body, which shifted the color of anima to that of lust.

"When we doing this?" he asked eagerly.

"You can start moving them in here anytime. Be discreet. This is just a temporary stop. Tell them to wait quietly until Francois comes for them. Leave only one or two of your main crew here to guard them. Make sure they have food and water. See if you can get them all here by the sixteenth. And I do mean all, Sergei. No holding out on me."

"Natasha too? She ain't going to like that."

"No. You can keep her and any of the other girls who have their own homes."

I examined him for a moment and added, "And I don't need you to give them the money anymore. I've got that handled. Francois owes me a big favor."

Sergei chuckled happily.

I said, "'Tis going to be a huge pay day."

"How big?" he asked eagerly.

"This building won't be big enough to hold all the women we're getting."

I stepped back as he stepped even closer; his hard cock pressing my leg.

"Just a few more days. And don't call me Lord Blackwood. Call me Lou. But don't mention me to anyone either."

I handed him all the cash I had on me.

"Have a nice dinner with Natasha on me. I'll be out of the country for a few days. Can I count on you to get this done?"

"Yeah. I'll have my bitches moved in here in a few days."

"Don't bring furniture or anything. I'll take care of that. They might need to sleep on the floor a few days."

He shrugged.

"No one can know we're in here. I'll leave this key by the back door. Send one of your men here to keep an eye on things. If anyone does show up, he's to hold them until I can handle it if he can't get them to go away."

"Right."

I offered him my hand to shake.

"You can go now. Thanks for meeting me. I'll call when I get a chance."

He ignored my hand, hugging me instead and kissing both my cheeks.

"*Do vstrechi*," he said enthusiastically.

When he'd left, I said to Francois. "All of the women he brings here need to be shipped out again. I'll get you a list of places in a few days. What's it going to cost?"

"Twenty grand a head usually but we can do it much cheaper."

"No. Follow the usual protocols. I don't want anyone to know this is a side deal."

"Then you should contact Rubio direct."

"Write down the contact info and how the scam works and drop it at the office for Emma. Mark the envelope private."

He nodded.

"Could you get them to Russia?"

"It'll cost you. We have a contact there, but he'll expect a hefty payoff for a big group. He'd need some of it upfront to pay off others."

"Get me that information too. Paris and Scotland are other possible destinations. I'd want them moved with as few people involved as possible. Never mention my name, company, or anyone who works for me to anyone. This is strictly between us."

"*Mais oui!*"

"I'll arrange for you to pick up the money. Don't contact me directly. You can leave a note at the office on the way in or out of your own, but don't let anyone you know see you doing it. Go. I'll call."

He left.

I called Jean and told her to meet me at the warehouse.

She was there when I arrived an hour later.

I headed to the office there, waving her to follow. "Vicky, can you join us a few minutes, please?"

The two women entered together. Jean stared in her stoic way. Vicky smiled. She wasn't wearing the pin. I wasn't sure if I was glad or not.

I closed the shades on the glass window that looked into the main room.

"I'm having the women moved to an empty apartment complex. They'll need some bedding. Jean, you'll bring in anything Vicky asks you to and give it to the man inside. I can make that man let you in to speak to the women. You're to get their pictures, their names, and find out where they'd want to go. Just ask them. Don't try to force them."

Vicky said, "Find out if any need medicine or drugs."

"Drugs?"

"They'll have been drugging them. We can help them get off it, but it's probably better to leave them on it until they're safely way."

"Damnation! Why didn't you say this earlier!"

"Because it's fucking obvious!"

"Not to me!"

Jean smiled as my anger brushed her.

I snapped, "I shall handle it. Is there anything else that is obvious?"

"They probably won't speak English."

My anger left me abruptly and I sank to my seat to rest my throbbing head in my hands.

Vicky said, "It's not a huge problem, boss. There's apps for that. She can just play a recording asking her questions, but they'll probably be afraid to answer."

"Then I cannot help them."

Vicky sat on the edge of my desk to pat my shoulder.

"Don't give up so easily. If they're on drugs, he'll probably keep giving it to them unless you told him you were going to kill them or something."

"No. He believes I'm moving them for his sake."

"Then it's probably fine."

I gestured Jean away. "Leave us."

When Vicky and I were alone in the room, I said, "When those men are murdered there'll be an investigation. Those women will be tracked down. There are too many people involved for me to be certain I've covered all of their tracks. So I shan't even try. My intent was to have their captors just release them. I see they cannot fend for themselves, but I darn't help because it could then become clear that I was the mastermind behind the murders. I've arranged to shelter them temporarily and can arrange transport but 'tis all I can do. Every person I so involve must die to ensure none will talk."

"Jean..."

"Yes. And Yusuf. I should probably kill the girl's at the club who saw me there, but they would have nothing of note to say except I was there, which could be explained seeing as I'm a man. But Jean and Yusuf stayed and participated. And while I'm certain they wouldn't have mentioned me, they *are* linked to me."

"Participated in what?"

"A party—an orgy on the floor of the bar before work started for the evening. Which is certainly odd enough to be remembered."

"It would probably be more suspicious if Jean and Yusuf were to die suddenly. You don't think they'd keep their mouths shut if questioned? I agree it's suspicious, but they could just say it's drugs or something if they had to say anything at all. Fucking is illegal here, but if they're home and questioned by police it shouldn't matter much."

"Maybe. I'll think on it."

Her expression hardened.

"You aren't who I thought you at all."

I laughed harshly.

"No. I'm not. But I'm not as cold as you imagine either. 'Tis true I could murder Jean and Yusuf without losing a wink of sleep, but 'tis because they're already dead inside. Ask her why my wife sent her here but do it privately least your fellow footmen take the law into their own hands. *She* is expendable. She was chosen to be expendable. My footmen are *not*. I won't risk them for these strangers either. I'm sorry for those women. I'm *infuriated* for them! But my fury could kill us all and I know it. So, if I must leave them to their fates, 'tis best done before I bring us to ours."

"Give me a few days at least."

"We have until the morning of twenty-sixth to act. After that 'tis out of my hands. They shall be freed at the least. What happens to them isn't my responsibility—was never my responsibility. Don't show yourself at that apartment or do aught that connects you. 'Tis imperative that my plan on that day be followed."

"So the club is our alibi?"

"I shan't answer. Speak of this to no one. And, Vicky, I need that Query Inc pin back."

"It's at my condo."

"Drop it at the office tomorrow."

I went back to my condo to pack up the gifts I'd bought for Julia. I was doubly glad now I hadn't told her anything of the plan. She'd be as furious as I was.

If I hadn't been trapped in the dark so long, I'd have been tempted to act despite the risk. But I *had* been trapped there. I knew just how precarious our lives really were. I'd not risk returning for these strangers. 'Twas infuriating to think the demon had planned for me to betray them, which leaving them uncaring to their fates would be. 'Twould be a sin the wrong thing done knowingly, but I also owed my footmen my protection and Julia. To do aught that would compromise her would be the evilest thing I could do. So, id do what I could for these poor women but only what could be done without bringing harm to those in my care.

The evilness of the men who had brought these women to this place and used them so foully confirmed my decision that none would be spared from this cleansing.

I laid out a sheet of paper and painstakingly drew the rune for fire.

I worked all night, tracing out the spell numerous times to making it as strong as I could, finishing ten new pages before it was time for breakfast.

I added the spells to the pile of them. They'd activate with just the merest touch of my anima. It wouldn't matter if Francois was able to get me the explosives or not. Everyone in that building would die.

Chapter 33

"Pip," Cassandriel said in surprise.

I kissed her cheek then shook Andre's hand, saying to her, "Perfect timing. I'd hoped to catch up to you."

I'd been waiting aboard Sandra's jet for hours to time my arrival perfectly with Andre's.

"'Tis good to see you both."

"Where have you been that you're so tan?"

"Dubai. I came back so as not to miss Valentine's Day with Julia—and I hoped to see you both."

Ryu stopped beside me, pulling a cart that held our bags.

"How'd you know I'd be here?" she asked laughingly.

"Drew told me. Ryu, this is Cassandriel, Sandra's daughter and my good friend, and this is Andre Ramirez. This is Martin Poole, or Ryu as we call him. He keeps everything running tickety boo."

Ryu shook both their hands, saying, "Pip has been just dying to get back to show you—"

"Let me tell her," I interjected as I held out my phone. "Look! Isn't she magnificent?"

Drew had found me the filly and she was a beauty. Pure white with a golden mane and brindle gray socks.

"Oh… she is!"

"And look!"

I showed her pictures of a litter of Turkish angora kittens.

"They arrive tomorrow. I vow, I can hardly wait! My Julia will be thrilled! I shall be thrilled! I adore cats and they're an absolute perfect match for the horse! Look at those beautiful golden eyes!"

Ryu said laughingly, "I think you bought them more for yourself, not her."

"Not so! Tell him, Cass."

"Jewels does like the white horses," she agreed.

"Besides," I said as I leaned to kiss her cheek, "'Twas my intent to gift you one. I think they would make beautiful kittens with your King. Can you stop by? Maybe even stay a few days? Julia would be thrilled to see you."

"Andre's only here for a few days, Pip…"

"As am I…."

I gave her my best pleading eyes.

Andre said, "I'd love to see your new babies."

I said to him, "'Tis more that I'd like Cass's opinion on the groom Julia has hired. I've no wish to upset her, but if you were to say he's unsuitable…"

"Is he?" she asked.

I could tell by the way her eyes crinkled that the idea of the horses being with an unsuitable groom worried her.

"I've no real idea. The stables appear to be running along smoothly, but Julia doesn't know enough to really *know*. Her new filly will need more training and care than the older horses. In truth, I lack experience training such a young beast. I was hoping I could ask you to stop by occasionally, perhaps come with friends to ride, and while there inspect the barns for me? 'Tis why I timed my flight to coincide with your arrival. 'Tisn't something I can ask in front of her."

I gave her my best charming smile as I added, "And I didn't think you could turn me down in person. It's quite selfish of me to take your holiday time, but she's such a darling little thing..."

Andre said, "You had her at new filly. The kitten was overkill. You're making me look bad."

"Not at all. I shall simply give the cat to you instead and you may then gift it to her."

I could see that she was still trying to think of a polite way of declining.

Ryu said, "If you don't mind, Pip, I'm going to leave you with Ollie and go see my girl. I've been promising to take her riding and maybe a romantic Valentine's Day ride through the woods there will be just the thing."

I realized I was gaping at him when Cassandriel giggled.

"By all means," I said.

"Nice to meet you. I hope I see you around the house," he said to them.

I was shocked—and hurt, which I knew was stupid, but the knowing didn't lessen the pain.

As soon as he was out of earshot, Cassandriel whispered, "He was nervous. Don't you like his girlfriend?"

"I'd no idea he had one."

"When do you go back?" she asked.

"In three days. Did your mother show you any pictures of my new project?"

Andre said, "No. But let's get out of here. You can tell us all about it tomorrow. We'll drive down and get a hotel."

"Don't be ridiculous. You'll stay with us. We have scads of room."

We walked out together.

Ollie was waiting in another rented limo.

"Can we drop you anywhere?" I asked.

"No thanks. I have my car."

She kissed my cheek.

"We'll see you tomorrow, Pip."

I waved as they walked away then got into my car.

Ollie said, "Your wife wants you to call her right away."

She answered on the first ring.

"I've got the animals through customs. Should I leave them at the airport or bring them home?"

"Home. And be careful, Jewels. She can see auras. She'll know if you lie."

"Oh... she isn't with you?"

"She's coming tomorrow. I tried but..."

"I better call Sandra."

"Did you know Ryu has a girlfriend?"

".... what? When did that happen? Who is she?"

"I have no idea."

"How do you not know her name?"

"She lives here. Should I ask him who she is?"

"Yes... no... I guess it's none of our business."

It somehow made me feel better that she was upset about it too.

I said, "Call me back and let me know what Sandra says. Ask her if I should drop by Honey's and have her call Cass."

"See you soon."

I said to Ollie, "Head to Oxford post haste."

"Should I stop for Ryu?"

"Where is he?"

"Don't know. He just said if you was alone I could pick him up."

I called Ryu.

"Where are you?"

"At the pickup for Delta."

"What... where's your friend?"

"There is no friend. I just thought if she thought it was romantic she might come along."

"Oh..." I was relieved, which made me feel foolish. I said hurriedly, not wanting to think on why I was so relieved. "Be careful with her. She can see auras. She can probably tell if you lie."

"What kinds of things see them?"

"We'll talk later." I covered the phone with my hand to say to Ollie, "Ryu's at the Delta pickup." I said into the phone, "We'll be there in a few minutes."

I hung up wondering if he were lying to me or if Cass had been being polite.

Chapter 34

Ryu followed me to Honey's dorm.

She looked very surprised to see us on her doorstep.

I said, "I have a small favor to ask."

"Lord Blackwood... come on in."

"Pip. I'm Pip to you and this is my friend Ryu. I think I might've ruined Andre's Valentine's Day gift to Cassandriel. I was just so excited..."

Ryu said, "He bought his wife kittens and gave one to Cass, which he thinks might have upstaged Andre... it's been bugging him."

I nodded agreement.

"I'm unsure how to fix it, but honestly I'm more worried that he might do something a bit *too* spontaneous that they'll both regret."

Ryu rolled his eyes at me.

"He thinks they might elope."

"Good grief," Honey said.

"Not elope, or at least I hope not... but maybe I've inspired him to give her a ring as to my mind that's the only thing that can trump a kitten."

She giggled, slapping her hands to her mouth and nodding.

Ryu said, "Or a horse."

I groaned. "'Twasn't my intent at all!"

"You didn't," Honey said with laughing horror.

Ryu nodded, grinning at her. "He did. A beautiful filly for his wife with a matching kitten."

"Oh no! And you told Cass in front of Andre? You are in deep shit! How can I help?"

"I was thinking, maybe if I gave one to you too?"

"I can't have a pet in the dorm."

"But you could ask her to keep it for you until you could send it home. That way he'd know I gave you one and maybe it wouldn't be so... awkward for him. I also have an ulterior motive."

I told her the same story of the groom that I'd told Cassandriel, ending with, "'Twas meant to be a bit of a bribe so that you'd bring her there..."

Ryu said, "And if Andre and Cass are planning anything, maybe we could stop them... Sandra would be livid, and Pip so doesn't need that."

"I'll call her right now."

I said, "You're a lifesaver. They're coming over tomorrow to see the horse and kittens. You should come too and pick one."

I handed her my phone with the picture of the kittens.

"Oh! They're adorable! I can really have one?"

"You could have two.... I'd buy you another entire litter if you smooth things over. If she says she can't keep it for you, I'd keep it there or have it dropped at your home."

She pulled out her phone and a minute later said, "Cass, I just talked to Pip and I'm so excited! He's giving me such a beautiful kitten. I think he's worried his wife will freak if he keeps them all, plus he's bribing me to check on the new horse. I was wondering if I could ask a favor though, could you keep it at your place or your mom's just until spring break? I can take it home then, but I really want to get to know it first." She listened for a minute then winked at me.

"Oh, I forgot. Tell Andre I say hey. Did you guys want to meet up with Rourke and me while he's here? We could ride down to Pip's place together? That'd be great. What's the plan for tonight?"

She listened, nodding then gave me a thumbs up.

"I'll see you in the morning. Thanks, Cass."

She said to me, "They're having dinner with her mom. She sounded pissed about it but excited about tomorrow. I don't think you have anything to worry about."

"Thank goodness."

Ryu said, "Why would she be pissed about dinner with Sandra?"

Honey smiled ruefully, saying, "I don't think she knew her mum was back. I'm betting she thought they'd have the place to themselves..."

"Oh..." He shrugged like it didn't matter.

I hoped she hadn't noticed my relief.

I said, "Bring riding clothes and an overnight bag. I'm hoping I can talk everyone into staying. My wife has been working way too hard—we both have. But she's been trying to organize the house and hasn't been able to get out much, and if you know Julia, you know she loves to go out. But a house party is the next best thing. And maybe you girls can convince her to join me in Dubai when I go back?"

Ryu squeezed my shoulder. "We won't be there much longer, man. We almost have things running without us. We'll be able to come home and just go check on things occasionally."

"What are you doing there?" Honey asked.

"Business. I'll show you tomorrow."

I kissed her hand.

To my surprise Ryu did as well, making her flush.

She said, "See you tomorrow and thanks, Pip."

"No, thank you. I'm in your debt."

We returned to the car.

I said to Ryu, "Don't trifle with her affections."

"Seriously? I barely said two words to her..."

"I know... I saw how she looked at you though. She's too young for you."

"I'm like two years older, tops!"

"Not in her world."

"You mean she's too good for me," he said angrily.

"I mean she doesn't need to be involved with this. She's Cassandriel's friend and we do nothing that would upset Cassandriel! Nothing! If your intentions were sincere..."

He laughed suddenly.

"I forget all the damned time who you really are!"

He took my hand, kissed it, then placed it on my knee and patted it. "I'll be a perfect gentleman. No trifling, I swear it. Besides, I'm not interested. I'm flattered you think she was..."

I'd no idea what to say. My heart thudded. The hand he kissed tingled. He'd seen me! It was terrifying and exhilarating.

Chapter 35

Ollie dropped me in front of the house.

Mrs. Roman opened the door as I mounted the steps.

"Lord Blackwood, how nice to see you home. Lady Blackwood is in the ballroom."

I said, "Have the new animals been settled?"

"My husband is with the filly as we speak. She's a darling. The kittens are in the kitchen."

"Very good. Did Lady Blackwood inform you to expect guests?"

"She did and has sent in menus already. I've ordered all of the rooms on the second floor to be freshened."

"Excellent."

I stepped past her then turned back to say, "Why haven't we a man on the door here?"

"Lady Blackwood has reassigned him. She asked me to choose another—is it urgent?"

"I suppose not. 'Tis just beneath your station to be answering doors. I'd prefer if you have one of the footmen do it until you decide who shall have the duty permanently."

Her eyes twinkled with mirth.

I said, "In the lady's absence from the house, 'tis you who should ensure all is done as it ought to be, and how will they respect you if they perceive that you are a servant of the same class as they? Nay, you give orders—you don't do."

"For the most part, they're a pretty respectful bunch."

"If anyone is less than instantly obedient to your requests, inform Mr. Poole at once."

"Yes, sir."

I set my coat and bag on the hall table.

"Have it brought to my room," I said pointedly when she reached for it. "I'll be with her ladyship."

"Yes, sir," she said, nodding and clasping her hands.

I winked at her, making her laugh and her shoulders relaxed. She nodded more firmly, removing her cell phone from her pocket. "I'll see to it at once."

I joined Julia in the ballroom where I found her talking to two women and a man, leaning over a table examining something upon it. A row of narrow tables had been laid the length of the room exactly where my mother had placed her buffet tables. These were much grander with beautiful carved legs and inlaid tops. They also possessed hidden outlets in clever posts that popped up when pressed. Two of which were being used to plug laptops into.

I paused as I passed to examine the pictures laid out in neat rows.

Julia hurried to join me, saying, "Darling, this is Ms. Vera Price and her associates. She'll be laying out the book for us."

She kissed my cheek, returning my embrace, grinning up at me as she continued, "We're just laying out chapters now. I've already gained the copyright on all of the photos I could locate. And, of course, we'll include photos of the artwork here and the home now."

She led me down two tables as she said, "Vera has already begun drawing the rooms and gardens based off of your notes."

Vera said, "The book is fascinating, Lord Blackwood. However did you find all of the details?"

Julia said, "A lot of the furnishings in the house are original and include makers marks, which can be traced. Luckily, Lou's grandfather kept a diary that stated why and when such things as the portraits were painted or the rooms redone. His great grandfather had kept a similar diary speaking of the doings in the neighborhood." She laughed lightly as she said, "It appears the writing bug skips a few generations before returning in full force. His great grandfather eight times removed left diaries and drawings."

I held up a drawing of the maze and garden path that led to the family cemetery as I remembered it from my youth.

"'Tis remarkably accurate..."

Julia gave me another quick hug.

She took the picture and laid it face down.

"I can handle all of this," she said firmly to me, then to Vera, "Lord Blackwood finds it distressing to view pictures of his family that he no longer recalls. Please don't include any when sending him the copy for approval."

"'Tis of no account," I said. "Someday soon I should visit that cemetery to pay my respects..."

Guilt assailed me that I hadn't gone to visit my family, but the thought of entering that graveyard made me break out in a cold sweat.

I returned to the first table that held old black and white photographs.

Julia leaned passed me to tap one that displayed the guest rooms in the west wing.

"The room with our ghost. Vera will have the sketches for that within the week?"

Vera nodded.

"Send them directly to Lord Blackwood. Pip, you can tell her what details need changing to keep it period appropriate. It should be portrayed as your research revealed the house was in the seventeen hundreds."

Vera said, "Do you know who the ghost was in life?"

I said, "Lady Violet Blackwood."

Julia inhaled sharply.

I squeezed her hand as I added, "'Tis good that she be remembered. She was a beautiful woman…"

"How did she die?" Vera asked.

"I know not. But 'tis indisputably her. Her portrait hangs in our dining room. Perhaps it could be used to draw some likenesses of her going about her normal affairs? To see her at her embroidery with her hair down in the early morning sun when she was oft sleepless and would creep into her sister's bedchamber and there sew quietly in her bed clothes so as not to wake her…"

"I wonder what they spoke of?" Vera mused.

"The usual things, one would suppose. Who would marry whom, where their papa had gone off to, when they would be presented at court… Violet was a woman who loved all of the womanly arts, writing, painting, sewing. She quite often drove her sister nearly mad with her prattle…or so she recalls it. I'm sure her sister adored her though else she'd have locked her bedchamber against those intrusions…"

Vera said, "We should include some photographs of her actual writing."

"Perhaps," I said. "If you can excuse my lady, 'tis long since I've seen her, and we have much to speak on."

Vera's assistant laughed, quickly stifling it,

Vera gave him a reproving glance as she said to me, "Of course."

She turned to Julia to say, "Just email me with the requested changes. The publisher is being remarkably flexible about the submission date, but if you want the book released for Christmas, we better get it wrapped up by September."

"I'll be in touch."

We escorted them to the door where I was happy to see a young man waiting. He had a faint red rind and wore what was obviously a borrowed suit but nodded politely enough as he held the door.

When our guests had left, I said to him, "Your name, sir?"

"John Mackay.

Julia said, "John is one of the parolees released into our care. He seems to be fitting in well here..."

"I appreciate the opportunity, ma'am."

I said, "Will you be keeping this position or is this temporary while Mrs. Roman finds permanent staff?"

"I've been offered the position as butler on a trial basis, sir. I hope it works out. I could really use the job and I like it here..."

"Then I hope it works out as well."

We shook hands and Julia and I headed into her office.

She stopped to take one of a matching set of vases that sat on a small table beside the door and placed it on another small table opposite the door.

Sound from outside the room became muted.

"There. We can talk freely."

I nodded my approval.

She grimaced ruefully at me.

"I didn't make it. I had Sandra do it. If you slide the vase out of the alignment, it'll deactivate it. I leave them on the same table though just in case a maid wants to clean and straightens them."

She stretched then sat in one of the wingback chairs by the desk.

She said, "John is one of the early release prisoners that I negotiated for. He murdered his wife's boyfriend. I'm certain it was self-defense. The bitch was trying to have him killed. Unfortunately the jury didn't believe him."

"And her? Are we doing anything about that?"

"He doesn't know that was her plan. I think he still has feelings for her despite the fact that she divorced him before it even went to trial and that during the trial it came out that she and the man John had murdered had been having an affair for months. He believed her when she said that she hadn't invited him into their home—he still believes it. I was tempted to make her confess to him, but it seems cruel..."

"You're certain 'twas her plan?"

"Yes."

"Something must be done."

"Must it?"

"To leave her free to do such again... nay. We cannot."

"Even if we make her confess, I doubt it would do anything at all since there's no proof. Any lawyer could probably get her off even if we made the prosecutor take the case."

"Knowing that people knew that she'd done it before would likely stop her from doing it again. 'Tis my thought that she confess it to him. We can arrange for Charles and Gifford to be present but unseen. Mayhap Gifford will know better if she can then be held accountable or him released from his servitude."

Julia nodded in agreement. "I'll handle it. I'd intended to make sure she knew how well he was doing that being the only thing I could think of that'd make her regret what she'd done, but that's even better."

"Make sure she doesn't attempt to cozen him into accepting her back!"

"I will."

"How many such men do we have here?"

"Six. Five of them are no problem. One I have to keep a tight hold on. He might run out of anima before I can legally let him leave the estate. I hate to send him back though when this is the first group and I know he's innocent of the crime that he was committed for. He's an ass but not a murderous one. I really wanted to show the parole board that the system is working."

"There are other ways to make a man listen. Send Ryu to speak with him."

She snorted with laughter.

I intended to have a chat with the man myself as I didn't like the idea of her using her own anima on the man and she lacked the skills to use another's without becoming drunk on it.

A hot flush heated my cheeks as I remembered my recent fiasco.

She hugged me again as she said, "God, I missed you guys! How's it going there? Can you return soon?"

"The marks will be in position next week for the final large fleecing. It should bring another twenty-four million in cash from each. I need at least one more week to ensure construction is going as it ought to. I'm unsure how often one of us will be needed to speed that up. All of the permits should be in order in another week or so.

"One of us will need to go there every five weeks or so to meet Sandra or Drew to replace the supplies at the tile factory and see the shipments dispatched. A four-day visit should allow enough time to check in on all of our projects there, assuming all is going according to plan that is."

"Good, then you can fly directly to Scotland when you finish there, and I'll meet you there. We're buying the brewery and the distillery. Sandra recommends we do it under a corporate name though so that when we eventually need to switch hosts, we can more easily regain ownership."

"I hadn't considered..."

"Don't worry about it, love. I'm setting up safe houses all over. Speaking of which, did you bring back any cash?"

"Three million euros, which is all that we could fit in our bags."

Her eyebrows rose and I snickered.

"'Twas simple. We've hidden some of our cash in Sandra's lair"—Julia pursed her lips at my choice of words— "but most is beneath the floor of the basement of the apartment house near the tile works. We'll have another such space put in under the new apartment complex and another easier to reach one in the new housing development we're building. You need to choose a mule for that. Paper money takes up a surprising amount of room and it's possible the authorities find it, so it needs to be someone who could believably have that sort of money but also someone above suspicion who would fit into that neighborhood."

"Why not keep it all in her lab?"

"I didn't think it wise to keep too much with her because I'm uncertain if she'd be willing to relinquish it."

"You really think she's a dragon?"

"'Tis likely she's descended from something similar. The gold *was* melted in place with no visible heat source, and she sees auras—or at least her daughter does, but 'tis likely she sees them as well. The gold bore claw marks, enormous ones... and you yourself told me her lair at her home had piles of trinkets and jewelry."

"But a dragon... can they be people too?"

"We know she's a powerful mage. She warned us quite pointedly that her daughter could lose her human form. Maybe 'tis a spell? To my mind it matters not except as a warning that we should be cautious with things that might tempt her, which we know by seeing her rooms that expensive trinkets do."

Julia said musingly, "Maybe that explains why she likes you so much? Don't dragons prefer virgin girls?"

A hot flush again scalded my cheeks.

I said, "That is a myth of unicorns. Unicorns and flying horses in other realms have no such fondness, or at least none I've seen written of. I think it a tale told here by man."

"Still..."

"She likes me because I remind her of her daughter. Drew told me himself he hopes that Cassandriel and I remain friends because we're alike in so many ways—ways that only someone who grew up believing themselves to be human and finding out it isn't so could understand."

"You are human—at least mostly..."

I kissed her brow then headed for the door. "I should like to shower and change to go riding."

"I'll join you. I haven't been in an age."

"What have you been doing for fun?"

"Who has time? I'm enjoying the work though, mostly, and soon I won't need to spend as much time on the accounts."

When we returned from our ride we found Charles, Mary—and Reginald awaiting us.

"Mum!" Julia said as she hastened to kiss her mother's cheek. "What a nice surprise!"

Charles said, "Reg told us of the new filly, and your mum insisted we come see it in person."

I was shocked that he knew of it.

Pansy growled low in her throat, stopping as soon as I lay my hand on her head.

Julia said, "Did he tell you Pip got me the most adorable kitten as well? Come see her."

Reginald looked puzzled or maybe annoyed.

I hoped it meant he hadn't heard of the cats, not that the detail mattered except to show he didn't know everything.

We all followed Julia into the kitchen.

"Can I get you anything?" our cook asked hurriedly, looking both worried and a bit put out to see us in his domain.

"Tea would be lovely and there'll be three more for dinner," Julia said.

She turned to her mother to say, "I insist you stay. In fact, I hope you'll stay the night?"

"She was counting on the invitation," Charles said as he squatted beside the large box to examine the kittens.

Pansy stuck her nose into the box and one of the kittens immediately tried to reach her.

Reginald said, "Why in the hell did you get so many?"

"We *like* cats," Julia said, rolling her eyes at him. "And they aren't all mine."

I squeezed her arm warningly. She glanced over her shoulder, shrugging a tiny bit, but I knew Reginald had caught it.

"Who for?" he asked me, his expression saying I'll find out one way or another so you might as well tell me.

"Friends," Julia said. "You can have one too, Mum, if you want."

I said, "If we have extra. I promised Honey she could have two."

"Honey?" Reginald said thoughtfully.

"Do we know her, dear?" Mary asked.

"Bruce Merck's daughter."

Mary said, "Oh, how lovely. I haven't seen her in an age. I didn't realize the two of you had remained close."

I said, "She's more a friend of a friend and the cat is a bribe."

"A bribe?" Charles asked laughingly.

"To come check on the horses while I'm away."

"Ahh."

Reginald's smile hardened. "I see... and who are the others for?"

Julia said to him, "Cass is a friend and the daughter of one of my biggest clients. So don't be an ass while she's here."

"Children," Mary said in the put-upon tone of a person who has often and futilely said the same thing.

"Have you chosen yours yet, Jewels?" I asked.

"I'd be happy with any of them."

I picked up the one that was trying most persistently to climb the box and kissed her nose. The others immediately began meowing and trying to climb out too.

"I shall call her Tamora, and she shall be queen of the household."

Julia kissed my cheek then the kitten's head before plucking another from the box.

"What should we call— "she, flipped the kitten over— "him?"

Reginald said, "Lear because you're crazy. You already have like ten cats."

"Four. The rest are barn cats and don't count. And four is hardly any in a house this size."

The cook said, "Did you want tea served here or the parlor?"

"Our sitting room, please," Julia said.

She led the way through the back entrance, and we all settled onto the yellow couches.

Pansy lay at my feet, keeping a watchful eye on Reginald who sat in one of the two new chairs that had been added to the room since my last visit home.

"The chairs are lovely," I said.

"This room is finally finished, I think," Mary said.

"We'll be wanting a cat tree by the doors and maybe a cat door put in. I was reading somewhere they make an invisible fence to keep your cat in the yard," Julia said as she served tea.

She turned to me winking then back to her mother.

I grinned back. Julia had a real knack with animal anima—or maybe she just didn't mind manipulating them. They never seemed to mind her doing it either. Our pets all loved her devotedly, which I wasn't certain was caused by manipulating their anima or the treats and affection she gave them.

She continued, "It'd be nice if they could go outside and enjoy the back garden."

Charles said worriedly, "Are you sure all of this expansion isn't too much?"

"We're fine, Dad. In fact, we're better than fine. Pip's idea has taken off. We have more orders than we can fill."

"Orders for what?" Reginald asked.

Mary said, "That's wonderful! I knew it would do well. There's a real need for high end tile—original pieces really set the tone of the room. I'm absolutely in love with the blue ones you picked, Pip. The bathroom will be just stunning!"

"It's a bit much for a barn though..." Charles said.

Julia rolled her eyes at him then kissed his cheek before sitting beside me.

"We get them at cost, Dad. It's cheaper than buying it here and it doesn't cost much to ship it if we wait until we're shipping another batch back."

Reginald said doubtfully, "You're making tile—yourself? Is that where you've been?"

Mary laughed dismissively.

"Goodness no. They purchased a tile factory." She frowned at Julia as she said, "You didn't invite your brother to the opening?"

"No. It didn't occur to me that he'd care about a tile store opening."

"And you'd be right."

Charles laughed, shaking his head apologetically at her as he said, "I thought the same, but I promised your mother that we'd attend the art show."

"Art?" Reginald asked.

I said, "One of the young men here has talent, and we think if given the chance, he'd do really well."

Julia said, "We'll be his patrons. Speaking of that, Mum, any word on a good studio space?"

"I looked over all four places that your agent showed me and the third looks the most promising to me. It *is* pricier than the others though, but I think the location justifies it."

"Fabulous. You'll be able to get it fixed up so we can open this spring?"

"I believe so."

"Leandro looks scary but he's a nice guy. You'll like him once you get past that initial impression."

Reginald gaped at her, and I thought him seriously alarmed when he said, "You're having our *mother* meet with one of your thugs? Are you crazy?"

"He's harmless."

I said, "'Tisn't the word I would choose, but Leandro has no reason to be anything except pleasant to Mary. He's quite excited about the opportunity. My man shall be watching him quite closely."

"Your man..."

I didn't answer him, instead turning to Mary to say, "We've already warned him that his appearance and manner need to be toned down, which he's assured us he can do for the showing in Dubai. Ryu will be watching him, and if we have any cause at all for concern, I'd assure he was never allowed unsupervised visits with you. But Julia is correct in saying his appearance is much more intimidating than he himself is. He's quite soft spoken and a bit shy. 'Tis my thought that he painted himself to hide that inner softness..."

"Good grief," Reginald muttered.

Charles said to him, "Then you should accompany your mother."

"I will—" his gaze at me was challenging— "assuming I'm invited, of course."

"Of course. I shall book you a room if you wish to attend."

Julia said, "I do hope you'll come, Mum. We plan to hold a big party with a raffle for charity."

"Will you be traveling overseas more often than for your charity work?"

"A bit. Maybe more in the future... we really haven't discussed it. Once we get our finances all in order, we'll probably travel more. We have plans to visit Scotland and look at properties there. We'd like a farm, something for the horses where we could ride and hold country outings."

"Another house?" Charles asked in the tone that said we were crazy.

I said, "Julia assures me our finances allow it. I leave all of that to her."

She said, "Do you remember my friend Frances Bolaños in New York?"

"The stockbroker?"

"Yes. She's been helping me out and I've been doing really well. Really really well. We invested all of that money that Mr. Fischer left Pip and have made some very good returns. So, in honor of Mr. Fischer who'd intended that money be used to rebuild an old estate, that's what we'll do with it. He really thought we were onto a good idea. So I'll take out that principal and put it into low-risk investments with the proceeds earmarked for this new property. I'm hoping we can get a loan and use the proceeds to pay that so we don't need to dip into the capitol, but either way, we can afford it."

Reginald listened with a puzzled expression.

I said, "The tile is in the green and our initial investment should be paid back within another year. If the art studio does half as well...."

"And don't forget the book," Julia added.

"What book?" Reginald asked.

"Pip has written his family history."

Reginald snorted derisively.

"I thought he couldn't *remember* his history?"

Julia rolled her eyes at him.

"There's plenty of papers in the attics here and news articles. He's been trying to relearn it." She turned from him to say to her mother, "Our ghost is Violet Blackwood and she's three hundred years old. The woman in the portrait in the dining room."

Reginald snorted but there was a hint of unease on his face that surprised me.

Charles said, "How did she die?"

"I have no idea. It's part of the mystery."

"Man, you think people will eat up any old tripe you serve…"

Mary reached from her chair to pat Reginald's knee.

"All of these old homes have a ghost or two. It's expected."

Julia grinned smugly at her brother. "Pip's already been paid a large advance on the book. We expect it to become a bestseller what with all the press it will get, which is another reason we want another home. This one will likely be inundated with tourists. So, we'll offer the tour and take ourselves off to Scotland or the apartment in Dubai to avoid the crowds."

"You have it all figured out, don't you? What would you have done if Fischer hadn't left you that pile?"

"Work hard. We could've done it without, but it did speed things along quite a bit. More than a bit actually. We were able to buy almost all of the original estate back. Our plan calls for opening enough businesses that the estate is once more a profitable business. We'll have the greenhouses, gardens, and the banquet hall, a riding stable that we hope can produce a winner or two, an organic farm, and a farm to table restaurant, and we're even thinking of tearing down the houses on the back road and rebuilding them as quaint cottages to let, which if the book is as successful as we think it will be should bring in people who hope to see Violet wandering the woods."

"*Hmm*," Charles said thoughtfully.

Julia said, "I think once the buildings are done and the town sees the sort of money that tourism can bring in, I'll be able to sell them on the idea of housing our boys to spruce up the town too. We'll make this a high-end vacation spot."

"You really do have it all figured out…. How long have you been planning this?" Reginald asked me.

"'Tis her plan."

His eyes widened then narrowed. A bead of sweat trickled down his cheek.

Julia said sweetly to him, "It's always been my plan, Reg."

Anima flared wildly from him.

I shook my head at her, saying to him, "She means it's all fallen on her since my accident. Luckily for me, she's a most accomplished woman since I no longer have a head for finance. I keep meaning to attempt to relearn it, but the book has kept me utterly distracted. And the tile works…I find the art of it pleasing. Mary, have you seen the newest offerings? 'Twas my thought that we might approach some local artists and perhaps let them design on commission? What think you?"

Julia went to retrieve our sales catalogs to show her mother.

The hair on my arms remained standing because Reginald remained coated in angry anima that his expression didn't reveal by a jot. He appeared perfectly pleasant and calm.

Pansy sensed his anger or mine own unease because she occasionally growled the barest sound and lay tensely against my legs. I kept my hand on her head, afraid she'd spring for his throat if he twitched—afraid that if he twitched it would be to spring for mine.

Julia returned and handed the catalog to her mother.

Reginald stood to peer over her shoulder; the anima slowly receding as he did so.

"Tile… I'd no idea you were into stuff like this."

"I think you don't know *me* at all."

We stared at each other until the cook returned to announce dinner was served.

Our guests had finally retired for the evening and I was glad of it. Dodging Reginald's questions was exhausting.

I slipped out the side door to take Pansy for her nightly stroll. She darted about sniffing the bushes while I followed, enjoying the solitude.

"Not that way, girl," I called as she approached the entrance to the hedge maze, which was just knee high now. There wasn't a chance of getting lost inside it, but I had no wish to visit that cemetery.

She returned to me then growled and darted away.

"Stay!"

She immediately halted, crouching and snarling at the shadow on the ballroom patio.

"Impressive," Reginald said. "You're just a font of surprises, aren't you? I think you really like that mutt..."

"Why are you here?"

"Is that any way to talk to a guest?"

"Why?"

"Did you come back because you were afraid *for* me or *of* me?"

I stared at him perplexed.

He stomped toward me, passing Pansy who snarled at his approach and kept growling, which was either very brave of him or very stupid. I couldn't decide which.

"At the casino," he said impatiently. "Don't tell me you forgot that too!"

"Nay. I remember."

"Well?"

"Well what?"

I crouched, snapping my fingers and hugged Pansy when she joined me.

She licked my cheek, but I could feel the rumble in her chest.

"My dog dislikes you."

"To hell with your damned dog! Why are you doing this? Just tell me and I won't bother you again. Did my sister... was this her plan all along? But why? It makes no sense! For the life of me, I can't figure out why you strung me along—unless it's her pulling the strings and you have no choice. I'd help you, Lou. You know I would!"

"Why?"

"I... love you."

"You don't know me. I barely know myself. You might have loved Lou although for the life of me I can't imagine why when he was a scoundrel—the most despicable man... but that man is dead."

"Did you come back for me?"

"I don't know what I intended as there wasn't anything I *could* do."

I stood to add, "It isn't *my* intent that you be harmed, nor hers. She loves you still."

"Shut the hell up about her! I'm talking about us here!"

"There is no us."

I brushed passed him and he grabbed my arm.

"Is it... do you need help?"

"Of course not."

His eyes were shiny in the dark. I thought his concern was sincere, but I didn't understand how that could be when Lou had been such a vile man.

I yanked away.

"This is bullshit! You know that right!" he called after me.

I stopped on the patio stairs to turn back and say, "I'm sorry that you ever met Lou. He was a bastard. Maybe try to see us as a stranger would... which I know is nigh impossible, but maybe we all need a fresh start? I wish I could help you but there isn't anything I can do."

"You could tell me the truth."

That made me laugh.

Anima swirled around him for a moment and then he laughed too.

"You're right, I wouldn't believe you."

He turned and headed to the maze.

I returned to the house.

Chapter 36

The next afternoon, Reginald joined me in the driveway to greet my guests, leaning close to whisper, "She isn't your normal type at all. Too old or too young—I guess it depends on how you look at it."

I ignored him, hurrying to open the door for Honey.

Cassandriel said laughingly, "Honey told me you bribed her. How come she gets two and I only get one?"

"Because 'tis getting you here that's the chore. I know once you *are* here, you won't be able to resist the stables."

Drew snickered saying, "He has you there, Cass."

I said, Everyone, this is my brother-in-law, Reginald Whitmore, this is Honey Merck, Lord Rourke Northrup, Andre Ramirez, Cassandriel Alder, and Drew Shangrün."

Reginald bowed over Honey's hand. "Enchanted."

Cassandriel said, "Kittens or horses first?" as she absently shook Reginald's hand.

Drew slung an arm around me, leaning close to mock whisper, "We've been trying to teach her manners but— "

She punched his arm then linked her arm in mine, hip checking him away.

"A promise is a promise."

"Kittens," Honey said. She linked her arm in my other one.

"Where's Jewels?"

"Seeing to lunch."

Reginald's gaze was a spot of warmth on my back.

I led them into the kitchen where Honey pulled me aside to whisper, "Can I give one of mine to Rourke?"

"Certainly."

She grinned, giving me a smacking kiss on the cheek then running to greet Julia who'd just entered.

Reginald stared sardonically.

I shrugged at him and joined the group by the box.

Drew took a pouch from his pocket and said, "I made these for my Valentine's Day gifts so we can tell whose is whose."

"Oh, it's beautiful," Honey said as she handed me one of the cat collars. "Dibs on purple."

She took the collar with the purple gems stones from Drew and handed the one with the green gem to Rourke.

"Gold for you, Jewels, and silver for you," Drew said as he handed them over. "Topaz for Cass. Topaz is a naturally healing gem."

It got them started talking about healing properties of crystal while they put the collars on the kittens.

Honey handed one of the kittens to Rourke.

"This one's yours. Happy Valentine's Day."

Drew said, "Let's go find yours and get their collars on. We'll meet you guys at the barn."

The intensity of Reginald's stare was practically burning a hole in my back when we left.

No one else seemed to notice. They continued chatting and jesting.

Drew and I went directly to my bedroom where I activated the rune of silence by the door by tracing the rune inscribed on the vase with my finger.

I was extremely proud of the spell because I'd written it myself.

He said, "Cassandriel's sure to try to wander off with him. I'd like to save us interrupting them for emergencies. Can you send one of your crew here after them?"

"Yes. They'll need a reason though…"

"Have someone go out and shoot and then have one of the others say they're looking for a poacher. She isn't stupid. She won't stay out in the woods if she thinks there's poachers out there. Add a few more grooms around the barns and tell them to mention they'll be there all night with one of the horses."

"'Twould be true. We have a mare about to foal."

"Perfect. Where does that leave?"

"The house itself but I think it would be simple to convince Honey and Rourke to stay up looking for our ghost."

"Will your security notice if they slip out of the house?"

"Yes. There are motion detectors on the lower floors of the main hall, and I can have the doors all watched. I shall set Pansy on her door. Julia had a collar made with a small camera. It often reveals nothing but floor, but I'd know if she moves, and it transmits sounds. Pansy can be told to follow. She does that often."

"You should get some hall cameras up here to record the motion they see at night."

"'Tis on our to-do list. The halls on the main floor are monitored but just in the main section unless Julia had more done that she didn't tell me of, which is possible.

"I brought cameras that I can set up. Just keep everyone out, including the help for an hour."

"I shall go instruct the help."

I exited my room and found Reginald right outside my door.

I said, "Shall we visit the stable?"

"Where's your friend? And speaking of that, where's your other boyfriend?"

I walked away.

He hesitated and then followed.

I said, "Ryu isn't my boyfriend in the way you mean it. He went to visit his family, but I expect him back any time now."

"And the new guy?"

"Drew is a friend, nothing more. This obsession of yours…. 'Tis getting ridiculous."

"Oh please, you're going to tell me she's just a friend too?"

"What… you imagine I fornicate with all of them?"

His face turned red. I was surprised no anima manifested.

"Fornicate?" he said, bursting into laughter. "That's a good one."

Still laughing he jogged away down the front stairs.

I called Ryu. "Are you on the estate?"

"Where else would I be?"

With your mystery girlfriend, I thought but didn't say. *Cassandriel had said he was nervous, not that he'd lied, although she might have chosen that word to be diplomatic, not that it matters,* I told myself.

I said, "Visiting your family, which is where I said you were."

"I'm in the barns. She just got here."

"Cassandriel?"

"Who else?"

I told him what Drew had recommended we do and added, "Tell the boys to keep an eye on them but to be subtle about it. Put all of the footmen on duty watching the house."

"They'll be chill. Hey, Jewels be careful!" he yelled in an aside. "I better go stop her from getting trampled."

He disconnected and I picked up my pace.

When I arrived, Cassandriel was in the paddock with Julia and the new horse that was sidling nervously, kicking her front and back feet sporadically.

Everyone was smiling except Ryu who was staring at Julia.

He loves her.

My heart sunk.

She turned and saw me and her eyes lit.

Ryu stared between us with a pensive gaze, caught me staring at him, and shrugged.

I shrugged back, which made him smile.

Julia said, "She's beautiful. I love her already!" drawing our attention back to her.

"She's a real beauty," Cassandriel agreed.

I reached the rail and Ryu shook his head at me, looking worried again.

Maybe he loves me too, I thought as he ran around the paddock to grab my arm.

"Should they be doing that?" he whispered as he pulled me a step away. "Don't go in too."

He raised his voice to say, "Jewels, come out of there!"

Julia didn't even glance at him.

"*Shh*, who's a beautiful girl?" Cassandriel said.

She continued to talk softly and within moments the horse had calmed enough she was able to slip a halter on her.

She and Julia led her around the paddock, and in no time the horse was accepting ear and neck rubs and was looking for more, nickering in the most endearing way at them.

"What will you call her?" Honey asked.

"I have no idea..." Julia said laughingly.

Everyone began offering suggestions.

Ryu jumped the paddock fence to join them, whispering something to Julia that made her nod and step away.

They both climbed back over the fence and joined me.

Ryu said, "I can see her now on a moonlight night. The ghost in the woods... you should call her Casper."

Reginald said, "Or maybe Viola. What do you think, Pip? It'll tie in with your ghost theme nicely."

His tone had been slightly mocking, *which could've been for the gift or the ghost or any number of reasons*, I thought sourly.

I smiled as if I hadn't noticed the tone, saying, "'Tis a beautiful name."

"Viola," Julia said musingly then softly to me, "A tribute to the beautiful Violet. I like it. What do you think?"

I kissed her hand and her eyes clouded. Her smile was forced when she turned away.

"Pip?" Ryu whispered and I realized I was crying.

"'Tis nothing. I'm just happy to have pleased my Julia. What think you, Cass? Will she be well here?"

"This is a great paddock, Pip. I'd like to go take a look at the feed rooms and the stalls in the smaller barn."

We all trooped after her.

I found myself walking with Andre and Reginald and surprised myself by having a pleasant conversation about the new plantings and future gardens, which even now men were working to install around the barns.

Honey and Rourke joined us as Julia showed Drew and Cassandriel the smaller feed and tack rooms and they discussed some minor changes with the grooms.

I remained pleasantly surprised by how charming Reginald was being.

Julia kept casting us hopeful glances that were heartbreaking.

She still loves him.

Ryu caught my eye, and I knew by his worried eyes he was thinking it too.

I said to Reginald, "I hope you'll come on the ride with us. We have two very nice horses perfect for beginners."

"You'd like me to come?" he asked slowly enough that Andre gazed at him in perplexity.

"If you'd like to."

"...sure, I guess. I've never really ridden before."

Honey took his arm. "Come with me. I'll get you all settled. Rourke, can you help Cass with Viola? She'll want to walk her around the paddock."

"Sure," Rourke said in obvious relief.

The three of us headed back to the bigger barn. I saddled Damocles and Julia's mare while Honey showed the rest of the stock to Reginald.

I said, "Thanatos and Pepper are on loan from Cassandriel. He's big, but he's a softie,"

Honey said, "All of her horses are sweet, except maybe Madori, but even he's settling down."

Ryu joined us while Honey was helping Reginald mount.

Ryu said, "I told Andre he could use my horse. I'm going to sit this one out. Leon heard poachers out back last night. We're going to go check it."

I said, "Maybe we should put another patrol on the houses out back?"

"Couldn't hurt. I'll stop and speak with Asa."

"Ask him to have one of the boys do a walkthrough of the empty houses every day. Speaking of which, has your mother set a date to move in?"

"Maybe we can drop by before we go back and iron out the details?"

"Of course."

He left and Honey said, "Does he work for you?"

"Yes and no. He's more of a partner."

"Have you known him long?" Reginald asked.

"I suppose not. It feels like forever though...mayhap because I don't remember a time here before I knew him..."

Honey said, "You're handling that better than I would. Although maybe forgetting my awkward teen years wouldn't be so bad…"

"I can't imagine you were ever awkward," Reginald said. "Now, how do I get this beast to move?"

I took the reins and positioned his hands then led the horse by the halter in a slow circle while describing what to do.

Honey trailed us leading Damocles, offering advice and encouragement.

"Take Julia's mare and we'll go for a short ride," I said to her.

We mounted and set off.

I said to Reginald, "We won't go far. Your legs will really feel it your first few rides. The best cure for the soreness is another short ride. Do that for a week and they won't hurt at all—at least not until you try the faster paces, but the same regiment will soon have them right."

"When do you return to—Dubai, was it?"

"In a few days. You're welcome to visit the estate here to ride whenever you like, whether we're in residence or not."

"Do you ride there?"

"If we have time, we rent horses."

Honey said, "I can't imagine they have many nice trails there."

"The desert is beautiful at the right time of day and the beaches, of course. We mostly stay in the rings though."

We began talking of the events that she and Cassandriel attended.

When we returned from our ride, Julia, Cassandriel, and Rourke were still with Viola. Andre and Drew had gotten mounted and were jumping in the outdoor ring.

We spent the rest of the afternoon there.

In our room while dressing for dinner, Julia said, "Reg seemed normal…pleasant even. I really had a good day. You think he's… better?"

I thought Reginald was acting or maybe he'd been legitimately happy, not for our company, but that he'd inserted himself so firmly in our party. Two of our footmen had reported to Ryu that Reginald had been looking up our guests on his phone.

Saying that would hurt her though, so I said, "'Tis a mystery to me."

I picked up Lear to kiss his nose then set him on the floor. His silver bell chimed softly, which reminded me to tell her of the security changes that Drew recommended.

"I'll call Asa," she said when I finished.

I kissed her cheek and left her to dress, taking Tamora downstairs with me.

Chapter 37

During dinner, Drew, Ryu, Julia, and I continually steered the conversation to our ghost.

Mary obliged by telling tales of moved furniture, fluttering papers, and an eerie sensation while working on the ballroom wing, which was where we planned to claim Violet was haunting the house.

Charles said, "You seem happy enough to work there though."

"I find it fascinating—the idea of a ghost, I mean, not the job although that's fascinating as well. I really am so pleased to be invited to lend my talents to this project."

Charles snorted.

Reginald and Julia laughed, exchanging what to all appearances were real smiles.

She said, "I couldn't have done it without you, Mum. You've been stellar."

Honey said, "We should camp out in that hallway tonight. Maybe we'll see her."

Cassandriel gave Andre an anxious glance, which he missed because he was looking at Honey.

I said, "We might as well or we'll all be up all night checking the halls at every odd noise, and we get lots of them what with construction not being finished and the cats."

Mary said laughingly, "It can be breezy in that wing. A good portion of the windows still need replacing and we have some plastic covered holes still. Bring heavy blankets."

"You're not joining us?" Julia asked.

"Your father and I are headed home after dinner."

Julia said, "You'll stay, won't you, Reg? I can drive you back or you can get a ride with one of the help."

He looked pleased, nodding his agreement as Drew said, "Do any of the help live in?"

"Ten of our tenants live in the east wing and the butler has rooms. Our footman have rooms in the house for when they're on duty and their own homes for when they're not. Cook lives on the estate, and the Roman's, of course. The rest are in the houses on the west road. Most of the housing on the east road is empty or has temporary renters. We've had some poachers recently, so we set guards on patrol."

"Where do you live, Ryu?" Reginald asked.

"It depends. I have rooms here, but I stay wherever I'm needed."

"You have no apartment or anything of your own?"

"I'm so busy that I haven't had time to look..."

I said, "He has a house that he hopes his mother will stay in..."

Ryu rolled his eyes at me, and I instantly felt stupid for chiming in.

Reginald smirked at me as he asked Ryu, "What is it you do exactly."

"Everything," Julia and I said at the same time, which made everyone except Reginald laugh.

Ryu said, "I mostly check up on the tenants and I accompany Pip although he's getting so he doesn't need me."

Julia said, "Pip is getting better with dealing with his condition, but I'm not comfortable with him traveling alone. I know it's a very slim chance that he'll have any further issues but... anyway, you're indispensable, Ryu. It was his idea, Mum, for the art gallery. He's a genius when it comes to investment ideas."

I said, "Our tenants relate to him better—or maybe just like him more, and I'm happier if he's around to accompany Julia."

Andre said, "I'll admit I was skeptical when you told us you were going to be working with early release paroles for such violent crimes, but they seem like decent guys."

"No offense or anything, Jewels, but I think you're crazy," Honey said.

"What if one snaps?" Rourke added.

Julia shrugged. "That could happen anywhere at any time. Who really knows what the people they live near are capable of? Besides, all of the parolees I have here are innocent of murder."

That began a debate of what constituted murder until we left the table to prepare for our campout in the west wing.

I stepped into Julia's office to call Mrs. Roman.

"I'm sorry to disturb you so late but could you please stop by Cassandriel's room and make sure she has enough blankets? We've decided to ghost hunt this evening, so perhaps Asa could bring some air mattresses from the pool or even some horse pads for the guests."

"How fun. I'll see to everything. Will Charles and Mary be joining you?"

"No."

"Then perhaps hot chocolate in lieu of tea? I'll drop off snacks, popcorn and the like, say at eleven-ish?"

"That would be wonderful. Include a few sandwiches and some fruit. I'll bring a carafe of coffee now and whatever pastry we have handy. Have one of the maids or John wait in the kitchen in case we need anything late tonight. And send someone around with some torches and a few candles."

"I'll have all arranged within the hour."

"Stop in and check Cassandriel first and again in an hour or so if she isn't in the west wing."

"Yes sir."

I stepped from the room, smack into Reginald.

"Excuse me," I said by reflex.

"Do you need a hand bringing bedding to the hall? Julia told everyone to bring their pillows..."

"I... that would be lovely...err, nice."

His eyes were laughing. I wasn't sure what had amused him.

He said, "Were you arranging a little ghostly surprise?"

"It hadn't occurred to me. Should I?"

"You're really asking me?"

I heaved an exasperated sigh without thought.

To my surprise he laughed instead of becoming annoyed.

"You're right. That was dumb. You're obviously asking me...but why? Why invite me at all?"

I didn't.

I was saved from a reply by Andre calling from the head of the stairs, "Hey, Pip, Ryu says we should take a few of the old mattresses from the closed-up rooms, but Cass really hates mice... are they mouse free?"

Reginald and I joined him.

I said, "I couldn't swear they are... I'd risk it for myself. I've sent Asa for some of the pool air mattresses that she can use.

Drew joined us as we were pulling another of the old feather mattresses into the hall.

Mrs. Roman had already made up two of them that we'd lugged out.

The girls had brought all of the kittens and were helping Asa blow up a stack of air mattresses.

John arrived with a bag full of new flashlights and a box of batteries.

Julia said, "I think that's enough, Pip. Let's show them the book and let Mrs. Roman finish."

She handed me Tamora and scooped up Lear.

Everyone else followed us, taking the rest of the kittens too.

Honey stopped in the entrance of the ballroom to say, "Jewels! I love what you did here! This is an amazing room! It'd be perfect for a wedding!" Her cheeks flushed and she hastily said, "When will you have a party?"

"We're planning the first ball for the fall. It'll be a costume ball with a Shakespearean theme."

"Tragedy and farce, how apt," Reginald murmured.

"Man...that's ages away," Honey said in disappointment.

I said, "We hope the guest rooms will be done or at least some of them... and the gardens. 'Twill be lovely to stroll there in the moonlight."

Cassandriel said, "They're already looking much better, no offense, Pip."

"None taken. Julia does a remarkable job of running the estate."

Rourke held up one of the drawings. "Is this what it looked like back in the day? Imagine having to take a horse everywhere you went?"

Reginald joined him.

Drew said, "It wasn't so long ago..."

"I wouldn't mind it," Cassandriel said.

Andre gave her a quick hug, grinning down at her. "You'd hate it because ladies weren't allowed to go anywhere or ride much."

"Yeah, that would've sucked," Honey said.

Julia said, "And they weren't allowed to ride astride."

I said, "They did though when no one was around..."

She shot me a laughing glance.

I continued, "'Twas a sedentary life then. Most people never went very far at all. There were no libraries unless you owned the books yourself and women weren't allowed to read much of anything anyway..."

"No libraries!" Cassandriel exclaimed in mock horror, feigning a swoon. "How could they stand it!"

She, Honey, and Rourke began dramatically overacting how they imagined a woman reading would've been treated, which except for the overacting was true enough to flush me with remembered anger.

I joined Drew who was examining the drawings of the old gardens.

"Will you rebuild them?" he asked.

"Some. We'll make improvements too, adding lights, fountains, and cobbled paths. 'Tis a shame the prior lords let it reach this stage of neglect. I wonder how they lost their fortunes..."

Drew said musingly, "It does seem odd. Have you looked into your father's finances at all?"

"I don't believe so. Have we, Jewels?"

"No. I'd no wish to upset you... I suppose we should though because it *is* odd."

She looked really worried, likely as worried as I was. It hadn't occurred to me to wonder why Lou's father hadn't used his power to keep up the house.

I said to Reginald, "Was my father here much?"

"I've no idea..."

Julia said, "I'll see what I can find out. The curate likely knows who was about, and maybe the old housekeeper."

"Did he have any particular friends?" I asked Reginald.

"Not that I recall you mentioning."

Drew said, "We're down a cat. I think it's Rourke's."

Everyone immediately began calling for it.

A few minutes later, Drew said, "Here she is, the scamp."

He handed her to Rourke.

"I probably shouldn't take her. My mom will freak…"

"Tilly likes them," Honey said.

"Outside…"

"She'll like this one," Julia said, not quite winking at me.

I said, "If 'tis a problem, she can live here until you've a place of your own to keep her."

"I'd keep her for you at my parents' house," Honey offered.

He petted the cat, not looking at Honey as he said, "We should get our own place, assuming, that is, Jewels was serious about the job offer."

Julia said, "Very serious. I haven't the faintest idea how to organize a corporation. Not that it'll be a big one, but someone has to run it…"

"What job offer?" Honey asked.

"As manager for their boutique and art gallery in London."

Julia said, "Black Whit will be a mix of projects from housing developments to coffee shops."

Honey hugged him excitedly, grinning over his shoulder at Julia.

"Why didn't you say anything?"

She released him to hug Julia.

"If you're looking for buyers…"

"We are actually. I'll email you the details."

"We could get a small flat right in London," Rourke said to Honey.

"I love you so much! This is just what you wanted!" she stepped back to gaze worriedly at him. "You really mean it? You're willing to leave that house?"

"Yes."

"I'm in! We need champagne to celebrate!"

"Then I shall call for some," I said.

I stepped away to call and order it.

Julia joined me while the others crowded around the table, talking about Rourke's job now.

I whispered, "You didn't nudge him to leave, did you?"

"No. I was tempted to but... it's a good job for him *and* us. Sandra wants Tilly kept friendly, and I agree it makes good sense. He's qualified to run Black Whit Corp—in theory, anyway. He can't really mess it up if we're keeping an eye on it and sending clients there."

"Problems?" Reginald asked as he joined us.

Julia linked her arm in his, grinning up at him, and it struck me how much weight he'd lost in the last few months. He'd aged, no longer looking soft but almost gaunt.

I worried over that until we returned upstairs.

Mrs. Roman had supplied coffee, donuts, and homemade cookies.

I grabbed a plate and sat beside Reginald.

"Do you do this often?" he asked.

"Ghost hunt or eat cookies before bed?"

"Both."

Julia said, "Chocolate milk with vanilla wafers is his favorite treat. The ghost hunting is new though."

"You never wanted to come look yourself?" Honey asked.

Reginald was staring at me in perplexity.

"You hate milk," he whispered.

"Lou hated milk. I don't. Try one of these cookies. They're divine."

He took a chocolate chip, staring at it like he'd never seen such a thing before.

"You eat cookies..."

I shrugged at him and offered the plate to Honey who grimaced and passed it to Cassandriel who took two.

Honey sighed wistfully, saying, "They look amazing, but I don't dare, or I won't fit into my jeans."

Ryu entered the hall followed by Pansy.

He carried two bottles of champagne and a stack of plastic cups.

"What are we celebrating?" he asked as he popped the cork.

"My new job," Rourke said.

Honey joined Ryu and helped him hand out glasses.

"To Rourke's new job!"

We all toasted him.

Honey said, "Jewels, you should combine the two bedrooms at the top of the stairs. The ones behind the lounges and put in a big fireplace and some bean bags or something, and people could rent it to tell ghost stories around while they wait for the ghost.

"Renting... no, but it'd be fun for private parties."

Cassandriel said, "Kill the lights, Pip. We can use the candles as our fireplace. Who knows a good ghost story?"

"I do," Reginald said. "I didn't know the ghost here had a name though... it doesn't feel like a woman either."

"You've seen her?" Honey asked eagerly.

"I saw something..."

"Here?" Rourke asked doubtfully.

"No. We were on the third floor. Lou and I, but I guess he doesn't remember it... maybe I shouldn't..."

His gaze at me was speculative and a bit worried with no hint of his usual mockery.

"You have to now," Julia said tartly.

I took her hand, finding it as sweaty as mine.

Ryu crouched in front of us, offering more champagne.

We both declined and he set the bottle by the wall then sat beside Julia, leaning over her to pet Pansy quickly.

She turned away from him to lay her cheek on my shoulder. Her body lay tensely against me. I cuddled her closer, it being the only comfort I had to offer.

Reginald said, "We were fourteen or so and had come here—well snuck in might be a better description. We hadn't wanted to go home, so we hadn't told our parents the school was closed for a voting holiday. So we snuck back here. There wasn't any staff or anything and I have no idea where your father was. We were just messing about like kids do, going through the place—even your dad's rooms."

His look at me was a bit challenging.

I smiled back blandly.

He continued, "When it got dark, we stole a bottle of wine and began daring each other just stupid things like going into the attic alone or spending ten minutes in one of the dark rooms—you know how kids are.

"Well, anyway, the third floor of the entire house had always been off limits to you, so of course that's the floor we picked to explore in the dark. This wing was really dangerous what with the holes in the floors and stuff, so we were mostly in the other one and the main floor. We'd been trying to scare each other, making noises, telling scary stories, and it was working. The lights didn't work at all on the third floor and half the windows were boarded over. We were both scared to cross that dark hall—you're sure you don't remember any of this?"

"I'm certain I do not. I suspect I was cowardly though and made you go first."

He laughed, darkly amused, nodding agreement.

"You boasted that you'd done it plenty of times, which even then I hadn't believed, but I wasn't going to lose face. So I went into the room to the right at the top of the stairs and spent the first few minutes looking around in a panic. It was really dark, but my eyes gradually adjusted and I saw there was a door to the next room, and I thought to myself that I could scare the crap out of you if I left through that door and snuck out and behind you."

They all laughed.

He wiped his brow.

He continued, "So I snuck into the next room and that room had a door too. It was locked but it was an old lock, and I was able to jiggle it loose with a pen knife I always carried."

He dug into his pocket and held up an old silver pen knife barely as big as a pair of nail clippers.

"This knife."

He caressed it with his thumb then returned it to his pocket.

"That next room was completely empty except for a table shrouded with a sheet. I, of course, was curious, so I pull the sheet away and as I'm doing it, I hear scratching noises behind me that I thought was you, but when I spun around, I saw red eyes in the corner of the room.

"I screamed like a baby and ran for the door. The next thing I knew, you were leaning over me slapping my cheek."

"You fainted?" Honey asked in a tone that said she didn't know if she should be appalled or amused.

"I have no idea. My shirt was ripped, my arm, chest, and little knife was bloody, and Lou—Pip—told me I'd been screaming for a few minutes before he could get the door open."

He forced a laugh.

"We, of course we're terrified and ran down to the kitchen where we stayed until it was light. Then, armed with kitchen knives, we went back upstairs."

"Did you find anything?" Andre asked.

"Yeah, Lou must've snuck back up while I was sleeping in the kitchen, although you denied that, of course, but written in what we thought was my blood was the word mine and scratched into the floor was the word leave."

They all gasped and laughed.

He forced another laugh and continued, "I was all for leaving post haste, but you wouldn't hear of it."

His gaze at me was his usual mocking one as he added, "You were terrified your dad would see the damage. So we cleaned it up and sanded the marks from the floor then tried to make a stain to match it with tea and coffee grounds. We made a mess and finally gave up and just put a rug over it. We spent the next night in the barn..."

Drew said, "What was on the table?"

"Books."

Reginald turned to me, "You really don't remember that?"

"No. It must've been terrifying."

I was terrified. It had happened in the room right next to mine.

"Was it rats or something?" Rourke asked.

Reginald shrugged.

Julia said, "Did his dad ever find out?"

"Of course. I swear that man had eyes in the back of his head..."

Pansy growled low in her throat, rising slowly and stalking away toward the stairs.

"Speaking of rats," Honey said nervously.

"Pansy, come here, girl," Julia said.

"Your story scared the dog," Drew said, and they all laughed again.

The floor at the opposite end of the hall creaked and we all stilled to listen.

Very faintly came the sound of wings.

The hair on my arms rose.

"We have lights," I said loudly.

"Probably a bat," Julia said as she stood to shine her flashlight down the hall.

Honey and Cassandriel shrieked when two pinpricks of red appeared at the window at the end of the corridor.

The sound of bats intensified. Dark shadows slid up the ceiling, obscuring the small red glow. It happened quickly, hopefully quickly enough that they thought it a natural shadow.

"Too much?" I tried to say as if I were perfectly calm and amused at them.

Cassandriel smacked my arm. "Jesus, Pip! You nearly gave me a heart attack!"

Honey broke into giggles. "*Nah*, it was great... you did rig that right?"

"Of course."

I grasped Reginald's hand and squeezed.

His hand was sweaty and his breathing fast.

I said, "Our effects are limited. 'Twas just chance they played so well to his story. There will be more in a moment..."

I carefully didn't look at Drew.

Julia said, "I forgot about that... I need a bathroom break. Who's with me?"

Both of the girls, and Rourke and Andre accompanied her.

I said to Ryu, "Call and tell the boys no branches against the windows. It seems Reginald's tale was scary enough on its own."

"Will do, boss. Excuse me a minute."

Reginald said, "You really rigged that? How?" Without waiting for my answer, he grasped one of the flashlights and headed down the hall.

"So..." Drew said thoughtfully.

"We'd no idea..."

He leaned closer to whisper, "It'll be angry over being driven out."

"Can we drive it out?"

"Just keep the lights on."

"Is it Blackwood...or Lou?"

Before Drew could answer, Reginald called, "There's no machines here or anything but I did find this."

He returned carrying a dead rat by its tail. His tone had been normal, but his eyes were too wide and locked on the rat.

"Pansy's rat," I said in distaste.

386

"How'd you do the glowing eyes?"

"Outside the window at the end of the hall. The bat might've been real... the kid holding the eyes probably spooked it. Maybe it was eating that rat?"

"Do bats eat rats?" he asked doubtfully as he dropped it onto the empty cookie tray.

"I've no idea."

"They probably do."

He wanted to believe that.

I rose to grab his arm, thrusting my anima on him, saying firmly, "It was just a bat and a rat. We're all having a good time. There's nothing at all to worry about."

"We *are* having a good time, aren't we?" he said, sounding puzzled but hopeful.

I leaned closer, putting as much of myself as I knew how into my anima that I was pushing onto him, saying, "We're having a really nice visit. It's fun to tell tall tales like this. No one is really scared. We all know there's nothing to hurt us here."

His body relaxed and he grimaced at the rat normally.

Drew said, "I'll take it. Don't tell the girls. It'd freak them out."

"Bring back popcorn," I said.

He nodded an acknowledgement.

Ryu returned. His eyes were almost as big as Reginald's had been.

He said, "I've called off the rest of the effects—if the dummies got the message passed in time."

I said, "They worked quite well though, so maybe we need a few more of the red eyes light kits? And don't forget to remind the night guards of the automatic lighting. We don't want the lights going off and startling a guest. Maybe it would be best to leave it on?"

He nodded, taking out his phone again.

While he was texting, Pansy again growled low in her throat, looking toward a closed door of one the rooms on the left.

I said loudly, "Rats, I suppose. We could turn the lights on there too to keep them away. I hate to ruin our evening though by running around flipping all the lights on."

Ryu said, "It's not worth the effort for this one night. This wing won't be used often. We can set some traps the night before a ball and the rats can have it the rest of the time."

"Not if they're going to be scratching up the furniture."

Pansy laid her head on her paws.

Her ears were still pricked and her eyes watchful.

The kittens woke and began wrestling.

On the pretext of playing with them, I drew a circle on the wall behind the beds with my flashlight, focusing my will and chanting the spell of holding to myself.

The effort to shift my anima into the spell at this distance left me feeling a bit dizzy.

I wished I was more accomplished. It was a large surface to cover. My spell wouldn't hold long if pressed.

But it couldn't know that. Maybe it would be enough to discourage it.

I was hoping the others had had enough and would want to leave, but when they returned Cassandriel said happily, "Honey was telling us about a ghost her mom had seen. It had red eyes too and long black hair. Tell them, Honey."

We settled back to the beds around our candle campfire as Honey told her story.

I thought Irene might've actually seen a shadow seethe as well.

Drew returned with popcorn while Rourke was telling a tale of a ghost on the campus.

"Who wants to play truth or dare?" Honey asked.

Uh oh, I thought.

Julia said firmly, "Not me. I'm not going into the attic alone."

"Me either," I said, which made Honey and Cassandriel laugh.

Ryu handed out cups of tea and began gathering the dirty dishes.

I stood to help him while Drew began telling a story.

We brought the dirty cups and plates down to the kitchen where we found Smalls and John having coffee.

John jumped up when we entered to take the plates from me.

"I've got the red lights you wanted, sir."

Ryu said, "Bring one of them up in a few minutes and give it to Lady Julia."

Smalls said, "The boys are in place—what are we doing?"

Ryu shoved him toward the door.

"Following directions! Just keep the outer walls lit until I tell you different!" He turned to John and said, "The lights are on everywhere else?"

"Everywhere except the west wing."

"All the closets?"

"*Um*...I'm not sure."

"Go check. Call everyone in the east wing in to help and if the closet doesn't have a light, prop the door open or leave a torch lit in it. You have forty minutes. I want everyone outside with flashlights by two."

"Yes, sir."

They both ran from the room and Ryu handed me one of the bottles of binding powder, the spelled napkins, and our silver daggers as he said "Drew, dosed the tea. They'll be asleep in a few minutes. I can't believe there's a fucking vampire in the house!"

I stuffed the items into my pockets.

He began jogging back to the west wing.

I followed saying, "Blackwood must have been letting it live here, but why?"

"Does it matter?"

"I suppose not… but why didn't it approach Julia or me? Why hide here and not just move on? And why show itself now?"

"Drew said he can place a holding spell around the beds along with a rune of silence, but he doesn't dare make it too strong in case they wake and need the bathroom or something. I had no idea he was a mage. Did you?"

I nodded and he pulled me to a stop to whisper, "Are you sure he isn't doing this somehow?"

"Yes."

"Are we really going to try to kill it?"

"I'd rather talk to it."

He began taking the stairs two at a time, saying over his shoulder, "You're crazy, you know that right?"

Chapter 38

Julia held a finger to her lips as Ryu and I approached.

Drew was describing a trip he'd taken where he'd encountered a village of people, none of whom spoke English but who'd managed to make it clear they thought him a ghost.

I stepped carefully around the beds to kneel beside Julia.

Ryu whispered, "I'm going to make the nightly rounds. Good night, everyone."

"Night," Andre whispered back.

I though Honey and Cassandriel were already asleep. I wasn't sure about Reginald.

I whispered to Pansy but giving Julia a pointed look as I said, "You stay here," pointing at Julia's feet, using my anima on the dog's to ensure she wouldn't follow me.

Julia bit her lip but nodded, gave me a quick kiss, and lay back on the pillows, feigning sleep.

Drew finished the story and stood slowly to blow out the candles. He turned on a flashlight and aimed it down the hall.

I tiptoed the other way and let myself into the room that Pansy had growled at.

Nothing seemed amiss. A thin beam of light from my footmen outside shining lights on the walls cascaded through the window across a sheet-covered divan in the center of the room. The light made the corners darker and hard to make out.

I waited a few minutes, hopefully long enough for Drew to perform his spells then said, "How can I assist you?"

I thought it might have gone and had turned to leave when it whispered, "...seethe..."

The sibilant hiss sent skitters across my spine.

"When he returns.... where has he gone... I shan't wait forever."

The cackle that followed that was terrifying.

"I'm almost free! Almost! Soon I shall hunt again!"

The tone changed completely when it said eagerly, "Has our master sent you to me? Is it time?"

Again the tone changed as it said angrily, "No! This is my house! Mine. 'Twas the deal!"

"Tell me of the deal."

It laughed a darkly vicious laugh.

"You trespass?" it asked haughtily and then muttered, "No 'Tisn't possible."

The darkness in the corner roiled.

It screeched in a rough whisper, "I see how you think to hold me here! Fool. Your pretty lights will be worthless!"

The darkness rushed forward, flowing onto the divan, standing directly in the light from the window that seemed to flow through it without appearing to do it any harm whatsoever.

It cackled again, leaping to the ceiling where it disappeared. A moment later an unearthly shriek sounded and it reappeared, looking surprisingly corporeal as it tumbled to the floor where it lay in what appeared to be tattered remnants of a long black coat.

"You dare!" It bellowed as it scrabbled to its feet.

In pure panic, I stumbled backward, flicking on my flashlight, shining it directly at the face. Red eyes glared from a tangle of black streamers of shadow that curtained the face, revealing glimpses of red eyes and smaller glints of light where a mouth would be as if saliva sparkled on its teeth.

It shrieked again when the light connected. Smoke billowed and the air immediately stunk of burned flesh.

I turned off the light.

"I'm sorry, you startled me—"

It ignored my babbling, running with an awkward gait.

I reached for the binding powder as it reached the window and crashed through.

A man outside yelled.

I rushed to the window.

Smalls stood almost directly under the window holding a huge flashlight that he was panning across the building as he yelled, "Was that you, governor?"

The shadowed seethe, if that was what it was, was nowhere in sight. The yard below me was brightly lit. I turned to peer above me. Someone had placed flashlights along the edge of the roof to fill in the gaps that the security lights didn't cover. The light fell along the house in bright pockets.

I didn't think a shadowed seethe could traverse the dimmer areas, but this was obviously no normal shadow.

I said to Smalls, "What did you see?"

"It looked like an old coat or a bunch of bats or something but when I shone my light at it, it just broke apart."

"Broke apart how?" Drew asked.

I leaned out again to see him staring from the window of the room beside mine.

Smalls shrugged, "Don't know, do I? It was just gone like birds flying away. What the hell was it?"

"Bats," I said.

393

Drew said, "Keep the lights on until dawn. We don't want them coming back inside to nest here again."

He withdrew his head from the window and closed it.

I said to Smalls, "Leave this window for tonight. I don't want to wake my guests."

I flicked my light on to examine the room.

A damp patch marked the spot on the floor where it had fallen.

The light was too weak to say with certainty what it was. More of the dark liquid that I thought could be blood dripped from the shattered edge of the window.

I tiptoed into the hall, meaning to go to my lab to retrieve the necessary supplies to take samples, and found Drew there.

He held a finger to his lips, jerking his head at the sleepers, taking my hand and pulling me further from the room.

I whispered, "It left blood or something behind. I should take samples."

"Blood? You sure?"

"No. It could be anything. It withstood the light coming into the room with no harm. What was in the attic?"

"Ryu was setting out lights there."

"Ryu..."

I turned and ran for the attic stairs.

Drew followed me.

All of the attic lights were on.

Ryu was surrounded by lit flashlights, standing by the window. He sagged in relief when we appeared, saying, "Blimey, I thought I was done for. Did you hear it scream?"

"Did it harm you?" I asked as I rushed across the room.

"Nah. Scared the bejesus out of me though. You okay? I heard it yelling..."

Drew said, "Tell us exactly what you saw."

"I didn't see much. I was facing the other way when it screamed. By the time I turned it was a...I don't know what it was. It was thicker than shadow somehow, but it wasn't solid. It was more like smoke, I guess, but black, really black. The black was a million strands making thicker ones and they flowed through the floor."

"Could you see the floor through it?"

"No. I couldn't. In fact, I couldn't see through it at all. Not the wall behind or nothing and it wasn't casting a shadow either that I noticed but it happened in like a second..."

"Is it dead?" I asked.

Drew said, "No. Or at least a seethe wouldn't be. If it was a shadowed seethe, it would be hurt and need time to make itself solid again."

I said, "It looked solid when it came through the ceiling."

"Tell me."

"It landed on the floor."

"Did you hear it hit?"

I thought back and nodded.

"It hit hard and left blood behind or something wet. It didn't have a face, just the red eyes and glints where a mouth would be but hidden behind shadowy hair so it was hard to see. The hair was moving like smoke—wafting about in hunks and thinner strands, not moving like real hair at all. The strands were mostly see-through but there were so many that where they crossed each other it was solid. I thought it could've been wearing a ripped-up coat or gown, but it could have been more of the hair. It frightened me and I shone my light at it. The light burned it. I could see real smoke and smelt it too."

"What'd it smell like?"

"Burned meat. It jumped from the window, which it broke, so it was solid when it went through. I wonder if it thought it had enough power..."

I told them what the thing had said to me, ending with, "It said it was almost free. Maybe it tried to free itself when it came up here into the attic and found itself in the light? Maybe it *was* able to make itself solid to withstand the light but didn't have enough power to totally free itself?"

Ryu said, "Can they make themselves a body like that, without taking someone else's, I mean?"

"I'd never heard of it but maybe. Lots of creatures can use magic to alter their shapes. Let's get those samples. I can try to track it by the blood."

I said, "Ryu, get the maps." I gave him a quick hug, which he returned. "Keep the flashlight handy."

His laugh ruffled my hair.

"I can't believe you fucking talked to it... you're crazy, you know that, right? Next time just light it up!" He squeezed me again then released me, muttering, "Talking to vampires...what's next? A pet werewolf?"

He headed to the stairs.

Drew grabbed my arm when I'd have followed.

"I'll need salt and a silver knife—purified if you have that."

"I do." I handed him one of the silver knives that Ryu had given me in the kitchen. "I have the sage mixture that Sandra taught us how to make. I'll bring that too."

"Take the samples carefully. Don't touch it yourself."

"I'll wear gloves."

He released me and headed to the window.

I ran for the attic stairs, slowing when I heard a lower murmur of voices in the hallway outside the door.

Julia was saying, "Pip can handle some bats. Come back to bed, Reg. Or you could return to your room if you want?"

Ryu said to them, "I'm calling it a night. See you tomorrow."

Reginald and Julia spoke but I couldn't make it out.

I stepped into the hallway.

Reginald and Julia were standing by the stairs that led to the ballroom.

Everyone else appeared to be asleep except Andre who was leaning up on one elbow over Cassandriel who appeared to be sleeping soundly beside him.

"Is everything okay?" he asked. "I thought I heard a scream and glass breaking."

"Probably my scream... The bats nearly startled the life out of me. I broke the glass more trying to open the window. I'm afraid I quite lost my temper and cursed a bit. 'Tis nothing to worry about." I said a bit louder, "Julia, love, I'm going for a broom so Pansy or the cats don't cut their paws. Keep them here."

She headed to me, trailed by Reginald.

He said to me, "She knows you snuck off with him."

"*Shh*, don't wake them."

Julia said, "Don't be ridiculous, Reg. Pip and Drew are just friends."

"Then why are they sneaking away together the minute you fall asleep?"

"We didn't sneak away. We went to see what Pansy had been growling about. But let's not talk about it here. I don't want to wake everyone."

He pushed past me to enter the room I'd been in.

"Mind the glass," I said as I grasped his shoulder.

"Why is it so light out there... what's going on?"

I leaned closer to whisper, "We had a rather large swarm of bats. A very large swarm... I'm hoping the lights will keep it from returning."

I headed down the hall to the main stairs, hoping he'd follow me before he could think to ask how that bat had gotten into the closed room and why there was no bat poop about.

Julia followed, glancing worriedly back at the sleepers.

Reginald stepped from the room then headed to us.

I said to Julia, "Drew could use help finding the shutters up there. Call and see if he needs a hammer or anything. Reg, want to give me a hand checking the attic in the east wing?"

I gave him my best friendly smile. "I've called already, and the lights should be on there but after those stories I'd still rather not go alone."

I grimaced at Julia as I said, "Ghost night wasn't the best idea. I vow I shall now have nightmares."

She laughed a soft of breath of nervous laughter as she kissed my cheek.

I headed to the main hall followed by Reginald. We stayed on the second floor, passing the guest rooms above the main hall and then heading down the corridor in the east wing where we ran into John coming down the stairs from the third floor.

"Any sign of bats?" I asked.

"We've seen nothing. We heard some shouts..."

"Have the attics been checked? Never mind, I won't be happy until I check them myself. Find me a broom and dustbin and a box to dispose of broken glass. Leave it by the door to the west wing, quietly mind."

Reginald followed me to the attic stairs.

"There must be fifty flashlights," he said in amusement as we ducked to enter the short door at the top of the stairs.

"John is new."

The attic ran the length of the wing with only a narrow stretch along the center of the ridgeline where we could stand fully upright. Thick beams held up the roof. The walls were all unfinished and uninsulated except for the farthest one.

Pink insulation covered the farthest wall except for a small window. There were only a few piles of boxes and some stacked furniture. Each pile was surrounded by flashlights that were casting broad swaths of light that made the dark seem darker.

It shouldn't have been scary, but the hair of my arms stood straight up.

Reginald said doubtfully, "Still..."

"I told him to make sure there were no dark corners. 'Tis good that he listens so well."

The corner of the eves were all brightly lit but the tops of piles of stacked goods were shrouded in gloom.

I headed to the window.

"What are we looking for?"

"Holes."

"We could see them better if we turned out all the lights..."

"I should've brought a candle to check for drafts, or Pansy..."

"What's really going on, Lou?"

I pressed my face to the glass.

Shadows swathed the yard. The barns were brightly lit, which made the surrounding pastures much darker.

"Lou?"

"'Tis no longer my name."

"So...we're pretending to be different people now?"

"I'm not pretending. I wish you wouldn't either. Can you not be the Reginald you wish to be?"

I headed back to the stairs, turning back when he didn't follow me.

We stared at each other for a moment.

I could see the indecision and pain on his face.

"As what... friends?" he asked bitterly.

"As family, I suppose..."

I ran down the stairs, down the hall, using the back stairs to reach the kitchen where I grabbed paper towels, a bottled water, and a box of plastic baggies.

I went outside through the kitchen door and ran around the front of the house, which was brightly lit by the light streaming from the interior rooms and every exterior light on the house and drive. The ballroom side wasn't as brightly lit, there being fewer outdoor lights installed, but I thought it enough to keep a regular shadowed seethe away. *This wasn't a shadowed seethe though...* the thought ran in a loop through my head. Blackwood had obviously been hiding—or raising—something here.

I punched in the house code on the double doors on the ballroom patio to let myself in.

The low beeps seemed explosively loud to me. I hoped our guests were sleeping through all of this commotion. What Sandra would say if this caused her daughter to lose her shape didn't bear thinking off.

A cold sweat made my hands clammy as I considered that our attempt to help her might have put one of my only true friends into serious jeopardy.

Light from the patio lit the ballroom well enough I could make out and avoid the tables.

I crouched to creep up the stairs and was just about to peek into the hall when Andre said, "Pip?"

"Yes. I didn't wish to wake anyone."

"They're still sleeping. Do you need a hand?"

"No. I'm sorry to disturbed you."

"It's three a.m. What's so urgent it couldn't wait until morning?"

I tiptoed up to him to whisper, "Bats. I've never seen so many... don't tell my wife. She'd be quite distraught. She thinks it just a few."

I held my finger to my lips, and he stifled a laugh.

I ran into the room to take my samples and found Ryu there already.

"How did you get in here?" I whispered.

"I walked."

He thrust a paper bag at me. "Take this to Drew. I'll clean this room."

I set my supplies on the sheet-covered divan and tucked the bag under my shirt.

He said, "The attic door is warded. One sec."

He stripped off the yellow kitchen gloves he wore to take out his phone.

"He'll open it in a minute. Where's your shadow—I mean Reg."

"Probably looking for me. Stall him if you can."

He thrust the gloves at me. "Gimme the bag then and you finish this."

"I wanted to see him do it, but I suppose you're right."

"I'll tell you all about it."

He grabbed the bag and frowned at me.

"You okay, Pip?"

"Shaken. Confused. Worried..."

"Back at you."

He kissed my forehead.

As always it warmed me when he saw the person I was inside this manly shell.

"Be careful," I whispered.

"I always am."

I donned his discarded gloves, which were still warm from his hands and somehow comforting because of it and knelt to examine the stain.

It had faded quite a bit already.

I used the bottled water sparingly, putting the resultant damp paper towels into another plastic bag. Then I laid out a strip of paper towels and began stacking the shattered glass on it.

Ten minutes later Reginald entered carrying a box, a broom, a dustbin and a battery powered lantern that he held aloft to examine the room.

I carefully bundled the glass on the paper towels and placed it into the box before I began sweeping.

He gazed from the window, saying softly, "Bats... *huh*?"

LORD BLACKWOOD

Chapter 39

After what had seemed an endless night of worry and waiting, Julia, Ryu, Drew, and I were in the upstairs study.

Everyone else had returned to their rooms to shower and dress for the day, except for Andre who I'd asked to help John put the borrowed beds back.

It wouldn't take them long at all, so I knew this meeting needed to be quick.

"Is it out there?"

"Not according to my location spell," Drew said.

"But you're not certain if it was sent deeper into the shadows or not?"

"No. I suggest you leave it a meal. A lamb with a fresh wound would likely appeal to it."

"In the house or a field or what?" Julia asked.

"Both. Turn off all the lights in the rooms around the one it was in and leave it the food and maybe it'll speak with you again."

"Why was it here?" I asked.

"That's an excellent question. Unfortunately, I don't have an answer. I'll speak to Sandra and see if there's anything we can do. Meanwhile, you can beef up the lighting around the house and barns. I think you should find out everything you can about Lou's father."

Ryu said, "I bet it's what attacked Reginald."

Julia nodded agreement as she said, "I wonder if it meant the books or the house was mine?"

Ryu said, "If Blackwood was trapping it here somehow, he must've had a good reason. I can't imagine he'd give up this estate on a whim."

I said, "But if he was trapping it, why didn't it leave when Blackwood died?"

Drew said, "Not all spells break when the caster dies. Sandra and I can check your home for spells, but it'll need to wait until Cassandriel is back in class."

"Of course. She's the priority," I said firmly.

Julia said, "I'll take her and Honey shopping or maybe we can go to London and look at the building my mum recommended and see if there any nice apartments available nearby?"

Drew pursed his lips, nodding thoughtfully. "London might be good. Andre hasn't gotten a chance to sightsee much there. Mention that when you make the offer."

Ryu said, "I could take them to the casino tonight. Pip, you could get us reservations at the Eye, and I'll tell them about my win here and we can go gamble, get dinner, and maybe catch a show. She'd be too busy to sneak off."

"Sounds good," Drew said. "But don't push it too hard. I don't want her to get suspicious, and no lying to her! She's bound to ask about last night, so be ready to change the subject."

Julia said, "Not that I don't want to help, but you need a better plan than this. Sooner or later you're going to run out of distractions."

"I know. We're working on it. We just need some more time..."

I said, "I'll speak to Asa about upgrading the house lighting and we'll give the staff the night off. Except for the footmen."

"The grooms in the back barns can stay too," Julia said.

I said, "I'll tell Patrick to place the sheep this evening. You see to our guests. Text me if they agree to visit London and I'll meet you there at the Eye. If Cass turns you down after Honey agrees, go with Honey and I'll be back up."

Drew nodded agreement.

I followed him from the room and headed to the back stairs.

John was with cook, Mrs. Roman, and two maids in the kitchen.

I said, "We'll be away this evening, so staff can have the night off. John, see that the kitchen doors remained locked in our absence. I don't want anyone wandering about."

Mrs. Roman said, "We'll see to it."

"Please inform your husband that I'd like to meet with him directly in his office and tell my guests I was unavoidably detained. John, if you would accompany me, please."

He and I left.

I said, "All doors and windows on the bottom floor are to be kept closed and locked unless we've specifically ordered differently. The kitchen doors that lead into the main hall are kept locked when Lady Blackwood and I are away from the estate or when you're away from the estate unless you've arranged for a replacement for yourself. The tenants who stay in the east wing are allowed in the kitchen and on the grounds but never in the rest of the home unsupervised unless you've set them a particular task."

"You want me to follow them if they come into the main hall?"

"Not necessarily. Just be mindful of what they're about. If one enters to borrow a book and you see him heading up the stairs politely remind him that the books are in the library off the sitting room and never my reading room. No one enters that room without my express permission, including yourself and servants. The library off of our sitting room can be used by you, staff, and the tenants. If someone is waiting to meet with Julia, and you don't see them in the parlor or sitting room check to see what they're about."

"Right. Got it. I can do that, no problem."

I laid my hand on his arm to be sure I was touching his anima as I said, "Protect Lady Blackwood at all costs. If force is needed, use force."

We reached the carriage house and entered the small office.

"Asa," I said, extending my hand.

"Lord Blackwood."

We shook and all took seats.

I said, "Last night showed me that we need to upgrade our security. Specifically, I want further lighting installed. Every room and closet should have a light. Further, I want a way to turn every light outside on at the same time. Ideally, I could turn the lights inside on and off throughout the house without needing to run about, but I don't want my guests having the lighting overridden in their rooms on a whim or by mistake. But perhaps we could install some sort of emergency lighting? Speak to an electrician and discuss the options. I'd prefer if there were independent backups so that a main wire couldn't be cut, or a power outage would leave us in the dark. The backup needn't have as much coverage as the main lighting."

"Yes, sir."

"We also want cameras in all hallways and covering all exterior doors, including barn doors. Lady Blackwood will want that working with the app she already uses."

"We'd discussed it in generalities before, but she'd decided to wait."

"We've decided it's best to move forward now that we have more art in the house and will be having more house guests.

Speaking of which, some of our guests will arrive with their own security who'll need to have workspace inside the house. Mr. Shangrün pointed out that our security is a bit too lax. He suggested a room that visiting security like himself could use to monitor the cameras."

"Mr. Shangrün is security?"

"He's one of Ms. Alder's personal bodyguards. She normally travels with two or more, but we'd thought she'd be secure here."

"Did something happen?"

"No. It was just a minor disturbance of no account whatsoever, except for the embarrassment it caused my wife. Luckily, our guests slept through it, and I believe the bats have relocated with no real harm done. But Mr. Shangrün was concerned, so I'm concerned. So speak to the company who installed the security and tell them we need to upgrade as soon as possible and that we'll want a control room somewhere in the house, perhaps in one of the smaller rooms in the west wing. That wing will be housing guests most often. Make sure we have at least three people trained in its operation and that they know that they'll be working with security from other firms as a regular thing. That means I want you to choose polite candidates from among our current security staff. Ones who could handle themselves if there had actually been an emergency. Send your recommendations to Mr. Poole who'll forward them to my wife and I."

I turned to John to say, "You'll be in charge of staff when they're inside the house. Keeping the house secure is your prime duty. If you think of something that could make your job easier, bring it to Mr. Roman's attention."

I turned back to Asa to say, "You're in charge of the entire estate. John will report to you as will your wife and anyone else you assign, including the head groom and all hired persons. I realize there are many more people about than we'd originally planned for, and you've been doing a very good job, but if it's too much…"

"Not at all. Things run very smoothly. Which is amazing when you consider the mix of people we have here…"

"I wished to commend you on the fast procurement of so many torches. Let's make a note to have one of the bigger type by each entrance and have everyone living on the estate issued a torch of good quality. Set someone to making sure that everyone is maintaining them in proper working condition."

"I'll add that to the checklist of monthly inspections."

"John, get that window replaced first thing. I want it done before dinner. If you require assistance, call for one of the footmen. I expect the guests will be wanting to go riding or maybe to London directly after breakfast. Have the house footmen waiting to assist with the guests' bags or the horses. You're dismissed."

That reminded me I needed to make time to meet Julia's footmen.

"Yes sir," he said and hurried out.

I said to Asa, "Ms. Alder will be coming over occasionally to check on the new filly. 'Tis a personal favor for me. See that her requests or recommendations are followed forthwith. She's never to go riding alone. Send at least one of the grooms, which leads me to a small predicament.

"Some of the men here aren't at all suited to accompany a lady. I don't wish to impede their progress or cast aspersions on their characters, but I darn't take a chance with a lady's safety. So always check with Julia, myself, or Mr. Poole if we haven't already cleared the groom to accompany her."

"Are any cleared?"

"Not at this moment. Julia will be supplying you with a list shortly. Remind her, please, that we need at least two female grooms on the estate capable of escorting guests about. If you have doubts about anyone on the list, bring it to our immediate attention."

"Yes, sir."

"Speaking of young ladies, my wife and I think the carriage house is more suited to John then yourself.

He paled.

I continued, "The cottage at the end of the drive would be the more fitting property for you. 'Tis, however, in a deplorable condition. To my knowledge John has no immediate need for his own home but he's a young man. I think it wise that we begin repairs on the cottage at once. Speak with your wife and see if she'd like to oversee that or if we should leave it to the architect. I'd like to keep it outwardly in the same style, but the interior will need to be gutted, so the layout could be changed to a more modern one."

He was smiling happily now, as well he should when the cottage was a nice size, two story home. It would likely cost more than the house was worth at the moment to fix it up, but I wanted him further away than this carriage house—and I didn't want Ryu to move out which he might decide to do with a new butler in need of rooms.

I said, "Julia will discuss the particulars with you of budget and requirements. But meanwhile, maybe you'd prefer to move into one of the empty homes on the back street for a bit more space until the cottage is habitable? Speak with John and the contractors and sort out the timing between you. And that reminds me, Mr. Poole's mother will be moving in shortly to number twelve. Make sure everything there is tickety boo. Offer a cash bonus to get it cleaned up and freshened. I just realized I have no idea how old his brothers are, but I think them young boys. Find out and make sure the bedrooms are suitably arranged."

"When will she be arriving?"

"In a week, I think, but I could be mistaken."

"I'll see to it."

"If anything occurs to you that would improve the security or the smooth running of the estate, send me an email, or call if it's urgent."

I shook his hand and went to the barns, calling Ryu on the way.

"Can you get away?"

"Yes. Jewels said you'd be needing a ride to London."

"I could get someone else to take me. I just thought we could stop and talk to your mother..."

"I guess..."

"We can go later if you'd rather?"

"No, it's fine. Better to get it over with."

"I'll try to convince her normally."

"It's fine, Pip. I'll see you in a few minutes."

"Pick me up at the barn. I want to check the filly."

"Cassandriel and Andre are there."

Which I knew because I could see them leaning on the paddock fence.

I disconnected and waved at Andre as he glanced over his shoulder.

He yelled laughingly, "Quick! She's plotting to steal her."

"Not steal...borrow."

Cassandriel nudged him with her hip, grinning at me.

"I was thinking, she's such a beauty and a lot like my white mare. They'd look so pretty together. Hargrove found this company that makes postcards and stuff with pictures of horses. I bet we could sell them some good shots of our two."

Andre snickered as he said, "It couldn't possibly make as much as the cost of flying her all the way there."

"No, silly. I'd bring Whisper here. To my mom's estate, I mean, and Julia could bring Viola there. Or maybe we should take shots at both houses? That'd be cool for the background. I bet I could talk Tilly into letting us take some shots there too. Beautiful horses on beautiful English estates."

I said, "'Tis a brilliant idea but don't sell those pictures. We'll make a calendar of our own. And a book! I have a wonderful idea! We'll make the calendar with the two white horses with some themed shots for the different months and then I'll send that to our prospective houses and ask them if they have a horse of their own that they'd like to feature in a coffee table book. Julia will love it! We can arrange to hold a hunt or a show at each house. It'll be fun and it'll give us a chance to place some of our tenants."

"It sounds expensive," Andre said.

I shrugged, "I shall offer to buy the pictures outright or give them a share of the proceeds of the book. Or maybe we should donate a set amount of proceeds to charity in their name... I shall need to speak with our accountant. But 'tisn't about making—or losing money. 'Tis about making connections."

"It sounds like something my mom would do," Cassandriel said doubtfully.

"'Tis my thought that 'twould get me invited to see stables that I'd otherwise not see. Between us, we have plenty of horses to stage any home we wished to visit."

"Yep—exactly like something my mom would do. You're hanging around her too much, Pip, you're getting all Machiavellian."

"You're saying you wouldn't be interested in seeing the Windsor Castle stables in person?"

She grinned, lightly punching my shoulder, "Well, when you put it that way..."

"Where is everyone else?" I asked.

"Packing up and taking another tour of the east wing with Julia. Rourke wanted to talk about his job. We're going to go see the building and then sightsee a bit. Are you coming with us?"

"I'm meeting you there."

We both turned as Ryu pulled up.

He waved.

I said, "We have a quick stop to make."

I gave her a hug.

"Thanks so much for coming. I'm sorry last night—"

"We had a great time." She winked at me as she added, "I don't think you need to add any special effects."

Andre interjected, "Especially scary ones. You just need a mysterious woman in the distance occasionally."

She said, "I wasn't scared. It was fun. I'd do it again. Next time in the attic."

"Sure," I agreed. "We should try it at your mother's place too."

As soon as I said it, I wondered if Sandra had a hidden inhabitant too.

"Not tonight," Andre said hurriedly. "I only have one more night before I need to go back, and I'd like a real bed."

"Not tonight," I agreed," as I headed to the car. "See you in a few hours!"

We drove away, passing the house where Reginald stood on the front steps. I debated the proper response and settled for holding a hand up as a wave seemed mocking somehow and to do nothing at all, rude.

"So... what's his game?" Ryu asked.

"I have no idea. 'Twon't be good though—will it?"

"I seriously doubt it. I hated leaving her there with him. She just *won't* believe he could hurt her, which means he probably can before she can react. I told Vicky to stay within earshot of him if he's near her. We should really do something, Pip."

"Kill him, you mean?"

"...yes, but I know we *can't*. She'd never forgive us."

"He can be so...charming."

"Don't tell me he's winning you over too! Come on, Pip! You know better than that!"

"'Tisn't necessary to remind me! I thought of nothing but the perfidy of handsome men for two hundred years!"

"Two hundred... I thought it was three?"

"The first hundred I spent thinking of ways I wanted to kill him."

He laughed.

I hadn't been jesting.

I said, "I think something very bad happened to Reginald that night."

"A demon?"

"Mayhap. I wonder if that thing last night was a shadowed seethe possessed of a demon? Perhaps such a creature would be able to withstand light? But it lacked...I know not what it's called—the *awfulness* that Pete possessed. He reeked of evil, but perhaps 'twas because I *knew* he *was* evil. This thing though, as scary as 'twas, lacked that same darkness. 'Twas sad and gibbering like I remember speaking to myself. Like one does when they don't expect an answer. I wonder now if it thought itself a shadow still? I'd no notion of my appearance—whether I was visible or not. I yelled and screamed and sometimes thought I saw a reaction. I imagined the words they spoke to themselves as they puttered around the room were spoken to me—I wished it to be true, so answered, making up the most outlandish stories to fit their narrative just to have the illusion of communication. What if it heard me and did the same?"

He said, "No. It knew the house. It knew itself. It *had* been living there. Maybe not for twenty years but it hadn't just arrived. It was responding to us—not hiding, but not showing itself either."

"I think it was there many more years. Many... I'm so glad I knew nothing of such things, or I'd have gone mad with the fear of it. It was fearful enough imagining myself falling into Hell but Hell, even when one believes, is still unimaginable as a *real* place. My mind never truly comprehended it as an actual place. Now... now, I truly can imagine the horror that lives in that darkness. I shan't go back. I shan't let Julia be sent there even if it means I must murder her brother and hence her love for me. She will *never* face that darkness! Never! We—you and I—will ensure that her soul remains pure and her body safe."

Chapter 40

Ryu's mother looked startled to see us, which was understandable it being barely nine in the morning.

I offered my hand, saying, "Lord Blackwood at your service, Madame."

She took it by reflex, and I kissed it, bowing as I'd seen my father do a million times.

She gaped at Ryu.

I said, "Might we come in a moment?"

Ryu said, "Lord Blackwood wanted to meet you, Mum. As part of my wages, I get the use of one of the houses on the estate, and you and the kids can live there rent free."

I said, "Martin is a valued employee."

"*Hmph*, I know what you have him doing."

"I seriously doubt it," Ryu muttered, which made me laugh.

She pursed her lips at me, folding her arms and tapping her foot.

I stepped past her.

"Ryu has contacts we need. My wife and I look for artists."

I sat uninvited at her kitchen table, taking out my phone, scrolling for a moment then sliding it across the table.

"We make our money in commissions."

Ryu said, "They're like agents."

I nodded as I said, "We look for up and coming artists who have something new and fresh to offer. We set them up, pay for their expenses and advertising, and take a large chunk of the profits for the first few years."

"*Hmph*, and then I suppose you just let them go on their merry way."

"Basically. Art has a lifecycle. It goes through stages. We ride that first hot stage, a stage that we arrange. Sales *will* slow, but the price of a piece will rise exponentially. So, we invest in the art ourselves too. The artist will either be good enough to have a following or they won't. 'Tis a gamble for us as much as for them. They sign a real contract, which they could buy out of. None have wanted to so far."

Ryu said, "They'd be crazy to. The Blackwoods have all sorts of posh connections. The rich folks flock to their openings... hang on a sec. I've got one of the brochures in the car."

He ran out the door.

I said, "You think I'm a criminal and 'tis a front for drugs. I swear 'tisn't. We *do* take advantage of these kids. They're too poor to do what we do and even if they could scrape up the money, they haven't our connections, but 'tisn't *all* one sided. We do our very best to make sure that their product sells."

"I heard how you be taking all the worst of the worst to work for you. They ain't artists unless you're counting con artists."

"*Ahh*... my wife's project. 'Tis a separate endeavor. Before you decide we're doing whatever 'tis you imagine we're doing, go to the estate and look around. Talk to whoever you like. Ryu does play a role in maintaining order but not by threats. He just speaks their language in a way we don't."

"I wasn't born yesterday. You got a nice spiel and all, but it's all bullshit! I don't want no part of it! My boys are good boys and I'm going to make sure they stay that way!"

"If you'll pardon me for saying so, then why stay here? The gang activity here is very high. My wife tracks those numbers across all of Britain. She'd be happy to show you her work. She could recommend a better neighborhood, but why not take advantage of free housing in a good school district?"

"I told you! I ain't getting involved!"

Ryu returned and handed her the brochure.

"What is this?" she said in a sneering tone that made me itch to slap her.

He said, "The sales catalog of our last opening."

"Is this tile... like bathroom tile?"

Ryu snickered. "Not like our bathroom, but yeah. That shit is three thousand dollars a square foot."

Her eyes widened.

I said, "You can read about the company on the website. If you call the business offices and ask for your son, he's the Vice President of Encore Enterprises, which is just one of his titles. He's a board member and junior partner. He handles finding the artists who make the tile. He's recently found us another form of art."

Ryu said, "You know Leandro, Mum. He and his crew have signed a contract. The Blackwoods are opening a new studio here in London that will showcase his art."

"Graffiti..." she said snidely.

I said, "We're still looking for artists, but he'll be top billing. The studio will be just one of three new outlets for us. There'll be a space dedicated to fine jewelry and a boutique selling custom one-of-a-kind products."

Ryu said, "The store will be managed by a future duke, Mum. These people are the real deal. They aren't criminals. They were born to wealth and power. Luckily, his wife wants to change the world. It's her idea to give kids like Smalls a shot. He's going to blow it, of course, but we all don't got to be so dumb."

"Has he been a problem?" I asked.

"Nothing I can't handle. Lady Blackwood is on top of it."

I said, "My wife works from home. Your son travels between all of our homes as necessary. We're constantly reassigning our new hires because we've found they adjust quicker to new jobs when taken from familiar territory. We try to use them to staff our businesses. I admit that I was swayed to hiring these young people with such long records because they *are* easier to fire if they don't work out, not that we've had to fire many. The trick is finding them work they enjoy doing and people they enjoy working with. My wife excels at that."

Ryu said, "Lady Blackwood opened a club in town, which is one of the favorite training sites. The people who go there to work learn how to mix drinks, deal cards, balance the books, wait tables, spin records, everything you could think of, and then she helps them find jobs."

She flipped through the brochure.

"People buy this stuff?"

"Crazy, ain't it? But they do."

She tossed the brochure aside, crossing her arms.

"Birdie told his mam that you was the butler there."

"I was."

I said, "He was my driver for a bit too. But then we got to talking and his ideas were really good."

Ryu said, "He could've just stolen those ideas, Mum, and never paid me a cent. Instead he not only paid me but hired me on as a junior partner."

I said, "My good friend and mentor invests in her employees ideas, and she's made a fortune doing it. It's a business model I strive to emulate—in my own way. My wife and I, and your son, will be opening more business as we get ideas and train staff. We aren't building a criminal empire, but we *are* building an empire. The idea is to diversify in lots of small businesses, but to do that I need people I can count on to leave in charge."

"Ones who owe you, you mean."

"I suppose. But I hope I'm earning genuine friendships or least genuine respect."

"You do-gooders with your grand ideas, thinking you can just waltz in and wave your magic wands—" Ryu burst into laughter— "like you got all the answers! And what's so damned funny!"

"Ollie said the same thing. Shit, we all thought it. But so what? Who cares what their motivation is? It don't matter to me none. I like this job. I'm a big deal now and I'm going to be an even bigger one someday. He ain't trying to stop me."

"Not now, but these kinds of men don't let you go. Once they got you, that's it!"

"You're the most stubborn woman!"

He held up a hand at me, inhaling a long hard breath and letting it out slowly.

"Even if every bad thing you think about him is true, how is that any worse than accepting money from your asshole of an ex who we both know made that dough by peddling meth?

"When he fucked up and got sent away, did his boss come looking for you? Hell no! Nobody cares! If I fuck up, nothing is going to happen to you at all, except maybe you inherit my shares. So what do you have to lose? My brothers can go to a good school and make friends with kids who are going places. They'll have the world at their fingertips! They can do anything!"

I picked up my phone, tapping the screen to make it light up again then handed it to her.

"This is Ryu's house. It's empty most of the time because he's busy. Call the local police and ask them about the crime rate there. Drive by and see it for yourself, then take a good long look at where you're living now."

Angry anima swirled around her.

I leaned away.

Inspiration struck me. Trying to act casual, I traced my rune of holding inside of a circle I drew in the air.

I didn't think either of them noticed as they were too busy glaring at each other.

When I held my hand out I couldn't feel the heat of her anima. Lifting my hand above the rune caused her anima to waft upward.

I hastily lowered my hand.

"My job is here. My friends are here!" she yelled angrily.

Ryu said, "There are secretary jobs there. I could get you a job or maybe you'd like to try something new? I make enough now to send you back to school or set you up doing whatever you want. Maybe you still want to open that flower shop like you always talked about? You can make new friends. Think about Harlow and Danby, please, Mum! Think what this could mean to them!"

"I'll think about it."

"That's not good enough!"

Her eyes narrowed, which made me laugh.

"Excuse me. "'Tisn't funny. You just look so alike. Perhaps if he knew you had a firm plan of action?"

"Like what?"

Her anger sought my own, flowing around the barrier of my holding spell. I worded my reply carefully because I was furious with her, and she was so close that I knew I could influence her whether I meant to or not. 'Twas clear this holding spell would need work before I could trust it utterly.

I wondered if my face was red from the heat of it where it was condensing—my holding spell being badly positioned to block it all.

I said, "Ryu would like his brothers to attend the local school, which is a very good one. My wife will arrange for you to visit it this week. Ryu can supply you with funds to travel there and arrange for the children to be properly supervised in your absences, or you could take them with you. Stop by the house and let them look around.

"My wife can arrange for you to tour the business if you wish. I think Ryu would be reassured that you were taking his proposal seriously if he knew you were acting. Then, if you decide against the move, at least you can have an intelligent rebuttal for him."

"Is he for real?"

Ryu snickered.

I erased my holding spell with a thought and said, "I'll let the two of you talk. I expect to hear from my wife that you've called to arrange that visit within the week. 'Twas a pleasure meeting you."

I strode outside before I was tempted beyond bearing to use my anger on her and just make her see sense.

Ryu joined me at the car ten minutes later.

"She ain't going to budge unless... can we stop by the beauty parlor? Her best friend works there. If they're impressed enough, she'll be bragging about the move in no time."

"What will impress them?"

"Be yourself."

He snickered occasionally as we drove down the street.

I didn't ask what he found so amusing because I knew 'twas me.

I followed him into the small salon.

Ryu headed right to a beautiful middle-aged woman in the back with coal black hair piled in tiny ringlets on her head. She wore a purple dress with stiletto heeled boots that reminded me of the posh woman in Dubai although hers were made of much cheaper materials.

He kissed her cheek then said, "Philip, this is my mother's good friend Evelyn Marsh. Ev, this is Lord Blackwood. He's looking for investment opportunities and I thought of you."

"Me?" she asked as I extended my hand.

I kissed it when she accepted it.

"Charmed. Martin tells me you're simply masterful with a comb. Lady Blackwood has been looking for someone to head up a salon. 'Twould be quite elegant with a drawing room and lounge. The sort of place a lady would go to be pampered."

"Me?" she asked again even more doubtfully.

Ryu said, "You know he's been hiring lots of the kids from around here. He wants to train some at this spa. It won't be no five-dollar cut kind of place. We're talking thousands for a visit."

Her lips pursed, which made him laugh.

"Not that sort of place neither just a high-class sort of thing. This is all still in the planning stages, but I can get you a chair."

I said, "'Tis a brilliant idea. Women will spend quite a bit on beauty... in fact we should open a shoe store directly beside it— and perhaps a hat store!"

Ryu nodded at me, saying to her, "This is a once in a lifetime sort of opportunity, Ev. He'll need a few good cutters, so if you have some friends you wanted to bring along... but they gotta be posh talkers like you. He'll be paying the overhead. Hell, it's too much to explain now. Gimme your email and I'll send you a copy of the contract. You'll see it's a great deal."

He leaned closer and whispered to her for a minute. Her eyes rounded, and when he straightened, she stepped back and examined him from head-to-toe.

He winked and smoothed his lapel. "Sometimes you're just in the right place at the right time. And it really is who you know. Philip counts on me to find him good people. I know you *can* do it. I hope you *will* do it."

He kissed her cheek. "Call me and we can talk. We've got to run now. I'll be out of the country for a few weeks, but when I get back, we can catch up. And talk to my mother. I want her to move into my house. Make her at least go see it."

I said, "'Twas a pleasure. I hope we meet again."

"Later, ladies," Ryu called out as we exited.

An excited babble broke out as soon as the door closed.

"Yeah, that ought a do it," he said in satisfaction as we got into the car.

I said, "A spa is a wonderful idea. The perfect place to send the ladies to spend money."

Ryu snickered as he said, "We can make the spa use our soaps and shampoos and lotions, which we relabel and make stupid expensive. I'll call Julia later and talk it out with her. Thanks for doing all this, Pip."

"'Tis what friends do."

"Yeah…"

"Are we not friends?"

"We are."

We drove without speaking for a few minutes as I marshaled my thoughts.

I finally said, "When I was a girl, I thought my father's lack of real friends was his position, which was true in a way. But I knew titled men who had real friends. All of them held roughly equal positions in society. I only knew one who counted someone of the lower classes a true friend. Their differences in wealth we're a true obstacle to that friendship in a way that their differences in titles was not. Many of the titled counted a wealthy man as a friend.

I think I'm not as patient nor kind as that man was. 'Twill likely be trying for you to remain my friend—a true friend, not someone who speaks in a friendly manner, but someone who can be counted on and expects the same. So I shall speak to Julia to give you legally what we give you in our thoughts—what we claim to give you to make ourselves seem less self-serving."

"It isn't necessary."

"I know it. 'Twill become necessary though as we adjust to this situation. 'Tis better to do it now before you think to resent us. I hope that if ever you do begin to resent us that you'd give us a chance to mend the rift. If we must part, I'd do it as friends."

"You would…"

"I'd not let anyone harm you. Sandra will know it would be war between us."

He nodded.

We both knew we hadn't meant Sandra.

Chapter 41

A blanket of stars cast shimmering radiance over the desert sand behind the tile works.

Not a person was in sight. The lights from the tile factory were just specs in the distance.

The ground rumbled beneath my feet. Sand fountained into the air, blocking my vision. When it cleared it revealed a narrow tunnel leading under the ground.

It took courage but I stepped into that tunnel and followed it down. Heat grew the farther I went and a dim light in the distance brightened.

I emerged into a golden cave. Battery powered lanterns hung from solid gold stalagmites that had been heated to have curved ends suitable for hanging things on.

Since my last visit heaps of trinkets, art, jewelry, knickknacks, clothing, and books had been stacked about. I added the two bags of cash that I carried to the closest pile.

A pentacle had been gouged into the floor in the far corner of the room. I itched to examine it but thought it would be rude.

She caught my gaze on it and waved me over, saying, "Don't step on it."

Nervous sweat bloomed on me when I read my real name written along the outer edge followed by Julia's and Ryu's.

She said, "It's a portal spell. I plan to put one in a building I just bought half a mile away. You'll be able to come and go as you need to even if I'm not here but it's best to let me know if you can."

"A portal? They work here?"

"To my knowledge magic works the same everywhere. It's the gathering of it that's different. Spells like this take a lot of magic and need to be replenished every so often. So don't use it unless you need to. It's cheaper for me to fly here to let you in."

I crouched to examine it.

Sandra said, "Take a look at this. Do you think you can use it in the tiles?"

She squatted to dump a bag full of gems on the ground. Most were very large and uncut. I picked up a hunk of ruby as big as my hand.

"Where... never mind. I know you can't tell me."

She said, "It's much too big to use as is but maybe we can get it cut down into a few gems or even a bunch of very small ones?"

"I'm sure I could find a gem cutter but what you need is a mine."

"I have one... humans can tell now though where gems are mined from. It's easier to mix these into end stage products then pass them off as coming from my mines. I was thinking we could work out a deal where you use them on the tile, because no one is going to be getting that appraised for anything other than authenticity. They won't care where the ruby comes from just that it's ruby."

"Julia and I are planning to open a jewelry store that we make our marks shop at. I can fence some larger pieces that way for you because we plan to offer top dollar for heirloom jewels. It should be simple to make a mark claim it was their piece. Then we just have them spend the money we paid them in one of our other stores."

She began gathering the gems.

I said, "As payment, I'd like another spellbook."

I took out my phone to show her a picture. "Can you make me inferno runes on poster-size paper that look like this on the front? I'd need twenty by the twenty-fifth."

"Fire I can do," she said laughingly.

She headed to one of the heaps of clothing and rummaged in it for a moment then handed me a leather-bound book that zipped closed.

"As requested."

I said, "Thank you. You're absolutely sure you only need thirty minutes?"

"What are you planning, Pip?"

"I'm taking that entire building down."

Her mouth dropped open.

I said, "'Tis needful. I've arranged for the street to be closed and the building empty, except for my targets. My footmen will be watching to stop anyone from wandering by at the critical moment. I've made my own spellbook with numerous small inferno runes that will be sent out in internal mail. Those posters are intended to ensure that no one on the thirteenth or fourteenth floor can escape.

"If it's fire you want there, I can do that without spellbooks."

"Still...I'd like them for the elevators."

"I can make you ones that will all activate at a set time, which would probably be easier for you to manage."

"Perfect. I shall have my mule put them out after closing on the twenty-sixth. There are ten exits from that floor. The eight elevators, and the two sets of stairs. If I place a few more along that main corridor, no one can get past it."

"The fire will need some mundane explanation."

"I have a mule planting human-style explosives. Ryu and I will remove the window as you asked and spread out your spells. We need a few minutes in the files on the top floor and on the fourteenth. The bombs will go off taking the building down.

I waggled the spellbook she'd just handed me.

"Then we'll jump out and float away."

Chapter 42

Ryu was with me in the office a week later when Julia called.

We'd been practicing with the binding powder, which we did every day for at least an hour. It was fun and both of us were proficient at it now. With a practiced wrist motion I released myself from the wall, dropping fifteen feet to the floor.

Ryu was crawling across the ceiling and released himself moments after me, dropping to the floor of the loft.

"Fool! You could hurt yourself and then where would we be?"

"*Nah*, it's like ten feet…"

"Still don't take any chances."

I glowered my displeasure at him, knowing he was unrepentant by his grin as I answered my phone, saying, "Ryu is here and you're on speaker."

"Evelyn is a treasure," she said as a greeting. "She's embraced the project and is working with my mother and Asa. They'll have the salon up and running by summer. Your mother agreed to relocate at the end of the next school term. I hate to say it when I barely know the woman but she's being… a snob with Evelyn. Not the Ev complained. She was nice as anything, but I'd have been pissed if I were her. I *was* pissed and it had nothing to do with me. You might want to tell her to tone it down a bit if she wants to keep her friends."

"She ain't going to listen to me."

I said, "'Tis none of our business—stay away from her."

"True... so I've signed the paperwork and sent the courier. You two sign at the lawyers and get it back to me. Encore and Elite Street are officially in all three of our names. Ryu gets ten percent this first year with a one percent increase each year until it's an even three-way split. We put in ninety percent of the capital, and you put in ten. The loan papers are being forwarded to you for your signature.

"Elite Street Corporation works the opposite way with Pip and I being the junior partners and you being the major investor. Right now, it's only properties are the spa, Elite Night Club, and the condo complex as yet unnamed, which won't be ready to open for at least another ten months and probably longer than that. In the future, we'll need to decide which corporate umbrella a property goes into. Black Whit Unlimited and Reset will be just Pip and me. You can invest in your own as well. Pip and I were discussing rates. You could hire us to host an opening night or attend a fundraiser."

Ryu said thoughtfully, "You're going to sell your services... to who? Me and Sandra?"

"We've been contacted by two shadowed seethes so far. Neither asked for a favor yet but it seemed prudent to plan. Speaking of which, Pip and I both want you to remain at the house, but we'd totally understand if you wanted your own place."

"It'd be pointless right now. But maybe later."

"The accountant needs the numbers for what we pay you. She offered some suggestions on how to work in room and board. I sent that list too, but we can change things if they don't suit you. I couldn't include the extra stuff you do for us, but I couldn't include the extra stuff we do for you either. Examine the numbers and really consider if it seems fair."

"You're kidding, right? "

I couldn't tell if he was being sarcastic, or if he really was shocked.

The entire conversation so far was making me really uncomfortable. I felt it driving a wedge between all of us. Reducing our partnership to shares and tax brackets made it seem a cold heartless transaction.

Julia said, "Neither Pip nor I have much experience with this sort of thing. We're relying heavily on Sandra for advice. She's supplying us the lawyers, accountants, and investment brokers. We pay her for those services. She also supplies us with lessons. We don't pay money for that. She has her reasons for showing us the ropes, and as payment we try to help her out when we can. But the end goal there is different. We don't want to be partners with her. We just want to be friends. Good friends—the kind who show up when you call and are in trouble, but her business and ours won't be meshed like ours are. So Pip and I need you to be happy with all of the arrangements. Or in a few years when you've built up your portfolio, you won't want us around. You'll resent us and we don't want that to happen."

"It's more likely to be you two resenting me..."

Julia said, "If we all know where we stand, we could break up our partnership if it became inconvenient for any of us—calmly without panicking. Your shares in the business would remain yours unless you sell them, and our partnership agreements give us all first refusal."

I said, "'Tis my hope that you'd trust that we'd act honorably in protecting ourselves. 'Tis unfair that we have no need to trust, but life often is unfair..."

He laughed, leaning forward to slap my knee as he said, "That's what makes this entire thing okay with me. I don't have to worry about you being nervous that I'm going to turn on you because I know you'll believe me if you ask. There's be no reason for you to worry about me."

Julia said, "Will you be finished with your projects there in time to meet me as planned?"

"Yes."

Ryu said, "Will you be finished at the estate?"

"I already am. I've stopped recruitment for the time being—actively, that is. All of our current positions are filled and so far our control group is conforming remarkably well. We've only had one minor incident involving drug use, which Doreen will soon have straightened out."

Ryu and I exchanged worried glances.

Neither of us asked.

She continued, "The rehab clinic opened last week and could use more cash. I think I'll hold a fundraiser and ask for donations. If there's enough honest interest, we'll open another rehab in town here."

Ryu said, "I think you should wait until we return."

"I agree," I said. "Spend a few days catching up on your reading. When we get back, the three of us will hold the fundraiser. Maybe a street fair to coincide with the opening of the studio? It would be the ideal time to see about getting the building beside the rehab donated to us. We could ask for volunteers to do the work cleaning and for supplies, and then house a few mules there to look after the place and see to the homeless who use it."

"I guess..."

"Which part of the plan displeases you?"

"None really. I just find it boring trying to wade through those books. It's just so much easier when you explain it to me."

"Which I shall do at the very first opportunity, but you'll have insights that I lack. I'd value your opinion."

"You're right, I should read them myself."

"Any news on Lou's father?" Ryu asked.

"I've tracked down his lawyer, Gerry Archer, and spoken to his accountant. Both sent me copies of all their paperwork. I have Vicky and Jacob going through it. We've tracked down a few accounts that Blackwood had that neither of his accountants knew about and have begun the process of claiming them ourselves. He was doing business in Switzerland and Russia. I think we can assume it'll be a long legal battle that we wouldn't win to retrieve those assets because we can't prove that Lou didn't sign them over when his father died even though I know the lawyer lied."

Ryu snickered.

He said, "You're making them give it back, right?"

"Eventually. I've no idea what they really know and finding out will be difficult seeing as they're there and we're here. I just thought it smart to find out everything we can before messing with them. Lou owns a small estate there, which has been vacant since Blackwood's death. I think he owned a car dealership there too but I'm still unraveling it—carefully so the man running it now doesn't get antsy. I think he's basically stollen it from us. I wish I knew if Lou knew of the assets and was just hiding them from me or if he didn't know."

I said, "And what of our estate?"

"He paid all of the bills. Gerry has access to an account to pay taxes and whatnot. Blackwood hadn't left a will. Gerry expected Lou to try to claim that account, but he never did. I don't think Lou knew about it. Gerry siphoned most of the money away over the last eight years. Lou was paying for the estate bills when Gerry should've been.

"Lou sold his condo right after his father died and moved back home. That condo was the only asset Gerry knew about and he looked once he realized Lou had no idea about his father's finances. The lawyer thought Blackwood was spending his money on travel and women and that he'd dip into the cash reserve soon or sell the estate to keep up with the traveling. He seldom knew where Blackwood was or when he'd be back. But Blackwood was checking in on the house and Lou. It wasn't until Blackwood died that the lawyer started embezzling. We could sue Gerry and win but I think him more useful as he is."

"You have plans for him?"

"Not at the moment, but he's a very respected lawyer with a prestigious firm. Blackwood had only a light grip on him. I think he was trying to keep the estate aboveboard."

I must have looked puzzled because Ryu said, "She means he was pretending to be less well off than he actually was and wanted it to look real, so he hired a company that does that sort of thing and left it to them. How often did he visit the estate, Jewels?"

"I'm not sure. Vicky will have a better idea once she has time to crosscheck his passport and reservations. I think he didn't come home often."

I said, "He visited Lou at the school. Maybe Reginald will know how often?"

"We can stop and ask at the school. Reg has been by a few times and has agreed to help run Reset. I'd like to make him an equal partner…"

"'Tis your decision."

Ryu said worriedly, "I don't know, Jewels. He could screw up your plans for them."

"I don't see how. At most he could disagree with a proposed assignment. I could just make them quit the program and assign them wherever I like."

"He'll know the names of all of your employees."

"He could know that already if he cared to look."

"Just make sure he can't steal it out from under you."

I said, "Is he being… pleasant?"

"Mum and Dad are thrilled we're getting along so well. I really hope he's getting over whatever the hell Lou did to him."

"Don't trust him," Ryu said before I had to.

"I know. I don't actually see him much. He sold the house in Paris, which I think is a good sign that he's letting that go."

I snorted softly.

She said, "I'll see you in a few days. Ta, darlings."

She disconnected.

I said to Ryu, "How difficult will it be to go to Russia?"

"She's right, Pip. We should stay away until we know more. He could've been working with vampires or even real seethes, or God knows what else."

"He was obviously working with magic—so he has books somewhere."

"Not all mages make spellbooks like Sandra does."

"But they'd all have books on it. I'm certain of that," I said.

"Knowing him, I bet he spelled them to burn up on his death."

"No," I disagreed. "He made no plans at all for his passing because he didn't think he could die."

"And that doesn't make sense either. Eventually he'd have had to let that body die to let Lou inherit and yet there wasn't a will."

"Because he still had years before it'd be necessary. He wouldn't have used Lou either because Lou would've been old by then too. I think those children were meant to practice on. I wished I'd thought to ask Pete if Blackwood Senior had visited."

"Reginald might know."

"Dare I ask?"

"...no or at least not without some planning. If Reg is recovering from whatever Lou had on him, he might decide he has to turn you in, especially if he thinks you might be considering doing it again."

"It makes me sick to think that this body did such things—my body...."

"You would never, Pip! And Lou wasn't blameless, but he *was* manipulated."

"I shall try not to dwell."

"Let's go see what the gang is up to at the gym."

I returned his smile—happy that he was so happy with his new friends.

Chapter 43

When we arrived at the warehouse the next evening for our last run through, we found Frankie and Jacob sweeping up the shattered remnants of the glass window that had looked into the small office on the main floor.

Vicky was laying on one of the old couches, buffing her nails. The rest of them were nowhere in sight.

She sat when she saw us.

"Hey, boss."

Frankie said, "We've got this... Did Emma call? I told her not to bother you."

"Got what?" Ryu asked as I shook my head.

Vicky heaved a hard sigh, flopping back onto the couch.

Jacob glared at Vicky as he said, "It was just a minor break in."

"I told the fuckers they'd picked the wrong spot," she said as she sat to shrug at him.

He rolled his eyes, bursting into laughter.

She returned his grin, laying back again to do her nails.

"Someone came here—while you were present? To rob you?"

I was too astounded to be angry.

Frankie said, "They were just dumb kids hopped up on something. We handled it."

"I did, you mean," Vicky muttered, making Jacob laugh again.

Frankie shot her an exasperated glance, cocking his head at her in a way that I thought meant shut up.

She said airily, "It wasn't any big deal. They've gone to drop the bodies."

"We didn't kill them," Frankie said hurriedly, shooting her another exasperated glance. "She just knocked them out. We thought it'd be best if we dumped them in an alley somewhere and let the local authorities handle them."

"And if they say we did it?" Ryu asked dryly.

"*Nah*, they were trying to rob us. They ain't admitting it."

"But they could lie."

"Want me to handle them?" she asked.

"No. Jacob's probably right, but just in case he isn't, take down the street signs on the model."

I walked over to examine the model. Magic glittered brighter as I drew closer. A complicated set of runes wound over the buildings and roads. I recognized some of them and knew it was meant to facilitate the placement of the real runes—or perhaps empower them or maybe deactivate them. Sandra hadn't volunteered the information, and I hadn't asked although I itched to know.

I said, "Leave this model untouched, except for the signs. And I mean completely untouched. Move nothing. Put the architect's models out and some streets or buildings but be careful you don't touch the original. Shred anything that has anything to do with the office building or the people there. We don't need any of that info anymore."

Ryu said, "Wipe the hard drives and then bring all of the backup computers to the tile work boxed and labeled as filler. Only official work on computers and paperwork remain here. Everything else is shredded. Have someone else takes the shreds to the tile works boxed and marked as filler. Vick, do a quick sweep to make sure no one missed anything."

"You think they're onto us for tomorrow?"

"No, but why take chances?"

I said, "We'd intended to clean up tomorrow anyway. This is probably better."

Jacob headed to the office, saying over his shoulder, "I'll put the license plates back on."

Ryu said, "Tell the gang they never saw those kids here. You can say you saw them around if you have. You three say you were here all night and that the others left to go clubbing."

"Remove the camera outside or replace the footage," I said.

"After we see it," Ryu said hastily.

Ryu and I headed to the office, passing Jacob exiting it.

He carried a box of license plates. We'd added magnetic frames around the plates that made it simple to switch them even though they appeared to be bolted on.

I said, "Send the plates to the tile works boxed and marked Storage. Put that box into the recycle pile behind the forge."

"Don't forget to wipe them all down first," Ryu said.

When Ryu and I were alone in the office, I whispered, "I'll have Sandra store them for me."

"We could probably reuse the computers."

"No. They go into the furnace. 'Tisn't worth the risk. Speak to Jacob privately about checking all of their work computers to make sure they don't have anything incriminating on them."

"You should just ask them."

"I will but maybe they don't realize what would be incriminating."

He huffed a quick laugh.

"You mean Ian." He sat at the desk to bring up the security footage as he said, "He's dumb, but he's a team player. I'll tell Vick and Jacob to keep an eye on him."

He fiddled with the controls for a moment, rewinding the tape and then said, "There."

Two men were sharing a bottle that they tossed before pulling knives and kicking at the door while giggling over how easy it was going to be to shake down the guard on night duty.

Vicky, who I identified by the sweatshirt because all I could see was her arm, had opened the door to yank one inside. The man yelling had drowned anything she might've been saying.

The other man had rushed in. A few minutes later one of our cars with Emma driving had exited followed a few minutes later by one of the vans.

I thought Jacob was probably right and that the men were on drugs—but I intended to ensure it at the first opportunity.

I wished I'd had a camera inside the building to see the fight, but I didn't dare.

I returned to the main room to say, "Were you injured?"

"*Nah*. I'm good. Stupid asses didn't even know how to use a knife."

Ryu stepped up behind me to say, "How bad were they hurt?"

"Well, he fell on his own blade, didn't he?"

Jacob snickered.

"She mopped the floor with them, but it was mostly bruises. Both were conscious when we dumped them in the trunk. Emma scared the piss out of them, and I mean that literally. I told her to stop and clean the car before coming back."

I glanced over my shoulder at Ryu who shrugged.

I wasn't sure if Emma could resist murdering them.

"We shall see," I said softly.

Jacob said, "Why are you here, anyway? I thought it was tomorrow night?"

"It is. We just wanted to go over it one last time."

"We know that shit backwards and forwards."

He added hurriedly, "Excuse my language, my lord. I meant no disrespect."

Ryu said, "Apparently you don't know, or you wouldn't have thought tonight was the night."

"I didn't think that. I thought you might've changed your mind is all."

I examined the model, which would be suspicious for us to be caught with but I didn't dare destroy it yet. Sandra had assured me that she wouldn't need this model again after tomorrow. I'd used it to mark where all security cameras were. Each one was marked by a red light that when turned on showed the area the camera covered.

I'd spent two weeks on that, talking to people in every building and examining old recordings to be sure I knew how far every camera saw.

I began setting out some unused model buildings as I said, "It must go like clockwork. To reschedule would require a new plan in its entirety. You know only the smallest portion of the entire."

Angry anima flared from him.

I was too far from Vicky to see if I'd angered her by her anima, but I thought I had by the tightness of her smile.

I continued, "Those others involved have not the slightest inkling that they *are* involved. They shall hopefully remain unaware of their small parts but 'tis tiresome in the extreme to find a suitable stooge and manipulate all to such a finicky degree."

Jacob relaxed. The anima of anger brightened to excitement before dissipating.

Vicky said, "When are you going to show us how you do that?"

I shrugged.

Ryu snickered as he said, "Who would dare disobey a request from Lord Blackwood?"

"Apparently no one," she muttered as she resumed her seat on the couch. She said to me, "It's weird though how everyone jumps to. I understand it for an asshole like Maamoun. The entire city is terrified of him, but no one seems at all scared of you. No one even knows about you."

Ryu's eyes narrowed.

"Don't go asking about him."

She nodded. Her smile hardening again—*this time in fear*, I thought.

I said, "We're all friends here. Ryu is correct though that I don't wish attention brought to myself. I'm just one of millions of visitors here. Do nothing that might make people suspect differently.

Chapter 44

The police hadn't shown up at the warehouse. No one at the office building seemed at all uneasy today, which had seemed to drag on interminably, but we were finally ready to go.

I popped a tiny, spelled emerald from the spellbook and offered it to Ryu who grimaced but took it. I removed another for myself followed by two spelled diamonds.

They didn't bother me at all to eat. I found it amusing. I wasn't sure why it bothered him. I thought it was because of the waste of the gem.

The spellbook was the size of a paperback. The leather cover had been spelled to only open for me. If the leather were breached in any way the contents of the book would burn—or so Sandra had told me, and I had no reason to doubt it.

The fire would need to be very hot to destroy the gems, which were glued to thick paper that had been painted to appear old, which was a ruse intended to fool anyone if I was seen using the book or asked to open it by a police officer.

Tissue thin papers interspersed the thicker vellum of the paintings. A spell was written on each of the thinner papers in melted metal that were meant to be torn out and used. All of them required a reagent to activate—blood, water, sand, spit.

I wasn't able to fashion such things yet although I could with effort shift the anima to infuse paper, but it took my—or Julia's—will to activate it.

"You good, Pip?"

A flush scalded my cheeks as I realized I'd been distracted by the spells instead of removing them, which I hated to do.

I handed him a paper with an inferno rune inscribed on it as I said, "Use care. It will burn hotly. Emerald is for falling. Diamond is for invisible. You have fifteen minutes to get inside before you're visible again." As I was speaking, I tore another of the spells loose and handed it to him.

He said, "I know. Place it flat on the glass and lick the top of the pentagram then back at least five feet away."

"If you fall…"

"Eat the green gem. I got this, Pip."

"'Tis important."

"I won't fall. Stop worrying about me and worry about yourself."

I handed him the diamond and emerald I'd removed for myself.

"Backups. Just in case."

"Take four for yourself too."

I hesitated but then took three of each, hating the necessity because once removed from the book, the spell would begin to deteriorate.

I carefully tucked the gems into the tight pockets of my black spandex clothing—emeralds in the left pocket and diamonds in the right.

I adjusted my goggles, tightening the strap to be certain they wouldn't slip in the wind or from sudden movement. I then carefully removed the spells I'd need, folding and tucking them into my pockets. I wasn't worried about these spells because unlike the gems, they could be returned to the book.

When I had everything situated to my satisfaction, I adjusted my empty pack, tightening all of the straps.

Ryu handed me a bottle of binding powder.

I said, "Take one of the envelopes of it just in case."

He patted his thigh pocket. "Way ahead of you. You ready?"

I nodded and he banged on the wall of the van.

It began to move a few seconds later and I giggled nervously as I grabbed for a ceiling strap.

He laughed too, moving up so he could peer over my shoulder out the back window, which was tinted black.

I watched the small GPS attached to the work bench.

"We're almost there," I said.

"Man, I done some shit before—but this… I have the best time with you, Pip!"

His grin made my pulse flutter.

The van slowed and pulled into a parking lot.

We pulled up alongside a dumpster and Ryu and I hit our stopwatches and swallowed the diamonds.

The world took on a hazy cast as if viewing it through smoke. I could no longer see Ryu at all.

"This is so cool," he muttered, making me laugh nervously again.

As I'd ordered him to this afternoon, Reid opened the van door and returned to the front, presumably to grab his gloves as I'd instructed him to do after he'd opened the door. He had no idea we were back here or what we planned.

His car would be seen by security cameras coming and going in the lot but I'd made certain no cameras would see us. I wanted there to be normal footage on the cameras, which is why we were entering in this manner.

While he was doing that, Ryu and I exited, darting across the parking lot to scale the building.

I glanced over my shoulder to see Reid had dumped a box of trash as he'd been told to do and was driving away.

I dumped a handful of binding powder into my palm that I rubbed onto the bottom of my shoe then dumped another handful that I dipped just my fingertips in before rubbing it onto my knees and other shoe.

I knew exactly where every camera on the street was and had adjusted all of them to be sure there wasn't the slightest chance we'd be seen climbing the building, camera's being the only thing that could see through the spell.

It meant we had to climb up on the left corner until we reached the thirteenth floor then climb under the window to the opposite side and then to the fourteenth floor where we'd break in.

Practice let me run with relative ease up the side of the building.

Sirens sounded in the distance—right on time. The first hint of smoke wafted into the sky five blocks away.

People were already crowding the street at the far intersection. I really hoped my footmen were in position.

"Setting the spell," Ryu said.

I grabbed his leg with the hand that had the binding powder.

The emerald's we'd eaten made us light enough so that I could hold him easily when he pushed away from the wall.

It took me a few seconds to release him. By the time I did, the glass was over halfway gone. It appeared to be melting as if it were paper held over a flame with the edges darkening and curling in. The metal edges of the window glowed with heat for a moment.

When I tentatively touched it, it felt warm but not hot.

I heaved myself over, followed by Ryu.

I took the portal spell from his backpack and placed it on the floor as he shoved furniture to the side to make room.

It took us five minutes to spread it and sprinkle the powder Sandra had prepared the way she'd instructed me.

I knew it was working when it began to glow.

A siren began to wail inside the building.

We bumped fists as he eased the office door open.

I glanced back at the missing window. Darkness blurred the view. Warm currents of air stirred the leaves of the fake potted plants in the corner of the office. Something enormous was hovering right outside the window.

Sandra, I thought in awe and quietly closed the door.

We ran to the elevator and took it to the top floor where Maamoun let us in to the Worthy Shipping office.

"Don't be late for the meeting," I said.

"The paperwork you asked for is on my desk."

He headed to the elevator. We ran into his office and stuffed my pack with the files.

On the way to Maamoun's hidden office on the fourteenth floor, Ryu paused a second to pull the fire alarm.

We ran down to the next landing, reaching it as the explosives detonated, sending a blast of hot air that smelled of metal past us.

Metal clanged hard somewhere close.

My watch beeped.

We ran for the newly opened door, reaching it right as the building shook.

"Too early," Ryu said accusingly to me.

"It wasn't me. That was up here somewhere."

Sharp pops of gunfire were drowned by a screeching of metal.

A man yelled in the distance.

Sprinklers came on and more sirens added their din.

The air was suddenly full of dense smoke and a harsh metallic smell.

"Go!"

I shoved him forward and we ran for the door we couldn't see, following a path we'd memorized.

He used a spell sheet on a metal door to burn a hole that we could crawl through. The man inside the room lifted his gun.

I yelled, "Run for your life! This building is going down. There are ten of us up here. We spoke Russian and you're sure we're after the safe. You barely got away with your life! Run! Run!"

He ran.

Ryu knelt to pull a gun from his bag. He shot up the wall, pulled out another gun and did the same thing as I ran for the filing cabinets and my true target.

A spell sheet got me through the lock on the cabinet. I began sorting through the files, stacking some aside but tossing most. I hadn't dared take them earlier, having no way to guarantee their absence wouldn't be missed. The only thing I'd dared do was disable their failsafe meant to destroy the files in the case of a police search.

Maamoun had kept complete records on the men he did business with. Forty years worth of criminal finances. If I ever had need, I'd know just who had dirty money that I could steal. I thought he'd kept these records for that exact purpose.

Ryu shot off a few more clips then began stuffing files into his pack. We gathered files until our watches beeped again. Sandra's fire would burn the rest.

"Where are you going?" he yelled when I ran up back to the doorway we'd entered instead of for a window.

"I just want to see. One quick peek."

He followed me.

I eased the door to the office open a crack where we'd left the portal spell, crouching to give him a view over my head.

Molten gold glimmered in a long spiral from an enormous hole in the floor. It flowed through the air into the center of the portal where it disappeared into a black abyss.

A roar echoed beneath us, and a man's scream cut off abruptly.

Flame glowed from the hole, revealing Drew standing with his back turned on the edge of the hole, peering down into it.

He was naked carrying a staff as tall as he was.

Before I could see what he was doing, Ryu closed the door and tugged me away.

We ran back down to the office, which was so densely full of smoke now that I couldn't see my hand in front of my face.

I gripped Ryu's hand tightly, running for the wall, feeling along it with my free hand to find a window.

I pressed his hand to the window before releasing him to slap a spell sheet on it.

The building rumbled as the first bomb detonated.

Ryu slapped my shoulder and I stepped to the side to let him jump out as I reached for my emerald.

The building rumbled again, glass crashing with a tearing shriek of metal loud enough I could feel it in my chest.

The tiny stone slipped from my grasp. I fumbled for the backup.

Another even louder tearing shriek of noise shook the entire building and something hard knocked into my back, pushing me forward.

I rolled with the impact and found myself falling.

"Pip!" Ryu screamed as I fell past him.

He reached for me, missing, and began cursing.

I got the second gem from my pocket right as the building began to settle. Ryu tumbled passed me from the force of the explosion.

Smoke and dust billowed around me. Laughing in giddy relief, I cast the spell of holding on one of the larger chunks. I grabbed it and cast again before letting go and landing on a circle of motionless sand with a thump hard enough to knock the wind from me. Smoke was so thick in the air that it was impossible to see more than a foot in any direction.

I gasped for a second, catching my breath.

Another wave of hot air accompanied by a new batch of debris and smoke rolled me off my platform.

I made another below me and managed to grasp the edge of it before the wind could knock me completely off.

The air above me stirred, strong downdrafts—*wings*—I thought in awe, but I didn't have time to gawk as much as I longed too.

I released my platform to have my hands free to grab that last emerald from my pocket.

I popped it into my mouth and immediately stopped falling down, instead being pushed sideways by the heated air below me.

I ate a diamond right as I cleared the thicker dust.

"Ryu!" I yelled as I scanned the dark looking for a darker spot or stirred dust that would reveal his position.

"Here!" he yelled. "I think I'm above you still. You scared ten years off my life!"

For some reason I found that hilarious.

My laughter cut off in a small shriek as I began to hurtle through the sky.

"It's just me," Drew said from right beside me. "Now, quiet down and I'll get you two out of here."

"I left two hardened patches," I said as I crashed into Ryu who grabbed me in a tight embrace.

"I dispelled them already.

We slid down, weaving between the larger buildings then picking up speed until we were going what felt very fast.

Our speed gradually slowed until we were drifting slowly above empty desert.

"I think he's gone," I whispered to Ryu.

Ryu said in a normal speaking voice, "There's nothing near us. You don't need to whisper. I hope we land before we get too far out."

I said, "Hold onto me. I'll cast a holding spell in front of us. It should stop our forward momentum and then we'll just sink straight down."

We hit the spell, laughing as we tried to push ourselves down from it.

"Do it again," he said. "I'd hate for this emerald to wear off while we're so far up."

We were only about fifty feet up now, but I didn't want to fall from this height either.

I said, "I'll aim below you about five feet. Feel around for it on my mark. Mark!"

I envisioned carefully and cast as quickly as I could, more nervous now than when I'd been free falling. I hadn't time then to worry about screwing up and the dust had made it easy to envision what I wanted. Now I was imagining him falling into the air as I was holding it.

His left foot landed on the spot, and I was able to grab it and him as he fell off of it.

We pushed against it to give ourselves some momentum.

Within a few minutes we were safely on the ground.

"We should've brought another diamond," he said as he dusted himself off.

"Why? There's nothing around for miles."

We began walking in the direction of the city, which we could see as lights in the distance.

"Because if anyone sees us…. Never mind. You'll just whammy them."

"Whammy… You mean hit them with my magic?"

"Close enough. You think anyone saw us falling?"

"No. We were over sand before the diamond wore off. I really want to learn that spell."

"I wish I could learn them. Still—I can do alchemy, which is cool. Is there an alchemy equivalent?"

"Similar, perhaps. We might be able to improve upon it. Smoked truffle gathered in the dark of night, if such can be found growing upon a node. Perhaps we should visit the standing stones of Calanais?"

We discussed possible alchemy solutions until we were within sight of a road.

He called Frankie, "Come pick me up." He listened for a minute then said, "Of course I'm aware, dumbass! Send me that list, no one else. I'll text you the street address. Don't dawdle but don't speed either."

"Problems?" I asked when he put his phone back into his pocket.

"*Nah*. They're freaking a bit is all."

"'Tell them 'twas my decision to keep the goal from them. They're blameless."

"Oh, he wasn't upset that we killed those assholes just that he couldn't take part."

"So—it worked. We're any innocents injured?"

"He'll text me a list."

"'Tis no need to coddle me from hard truths. I knew the risk as well as you."

"I'm not being coy. I just don't know. There's been five reported fatalities so far, but no names given. It could be our targets."

"I expect to be told truthfully."

"Of course."

"'I shan't force you to answer," I said stiffly.

"I know..." he grimaced ruefully at me as he added, "I like that you trust me, but you shouldn't trust anyone, Pip. Ask us all, all the time."

"Then I'll never have a true friend..."

His phone rang.

"Jewels," he said happily when he answered. His expression darkened as he listened. I only caught a few words, but the tone was angry.

I held out my hand.

He said, "Pip wants to talk to you."

He covered the phone with his hand and whispered, "She's in a snit. I told you we should've told her the entire plan."

I took his phone and said, "'Twas my order. I'd not have innocent deaths on your head, which they *would* be if you knew of my plan. The men were simply too dangerous to leave loose."

"Sandra had no right to ask you to do that, Pip!"

"Sandra agreed with me, nothing more. She didn't ask me to blow the building. 'Twas my idea to cover our tracks. She knew nothing of my desire to use the explosion as a means of disposing of them. They were too deep in my thrall to behave normally. Something had to be done. I positioned my footmen to block the streets and spoke to everyone I could in the nearby buildings before the event telling them to stay home or to leave early or run when they first heard sirens."

"They're calling it a terrorist attack, Pip!"

"It was such... those men were terrorists. They terrorized everyone they could all of the time! My hope is no innocents were injured in my attempt to stop them, but they *had* to be stopped!" Ryu took the phone back to say, "Pip's right, Jewels. We couldn't have left them even if we wanted to. They were too far gone. Someone was bound to notice them acting very oddly but we didn't do it to hide our thefts. We did it because if we left them alive they'd have murdered many more people."

He heaved a hard sigh as he tapped speaker phone.

Julia yelled, "We don't keep these huge secrets from each other! You don't get to protect me by keeping me in the dark!"

"I love you—truly. I *must* do as my conscience dictates to protect your soul, whether you wish to be protected or not."

"My soul's just fine!"

Ryu said, "You're making her cry, Jewels. Can't you just let it go—at least for now. We'll be more careful in the future not to make too many zombies and it won't be necessary to get rid of so many all at once again."

"I'm sorry, Pip. I love you too. I'm not angry at you, just worried that you're taking on more that you should. It's my soul to worry about. You don't need to worry about it for me. I promise I'll go to church and sincerely pray."

I dashed my angry tears away.

"Do as you will."

"Pip...."

Ryu said, "I'll call when we find out what's going on here. We're fine and will be on that plane. See you in a few days, Jewels."

He tucked his phone into his pocket.

We didn't speak until we were in Frankie's car an hour later.

"She's right, you know," he said as we reached the warehouse. "It has to be her choice. You can't force salvation on her."

My glare made him flush.

"Are you wearing your amulet?"

He bit his lip, nodding.

I thumped his chest with my finger to emphasize my words as I yelled in his face, "We protect Julia—even from herself! I care not if it makes her unhappy with us! I shall act before she can commit an offense that God will not forgive! I will never forgive you if you lead her to damnation! Never!"

I stalked away before I was tempted to rip the amulet from him and ensure he'd listen.

Chapter 45

I took a cab to the warehouse early the next morning and was surprised to see everyone, except Ryu and Ollie already there.

The sparkle of magic was gone from the model. The faintest outline a pentacle was through the window of the thirteenth floor, although perhaps twas only my perception because I expected something to remain. It had been a powerful spell.

Awed goosebumps rose on my arm as I considered Sandra's power.

I disassembled the model of the office building, throwing the pieces into the pile of scraps of similar pieces, except for the thirteenth floor. I painted it with the black paint that we used to lay ou5 the roads then broke it into pieces and mixed those pieces into the trash. While I was doing that Ryu placed one of the spare models in its place.

My footmen watched with puzzled expressions, likely wondering why I bothered.

"Gather around, please," I said.

"Did we have anything to do with that, boss?" Jacob asked as they took their positions in a tight circle around me.

Their anima was a familiar warmth.

"Of course not," I said. "We've all been working really hard getting the tile factory up and running. You've been busy taking messages to the contractor for the new apartment building and getting the art show ready to open. Does anyone have any reason to think any of us might be involved?"

Emma said, "Vicky was sneaking off to meet with someone at an apartment building and it was supposed to be empty."

"You're mistaken."

I took her hand to tug her from the group.

"Vicky would never be involved with something illegal. You've only seen her here, the office, the condo, and the tile works, or when the two of you shared meals or went for drinks."

She stared at me without expression. The rest of them looked confused or annoyed. No one was angry enough to make their anima appear on their rinds.

I pulled her back into the circle to say, "If anyone asks you, you only ever saw official business being done. No one acted suspiciously at all. Yusuf quit the week we arrived, and we haven't seen him since. None of you liked him, so we never gave it a second thought."

They nodded or murmured agreement.

I said, "Emma, book a flight home for yourself. That attack scared you and you want to go home. Jacob, Nick, Frankie, and Vicky will stay here with me. The rest of you leave as planned on the first for Scotland."

"Are we still holding the art opening?" Jacob asked.

"Why wouldn't we? The explosion had nothing at all to do with us. Insurance should cover our losses, not that we had much invested there to lose. Frankie has copies of all of our office files. We can work from here until our suite at Gryphon Tower is ready."

Vicky frowned at Frankie, scanning the group and looking puzzled.

"That will be all. Frankie will keep us informed if we need to make official statements. Frankie, Vicky, a word, please. Nick, collect all of the burner phones, seal them in an envelope, and leave it with me."

I headed for my office here, which still lacked glass from the window that had broken.

Frankie and Vicky followed me.

Ryu said, "Frankie, call the police station and see if they need a statement or anything from us. Inform them that all of our employees are accounted for. If they do want a statement, make an appointment and inform Jacob."

"Right, o, boss."

He jumped up, reaching for his cell phone.

I said to Vicky, "Are you wearing the Query Inc pin?"

"What...oh yeah. I forgot about it."

She took off her blazer to remove the pin.

When she handed it to me, I said, "Tell me what you think happened?"

She glanced over her shoulder and leaned closer to whisper, "I think you blew that shit up."

"'Tis true but never tell anyone else."

"Like I would..."

"The women?"

"Are on their way to America. Are you sure you can trust that guy to let them go on the other end?"

"He's just transport. I paid all of the fees. They should be released on their arrival; free to go wherever they wish, but of course I can't guarantee that someone else in the loop of whom I'm unaware doesn't take advantage."

"I gave them the directions to the embassy and a women's shelter."

"You gave them..."

"I meant I told Jean to. She said she did."

"We're you aware that Emma was following you?"

"No and it worries me. I don't trust her to keep her mouth shut."

"I don't think it would matter overmuch since the women don't know where they were being held, but just to be on the safe side take Jean and go clean it up."

"They could probably describe Jean."

"Jean might have to be sacrificed."

"Is Yusuf dead?"

"Yes. He was in the building."

"Even if you kill her, she's still a link back to you."

"If pressed, Jean will say she was working with Yusuf trying to steal those women and that she didn't know anything about what the men had planned. Yusuf's body will be found on the first floor, and he'll have died from a gunshot to the head. My hope is the police infer that he was murdered by the gang he was trying to swindle."

"And she's just going to admit that..."

"Yes. There will be some small pieces of corroborating evidence in Yusuf's apartment. Nothing that should link her without her testimony. I'm hoping neither is identified."

"... How do you do that?"

"I'm debating telling you, but I think right now you have no need to know. Do you plan to tell anyone of what really happened here?"

"No. As far as I'm concerned it was all official business."

I pocketed the pin.

"Very good. I'm extremely pleased with your service. Might I suggest you take your quarterly bonus and speak to Leandro. You'll find him quite happy to give you the piece that you were his inspiration for. You can then keep it, leave it in the show and see what offers it gets, or even put it into our auction, whichever pleases you to do. I think you'd be amazed at the prices that our little auction will bring in."

Her eyes widened.

The buzzer sounded, announcing a car had pulled into our driveway.

Jacob yelled, "It's the police, Lord Blackwood!"

"Let them in. We have nothing to hide."

Vicky said, "I'll check to make sure of it."

She ran from the office.

I went to make sure the portraits had all been removed from the wall, which they had.

Nick flipped off the television and all of them ran up into the loft, except for Jacob who escorted the police inside.

Ryu had been rearranging the the model on the table to that of the new apartment building. There were still a few buildings and streets but there wasn't anything to say which streets.

I was still examining it when the two officers entered.

"Lord Blackwood," the older of the two said in English. "My name is Sergeant Saadeh, and this is Sergeant Mohamad."

"I assume this is about the Maamoun building?" I asked as I shook the offered hand.

"Yes."

"My secretary was supposed to phone to inform you that all of my staff is accounted for."

As Mohamad and I were talking, Saadeh circled the table, examining the model.

He said, "That's good to hear. Can I ask what your business is here?"

"Art mainly. Please, come into my office, such as it is."

I led them into the office, gesturing them to seats as I took mine behind the desk. Jacob sat on the windowsill.

I took one of the tile brochures and one of the flyers announcing the art show from my desk and slid it across the table, saying, "We only had a short lease in that building. We'd only arrived in town last month. Our permanent office space isn't quite ready yet."

Mohamad flipped through the brochure while we were speaking.

"Oh, where will you be?"

"Gryphon Tower. It's undergoing some renovations at the moment. We have a three-year lease there."

"I see."

Jacob said, "Is there an official casualty list? We do business with Xion shipping."

I said, "I'm sure someone from the office will be in touch to reschedule."

Mohamad asked, "You sell much of this?"

I nodded.

"We've begun updating the equipment. I believe sales will increase when we offer the Leandro line, which we plan on doing once all of the equipment is up to date and can handle the increase."

"*Hmm.*"

He picked up the flyer, frowning doubtfully at it.

"Gorgeous, isn't it! So original, so alive! It has such passion!"

He shrugged as he dropped the flyer onto my desk.

"Had you done any business with Worthy Shipping?"

"We approached them, but Xion is smaller and so more personal. She was quite obliging about our security needs. Worthy's security was a bit too opaque for me."

"How do you mean?"

"I requested to have my own security men run background checks on the men who'd be escorting my tile and was flatly refused. It seemed a simple request. One Xion was happy to oblige.

Vicky approached with a tray and tea from upstairs.

"Gentlemen?"

"I make the tea myself," I said as I accepted a cup, nodding my thanks to Vicky.

She set down cups for them on my desk and handed Jacob one.

She said, "The manager at the factory called. If you don't need me, I'll go settle the paint dispute."

"Take Nick and stop at the apartments. Inform the contractors that we'll be working from here for the next few days and remind them I'll be in Scotland for three weeks, so all the permits need to be in order."

"Yes, sir."

"You're leaving the country, sir?" Saadeh asked.

"Right after the auction. My lady wife insists that I don't miss Baron Fardenay's ball. Nick Kane will be in charge here while I'm gone. He'll know how to reach me should the need arise although I can't imagine I'd be much help."

"Did you notice anything odd or..."

I snorted. "I assure you, sir, if I'd have noticed thugs about planting bombs, I'd have called forthwith!"

Jacob said, "His lordship doesn't spend much time in the office."

I nodded agreement, saying, "Frankie, my secretary was there most days. But if he'd seen anything, I'm sure he'd have told me."

"We'll want him to make a statement."

"He's upstairs."

Jacob said, "I can get him."

"No need to disturb yourself," Mohamad said.

He left the office and headed upstairs.

Jacob followed him.

I said, "Do they have any leads on who the perpetrator is?"

"We believe it was a Russian gang new to the area."

"Why would anyone do that..."

"We'll find out."

"Do you do business in Russia?" he asked.

Unease shivered through me. I had no idea if Lou had done business there.

"No. This is actually my first business venture. I was in banking until my accident. I now find I quite enjoy art. I've designed a few of the tiles myself. My wife and I are using quite a bit of it in our home. Mary, my mother-in-law, designed the most exquisite tile for the summer room."

"I'm sure. We'd like a list of your employees."

"I assume you mean just the ones that are here? We have quite a few of them elsewhere."

"Really? I thought this was your first business venture?"

"It is. My wife also has employees. And then there's the houses. We have a large personal staff, grooms, gardeners, cooks, maids, drivers."

"Just the staff here will be fine."

I opened my top desk drawer to remove our official day planner.

He stood to lean across the desk and read the entries.

I flipped to the last Friday page then copied the names listed to hand it to him.

"Frankie can get you copies of their timecards if needed."

I handed him one of my business cards.

"We all stay at the same condominium complex."

"What's the model there for?"

I laughed lightly as I said, "I couldn't find a place that would suit me. So we're building a luxury housing complex."

His lips pursed. "There's plenty of luxury apartments available."

"None have the stables and barns that I and my friends require. It shan't be a high rise but more a sprawling hotel with its own everything, including two indoor horse rings."

"I see."

I showed him the plans and let him flip through the maps while I gushed about our projects.

Ian joined us while I was showing him the model.

He said, "Excuse me, but the caterer is calling again. They need a firm answer."

"Then tell them to continue as we'd planned."

"Yes, sir."

He stepped away and Jacob leaned over the upper rail to say, "Should I call and reschedule at the bank?"

I said, "I think I'm done here."

Saadeh said, "Thank you for your time. If anything occurs to you..."

"My secretary always knows where I can be reached."

We shook and he left, heading up the metal stairs where his partner still was.

Jacob ran down the stairs and whispered, "Mohamad is getting everyone's statement. Emma—"

He broke off when the two detectives appeared on the stairs.

He joined them and escorted them out.

I went upstairs to see what Emma had said.

Frankie handed me one of the briefcases. I could tell by the weight it was still full of money.

Everyone was glowering at Emma.

She crossed her arms, saying, "I told you; I never saw it before! Someone rigged that security tape! It wasn't me! I'd remember something I was supposed to have done last night!"

Frankie turned his laptop so that I could see the security footage that clearly showed Emma placing the case by Vicky's desk. The smirk on her face was infuriating.

Frankie said, "Vicky found the case wrapped in a blanket and she was seriously pissed. She told me to make it look casual, so we put the blanket on the couch here and just left the case beside the couch."

I said, "No harm done. We can all just forget about it."

My anger made them sway toward me.

I said to Emma, "Don't trouble yourself by thinking about it. It never happened. Did you call to make those reservations?"

"Yes. Thanks for letting us go home."

"This trip was a bad experience that I'm sure you want to forget. But don't forget that you had some good times here too after the boring office work was done. I'm sure you want to remember the lovely dinners and getting drinks with your coworkers."

"She didn't come out with us much," Frankie said.

"Where did you go?" I asked.

"I stayed home. It isn't like they wanted me along."

"It's nice that you enjoy quiet nights in reading. Pick a few books to read on the plane on the way back and remember them so you can tell me all about them."

She grinned at me.

I wanted to slap her.

I smiled back.

Chapter 46

Ollie was the only footman to accompany Ryu and myself onto the Query Inc jet.

I expected Drew or Sandra to appear aboard after the plane took off but neither did.

Ryu fell asleep within minutes.

Ollie was playing with the tv, switching channels with the eagerness that most people displayed when shown a new television.

I'd never understand the modern fascination with machines that they already owned but of a different size. Smaller or larger— it appeared to make no difference as long as it was newer.

I settled into my seat to read my paper, which was full of speculation as to the reason why a Russian gang had attacked in the manner they had. The obituaries were full of glowing praise for the men I'd murdered. The two innocent people who were killed in a car crash, a crash that was assumed to have been caused by the driver gawking at the buildings in the distance, not the road, got barely a mention.

I texted Emma, ordering her to follow up to be sure there were no orphaned children left behind. Moments after I sent the text it occurred to me that she might think I'd meant to murder them as well.

I texted her again, saying, *'Take no action at all. I just wish for information.'*

I stared at the text, debating if she were worth keeping around because the only reason that I could think of why she'd have put the money and blanket there was to get us caught.

She'd have gone inside the apartment to get them. *She'd been planning something.* I wished I'd thought to ask the officers why they'd come when they had. They hadn't appeared to take any particular notice of Emma or anyone. They'd seemed to believe me, showing no strong emotion at all, which I didn't think would've been the case if they'd thought we were involved. It hadn't occurred to me to question them, and it was too late to question her when I'd told her to forget.

I finally leaned across the aisle to say to Ollie, "What's your opinion of Emma?"

"She's fucking nuts, if you'll pardon my bluntness."

"'Tis my thought to reassign her somewhere else. How would the rest of the team react to that?"

"Reassign her or..."

"A job at the estate, I suppose."

He said, "I wouldn't trust her if I was you. Especially if she thinks you're going to demote her."

"You don't trust her," I asked thoughtfully.

"Who would?"

"Who would, indeed."

I sat back in my seat and stared at my newspaper, debating what to do with the problem that was Emma.

Ryu woke as the plane was landing.

We'd each brought just the one carryons, which were full of cash, and were through customs in moments without me needing to do a thing.

Ollie glanced wistfully back at the airport.

"You should buy your own jet, Lord Blackwood."

"I've no need of one."

"But they're so cool."

Ryu said, "Take his Lordship's bag and see about our rental car. Call me when you've got it."

Ollie took my bag and his own and sauntered off.

"He doesn't like Emma. Said she can't be trusted. Is that his normal sort of reaction to a woman?"

"No one likes Emma," Ryu said absently as he stopped to read an airport map.

No one likes her.

"There's a restaurant here where we can grab a bite while Ollie gets the car."

He began walking, saying, "He doesn't dislike women in general if that has you worried."

"It hadn't occurred to me to worry over that..."

We reached the restaurant and ordered our food.

"You're... distracted. I hope you're still not angry about Julia. I agree with you, Pip. I'd never do anything to hurt her."

"Why don't you like Emma?"

He opened his mouth then closed it again, his eyes narrowing and his fingers tapping the tabletop.

"What's the sudden fascination with Emma?"

"Why don't you like her?"

"Cause she's a sociopath. She's getting worse at hiding it too. Or maybe she's not bothering to hide it. I think in her mind we're all like her. I see her try to mimic Vicky and it's creepy as hell."

"Mimic her how?"

"Vicky is funny. She's nice. She's normal except for her temper, which we all know how to avoid. She's real with us and comfortable with who she is. Actually, now that I think about it, she's a lot like you..."

"And Emma tries to be funny and nice?"

"Not really—maybe. It's more she mimics Vicky's mood. Like if Vicky comes in and lounges around, so does Emma. If Vicky is studying an op, Emma tries to mimic her intensity but it's all just surface mannerisms. She isn't really interested like Vicky is. I think she's trying to learn to be her, but she doesn't see the real her, she just see's the surface."

"I see."

"Are you going to tell me why you ask?"

"I don't like Emma. I never have. 'Twas my thought that I might've influenced you to dislike her as well. But I think not as I never noticed she was stalking Vicky."

His eyes widened then narrowed.

"Son of a bitch!"

"Quite... I'm uncertain how to proceed. I want her nowhere near Julia."

"Jewels ain't going to mind if we cancel the test on her. Just make her behave."

"'Tisn't Julia who concerns me. My footmen would rightfully distrust me were I to permanently fire one of them—without cause at least. I hate to manipulate any of them to the degree would be needful to make them forget her. I could manipulate her and leave her in the group but I've no wish to see her and 'tis clear she finds loopholes in my commands."

"Can't we just manipulate her and leave her in Dubai or send her to London to work?"

"I think not—or not without checking in on her frequently. If I were a demon looking to inhabit someone, especially if I wished to infiltrate my enemy's stronghold, she's exactly the host I'd look for."

"You think she's possessed?"

"I think she'd accept a possession—mayhap even seek one out if it ever occurred to her that such was a real possibility, which it might do if she begins to think on the things she's seen and knows we've done. She was clearly plotting something if she stole that briefcase. Her training should've made her bring it to me immediately and yet she put it in the loft, which is a loophole... one I believe she intended to use to do serious harm although I'm not certain if that harm was meant for myself or only Vicky."

"Then you have to make her forget."

"I did."

I gestured to his untouched burger.

"'Tis my problem. I can handle it."

Ollie called while we were eating. Ryu ordered a hamburger to go, which arrived as we were finishing.

He paid in cash, and we went to the car where he gave Ollie the bag, saying, "I'll drive. We ate."

"Thanks, man."

Ollie got into the passenger seat.

Ryu said, "This is just between us, would the rest of the gang give a shit if I were to whack Emma?"

Ollie shook his head and kept eating.

Ryu continued, "The boss doesn't want to do it because she—he—doesn't want to upset anyone, make them antsy like, but he's worried that Emma might try to kill Vicky."

"Good luck with that," Ollie said, and Ryu laughed in agreement.

Ollie said, "Still, it'd suck if she got lucky. Vicky's cool as shit. We should warn her at least."

Ryu said, "Maybe—it ain't that I don't want to warn her, but I have no proof. It seems to me that would start a feud and maybe splinter the group because why the hell would I leave Emma there if I really thought she'd turn on us?"

"Good point," I said. "'Tis my belief she could be turned. No words of mine could hold against such a soul... 'twill have to be the ax."

Ollie shrugged and began eating again.

Ryu glanced at me in the rearview.

"That's how it is in our world. You cross a line and you die."

Julia was waiting at the hotel when we arrived and greeted all three of us with quick hugs, even Ollie who gaped at Ryu then grinned at her.

She didn't notice, being too intent on hugging me again.

She said, "Baron Fardenay has invited us to dinner, and I've accepted on our behalf. We were offered rooms at his home, which I politely declined with the excuse that we had too much staff that we needed access to. Ollie, I've rented the entire floor."

As she was speaking, she handed a keycard to Ollie and one to Ryu."

"If you prefer a different room, just ask at the desk."

Her cheeks flushed as she said to Ryu, "Your suite is across from ours. We have it for two weeks. You could take those weeks off, not that we want you to leave..."

His cheeks were just as flushed as hers.

My heart sunk as I realized she'd given him his own suite so that he could bring a date back.

It hadn't occurred to me to offer him time off. It hadn't occurred to me that of course he'd have his own interests that he'd want to pursue.

I said, "I'm unused to the modern way of managing staff and have been remiss about arranging for time away. Please, feel free to make arrangements that are pleasing to you."

He laughed as he cuffed Ollie on the shoulder.

"This ain't no job, it's a way of life. We don't want to miss anything, do we?"

"No siree bob!"

"There won't be much to miss," Julia said. "If you'd like to go home for a visit or have them here in your room, it's fine with us. Just work out a schedule that puts one of the footmen on duty for driving and one for running around should the need arise. The rest can do what they like."

I said, "Except for Frankie and Jacob. Leave them off the schedule entirely as their time will be spent doing their regular jobs for me but arrange to give them time off."

Ryu surprised me by giving me a smacking kiss on the cheek.

"See, you can't do without me!" He bowed extravagantly. "Your wish is my command."

Julia grinned at him—a real smile that lit her eyes.

Ryu's eyes darkened when he met hers.

I was shocked when anima appeared around her lit the color of lust.

His anima darkened to a matching color, a thin line between them brightening.

I hastily looked away, saying hurriedly, "I'm for a long soak. You can fill me in, Jewels."

A hint of embarrassment shadowed her normal smile.

I was just as embarrassed because it hadn't occurred to me until that moment that she'd have seen me lusting after him too.

"Have you found an estate you like?" I asked to distract us both.

Her smile gained depth.

Ryu said, "I'll catch you later," and he followed Ollie.

"There's a few I want to see," she said.

471

I let her happy talk soothe my embarrassment. We could talk later—much later—about my growing infatuation. *Or perhaps I could find a more suitable man, someone who'd return my interest.*

I laughed in sudden excitement as I realized I could date too.

"I'm so glad you're home and happy," Julia said.

I laughed again as I hugged her.

"Me too. We shouldn't part for so long. I missed you like crazy. Show me your dress. And wait until you see the jewelry I brought you! It should be arriving with my footmen."

She laughed with me.

It hardly bothered me at all when she glanced down the hall to smile after Ryu.

Chapter 47

Baron Fardenay bowed over Julia's hand.

"We're so pleased you could make it, aren't we, my darling? Lord Blackwood, Lady Blackwood, might I have the honor of introducing you to my wife, Beatrice, Baroness Fardenay.

"Charmed," I murmured as I kissed her hand. "Please, call me Philip."

"And I'm Julia," Julia said as she and the baroness shook hands.

Beatrice said, "Please, come meet our guests. Sir Horace Sheld, Margret and Thomas Dale, and the honorable Fredrick Maiser and his wife, Doctor Gwendolyn Maiser. Lord and Lady Blackwood, the Earl and Countess of Horsham."

The doctor and his wife were just a bit older than Julia and I.

Horace was a very old man in a wheeled chair. He reminded me strongly of Mr. Fischer, except he had a very pale rind.

I leaned to shake his hand and he clasped it a moment in both of his. "You've the look of your father, sure enough. Peter tells me you're one for the books as well."

"You knew my father?"

"Oh, aye, he bought the old pile from me, didn't he? I'd have thought you'd have been by before this—it's been what, six years or more since he passed?"

Julia took my arm as she said," My husband has no recollection of his father at all since his accident."

"Aye, we'd heard you'd conked yourself right proper."

Gwendolyn offered her hand to me, saying, "You've had no recovery then?"

I shook my head as Julia said, "No, he hasn't. The doctor assures me there's still hope but we've become accustomed—or at least I have. It's harder on him, of course."

I said, "I shan't complain. I'm grateful I retained my faculties."

Peter said happily, "He's a right dab hand at translating the Greek. I promised to show him my books."

Beatrice said, "After dinner, dear, or it will grow cold."

A woman wearing a blue dress with a white apron entered and began handing out glasses.

"It's duced good," Horace said approvingly.

I said, "My wife found the most amazing vintage recently."

The talk turned to favorite wines for a few minutes as we settled into our seats.

Horace leaned over to say, "Peter's cook makes the most amazing Cullen Skink."

"The secret is to catch the fish yourself," Peter said. "Have you any interest in fishing?"

"I've no idea... it hadn't occurred to me to try it."

They all laughed.

Julia said, "He enjoys riding. In fact we hoped to buy a property here to keep some horses."

"I see," Horace said thoughtfully. "You're keen for the hunt then?"

I nodded.

He continued, "I don't suppose my old place would do at all for that…"

Julia said, "We didn't know his father had a place here. We just recently learned that the lawyer his father had hired to manage the housing trust scarpered with the funds."

"Good lord!"

"We aren't sure how far back his thievery goes or if others were involved because Philip has no memory of the events at all. It's possible he'd made alternate arrangements that he just forgot about. Straightening out the finances has become my full-time job…"

I said, "'Tis much to ask, I know, yet I haven't the heart to face it."

She patted my hand.

"It's further complicated because Lou went through a bit of a wild phase right after his father's death."

I said, "I believe I was a bit of a bounder, drinking, gambling… I eventually settled down and got a degree. 'Tis a miracle that I found my beautiful Julia…"

Julia laughed lightly.

"We met completely by chance in New York City. It was love at first sight—at least for me."

"For me as well. If not at that precise moment—surely when I awoke at your feet."

Gwendolyn said, "You didn't recall her either?"

"I recall nothing, except for some plays and strangely the languages I spoke."

Julia said, "We'd been reading the plays directly after the accident. He fell asleep, and when he woke… it was all he remembered."

"How very strange. I'd heard of something very similar recently."

Fredrick shook his head, saying, "The man was gravely injured and died soon after, so not, I think, *too* similar."

"I'd meant the recall. He vividly recalled the show he'd been watching; thought he was living that show. So much so that he was convinced he was married to the woman in it."

Julia said worriedly, "Did he die of the brain injury?"

"Heavens no! I shouldn't have alarmed you, my dear. It was just such a strange occurrence—one I thought to never encounter again, and yet here we sit."

Fredrick said, "He died of sepsis."

She gave him a wounded glance as she said, "We knew his chances were small since the accident had badly injured his intestinal tract. Within hours of arriving he had a massive infection that we were unable to stop."

"Lived for over a week, the poor chap. Quite out of his head the entire time, which, I suppose, was a mercy. In the end, he went peacefully enough."

Beatrice said, "My, the talk has grown morbid. Tell me, Julia, have you plans to move here permanently?"

"No. We'd like something we can refurbish and come for short visits to ride and admire the scenery."

"Plenty of such around here," Horace said cheerfully.

She grinned at him as she said, "We'd like to have guests for long weekends and maybe balls. I do so love balls. I was just thrilled to be invited to yours! We've begun restoring our estate and hope you'll attend our first ball in the fall."

I said, "Assuming the roof is quite firmly attached by then..."

Julia laughed, saying gaily, "It will certainly be ready by September, darling. We plan to have a costume ball with a Shakespearian theme. The ballroom itself has been repaired but the guest rooms above it suffered extensive damage from an unnoticed hole in the roof."

I said, "We had to basically rebuild it."

"It wasn't quite that bad. It needed to be gutted to update the wiring and plumbing, which feels like a never-ending process..."

"You Blackwoods sure do like a project," Horace said.

Margret tittered.

Her husband, Thomas, said, "We all thought your father was a might barmy for wanting Horace's old place..."

"Here now! Don't go disparaging my family's keep!"

He snickered, clearly not at all angry at the disparagement or that he'd had to sell it.

He continued, "His lordship will be thinking I sold his father a pig in a poke! 'Twas a right decent deal!" his lips pursed as he considered me. "It's strange though that you never came. I'm wondering if it's one of those properties your crooked lawyer fella stole away?"

"Has anyone come?" Julia asked.

Horace said thoughtfully, "Colleen stays to herself. She has to be what... eighty if she's a day. Her son comes to town to do the shopping and whatnot, but he's a quiet one too and must be pushing sixty."

"Colleen?"

"Oh aye, she came with the place or close enough. It was deserted for a good many years. I'd let her have the run of it for her sheep. She was one of the traveling folk. Her folks kept a caravan wherever they could cage a spot. She ended up marrying a local, but her husband died soon after the boy was born. She counted on them sheep. Made soaps and such and would sell it at fairs and she did some light housekeeping for me.

"Her husband had been a mate of mine in the war. He was a good fellow... When Blackwood bought the place, he kept her on as groundskeeper and cook and she sold her old place that was falling down around her ears. He wasn't around much those first few years while the rebuilding was going on. Don't be thinking it's a grand castle. It's just a small croft on the edge of the moors. It do have a grand view though. A grand view!"

Margret said, "It's a chore to reach it though. I've been there twice collecting for the church. Colleen's a nice old bird if a bit daft. I can't imagine her being a party to stealing... That son of hers is a bit slow too. My bet is they just kept on keeping on thinking he'd be back."

A shiver rose goosebumps on my arms.

Julia clasped my arm hard for a second.

I said, "Did my father have a solicitor locally?"

Horace sipped his wine, rubbing his chin as he thought.

"I don't rightly know. The man I'd used for the sale passed away a good fifteen years ago now—days after that sale. His office is still there though. I can inquire to see if they have copies of the paperwork, which would likely have your father's attorney's information."

Thomas said, "Inquire at the city hall. They'll have a record of who's been paying the taxes. I can't imagine Colleen managed to scrape up the necessary herself."

"Does she have other family living locally?" I asked.

"No. Her son, Archie, be the last of the Baties from here abouts."

Talk turned to gossip about the local gentry, which led to gossip of friends and acquaintances they had in common with Julia.

When Julia and I were on our way back to our hotel, "I said, "We need to visit his home here."

"Maybe Reg will know if Lou knew of it?"

"He's unlikely to tell us."

"I don't know, Pip. He's mellowing. He's stopping by and acting normal. He even apologized. I think he was honestly upset and confused, not only over what he'd done but why he'd done it. His tears break my heart... and before you say he's playing me, he's seeing a therapist. I believe him when he says he doesn't know why he did what he did and he's trying to get better."

I hesitated, not sure what to say.

She continued, "We'll go check out that house tomorrow. I think I'll stay up tonight to finish reading the papers the realtor sent. There were a few good options. I thought I'd make a comparison list now, before we see them so that we have a rough idea of what the real cost will be to get it how we want it."

"Real cost?"

"Any place we buy that we plan on spending a lot of time at will need a lab space. I was thinking that space should be big enough to hold Sandra. It'll also need a cage in case we need to hold a mule, so we need to factor in the construction cost and how difficult it would be to hide that construction."

"Sounds good to me."

"Plus it has to work for what we want it for. I was thinking at least five bedrooms and there needs to be room for live-in help close by. I'm hoping we can find another couple like the Romans to live there, although it only really requires a housekeeper. I suppose, we could hire a chef when we have house guests."

I said, "We could always add a small guest house if the main house wasn't large enough but everything else suited you. It would be a good excuse for construction."

"I'll add that to my list," she said happily.

She talked excitedly about her ideas until we reached the hotel.

It worried me that she had yet another project to spend her time on instead of learning the basics of magic, but I didn't have the heart to lecture her when she was clearly so happy to begin this project.

I kissed her cheek, saying, "I have a bit of studying to do, which will probably put me right to sleep. I'll see you in the morning, beloved."

"Sleep well, Pip."

I headed to my room, saying over my shoulder, "You should consider working with your mother, you love designing so much."

She flushed, waving a vague agreement.

Chapter 48

The next morning Ryu drove us to Lou's father's secret getaway.

It was very secluded and very picturesque. A small rock house on a cliff overlooking the ocean.

A flock of scraggly sheep grazed as they wished over the hillside with an equally scraggly dog watching in a desultory way.

The barn roof had fallen sometime in the past and been fixed with the simple expedient of draping a tarp over one corner.

An older man exited the house as we pulled up. His clothing and beard were equally unkempt. A faded anima rind coated him. It was so faded as to be barely visible.

"We don't want none of what you're selling," he said crossly.

I exited the car to offer my hand.

"I'm Lord Blackwood. Louis Blackwood."

"Archie Batie," he said reluctantly, eyeing me suspiciously. "Aye, you've the look of your father, sure enough."

"This is my wife, Julia, and our assistant Martin Poole. Might I speak with your mother?"

"You can try. She don't hear so good no more."

He held the door for me and bellowed, "Mum, we got company! His lordship has come!"

There was no reply.

He shrugged at me.

Julia said, "We've just recently learned of this estate and I'm afraid we've no idea what your contract with his father entailed."

"We gots no contract. Was a gentleman's deal, wasn't it. Me and my mum took care of the place for him when he wasn't around and made ourselves scarce when he was. He never minded if we used the house and all. You come to evict us?"

His tone gave me no hint if that worried him or not.

I said, "Not at all. I intend to honor my father's wishes."

Archie's shoulders relaxed.

I said, "How have you been paying the bills and the like?"

"He left money for the upkeep and what not. It's been running a bit short, but we make do."

"Did he come often?"

As we were speaking, we followed him into the house. The front room, which was the sitting area, was open with a staircase in back beside a hall that led to a kitchen. Piles of unopened mail covered a table beside the door and were stacked beside it on the floor. Dust coated every surface, except for a path that led to the back of the house and a rocking chair by the window that overlooked the drive.

There were two closed doors visible to the left, one of which sparkled the tiniest bit the way spells did before they sank into the paper.

Archie was saying, "Three times a year like clockwork. Mum and me would spend those weeks in our old caravan. We were good caretakers. Not one time did we break his rules. Not one time. It be just like he left it."

He said that proudly, almost as if he expected my father to exit the car and demand to see it.

Julia said, "Perhaps Martin and I can make us all some tea?"

"There be some in the kitchen," Archie said agreeably.

I said to Julia. "You have yourself a sit down, darling. I can make the tea."

Ryu said, "Would your mother care for a cuppa?"

He trailed behind Archie as he headed down the hall to the kitchen.

I whispered to Julia. "Can you see the marks on the door? Don't touch them."

I hurried after Ryu.

Colleen appeared to be sleeping in a tiny room beside the kitchen that held two twin beds with a chair between them and a small television. She had to be at least ninety. I thought the two of them probably shared the room.

Ryu glanced over his shoulder, and I beckoned to him, taking his arm and pulling him toward the kitchen.

I whispered, "Don't touch any doors. I saw a spell."

The kitchen was clean with two cups and plates on a drain board.

I said, "I'll make the tea. Warn Julia not to try anything with either of them and keep her away from the doors."

He hurried back to the main room.

I set a pot of water on the stove and examined the room without touching anything.

It all looked perfectly normal.

Archie joined me a few minutes later.

"Mum be sleeping now."

I said, "I think you'd better show me the money my father left so I can be sure you have enough."

He frowned for a moment then nodded. "You be the lord. I can open the door for Lord Blackwood."

I followed him back to the main room where he headed for that magicked door.

"Stay here," I said to Julia as nonchalantly as I could.

She was biting her lip; I thought maybe debating arguing.

Archie opened the door.

I stopped in the doorway to examine the room, which was perfectly clean.

The desk had a hint of that same sparkle.

I said, "Bring it to me here where the light is better."

Archie Removed a painting from the wall, revealing a safe that he opened. He withdrew two stacks of money and brought them to me.

As I reached for them, Julia said anxiously, "Pip?"

"'Tisn't enough left," I said to Archie, waving the offered money away without touching it. "My assistant will bring you additional funds. I'll take the correspondence with me."

Archie nodded agreeably, saying, "I'll fetch a sack or two."

I said, "Could you please pack up the contents of the desk for me?"

He halted, scratching his head for a good minute before he nodded and continued to the kitchen.

I whispered to Julia, "Can you see it?"

"Yes. Can you tell what it does?"

"No. But I don't think we should go in there. We'll send a mule for whatever he packs up. I think the mail is okay to take now though."

Ryu shook his head, saying, "Maybe. Who knows what sorts of things get sent to him. I think it's probably safe to touch it but be careful opening it."

Julia said, "We should call Sandra."

I nodded agreement.

"Do it outside away from the house though."

She headed for the door.

"Go with her. Keep an eye on that dog."

Ryu ran after Julia.

Archie returned a few minutes later.

I helped him pack up the mail, saying, "Mr. Poole will return with one of my assistants to retrieve everything from the desk and safe. I'd also like any books, notebooks, anything he might have written. I'd like to send a woman to do some cleaning. I see your mother is getting on in years. If she'd prefer to go to a retirement community, that could be arranged. If she'd prefer to stay here, I'd like the woman who comes to do some cooking."

"Aight."

"You can use this front room however you like."

"Thank ye, sir."

The tea kettle shrilled.

I said, "I think I'll take a rain check on that tea. My man will be back this time tomorrow." I set my card on the now empty side-table. "You can contact me at that number. Good afternoon."

I let myself out, taking the bags of mail with me. They made an awkward armful that I was glad to dump into the trunk.

We all got back into the car.

I said, "I don't think we should mess with either of them until Sandra takes a look. I told him you'd be back for the contents of the desk and any books this time tomorrow. Don't touch them yourself. Have Patrick and Jean move everything. Bring some groceries. See if he'll tell you anything but don't push. I'll speak to Vicky about arranging help for them, but I don't want anyone in there until Sandra can come."

Julia said. "She said she'll come the day after tomorrow and that we shouldn't open any of the mail until she examines it but that we should examine it ourselves to see if we see or sense anything."

"Did he have a rind?" Ryu asked.

"Yes. A faded one."

"Couldn't you just make him tell you what you want to know?"

"It would be risky. He's worked for my father for years. It's possible my father would know if I used him."

"Your father is dead."

"Is he? How do we know that? It would be really hard to kill a seethe, so how did they manage it? If the body had been floating a while, maybe the corpse wasn't him. Maybe he just wants everyone to think he's dead. We need more information. Who identified the body? What injuries did it have?"

Julia took my hand. "Let's not panic, darling."

"I'm not panicking. I'm being prudent. Sandra told us we could infuse our essence into our servants. That man has been following directions for years. He's following them so well that he hasn't deviated in the path he takes from the front door to the kitchen but he's aware enough to care for his mother, so he isn't a mule."

"Unless your father told him to take care of her," Ryu said.

Julia snorted softly. "Pip's right. That isn't something Blackwood would do. Besides, it doesn't hurt anything for us to proceed cautiously."

She clasped my hand a moment before releasing it.

"We might as well drive through the town and have a look. We can see a few of the properties, have some lunch, then go back to the hotel to sort the mail. I'll arrange for another room so we needn't sleep in the same room with it."

"'Tis a good plan," I agreed. "First, we should both sketch out the symbol we saw so that we don't forget it."

She rummaged in her bag and handed me a small notebook.

I sketched it quickly, making a mental note to bring drawing materials on my next visit to draw it while looking at it.

I handed the notebook to Julia, watching over her shoulder.

She drew just a simple circle with a few flourishes.

I said, "Did you not see the detail or are you just unsure?"

"I saw it. It looked like what you drew."

"I don't mean to nag, but I think perhaps you should draw it out as you saw it so that we can compare to see if we possess the same strength. 'Tis possible my penchant for studying the magical arts has increased my awareness of such things. Mayhap I saw detail that you did not. 'Twould be good to know if such things are possible."

Julia said, "Did you see it, Ryu?"

"Nope. Looked like a regular door to me. I noticed that old dude was spry as shit though."

I said, "I saw no marks upon him, nor noticed any amulets, but 'tis possible his clothing hid it."

Julia said, "He's probably spry from living out there and taking care of those sheep his whole life."

"I should arrange for the barn to be repaired," I said.

"Do you intend to keep that place then?" Ryu asked.

"For the time being. Besides 'twould be wrong to sell it when it might harbor traps."

"I doubt he'd leave anything that anyone might notice," she said absently. "What a charming village. I think that first place is right down that lane there."

Ryu met my eyes in the rearview, shrugging lightly.

He looked worried, which was a bit reassuring that he thought she should be taking this more seriously too.

She heaved an exasperated sigh, squeezing my arm. "Come on, Pip. Can't we just have a day off, please! One day. Not even a full day. Let's just have some fun. Look! Isn't that a great old house?"

I smiled my brightest smile, leaning to kiss her cheek.

"Yes. I'd prefer a more secluded place though. 'Tis too close to town. Although it might make a delightful hotel."

"Now you're talking. Let's see the next one!"

"As my lady commands," Ryu said cheerfully.

I forced a laugh.

Chapter 49

Sandra examined the stacks of mail, picking up each piece, opening it and placing a pinch of white powder inside. I'd spent the night examining them and hadn't seen or sensed a thing. Julia had only given them a cursory appraisal. She'd been more interested in who'd sent them than in if they might be magicked.

"They seem perfectly normal. I think it's safe to open them."

She handed me the last envelope and picked up a leather-bound book from a stack of them that Ryu had brought back.

Archie had sent six boxes of books and papers that I'd been afraid to read. I hadn't done more than open the box to gaze at them and was itching to examine them all.

Sandra lifted each out to examine, sorting them into piles. I leaned over her shoulder to watch.

My breath caught at the contents displayed as Sandra flipped through them.

One of the piles was ordinary sorts of books. She set aside a pile of notebooks that contained writing in a language I couldn't read but recognized the same symbols that Sandra used in her spells. The leather bound books where certainly grimoires.

She held one out to me as she said, "This on the other hand... it doesn't appear to have protections, but I'll need some time to translate the texts."

"Can you translate it?"

"I believe so. It appears to be a combination of Salazar and Latin."

She handed me another similar book and picked up one of the notebooks.

"I'd like to take them all with me, Pip. These notebooks will tell us a lot about the author and his intent for those spells."

"You don't know what the spells do?" Julia asked.

"The spell in the first book is a blood pact for mutual assistance. It's a common spell in Salazar. Not to say that it's used often but it *is* well known. That second book is common portal spells. The notebooks tell me that the author was attempting to make new spells. I think he was trying to weave in a back door to weasel out of the consequences of breaking the blood pact. There's a few versions of a spell in these notebooks that I think was meant to force someone to do his bidding.

"Those sorts of spells are considered black magic. They exist but to own a book with one would be a death sentence if you were caught with it. It isn't the sort of spell people want mages to know. It's also a difficult thing to pull off. I'm not sure if he managed it or not. I'd need to break the spell down to the base runes. I think the different color inks signify hidden runes within the spell. It's complex and I need time to read them all."

I said, "Will you be able to tell what the spells at the house do?"

"Let's go see."

"Well?" I asked anxiously.

Ryu and Archie had gone outside to discuss the repairs for the barn, leaving Julia and I to examine the house with Sandra. Colleen was sitting up in bed, dozing in front of the television in her room. I didn't think she could hear us or that she'd care if she did.

Sandra said, "It's a nasty piece of work. I can remove it, but should I?"

"What's it do?" Julia asked.

"It's a suicide spell."

"Holy cripes!"

Sandra nodded, grimacing her displeasure as she said, "It's actually quite ingenious. If you entered without the lord's permission, you'd feel a growing compulsion to eat hemlock. The clever bit is he could easily reverse it if he cared to." She pointed to a swirl along the bottom.

"He can turn it on and off easily himself. This symbol here would allow anyone to turn it off. My bet is Archie has been told to place his palm here when given the correct phrase. That way Blackwood could call if he needed to allow anyone access. But he's a tricky devil, so I'd also bet there's a hidden key."

She withdrew a vial of purple powder from her purse and blew a pinch of it at the door.

The spell fluoresced, new writing becoming visible.

"Wallah! See? He keyed it. A mage who saw it and placed his palm there would trigger these runes here."

Without touching the door, she traced a symbol that was now visible connected to the little squiggle.

"That is an inferno spell. It would burn you up in seconds. It would burn you even if you were underwater. He was serious about keeping people out."

"What if I went in through a window?"

"This is a powerful well written spell. It isn't guarding this door but the room. There's no way to enter this room that wouldn't trigger the spell."

"How do I break it," I asked.

"There's a few ways to break a spell. You can rewrite it if the author of the spell left a loophole. You can trigger it and fight the effects. You could dispel it if you were strong enough."

"Are you strong enough?" Julia asked.

"Oh yes. You, however, aren't—at least not yet. There are two ways to dispel it. I could take the power out or burn the power up. You need to know the strengths and weaknesses of a caster to choose the correct option, assuming, that is, that there is an option. In some cases your power might be completely incompatible with the spell. In this case, I'm going to burn it because I don't want there to be the slightest chance that he contaminates me."

"Can it do that?" Julia asked anxiously.

"That magic within the spell is *his* magic the same way anima belongs to the person it encompasses. It's a part of him."

"'Tis God's honest truth you want no part of that fiend."

Sandra nodded agreement.

"Watch carefully," she said.

She laid a fingertip against the topmost loop. A brilliant white light flashed along the length of the spell. A second later she withdrew her fingertip. The door was just a door now. The removal hadn't left even a soot mark.

She said, "I'm very adept. A novice would've likely scorched the wood. That spell was well written but if I thought he might return, I'd place my own spell upon the door that appeared in all ways similar but keyed for him."

"You can do that?"

"Yes. It would take time to write out the spell because all of the additional runes and changes to his spell would need to be hidden. I don't think it worth the effort because I don't think he's the type to ignore the removal of the spell."

"He'll be able to tell it was removed?"

"He'll have felt backlash if he was close enough. The spell was strong enough that he could be a good mile away or more and feel it. I doubt he'd know it was this spell in particular, but he'd know a spell of his had been broken. Now, let's see what other protections he's laid."

We spent hours searching the house and grounds.

She removed two similar spells, one on the door of his bedroom and the other on a small shed by the barn that had an old rock floor with one rock recently removed to reveal a plastic bin. When questioned, Archie told me that's where the notebooks had been kept.

In the car on the way back to the hotel, Sandra said, "The house should be safe now for anyone to enter. I'd recommend keeping it as it's built over a ley line, which is likely one of the reasons he chose it. Your magic doesn't lend itself yet to earth magic, but it might given time and training. But it's always good to have a place like that to lend a friend should they have need of a secret place to recuperate. Or even an acquaintance you wished to make a friend."

"Feel free to use it whenever you like," Julia said.

"Thank you. It would make a lovely vacation spot. I'll need to return home for a few supplies and to hide these books. Pip, I know you're anxious to study them yourself, but you aren't yet ready. I promise I'll return them though and meanwhile I'll do all that I can to get you ready."

"I'd like the evening to examine them."

"Tell you what, we can meet at your estate in two days. I'll search it for similar spells. Meanwhile, my team will look into the facts of your father's death. I assume you'll make copies, which is fine, just don't leave your notes where they might be seen. I don't think you should even keep something like this in your study at home. These should be kept in a secret locked room in a warded box."

"The lab?" Julia asked.

Sandra nodded her approval.

I was itching to keep them myself, but she was right that I lacked the strength to use them or keep them safe.

I intended to remedy that by studying even harder.

Chapter 50

Julia led the way to the third floor.

As promised, Sandra had come to examine the estate. Julia had been annoyed to cut our Scotland trip short.

I hoped she wasn't still annoyed with me for staying at the hotel to study when she wanted to shop but I was afraid she was.

We'd bought a new estate, which I was more than happy with. I wasn't sure if she was truly happy with it too or just tired of begging me to go see more houses.

Ryu, and I carried Sandra's equipment. Sandra had arrived this morning and we'd been searching the house all day. We'd checked both wings and the two floors of the main wing of our estate. She'd wanted to leave the third floor for last in case there was a spell there linked to others in the house.

Ryu said, "Why were your rooms way up here and not on the second floor?"

Sandra said absently, "Children were frequently quartered on the top floors, those floors being the warmest rooms and easiest to defend as well as children being able to navigate stairs that adults might have trouble with. Most homes, even if they were only one room, would have a loft for the children."

I said, "This floor was dedicated to us. Our servants all lived on it. The nursery room with nurse, our classrooms and our teachers, our governess and our two maids were all quartered here. Plus we had the upper music room, the sewing room and a parlor. Most of our friends had the same sort of thing on a smaller scale. 'Twasn't unusual."

"Pip's brother used her room until he moved out," Julia said.

I said, "I hadn't wished to take it, but my father had insisted— or at least that's what my mother told me. But that was oft her response when she wished to brook no argument. In this case though I believe it to be the truth as to my mind I can think of no reason that she'd have cared if Violet and I had continued to share a room."

Sandra opened the door of what had been our music room, which was the room closest to the west wing, and began to examine it as she said, "She might have thought you'd need the room to hold your clothing and trousseau. You'd have been attending events that your sister wouldn't have yet been invited too."

The room was empty of furniture and had recently been painted white.

I said, "True... I think I was a trial to my mother, having no interest in fashion. 'Twas Violet who kept my clothing in good repair. She sewed nearly every gown I had, except for the few my mother insisted I have from the dressmaker."

Julia said, "But you love fashion..."

"Fashion then was an entirely different thing. There was one style, and it was wildly unflattering on me. I looked ridiculous in the ruffles and bows of that day and always felt the fool wearing it. I much preferred my simpler riding habits and my day dresses."

Ryu laughed, shaking his head at me as he said, "That must have sucked." His expression became thoughtful as he added, "And then you were here, a man, forced to wear trousers. If it had been me and I'd come back as a woman, it would have freaked me out to have to wear a dress."

"The trousers aren't the difficult bit," I murmured, making Sandra laugh ruefully.

She returned to the hallway to take the bag Ryu carried then knelt on the floor to open it.

We all fell quiet as she removed a glass jar and sprinkled a bit of the powder it contained onto her palm. She blew it off and we all watched it waft away.

In seconds, I couldn't see it. It had flown up, spreading out in an unnatural way.

We waited a few minutes then she stood, shaking her head.

Ryu said, "Would painting over a spell ruin the spell?"

"Some spells. There could've been spells worked into the woodwork that were recently broken when that woodwork was torn out or repaired."

I said, "There wasn't much woodwork up here. It was mostly plastered walls, except for the hallways."

Julia said, "Since we didn't want people up here, we decided not to furnish any of these rooms and just paint them all white for the time being. None of them needed any major repairs, except for the bathrooms. Two of the baths we updated and one we enlarged and then we put in another between the two rooms across the hall from Pip's old room—mostly as an excuse to put lights in the walls.

"We didn't want to disturb her old room, so there aren't any lights on that side of the hallway until the bathroom. Those rooms don't have lights in the ceiling, but they do in the floors. Every room up here except for these two have night lights on all the time."

Julia showed Sandra the floorboards that opened to allow the lights to be serviced. Battery powered LED light strips were threaded through the sound proofing insulation.

She said, "We only did this in the main hall. The rest of the house has to make do with leaving lights in the rooms on."

I said, "I think the night lights are enough of a deterrent, but I'll admit that the lights in the floor let me sleep better at night."

Sandra reached into her bag and withdrew another glass bottle, this one full of blue powder that she sprinkled onto her hand and blew off as well.

"I sense nothing in here. If there had been a spell that first powder would have found it unless the spell was written to make it unfindable. There are runes that can hide from sight, from senses, and even from other magic, but it's costly and time consuming to do that. I can't imagine anyone in this realm bothering when the chances are so low that another mage would stumble across them. This is a private residence. It would have been simplicity itself for him to keep anyone he didn't wish to see his work out of this building and even simpler for him to keep them off of this floor. The blue powder would have shown me if there was a partially written rune. Granted I didn't use much of it, but I haven't a lot and partial runes would be mostly useless."

She handed me the bottle.

"I'll show you how to make it and then you can sprinkle it about to your heart's content, assuming you're able to make it, which I can't guarantee."

All of Sandra's spells used gems or precious metals as a base and it suddenly occurred to me how much a bottle of what I believed to be amethyst dust must cost.

We headed to the next room, which had been the music teacher's bedroom but was now a bathroom where she again examined the room and then used her powders.

I pulled Julia aside while Sandra was examining the schoolrooms to whisper, "It hadn't occurred to me to ask the cost of this."

"The cost doesn't matter. It needed to be done. Besides, it really cost us nothing. I gave her all of the jewelry and gems that you got from the marks in Dubai and told her she could keep the cash that we'd stored in her lair. She agreed it was more than fair payment and would throw in a few more copies of her books."

"It seems unequal."

Julia said, "She told me that she'd learn quite a bit from the notebooks we found. Mages seldom share information, except with their apprentices. Those apprentices normally take oaths that bind them to the mage who teaches them. We're unique because we're paying her in skills for her tutelage. The books have worth. She's trying to be fair to us, not take advantage of our ignorance, so I asked for books that pertained to demons. She said she'd look."

She took my hand and went to join Ryu and Sandra who were about to enter the room next to mine.

Sandra said to me, "Have you been inside this room at all?"

"No. We never come up here."

Julia said, "No one comes up here, except for the painters and stuff. Are there spells to keep things out of your house?"

"Yes. That's advanced magic though." As she was speaking, she headed into the room to examine it. "You shouldn't attempt it until your absolutely sure your proficient enough because you could make it impossible for yourself to leave or enter or even keep out air and light. In my realm, mages rarely cast spells like that. They'd hire an inou if they really felt they needed that protection. Most were content enough with simpler alarms."

"Would the alarm warn of shadowed seethes?"

"They could be set to warn for almost anything."

The hair on my arms rose when I stepped into the room.

I said, "There—on the wall."

Julia said, "It gives me the willies too."

Ryu said, "You're letting Reg's story scare you."

Sandra shook her head.

"No. I feel it too. It's a powerful spell."

She closed her eyes and spread her arms, taking tiny steps.

Julia pulled me back into the hallway.

Ryu retreated to the doorway.

Sandra said, "I can see it. Hand me that purple powder, Ryu."

Spell-sparkle covered almost the entire wall to our right.

Ryu opened the bag to get the powder.

She set a pinch of it on her palm and blew.

The powder appeared to expand into a thick cloud, much thicker than the small amount of powder should be able to make. The cloud covered the wall between this and my room and sank in leaving a large pentacle with small writing and runes around it surrounded by three circles, each inscribed with runes.

"Holy shit!" he exclaimed, taking a quick step back. "What's it say?"

Julia released me to peer past him.

"Die ye who enter here, would be my guess," Julia said.

He put his arm around her and took another step back, pulling Julia with him, laughing nervously.

Sandra said, "No, nothing like that. Pip, can you read it?"

"I recognize some of the symbols from your books and I think that's a name there by my surname. It looks a bit like the pentacles in the notebook, but I see differences."

I eased past Julia to peer closer.

"It says Lord Blackwood in the center and again on the outer edge and then Blackwood by the word Silah."

Julia pulled me back again as she said, "I can read it too. Can you Ryu?"

"The names yes. I see the little symbols but don't know what they mean. I'm guessing nothing good though. We should get out of here..."

Sandra said, "It can't hurt you—unless you happen to die in here."

Rage caught my breath so hard it made me see spots.

"He did it on purpose?" I asked when I could finally draw a breath.

I'd sounded remarkably calm to myself.

I'd never been so angry in my life.

Sandra said, "I don't know. It's an old spell meant to hold a shadowed seethe. Maybe we've got this wrong. Maybe that thing that was locked in the house was the original Blackwood and another seethe killed him and locked him in here?"

She beckoned to me, pointing at the glowing purple lines along the bottom of the pentacle.

"The center where the crest and the word Blackwood is written was written in a different hand than these two lines here. This top line is meant to transfer power to the second. It basically says to you I bequeath the power of my blood. The next line says the same. This is a blood pact. A powerful one between three people. The shadowed seethe might have agreed to it because I can't see anything in this original spell that would keep it right here, which it would've had to have been to take part in the spell."

She pointed out a line of small symbols.

"Those are protections. It's a modified portal spell. I think this was meant as a sort of anchor in the void. A way to pull itself back. See how that same symbol is on each of the points? My guess is there are four other matching pentacles that would allow travel between them. The outer rings were added later. My guess is one of the partners had a change of heart and since they couldn't kill the seethe, they added this to trap it here."

"Why couldn't they kill it?" Ryu asked.

"The pact they made had protections worked into it. Breaking it would kill you. See how the names are entwined here? Blackwood, Blackwood, Silah. I think there were two Blackwoods."

I said, "So, Silah and the new Blackwood trap the original Blackwood?"

"Or the third was a Blackwood by birth or maybe marriage. You have to use the name you call yourself. It can't be faked, or the spell won't work. It might just fail, or it might backlash strongly enough to destroy you. A spell this powerful would certainly maim you at the least if you screwed with it."

"So it's possible it just caught me by accident?"

"It would catch any Blackwood in spirit form."

"Lou..." Julia said thoughtfully with a hint of horror.

Violet, my heart screamed.

I said, "What happens if we break the spell?"

"That depends. My guess is that the Blackwood being held here would be free to go, but that might not be good for it. If it has been using this spell as an anchor, it'll be adrift in the void. Any other Blackwoods caught in the spell would be released to either Heaven or Hell or maybe the void if they were seethes."

"And to us?" Julia asked.

"You can leave the house, so it isn't affecting you in that way but it's possible it's linked to you as Blackwood number two in this equation. I on the other hand, have no link to it at all. I could break it."

"Would that hurt us?"

"No. There's no clause worked into the spell for that. Most blood spells skip that because it would be too simple for a more powerful mage to break a spell and kill you that way. The danger is only if the participants break it, not if a third party does."

"Can you break it?"

"Yes, but maybe you should think about it a bit. They would know this spell was broken."

I said, "No. It needs to be broken. Too many of my family will have died in this house. They could all be trapped as I was. It *must* be broken!"

"Lou will be free..." Julia said worriedly.

Ryu took her hand.

I said, "Lou will be sent to Hell as he deserves!"

Sandra said, "It's possible that he has enough seethe ancestry to return as a shadow. It's possible that the spell was made precisely because the Blackwood line was producing too many seethes. Breaking the spell could release hundreds of shadowed seethes."

Julia said, "Hundreds seems a bit much. There can't be too many that actually died in the house."

Sandra said, "I have no real idea of how a seethe is born. It's possible it doesn't require an adult soul, although I think soul is the wrong word."

Julia said with dismay, "So every child who died..."

I said, "All the more reason to free them."

Sandra said, "First, I'll finish the search."

While she continued her examination, I sketched the spell.

She spread about an assortment of colored powders but nothing else in the room reacted.

She examined my room next.

It took more courage then I liked to admit to myself to enter that room.

The room seemed purely mundane, but I could feel the heat of the spell through the wall.

"Do you feel it?" I asked.

"I hate this room," Julia said, and I was struck with how difficult this must be for her.

I said, "I shall never be happy to enter here. It is an evil place— but it does hold a few sweet memories. I shall never forget when I first felt that warmth of your touch. I hate that our destiny required the hard road to our meeting but am beyond glad that we *did* meet."

Sandra said, "I can feel the power of the spell too. Did you ever sense anything when you lived here?"

"Not that I recall. I spent little time in here. There was an armoire against this wall that held the dresses that I despised. 'Twasn't a place I dwelled much. I would occasionally read in here but always in the chair by the window.

"Most days that kept us indoors were spent in my sister Violet's bedchamber. I would read there more often than not while she and her maids fussed with her hair or clothing. She disliked being alone and would wake me most mornings... we cannot leave that cursed spell upon the wall!"

Sandra said, "I'll remove it. Just in case though, I think the three of you should leave the estate. I'll call when it's gone—or better yet, go to my estate. I have books there you should read. The ones you truly need to read are written in Salazar. I'll lend you a primer and begin preparations for an amulet. It will take time and work best if you have at least a tiny understanding of the language or culture.

"Pip, this sort of teaching can have repercussions. I won't ask you to swear the oaths of apprentice to master but I would ask that you think of me not as your friend in this but as your magister. In this we aren't equals. My words must have more weight than even your own thoughts."

"I'm honored and do swear to hold your words in the highest regard, magister," I said as I bowed to her.

Julia looked uncertain if she should be worried or not.

Sandra nodded, turning back to examine the writing on the wall.

"Is this room safe to enter?" Ryu asked.

"As far as I can see."

He said, "I vote we keep both of these rooms locked and empty."

Sandra said, "People would notice and think it odd. But if you store building supplies in it or old furniture or something, no one would give it a second thought."

I said, "I should like to do the cleansing spell you taught me here and perhaps pray."

"I'll perform the strongest ritual of cleansing that I know," Sandra said.

"Leave the windows open and unshuttered. Perhaps it will help..."

"It couldn't hurt," Sandra agreed.

She clasped my hand for a moment.

"She wouldn't have died here. She'd have been married and gone to live in her husband's house."

"I pray God 'tis so and that he was a kind loving man—but here I am."

Ryu gave me a quick hug. "You escaped the spell, Pip, so it can be done."

"How did she escape it?" Julia asked.

Sandra frowned thoughtfully, "That's an excellent question. One I don't have an answer for. I have an educated guess though. Blood and a strong will can affect spells. When you add in Lou had Blackwood blood that he believe himself to be Lord Blackwood, it seems a reasonable assumption that the spell recognized him as such. The spell was originally cast by Lord Blackwood to hold Blackwood. It was Silah who added the trap to it. But Lou was outside that trap. Pip never thought of herself as Lord Blackwood. She probably didn't think of herself as a Blackwood at all by then."

I nodded agreement.

"Lou was ranting about hating this place," Julia said thoughtfully. "He kept saying he'd be free of me and this place, and I know I cut him in the struggle. There were more pictures in the room with the spell. He could've got blood on the walls when he went to retrieve them."

I said, "Or maybe that thing locked up here helped? It was almost free. Maybe it had weakened the spell?"

"It was probably close," Sandra said thoughtfully. "The smell of the blood would've enticed it. It would've had to wait until it was dark, but it was probably lurking. I wish I knew how it was breaking free!"

"Why didn't it break the spell?" Ryu asked.

"It's really hard to break a spell like that when your one of the participants. It would've taken this Silah person a lot of power to write in that holding spell without getting trapped in it himself— although maybe Silah didn't write it. A friend could've done it or hireling or even an enemy, I suppose."

She headed back to the other room to examine the wall again.

The glow had disappeared leaving just the faintest sparkle.

I offered her my sketch.

She spread more of her powder to make it show up again then took the sketch from me to say, "The curved line here is the rune of connecting. See how you have it drawn under the small t-branching? but on the wall it's almost at the bottom of the stroke? That small difference is a big one in the meaning of the spell. The length of the stroke symbolizes the length or tightness of the connection. A short line is more forced than a longer one. If I were reading your spell, it says something different than the actual one. You have the rune of movement wrong too. Look, see how the end circle kisses the point in the pentagram? If you look closely, you'll see the mirrored rune matches perfectly. That Isn't three waves but four with the ends overlapped."

She continued to point out and name all of the runes.

Julia said, "It's much more complex than it looks, and it looks pretty darn complicated."

"It was written by a master," she agreed. "He's probably dead now though. Unless, of course, he practices very dark magic. I'd guess he befriended the seethes to become their servant or maybe to learn to mimic their power."

"Can it be done?"

"Not to my knowledge. Countless mages have tried. But a powerful enough mage could prolong his life by stealing the life force of another. There are countless ways of adding years to a human life span but most of them require the death of something or other, which is considered very black magic. The belief is that God would revile you to use those methods. In effect, you'd live a long time but be damned when you died. The easiest way to preserve your life if you're a human is to offer that life in service to a being that can help you. Again, the human belief is that doing so will damn you but there *are* exceptions. It was commonly believed that the love of an inou was free of evil taint if that inou wasn't bad.

She made air quotes on the word bad.

"Bad, of course, was whatever the humans deemed bad. Seethes were sometimes seen as being good"—again she made air quotes—"but were most often seen as being bad. Pixies were often thought to be the best choice although in my opinion they're right up there with demons, although that's probably my own prejudices. There are probably pixies who are perfectly pleasant, but I found them all to be sneaky lying creatures. Of all of the spirit creatures, they can slip from an oath the easiest. They're masters of the loophole. Never trust a pixie! It would think it a great joke to see you torn limb-from-limb by a pitchfork wielding crowd."

Ryu said, "All those things can make you live longer though?"

"Yes. Every creature of spirit can in some way or another add to a human lifespan. It's why we're always hunted. Which is why we keep ourselves so secret here in this realm. Well that and it makes it much easier for us to blend in and use magic."

"I'm surprised more of you don't come here," he said.

"Most couldn't make the trip. But even if they could, most wouldn't want to any more than you'd want to live in Hell."

"That's a bit much," Julia said indignantly.

"You're thinking like a human. Spirit creatures don't live in cities or houses. There are few of us. Our native lands aren't the sorts of places a human would like. Humans come to our realms and make them more like this earth and we adapt. We can appreciate the human machines, but we aren't human and have no real need for them, except when we're pretending to be human. Some of us pretend better than others. A fairy for instance could never live here. This world lacks the right sunlight and is too polluted. It could live here only with great effort, and it'd be miserable—as miserable as you'd be in a land of fire."

"But some of you like it here," Ryu said.

"As opposed to being hunted to death—this place is great." She wrinkled her nose at him. "It's beautiful in places and even the cities are growing on me, but I have skills others of my kind don't."

Julia said, "The mage is from your realm though."

"He appears to be. Salazar is a common language there, but he could've been born here and taught by someone like me."

"Did you teach him?" Ryu asked.

Shock stole my breath.

Julia rolled her eyes at him, and my heart resumed a normal rhythm.

Sandra said, "No. I've met no other mages in my time here. This first part of the spell was written way before I arrived. I plan on looking for him now though. I hadn't heard of a mage of that name before I left home, which is why I think he's from here. Most of the very powerful have at least heard of each other. We change our shapes so might not be recognized, but powerful spells require a true name. If he'd been practicing powerful magic in my realm, I'd have heard of him. Of course, he might have been in hiding, lots of mages hide what they are there at least until they're powerful enough to fight off mage takers or demand a good posting."

"Sounds charming," Julia said.

"You'd hate it there. Unless things have changed since I left, which is possible, seethes we're being shadowed as soon as they were found. Plenty of humans have been murdered in that hunt. You'd need to be really careful not to give yourself away."

Ryu said, "They should be more careful here."

Sandra nodded agreement. "Too many big deaths like that is bound to draw attention."

"We're content now with what we have," I said.

She nodded again.

"Good. Take the time to learn. I knew when I sent you there that Maamoun was an evil man and was hoping we could remove him. I hadn't intended such a large-scale operation. Not that I'm complaining, far from it, but it does lead to suspicion. I hadn't realized how personally angry it would make you to be confronted by their greed."

"'Twasn't their greed I found offensive but the manner in which they pursued their endeavors."

"In the future, I'll be more careful of the favors I ask. Speaking of which, I checked on Bob's story and found nothing at all unusual, which, if he's a demon, means absolutely nothing. I recommend you study up on demons before you go looking for him."

"We will," Julia said firmly to me. "We're leaving him alone."

"For now," I agreed.

She sighed in exasperation.

Sandra said, "I'd like to get started since I don't want to be away from home too long."

Julia said, "Give us an hour to pack and we'll be out of here. It'll be nice to see Cass."

"It will," I agreed. "I can't wait to show her pictures of the new estate."

Sandra said, "She'll be glad to see you both as well. My housekeeper has standing orders to admit you, but if you have any problems, call Drew. My phone will be off for a bit."

"Thank you for the help," I said.

She waved me away.

The three of us headed for the stairs.

I said to Julia, "Pack me a bag, please. I'm going to round up the pets."

Ryu glanced over his shoulder then leaned closer to whisper, "You believe her about the mage?"

"Yes. She has no reason to lie about it."

"That you know of."

"You think we should do what?" Julia asked.

Ryu shrugged uncomfortably. "This, I guess. I'm just saying keep our eyes open. Even if she don't know him now, she might prefer to be friends with a powerful mage."

I said, "She *is* friends with a powerful mage and Drew likes us. Her daughter likes us. I can't see her turning on us without good reason."

Julia said, "Besides, we don't know that the mage wouldn't make a good friend. Just because he tried to lock Blackwood up here doesn't make him a bad guy. I'd do the same if I could."

"True..."

I said, "I hope he had no notion that he was trapping all Blackwoods."

"We don't know that it did. It might've just caught you because of the manner of your death or maybe the spell had nothing to do with you being trapped there."

Ryu said, "This is giving me the jitters. Let's not talk about it anymore. You guys shouldn't think about what happened in that room. Don't go pray in there, Pip. I'll do it for you. I promise to say sincere prayers. I'll get the room staged and locked and you two don't need to think about it again. Whatever happened there happened long ago. That mad thing will be free and hopefully it'll return to wherever it came from, but if it does come back, we should think about building another spell like that but this time we do it in a smaller place like the barn. Somewhere it can eat but where it can't hurt anyone else and no one else will be trapped there."

"A way must be found to release the creature to eternal peace."

Julia paled, clutching my hand tightly. Tears trickled to her cheeks as she said hoarsely, "I think there is no eternal rest for us. It's our blessing and a curse."

"We'll always be together, my beautiful Julia. I shall be your light in the darkness as you are mine."

I hugged her for a long minute, feeling the fragility of her—us— these human shells. Contemplating the endless cycle of escaping the void made me clammy and cold.

I said, "We need never go into the void. We can simply move— or stay if we can learn to change our shapes."

She choked on a sob and then was crying hard.

Ryu said, "Jewels..." patting at her and trying to kiss her cheek, trying to take her from me.

I shook my head at him, saying, "Tis terrifying but there are two of us. We'll find each other. I shall practice until I too can craft a spell to anchor us. I swear, I'll never let the void have you. I swear it!"

Ryu nodded grim agreement.

He hugged us both.

Chapter 51

A week later, Ryu entered the reading room saying, "Come on, Pip! You've been inside here for days. You need some fresh air and exercise. Cass and Honey will both be here in a few minutes. Come riding with us. The books will still be here when we get back."

I put the thick tome on demons aside beside another similar tome that I'd just finished.

"A ride sounds lovely. When we return, I'd like to work out a way for me to feed as I did in Dubai."

"Absolutely not!"

"No. You misunderstand. I've no wish for mules or even marks, except that I need the anima to eat so that I might continue my studies. I'd prefer not to consume the rinds of my footmen, although, I suppose the smallest sips here and there shan't hurt. But I'd prefer to dine out, as it were. Take out would be ideal."

"I don't know, Pip. Finding a steady stream of killers to bring home isn't going to be easy. Especially if you don't want to order them about but just snack on them."

"Priests perhaps? Maybe doctors? Or veterans? Perhaps we could arrange a weekly or even monthly lunch? I can shift the anima from them to my mules."

He nodded, looking relieved. "Yeah, that sounds good. But you need to eat real food and sleep too."

"I'll study for two days and nights while sipping the anima and then refrain for the next day as I did in Dubai. After my sleep, I'll eat real food and exercise and do whatever mundane chores await me for one day and then it's my two days and nights of study again."

"Does Julia know you plan to do this?"

"Not yet. I don't see how it could alarm her."

"Your panic is going to alarm her."

"'Tisn't panic. 'Tis prudence. Blackwood is now free. He *will* return. I wish to be prepared is all. My hope is that we can speak to him and offer help, but I think he will hate me. So, just in case, I'll learn to make a holding spell of the strength needed to hold him."

"How's that going?"

"Slowly—which is why I shall study as much as I may. Besides, I quite enjoy it. There's so much new information to think on."

"There's fun to be had too, Pip. Don't be afraid to make new friends. None of us know how long we have. We can't be afraid to live while we're alive."

He left, whistling jauntily.

Pansy followed him to the door, turning back to me with pleading eyes that made me laugh.

"We're going, silly dog."

She danced happily around me as I went to dress, putting on the riding clothes Cass had given me for Christmas. That she'd picked clothing I really liked still surprised me.

I still detested this male body but perhaps in time I could grow accustomed—maybe even enjoy it for more than the strength of the arms. Or trade it for one more to my liking, although I'd be loathed to give up my title, but I'd need to relinquish it eventually...

Thoughts of the distant future kept me distracted until I joined the others.

To my surprise Reginald was there.

He greeted me civilly—and it *appeared* sincere. He was charm itself to Cass and Honey.

I caught Honey eyeing him thoughtfully a time or two, and it occurred to me that Reginald appeared a good catch. Sorrow pierced me for what might have been for him if he hadn't had the misfortune to meet Lou.

The charming façade that he was displaying might have been his real one. He might've found a woman like Honey and been happy.

The thought occurred—*a man like me would make him happy.*

My own wistful response shocked me. I hastily turned my attention away, knowing that it would only be the shell I wore, not myself that would entice him.

I don't wish to entice him, I told myself firmly.

Cass asking about Viola was a welcome distraction.

Reginald's weighing gaze as Cass and I laughed together reminded me how the world would see her and I. My casual hugs and quick pecks on her cheek would be taken for flirtation at the least and more likely an affair—not the close camaraderie of women friends.

I suddenly couldn't wait to return to my books where I could be myself.

Vicky was waiting in my reading room when I returned.

She handed me a folder.

"You better not let anyone find this, my lord. It would be clear you must have stolen the information, and it wouldn't be that big of a leap to guess where you stole it from."

"Are there copies anywhere?"

"No."

"And the original documents?"

"Destroyed as you requested, except for the ones Julia took."

I opened the folder.

She leaned over my shoulder to tap the first page.

"This is a complete list of the relatives of the men killed in the building, but we only checked the names highlighted yellow."

"And?"

"It's all in there. Except for a few exceptions, it's happening as you foresaw. Are you clairvoyant?"

"I wish..."

She snorted with laughter.

"The discrepancies?"

She perched on the edge of my desk as I took the folder and sat in the seat.

"Small deviations. Except for in Paris. Tussaud's son was killed in a car accident two weeks ago. It appeared to be a real accident, but it put that pack of thieves into a spin. I put a complete list of the men killed in the following panic in the report. Claudia is there with Frankie checking the obits. Some deaths we can clearly link to the power struggle, and some are clearly unlinked, but there's a few that we aren't certain."

"Keep me updated. I want to know if the general feel is one of unease or relief."

"From Maamoun's men or the populous?"

"Both."

"I don't think I need your crystal ball to say that the men who owned the sex dens are going to be really unhappy about the new managements change of orders. I think you can expect a few more murders there. Are you ever going to tell me how you got them all to agree to let that part of the business go?"

"I didn't. I simply pointed out that there are plenty of women willing to work in such establishments and it would be cheaper, more efficient, and less likely to lead to criminal charges to use them. The money spent on the drugs they use to keep the women enslaved could be spent on other things. Speaking of which, has there been an increase in the drug traffic?"

"Not one that's showing up yet. But it's going to take them time to shake down. And you can bet your ass they're looking for Tussaud."

"They shan't find him."

"They won't stop looking for that money, boss."

I shrugged.

She laughed, sliding from the desk to stand.

I said, "I want the situation watched. Speak to my wife if you require more assistance. Inform me, not her, if the violence between them begins to affect civilians. And notify me at once if any rumors of my involvement are heard. Inform me of the merest whispers and who has whispered them."

She nodded as she said, "The links between those separate gangs are clear, but we haven't even scratched the surface really."

"As long as we know who the top man is than I'm content. Change will take time and can only be done through that top man. Removing the smaller men just leads to different men who will do whatever the top man says to do."

"Maamoun might not have been the top man."

"True. But one must start somewhere. We shall see who emerges to take over his holdings and that city."

"I hope you know what you're doing, boss. Jacob told me to remind you that you have a meeting with the police here at four."

"*Ahh*, yes. Our rotten apple has been in twice now to speak with them. Have you been watching Emma as I advised?"

"She doesn't go out, except for necessary trips to the grocery store after work. If she's plotting, she's doing it quietly at home."

"Did you see her yourself?"

"No. I didn't see the point. She isn't going to admit anything to me, and my showing up would make her realize I was sent to check up on her. Which I think would confirm what can only be suspicion that you sent her there to keep her away from us."

"Keep a team on her. I think perhaps we should find a new team member. One proficient in searching computers. Speak to Julia. 'Tis Emma's nature to plot. Until I can permanently remove her, she must be watched least she plot against some unsuspecting woman."

"She's more likely to try to take us down."

"'Twould be extremely difficult for her to do. I have absolute certainty that she hasn't yet deviated in the story she's telling the police."

"Just don't get cocky, boss. Whatever you have on her that's keeping her quiet might not work if she gets it into her head that she doesn't care if ruining herself ruins you too."

"Removing her might make the police more suspicious. 'Twas our thought that leaving her to answer their questions would be better—for now at least."

"That's just it. She might decide to tell them what we were really doing or even lie."

"She doesn't know what I was really doing."

"She has to suspect we were behind that."

"Perhaps... I shall speak to her again and offer further inducement. Meanwhile, we're working on setting a small event into motion that should discredit her should it become necessary."

"Your crystal ball was broken when you picked her, boss, which just goes to show that you aren't infallible."

"Emma was my wife's choice. She thought, or perhaps hoped would be a better description, that we could turn her from the evil path she was on. 'Tis my thought that she will never willingly leave that path. For every urge of hers that we nip in the bud, a new one grows. 'Tis exceedingly wearisome to keep abreast of whom she means to murder. Her murders have no merit at all. They would gain neither herself nor anyone else a thing and would harm many. She's an evil creature…"

Vicky trailed her hand along the leather cover of the book I'd set aside when she'd entered.

"You think she's possessed?"

"It might be easier to deal with her if that we're true… I'm certain she is not. 'Tis her own folly. It worries me though of what she might do should she find a demon to partner with."

"You believe all this mystical stuff?"

"I know it to be true."

"I'm not going to lie. That worries me, boss. You start believing in stuff like this and anyone can sell you a pig in a poke."

"A pig in a poke… an expression of gullibility, I take it… it isn't blind faith that leads me to my conclusion but certainty. I have seen a demon, which I know is unbelievable but 'tis true, I swear it. Not that it matters a whit if you believe me or not. Your relationship with God is your own. What you believe is irrelevant to me as long as you obey."

"You think Maamoun was possessed?"

"He wasn't. None of *his* men appeared to be possessed either. I think their level of evil would have eventually brought a demon or perhaps one was there but remained hidden from me."

"You really believe that don't you?"

"I believe there are many things hidden from me."

"No. I mean that you can see demons."

"I wish that I could—or perhaps I should be grateful I cannot. I'm unsure if all would be as apparent to me as the one who revealed itself. None of Maamoun's men appeared possessed but since I can't say with certainty why that one had become visible, I tested all of his men with Holy water, and none reacted in the slightest. I have too little data to be certain of my hypothesis of how I might spot one, but I *am* certain that where there is one there is always another. My hope is that they're as rare as hen's teeth."

She snorted with laughter.

Chapter 52

"Sergeant Saadeh, what a surprise," I said as I entered the interview room.

Inspector Brantwold gestured us to seats.

I was surprised and worried to see him there.

Saadeh said, "We had a few follow up questions."

"And a phone call wouldn't do?" Jacob asked.

Saadeh ignored him, sliding a photograph across the table.

"Do you know this man?

"Yes. His name is Yusuf Keita."

Jacob picked up the paper and tossed it down.

"He was an unpleasant ass..."

"Was?"

"I'm sure he still is for the unfortunate people he works with now. I was glad to see the last of him."

I said, "Why do you ask?"

"He was one of your employees, correct?"

"For a short time. He left my service days after we arrived in Dubai."

"What was his job description?"

"Driver. He was one of my wife's placements."

Jacob laughed as he said, "He means her charity cases. Lady Blackwood runs a school for socially challenged people with rap sheets, mostly young ones who'd otherwise have a difficult time finding work."

"I see."

Saadeh flipped through his papers for a moment then folded his hands on them to lean across the table.

"When was the last time you saw Yusuf?"

I said, "I'm not certain of the date but he'd accompanied me to a private club. It wasn't my sort of place. I left it within minutes. He declined to join me. I had to call for a ride and fired him forthwith."

"The name and address of the club?"

I told him."

"And how did you hear of it?"

"Francois Tussaud."

"The context of the conversation?"

"My assistant, Martin, had commented on a poker tournament we'd been thinking of entering. He'd had a recent big win. I believe I asked if there would be gambling establishments here in the future and he told me of the private clubs."

"Did this club offer gambling?"

"I didn't stay to find out. The host was a bit too enthusiastic in offering me female company. I found it quite tasteless."

Brantwold said, "Did you have any further dealings with them?"

"No."

"Did Tussaud?"

"I have no idea. I expressed my displeasure at my next meeting with him a few days later. He thought it amusing. I don't believe he mentioned that establishment to me again. I told him quite clearly that I wasn't amused. He, of course, apologized."

"Did anything about that meeting stand out as odd?"

"Odd... not really. When he apologized, he said they had their uses, which made him laugh. I thought that was strange but assumed he was laughing at me."

"But you thought it strange at the time?"

"People rarely laugh at me to my face," I said dryly. "I thought he'd been amused at sending me to a brothel."

Jacob said, "What's this all about?"

"Yusuf's remains were recovered from the building."

"Son of a bitch!" Jason exclaimed.

I said, "And you think he went there with that group? Because it was a Russian run facility or was the connection closer?"

"Much closer. The owner of that club was the mastermind behind the attack."

"Goodness!"

"Your x-employee was shot in the head. One of the witnesses heard the man who shot him say something to the effect that he hadn't come through or maybe you're through. She isn't certain which. Had he contacted you?"

"I have no idea. He wouldn't have been put through if he'd tried calling. You'd need to ask my secretaries or assistant if he attempted to call. I never saw him again after that night. To my knowledge he hadn't shown up at the office or our warehouse. You can ask there because it isn't the sort of thing the help would bother me with."

Jacob said, "It's our job to keep the riff raff away, which a disgruntled employee would certainly be. Otherwise his lordship would be knee deep in beggars. I don't recall seeing Yusuf again. I spent most of my time at the warehouse when I wasn't wrangling the permits. I can ask everyone else if they'd seen him or give you their current contact information?"

"I'd appreciate the contact information."

I said, "Some of the people who attended me there are still in Scotland seeing to another project."

"When do you plan on returning to Dubai?"

"Within the month, but it will be a short visit. My wife will accompany me there again next month for a slightly longer visit, assuming the manager she's hired is suitably trained by then."

"Another felon?"

"I've no idea. She handles staffing. She wouldn't recommend an unsuitable person for a job of the importance as this will be. If the person she's chosen is a felon, they'd be a reformed one."

"Like Yusuf?"

"I believe in second chances, but we do have a firm one strike and you're out rule."

"It didn't occur to you to send him home?"

"It was clear that I'd lost all control of him when I couldn't get him to return to the car…"

"Leaving a felon loose on the streets."

Jacob scoffed.

Brantwold said, "Did he receive severance pay?"

Jacob said, "I can check but I doubt it. He'd have been given his return ticket and a week to find new lodgings. But I don't think it took him a week because I never saw him at the condo again after that night."

"We're you aware he'd been fired?"

"We all were. Lord Blackwood was pissed that he had to call for a ride. He'd ordered Yusuf's locker cleaned out and his things dropped off at his condo, and we were told we weren't to let him back into the warehouse."

"Did he pick up his clothing?"

"I have no idea. Frankie or Emma or maybe Nick would know."

I said, "My assistant might know as it's his job to be sure all of my help gets where they're supposed to be, which includes arranging their lodging, transportation, paying the bills and whatnot. He's here in town if you need to speak with him. Frankie is in Scotland, Nick still in Dubai, and I believe Emma is in London."

"Did he have any particular friends in your little group?"

"I wouldn't know."

Jacob said, "He was an ass. No one acted like they missed him or were sad to see him go. To be honest, Ollie is the only driver we like."

"How many do you have?"

"I have no idea. There are four assigned to me, but I know we have more than that because my wife has her own drivers and then we have the ones in training and the ones assigned to our managers."

"Why so many?"

"I don't drive."

Brantwold raised an eyebrow.

I said, "My accident left me slightly disabled."

"Your accident..."

"Isn't relevant," Jacob said. "If his medical records are required, you can get a warrant. He keeps two drivers on duty so one is available to run errands while one is available to drive him."

Brantwold said, "So if you hadn't needed Yusuf as a driver for the day, he'd have been free to do what he'd wanted?"

Jacob said, "It depends. Lady Blackwood gives bonuses for completing online courses and she allows the help to do that when not assigned specifically to another job. Drivers also keep all of the vehicles and garages clean and help out in the mail room. Lady Blackwood lends hers out to friends occasionally. They sometimes do duty as waitstaff, or in the barns, or other odd jobs around the estate. There's an app that we're supposed to check that lists the jobs that need doing. We sign in and out. So if Lord Blackwood had said he wouldn't be needing him for a few hours, Yusuf would've checked the app to sign off of active duty and checked to see if there were any jobs waiting. If there weren't any, he could sign into the online courses for bonus pay. If there were jobs, he was supposed to go do that."

"Was anyone checking to be sure he was where he was supposed to be?"

"The secretaries check all of that. It's their job to be sure no one is taking advantage and claiming a simple job lasted all day or something. Mr. Poole checks the drivers as he's usually with my lord, so he knows when the drivers have been excused. Not that he needs to do that much because my lord's schedule usually makes it clear when a driver would've been unneeded."

Brantwold said, "So if you hadn't needed Yusuf as a driver for the day, he'd have been free to do what he'd wanted? Do you sign in and out of this app?"

I said, "I check it in the morning to see the schedule. I enter requests occasionally, but usually my secretaries or assistant make the entries as needed."

"Does the app track your physical location?"

"I have no idea."

Jacob said, "Not to my knowledge but we all use a location sharing app."

Saadeh brightened.

"Do you save those records?"

"I'm not sure. I know it sends the information to a cloud, but I don't know for how long it keeps that information."

I said, "Give him the password and let him look."

Jacob said, "He can get that same information by subpoenaing the phone records."

Saadeh said, "We'd appreciate the password just the same."

Jacob shrugged and wrote on a piece of paper that he handed to him.

"Does your wife monitor the online classes your employees take?" Brantwold asked.

I said, "I wouldn't think so. She might have a secretary do it, but I'd think she'd just be concerned with the end grades, not how long it took to get a passing grade."

Jacob said, "That's a good idea. You might be able to tell where he was if he signed in again after he quit, except I don't remember him taking any classes."

"Do you take classes?"

"We all do. It's sort of a hobby with us. The bonus for successfully completing a class is really good, so we're always joking about them and finding easy ones we can do in a few hours. We sometimes get together after work at a bar and take the classes together for fun. Just last week we all took a class on mixology."

"And they pay you for that?"

He laughed, shrugging.

I said, "An assistant who can make the perfect martini or can recognize when inferior wines are offered is priceless.

Saadeh snorted softly.

Brantwold nodded thoughtfully.

I said, "We encourage our staff to study anything that interests them."

Jacob wrote again and handed the paper to inspector Brantwold.

"That's Lady Blackwood's secretary, Allison Hardy. She'd know Yusuf's login info and what classes he was taking, if any."

"I'd like a list of the current whereabouts of all of your employees who were with you in Dubai. Even if they were just there very briefly."

Saadeh said, "Have any others quit or been fired since then?"

"I couldn't say for all of the different branches, but Yusuf was the only employee assigned to me who left my employment."

"When you say assigned to you..."

"The ones who I personally interact with. We imported quite a few construction workers, electricians, plumbers, architects, and so on to work on our myriad of projects. We brought in maids, cooks, gardeners. I've no idea how many were fired or quit."

"Why not hire locals?"

"We do."

Jacob said, "It's easier on us to use our own base crews and work in the locals as we become accustomed to the area, especially when there's a language barrier, but even here in England we do the same thing."

"And these construction crews are all parolees?"

"Some will be."

"You're bringing in these criminals…"

"Who've served their time and been released. They're now law-abiding citizens."

Jacob said, "They apply for passports and work visas as the law requires. We aren't breaking any laws at all. We haven't had even one incident with one of our employees."

"Yusuf—"

"Wasn't working for us when he did whatever he did."

"How convenient."

"How many men involved in that incident were former police officers?"

Saadeh flushed.

Brantwold scoffed. "Russians…"

"Still… if you aren't holding *their* former employers against them…"

"We'll be in touch," Saadeh said as he stood.

Brantwold offered his hand. "Thank you for coming in. If you think of anything, don't hesitate to call. We'll be reaching out to the others who accompanied you, and I'd like to speak with your assistant and secretaries to see if Yusuf tried to contact you again."

Jacob said, "And why would that matter?"

"Maybe it doesn't. But maybe he was murdered because he couldn't get his boss there?"

Jacob's eyes widened.

"You think the men killed were killed purposefully? That they were lured there somehow?"

"We're certain they were brought in purposefully but whether the person who arranged it knew what would happen that night is still up for debate."

"What did happen?"

"I'm not at liberty to say."

"But you think Yusuf was trying to get my lord murdered?"

"It's possible. Do you think he disliked the Blackwoods?"

"He didn't act like it. He hardly said a word. He spent most of his time on his phone playing games. He was an ass…"

"Did he ever make threats or boasts or anything?"

"Not that I recall. He was polite in a disinterested way. I mean, he made all the right responses, but he didn't mean it. It was just the correct response, if you know what I mean."

Brantwold nodded.

I said, "He usually fell asleep while waiting for me. He was efficient enough when sent to pick things up. I don't recall him taking overly long. There wasn't anything that stood out as off. I was shocked when he refused to leave."

Brantwold snickered, mumbling, "I bet."

"It was quite inappropriate behavior from everyone there!"

"So you knew it was an orgy?"

Jacob gaped at me.

"It was clear it was going to be," I said primly. "The men were extremely drunk when I arrived. I saw immediately the type of establishment it was but thought perhaps I'd just gone to the wrong entrance. But they invited me to stay. I got the impression they'd been expecting me, not that they ever said my name, but they were too welcoming—too jovial. Too quick to offer me hospitality."

"Drugs, you mean?"

"Pretty much anything. When I'd knocked, I'd said Francois had sent me and the reply was yes yes welcome, comrade, we have girls, drink, anything you require.

"What I required was a shower. The place was disgusting. I was very angry... Francois had thought to make me a fool as only a fool would have stayed to partake. But I'm *not* a fool, so I left immediately."

I was waiting for him to ask about Jean. Before I could make up my mind to mention her myself, he said, "You'd probably be dead now if you'd have stayed—or in jail. I think Tussaud was trying to make you his patsy by sending you there."

"You think he was behind it?"

"I'm not sure. There's a good chance they double crossed him or maybe he double crossed them. If I were you, I'd be watching my back while I was there."

He nodded at us and held the door.

We took the hint and left.

In the car, Jacob said, "That stupid fucker!"

I wasn't sure if he meant the police or Yusuf.

He continued, "Still, if that's all they've got, I don't think you need to worry."

"'Tis plenty of other things to worry about."

He laughed.

I hadn't been jesting.

Chapter 53

Mrs. Roman said worriedly, "Excuse me, sir. I'm sorry to interrupt, but the man at the door was quite insistent that he speak with you at once."

She glanced back to the stairs, leaning closer to say, "I think you should maybe call for security to handle him. He was very rude. Very..."

"What on earth..."

She flushed, leaning even closer to whisper, "He said it was about your bitch of a wife. Then he laughed but it wasn't a nice sort of laugh. I'd have called security myself, but he said if I didn't get you that he'd go direct to the press."

I took her hand to say, "Think no more of it. Everything is fine, Kathleen. Continued with your duties."

The tight expression eased on her face.

I said, "I believe Oscar has gotten into the suit closet. Could you please roust him out and see which suits might need cleaning?"

"Of course, sir."

She hurried away.

I returned to my study to grab a vial of binding powder, the antidote, and the spelled napkins, putting them all in my pockets then headed to the door.

The man in the hallway was unfamiliar to me but I knew he was a killer by his thick rind.

He smirked at me when I appeared.

"Come with me and no bullshit or your wife gets it."

"Who are you?"

"Does it fucking matter?"

"No, I suppose it doesn't. Where is my wife?"

"I'm not dicking around here. Come with me right now if you ever want to see her again."

The heat of my anger brightened his rind.

"Where is she?" I said again.

"I've got her on ice. We get the call when you're in the car."

"Then by all means. Let us be away."

He laughed, apparently not realizing I'd forced the answer. Although maybe I hadn't. 'Twas a good chance the man was a psychopath to have that thick of a rind and we hadn't been testing long enough to be certain those sorts with a rind could be controlled.

I began to sweat as I considered this man might know exactly what I was.

He snickered as he stepped forward and began to pat me down.

I said, "I have nothing that concerns you. Let's go."

I was relieved when he turned immediately.

He took two steps then halted, glancing back at me with a puzzled expression.

Terror took my breath.

If I'd made him forget where he was taking me—

Before I could truly panic, he said, "No funny business. You try to signal or crash the car or any shit, your wife gets it. And before you start thinking who the hell cares, we got it figured so you'll be blamed."

I followed without speaking because I was terrified that my anger was strong enough to make him instantly a mule and perhaps make him forget what he was about.

We got into his car, which was an older model SUV that apparently had never been cleaned. Trash covered the backseat, old clothing, discarded takeout containers, smashed and ripped open boxes, and it stunk of stale beer.

There wasn't a sign of Julia. I sensed nothing from her either.

His phone rang as we took the turn that led to town, not the motorway that led to London.

She was close then.

He snickered as he said, "I got him and he's crying the stupid fuck."

I hadn't realized I was, so great was my distress.

He listened a moment and then said, "You fucking stick to the plan. I know what I'm doing."

He pocketed his phone.

"This can go two ways for you. If you're smart, you'll do what you're told and walk out maybe a bit poorer and with some new friends you need to keep happy, but you'll be fucking alive. Be a dumbass and we'll waste all your stupid asses."

All... he had more than Julia.

I said nothing.

He leaned closer, saying loudly, "Did you hear me? I'm trying to save your stupid life here."

"I hear."

He chuckled as he said, "Man, Bootsie is going to love you. Maybe I'll take a turn too..."

My surge of anger was accompanied by his ragged inhalation.

I knew he felt my anger and coveted it, that it aroused him. His aroused state was very apparent. 'Twas infuriating to know he thought himself able to do whatever he wished to me and mine without consequences.

My anger billowed about me in a red cloud that I knew that he felt by the way his hands loosened on the wheel as he turned to me.

"Watch what you're about," I said angrily.

He grabbed the wheel in time to avoid going completely off the road.

The car skidded into the parking lot behind the warehouse that Julia had purchased to turn into a club. My heart pitter pattered hard as I scanned the lot for Mary's car.

There were only two other cars in the lot, and I recognized neither.

He parked right in front of the back door.

I said, "Is my wife inside?"

"Yes."

"Who else?"

His eyes were huge and dilated as he swayed toward me.

"My men and yours. Hugh's—"

A man stepped from the door, saying angrily, "Get in here before someone sees us."

Hugh, I thought in rising anger at myself.

I exited the car.

The man at the door wore jeans and a blue shirt. He looked completely normal, except for a mostly covered tattoo on his throat, which was the only visual clue that he wasn't as harmless as he appeared. His rind was much thinner than my escorts.

"Your name?" I asked with intent.

"Rufio Palma."

Palma stepped back as he said it, holding the door open with one hand to gesture us inside with the gun in his other.

"Release my wife."

He released the door to take another step back, turning to say to someone out of sight, "Is the bitch awake yet?"

A woman screamed a terrified breathless cry that ended in a gurgle.

I rushed past Palma.

"She's finished," another man said.

"Julia!" but I knew it wasn't her even as my knees hit the floor.

"Told you he loved her," the new guy said complacently, snickering as he rose from the corpse, grabbing for his pants.

The woman was too bloody for me to recognize her through the haze of my anger. She was naked with a shirt tossed carelessly over her face bleeding from several wounds on her neck and torso. She lay at the end of a short hall that led to the main room.

I would feel a mortal wound, I told myself, but 'twasn't as reassuring as I wished it to be because I'd no idea if that would be true if she'd been knocked unconscious.

I'd been here once before so knew a door on the left led to the kitchen. Two doors on the right led to small bathrooms. All three of the doors had been propped open so I could see they were empty as we passed.

I averted my gaze from the dead woman as I stepped over her to enter the main room.

Fear was making me nauseous. I couldn't control the tremors that wracked me.

My escort crowded against my back. I thought it was the heat of my anger drawing him.

"What's his name?" I asked.

"Bootsie," he whispered as one would to a lover. "I'm Joe."

"Now that we're all friends," Bootsie said cheerfully, stepping away from the corpse as if she'd meant nothing. He ignored the blood on himself, pulling his pants on but not doing the button, smirking at me as he continued, "I got plenty more for your bitch and you. Bring him in. The boss wants to have a talk."

My shaking stilled. I hoped he'd meant he hadn't yet raped Julia, that he'd been waiting for her to wake.

I strode forward eagerly. All three of them followed close on my heels.

"Pip!" Ryu said in great relief,

My gaze swung from Julia who was laying on the floor to him.

He'd been tied to one of the metal poles that held up the roof. New bruises covered his face. Fresh blood marred his cheek. I thought the blood was from the hand that was clutching his side. A puddle of blood was growing around him. 'Twas a serious injury.

"You fuckers are in for it now," he said weakly and slumped.

I gathered the heat of them and thrust it at Ryu as I knelt to feel the pulse in Julia's neck.

All three of them moaned.

"Release him and bind his wound," I said.

Palma and Bootsie rushed to do my bidding.

From behind me, Stan said, "You're going to tell me whatever the hell it is you got on Hugh and Brent," and I realized who the other woman was. She was Amber, Hugh's wife.

"Why did you murder his wife?" I asked.

Joe said, "To frame you."

"Shut up, fool!" Stan said angrily without leaving the doorway across the large room.

Paper covered the entrance doors, making the entrance way dark, but I could see he had a gun. He was too far for me to reach.

Joe shrugged at him, not taking his gaze from me as he said, "The plan was we tell him."

"Tell me the plan," I said.

"We kill your bitches, and you either help cover it up, in which case we own your asses forever, or you go away for life, in which case we own your ass forever."

Stan snickered.

I leaned over Julia to feel her pulse again then went to check Ryu.

Palma sat back to let me see the wound he was binding with his own shirt.

"You goddamned bastards!"

A wave of anima accompanied my words. I grabbed the sparkling anima coating Palma and thrust it at Ryu. Palma lost his footing and fell or perhaps wished to be closer to me, but I thought he was dead because there wasn't a spec of anima remaining on him.

I pressed that heat into Ryu who moaned.

"Did he fucking faint?" Stan asked as if that was the most ridiculous thing he'd ever heard of.

I ripped the last specs of heat from Palma out. My own anger was a cloud around me that lit with sparkling motes that I guided to the wound in Ryu's side. His anima took on a healthy glow.

I didn't need to examine Palma. I knew he was dead and was glad of it.

I clasped Ryu's hand to feel his pulse.

Stan said sneeringly, "I thought he was your new boyfriend. Does your fucking wife know?"

"What difference could that possibly make to you?"

I released Ryu, leaning forward to kiss his brow.

"All will be well."

Blood had stopped flowing, which I thought was a good sign. His pulse was fast but strong. He was still laying limply but I hoped he could recover if not from the anima I was directing to him then perhaps human medicine.

"Give me your phone."

"What the fuck man?" Stan said angrily as Joe passed his phone over.

I called Doreen.

Stan peered between Joe and I worriedly, his gaze drawn to the gun in Joe's hand, which made me laugh in angry amusement.

Stan was still too far for me to reach unless I had one of my new mules shoot him. And as angry as I was, I didn't want him dead—yet.

Stan said angrily, "Don't you fucking forget who's in charge here. Who holds the goddamned purse strings!"

"I shan't," I said as Doreen said, "Who—sir?"

Stan stepped backward as if considering running.

I said, "Come at once to the new club Julia has in town and bring medical supplies for a serious knife wound in the abdomen."

I tossed the phone down.

"Where is Hugh?"

"On his way," Joe said.

I said to Stan, "Does he know what you'd planned or was this meant to hurt him?"

Stan shrugged at me, narrowing his eyes at Joe.

"Go see if they're here yet," he said, waving his gun in our general direction. I thought he was afraid to point it at us because he wasn't certain if his hired thugs were still working for him.

"Do as he says," I said.

Stan frowned.

"I'm in charge," Stan said forcefully but with a tremor in his voice that belied the words. He knew I was but was hoping he was wrong.

I laid my hand on Joe's thigh, and he stopped to peer back at me.

"If he raises that gun, kill him."

Joe nodded.

"What did you give to Julia?"

Stan backpedaled away from me, licking his lips and casting nervous glances around.

I stopped walking afraid he'd bolt. I needed to cozen him to get within range.

He said to Joe, "Whatever he offered you, he doesn't have it. You know I'm good for it. We go way back, Joe."

Joe didn't glance away from me.

"Tell me what you gave Julia," I said as forcefully as I could.

Joe said, "I don't know. Amber was told to slip her something over their lunch to get her here more easily."

"Go search her bag."

Joe ran off.

Stan still stared between us as if he couldn't decide if they were working for me or him.

I walked closer and he pointed the gun at me then shifted it to point at her.

I said, "Don't be a fool. I *will* kill you."

"It didn't need to be like this, man. You brought this on yourself with all that amnesia bullshit!"

"And Hugh?"

"Is fucking in it with you!"

"Brent?"

"I don't know... is he?"

"What have you done to him?"

"Nothing—yet."

I couldn't tell if that was a lie.

I said, "So Amber.... Why murder her if she was willing to help you?"

"She wasn't fucking willing until I told her Hugh was going down anyway. Then she was onboard. It was her fucking idea to bring your wife here. She thought it would make you talk, so I thought why not make her prick of a husband talk too!"

"I thought you were friends..."

Stan scoffed.

"He thinks of you as such."

He wiped his sweating brow, saying angrily, "Enough of your fucking bullshit. You got him covering your ass. We know he gave you all of the inside info on Shipley!"

"But you murdered *her*!"

"Bootsie gets carried away, but we did Hugh a favor really. He wants her gone. Granted, he didn't want to go away for her murder, which he'll sure as shit do if he doesn't smarten up, but he'll be glad I wasted her."

"Wasted... you're despicable."

"Like you're one to talk. I have shit on you, Lou. And I don't mean your fagot boyfriend who's going to be pissed as hell at you for outing him, but real shit that would get you life."

"Like what?"

"Like you're working for Jerome Pruitt, and I can prove it!"

"How?"

"How what?"

"Could you prove it?"

He stepped back as I stepped forward.

"I will fucking shoot you both!"

"Put the gun down."

He lowered his hand then scrambled backward and lifted it again.

Joe returned, saying, "They're here."

He handed me a pill bottle.

"What is this?"

He took the bottle back, opened the cap and poured the contents into his hand.

"Ambien and benzos, I think."

"What does it do?"

"Makes you sleep. Relaxes you and shit."

Stan said, "Are you double crossing me, you asshole?"

I said to Joe, "Who do you work for?"

"Pruitt."

"No fucking way," Stan said, sounding shocked and terrified. "He can't fucking want this cocksucker to live! Lou fucking screwed him too!"

I was surprised too. I'd thought he'd say Stan or Shipley, which would've hopefully relaxed Stan enough I could get closer.

I said, "Maybe Lou only pretended too..."

Ryu groaned and I glanced back to see he was tugging at his wrist that was still shackled to the beam.

"Release him."

"Stan has the key," Joe said.

"And you aren't getting it! What the hell is going on?"

I laughed an angry growl of laughter, saying, "This is your show. You tell me."

He gaped at me.

I said, "Give him the damned key or he'll shoot you in the fucking face."

Joe lifted his gun.

"Get the key," I said to him.

Stan tossed him the key, saying, "Look man, call your boss, and tell him he's got this all wrong. It's Lou who's the problem! I don't know what bullshit lie he told Pruitt, but Lou isn't running Shipley or anything else. He's fucking broke as shit. His fucking wife will toss him to the curb when she finds out he's screwing her brother. His money is going to dry up! Every cent he gets he spends on his fag. Whatever the two of them are up to, it's never going to pan out because they're both stupid fucks. This was my plan. Mine! It won't work without me. None of them know who the contacts are."

I said, "Give him the key or I'll have him make you wish you had."

We all paused, tensing as the door opened, letting in a swath of bright sunlight.

The door banged shut as Hugh yelled, "Oh my god!" from the back hall. "Amber! Jesus God what did you do!"

"He doesn't sound happy with you," I said.

Two new men entered the room.

Both had guns out and looked pissed. One had a rind. Both looked like the sort of men who'd done serious time.

"Pip," Ryu said worriedly.

"What are their names?" I asked Joe.

"Higgs and Stoll."

"He's trying to cut us out," Stan said angrily to the new men, or maybe Hugh.

Higgs, the rinded man, pointed his gun at Joe.

I held my empty hands out as I walked close enough to see the threads of anima that I could feel as growing heat.

"What happened to Palma?" Stoll asked.

Stan scoffed, saying, "I think he fainted or something. I don't fucking know. All I know is that Joe is working with Lou and Lou thinks he can talk his way out of this."

I was close enough now to firmly grasp Higgs' anima, which I did as I said, "Kill Stoll."

"Fuck!" Stan exclaimed as Higgs turned and fired. Stoll gaped at him. He looked shocked and hadn't even lifted his own gun.

"What..." he trailed off gasping as he slumped to the floor, clutching at the bullet hole in his chest.

From the entranceway to the room, Hugh said, "What the fuck is going on!"

I said, "Stan had your wife murdered."

"He did it," Stan said as he began walking backward, waving his gun between us as if he couldn't decide where to point it.

I said, "If he takes one more step, shoot him. If he doesn't drop the gun, shoot him."

"You fucking killed my wife," Hugh said as if he couldn't believe it.

Stan opened then closed his mouth, clearly debating claiming again that I'd done it. He finally said, "I did you a fucking favor! We needed something on Lou, something he couldn't weasel out of or get you to cover for him!"

Hugh snorted angrily.

"Free my man," I said to Joe.

"Your man," Stan said in derision. "I told you he was a fag."

Hugh peered between us looking very worried.

He said, "So now what? You blame me for killing our wives? Is that it? Why the hell would I do that, Stan? The police would never believe you! Never!"

I said, "Ryu, can you get to the car?"

"We can't leave her in here, man."

"I shall attend to my wife."

"She's going to be so fucking pissed when she wakes..."

"True..."

She would be pissed and neither Stan nor Hugh had a rind she could use.

"She doesn't know about you two, does she," Stan said triumphantly.

"You're a fucking idiot," Ryu said. "Why the fuck don't you just end this now, Pip? None of these assholes deserve another moment."

"I tend to agree, and yet I see there is more here than meets the eye."

Stan said, "Look, man, I think we both got the wrong end of the stick. We can clean this shit up and it'll be just like it never happened."

Hugh said angrily, "Except my fucking wife is dead! You think no one's going to notice, asshole!"

I said, "Joe, take my wife, gently mind, to the office here and make her comfortable."

Ryu staggered to his feet.

"I'll stay with her."

Stan scoffed, saying, "He's fucking stalking her, Lou. Or maybe they're having an affair or some shit. You'd be a fool to trust him. I bet he wants to whack your ass!"

"Take his gun," I said to Ryu. "Tell me truly, how badly are you injured?"

"Not too bad now, I don't think."

He winced as he dropped his hand from his side, leaving me to believe that he was still hurt.

It made me furiously angry.

Joe and Higgs moaned, stepping closer to me.

"Go," I said to Joe, and he turned back to Julia.

I said to Ryu, "Doreen will be arriving shortly, and she can see to you both. But I'd rather stop at the hospital myself then have you drop dead."

He snorted with laughter.

"I'll be fine. Deal with this, but be careful, Pip. He's a lying ass."

Hugh said, "What the fuck, man..."

I said to Stan, "How did you imagine that you could make the police believe that Hugh had naught to do with his wife's demise?"

"Lay off the goddamned act, asshole!"

"Seriously, we're going to argue about whether he's faking his amnesia now!" Hugh yelled angrily.

"How?" I asked again.

Stan's angry gaze passed over all of us before he said, "We'd give him an alibi. My wife will say Amber was going to meet her."

"Your wife is aware of what you intended?"

"No. Amber called her to set it up. She'd made arrangements to take Brent's boat out for a girl's night. It was all her idea. Everyone knows my wife is always late for everything. She'd just say she was waiting for her and everyone else went ahead, and then she'd act realistically annoyed that Julia wasn't there if we'd decided to let her go or horrified that she'd fallen over with Hugh. Brent and Leif will say whatever I tell them to and since they have no motive to kill either of them, everyone would believe it had happened just like they said. My wife wouldn't know what had happened, but she could truthfully say they'd made plans to go out and she'd believe what we told her had really happened."

He sneered at Hugh as he said, "And if I told her Hugh and Amber were fighting, she'd believe me and tell the cops that."

Hugh said, "What the hell are you talking about? Me and Julia drowned! Like hell my wife set that up!"

Stan glared at him as he said, "Your wife was onto you. She knew about your other accounts and was pissed as shit. I told her Lou was fucking with all of us and you were going to get us all arrested, which you fucking are if you keep telling Lou's wife shit that she doesn't need to know. Amber agreed to help us disappear your ass! She thought the fucking boat was to get rid of your corpse."

"She wouldn't..."

Stan smirked, "Then why the hell did she poison his fucking wife? She knows you're having an affair with Julia. I showed her the transfers from your account to Julia's and she wanted you both dead. We all knew you had to be screwing her to keep lying like you were. Amber was talking shit about how she was going to bring you to the cleaners—take everything. She didn't care if there was an investigation into your finances. She told me plain as day if I didn't make you give her everything, she'd ruin us all. So I told her I'd have you killed, and she was totally onboard with it!" He snickered at his own joke. "So you can thank me for whacking her ass for you."

"Poison?" I said as I examined the bottle of pills Joe had handed me.

Stan shrugged, "I've no idea what she gave her. She just had to get her into the car and keep her quiet."

Hugh said, "You were going to kill all of us, weren't you... Did Brent know?"

I said, "Who else knew of the plan?"

"Just these guys here."

He hadn't hesitated at all, but I knew I hadn't compelled the answer. He was still too far for me to reach him with my anima.

"Did you plan to kill us all?" I asked.

"Not you. I needed a patsy and you'd have inherited her dough, which would maybe pay back the money you stole."

"But the rest of your little group?"

He shrugged, saying, "I had to, didn't I. They know too much, and it was my fucking money they were giving to your bitch!"

I wasn't sure I believed him. I thought he might be saying what he thought I'd wanted to hear.

He let Joe pass him with Julia.

Ryu gave me a worried glance and limped after them.

We all stared at each other until the office door closed and I said, "And now? What do you imagine we could do to cover this up?"

"Same thing. You go on the boat and claim Amber got drunk and fell overboard."

Hugh grunted in annoyance or maybe disbelief.

I said, "I suppose with enough witnesses of impeccable character that you'd be believed. Let's leave that for now. Tell me why you were surprised to find that Joe works for Pruitt."

"He's been our guy forever. Me and him have been friends since grammar school."

"But you don't work for Pruitt?"

"No. I do business with him but I ain't his bitch."

"But you're afraid of him?"

"Anyone sane would be. We keep out of his way and treat him right. There's no reason he'd be after us, so it must've been you're idea. What I don't get is why? We had a good thing going, Lou. Why'd you go and fuck it all up?"

"I truly do have amnesia. Not that I care a whit what you believe. You're an evil man who needs to be stopped." I glanced back at Hugh, saying, "You all are. Do you even care that he murdered her?"

"Of course I care!"

Higgs fired and I turned back to see Stan disappear through the front door.

"Damnation!"

I chased him but by the time I reached the door, Stan was driving away.

"Higgs, begin cleaning. See if you can find something to wrap the corpses in. Do whatever you can do to hide that your stacking corpses in Palma's car."

I hesitated when I glanced at Hugh, feeling bad for him even though I'd believed Stan hadn't lied about Hugh being grateful to be rid of his wife. She couldn't have loved him if she'd been willing to murder him although maybe Stan had lied about that... not that it mattered.

I said to Hugh, "Help him clean up. Start with the blood there by the pole. Do a good job. You don't want anyone to know this happened."

He nodded agreement, which I thought he'd have done even if my anima wasn't thick around him.

"Bootsie, come with me."

I went to check on Julia and Ryu. Joe had placed her on a ratty couch in the office. Ryu was sitting beside her holding her hand. He looked terrible, sick and shaky. She appeared to be sleeping.

I felt for her pulse again.

Ryu said worriedly, "She's really cold, Pip. Is this normal?"

I snorted and he winced.

"Are you recovering?" I asked as I reached past him to feel her forehead.

"It hurts," he said shortly.

"Hug her," I said to Bootsie.

He did as I bid him, and I pressed the heat of him into her.

He fell to the side.

Ryu exclaimed a wordless worried sound when I dragged the corpse away from her, letting it fall.

"Take Joe's hand," I said to Ryu who hesitated the smallest moment before nodding and doing so.

I shifted Joe's rind to him, pressing it on the deep dense core of him.

Ryu exclaimed, shaking his hand as he tossed Joe's hand aside.

"Too hot," he said. "I'm... better, I guess."

He grabbed Joe's hand and placed it on her heart.

Julia absorbed the rind in seconds. I guided the heat of him onto her until Joe fell over, knocking into Ryu who laughed a nervous relieved laugh.

I pulled the corpse away.

"When Doreen gets here, have her examine my lady and yourself. If a hospital is needed, go forthwith. We can worry about covering that up later. If she thinks my lady will sleep this off, bring her home and make her comfortable in the study. Remain with her until I return. Do all that may be done to keep her calmly at home."

"People are going to talk, Pip, if I bring her home in this state."

"'Twill need to be dealt with on my return."

"I should stay and help you."

"I've no need of assistance. Although, perhaps send two of the boys with cleaning supplies."

"What are you going to do with the corpses?"

"Bring them to Brent's boat."

"People will think it's weird if they all die there, especially if Julia was the last one seen with his wife."

"I suppose... "

"Maybe Sandra could help?"

"I'm quite capable of disposing of them."

"I meant, maybe she has an idea about what to do with them. There must be somewhere they could be sent that wouldn't arouse suspicion or disrupt whatever plans they were working on. If we could handle it before Jewels wakes..."

"'Tis an admirable thought."

I called Sandra.

"I'm sorry to disturb you." I filled her in on what was happening.

She said, "I'm glad you called me because we do need them for a while longer. I think you can safely dispose of the wife though. Call Brent and have him and his wife meet you at the boat. Give them the command and make sure there's plenty of booze on board. Make sure one of your mules brings a few cement blocks to weigh down the body. Stan and Hugh can drop it. If you tell Brent to take his wife to the stateroom before you bring the corpses on, it shouldn't be that difficult to make her believe they were all partying and that Hugh and his wife were getting along fine. Tell her she saw Amber slip and fall. In fact, give her a signal. Like tell Hugh to flick the lights at three or something and that she saw Amber climb onto the bow to see and she fell. Tell her to call it in and have them all search as if it had happened."

Ryu said, "Don't forget to tell her that she's upset and describe the scene enough that she has a believable image in mind."

Sandra said, "Make sure you check for recording devices. In fact, I'll go check it. Text me the dock info. I don't trust that asshole. God knows what other loopholes they found in Julia's commands."

"Loopholes?"

"She spoke with Stan. I was there when she told him you had nothing to do with the missing money. It didn't occur to either of us to tell him that she didn't. You can stop by his house once you officially hear Amber died and reinforce the commands to make sure this won't happen again."

"I want them dead."

"As soon as we can without arousing suspicion. I'll call you when I'm certain the boat is safe to board. I think you should probably burn the other corpses though."

"Why not burn her too?" Ryu asked.

"The fish will clean her up and we might need to really prove she's dead, which we could do by having someone find the bones."

He shrugged at me. I could see he was really worried.

"Thank you for your assistance," I said to Sandra.

"Keep a cool head, Pip."

She disconnected.

I set the phone down.

Ryu said, "I don't think it's a great idea to have that corpse floating around, especially if you're going to that boat. I think it'd be smarter to burn them all. We don't even need to tell Sandra that we did."

"I'll think on it."

"The only reason anyone would need to see that corpse is to set someone up. I'm not saying she'd set you up, but why leave the slightest clue? I can take all of the corpses home and you can use an inferno spell. We dump the ash, and no one will ever be able to say where the body is. Besides, the chance of a diver finding it if we ever needed it are minuscule."

"Sandra could find it. But I agree, it seems a large risk for little gain. Twould be better to dispose of the corpse ourselves and then only have the lie to plant. My appearance at the dock should be unremarkable. I can simply say I'd gone to meet my wife and accompany them on their outing but that she'd gone home with a headache of which I was unaware until I arrived."

Ryu nodded agreement, saying, "Maybe I should take her to the apartment in London? It would give her time to cool off…"

"Do so if Doreen thinks you're able. How did they grab you?"

"I was there keeping an eye on her on the down low and saw she was acting tipsy when she left the restaurant. I wasn't too worried because I thought it was an act. She hadn't had more than a glass or two of wine. They got into Amber's car, and I could see Julia had fallen asleep, which wasn't like her, but I still wasn't that worried. I followed her to the club, and they jumped me when I reached the car. They meant to kill both of us. I was hoping she'd wake up and was terrified she would... What will you do with Stan?"

"I'm not certain. He might be able to elude me."

"Elude you? He got away!"

He released Julia's hand to stagger to his feet.

"We need to get out of here!"

"I doubt he would call the authorities when 'twould be our word against his."

"He could have more thugs."

"I'm certain I have many more than he."

Ryu snorted in annoyed laughter.

I said, "I'll send Higgs or perhaps Hugh to bring Julia to your car. Where is your car?"

"Out front. I left my keys in it, but he could've taken them. He took my phone."

As I was speaking, I began rifling through Julia's purse that was dangling from her arm. I handed him her cell phone. "Call Doreen and arrange for her to meet you."

He squatted by the corpses, removing two phones, one of which he waggled at me then made a call while searching the other corpse.

I went to see how the cleanup was progressing.

Amber's corpse had already been removed. A pile of blood-soaked clothing lay on Bootsie's chest. Hugh had apparently been using the clothes to mop up the blood. He was using glass cleaner and paper towels on the pole when I arrived while Higgs was spreading an old tarp beside them.

He must've brought it with him, which angered me all over again.

Both stopped to stare at me.

"Higgs, bring Julia out to my assistant's car. Treat her gently. Quickly now."

I was a bit worried now that Stan would call the police. If the authorities arrived while we were cleaning up, it wouldn't look good for us. If Stan claimed he'd escaped us, he might be believed.

I said to Hugh, "I have two men coming to help clean up, but we need the bodies out of here. Help Higgs get them all into Palma's car. I'll text Higgs an address to bring the car. Speaking of which, did you find any phones or anything?"

He shook his head.

"Check the bodies. Keep the wallets and phones for me. Bring Amber's phone with you to the boat and toss it over when you're a mile or so offshore. As soon as my men get here, go home and clean up quickly then dress in something you'd normally wear for an evening on Brent's boat."

"I'm not sure I could trust Brent to lie for me."

"We can discuss your concerns later. Act in a manner appropriate for someone on the way to a pleasant evening with friends. If the police accost you between now and when I see you again say whatever you like that doesn't implicate me, Julia, or Ryu. Do your best to get this mess here cleaned before my men arrive but go move the bodies first."

I ran through the room to peek out the back door. The same two cars were there.

I ran back to speak to Ryu, but he was gone already.

Higg's entered the front door as I was headed to it.

"Lock that door," I said, which made me wonder how they'd gotten in.

"How did you get in here?"

"Stan had a key."

550

"Did anyone notice you bring Julia out?"

He shrugged at me.

"Help Hugh move the bodies and then do your best to hide what happened here. I have two men coming to help clean. When they get here, you take your car and drive away. Drive carefully and find someplace where no one will notice you have bodies in the car and wait for my text. We don't want anyone to know anything happened here."

He nodded.

I grabbed his arm and his anima to say, "You want to please me. Don't get caught with the bodies. Do exactly what I tell you. Hide the bodies in Palma's car, and when I text you, you'll meet me. You'll know it's me texting because I'll say come at once. Now give me your phone number."

He grinned at me as he gave me the number.

"If anyone stops by just say you came to take measurements to give Lady Blackwood an estimate on new siding."

He nodded.

"Go."

I ran out to Palma's car to get my phone and called Ryu.

"'Tis me," I said as a greeting. "Send someone here to move these vehicles. I shall leave the keys on the seat."

"Ollie is on the way to pick you up."

"Thank you."

"Bent and Smalls should be there any minute. You don't need to wait for them though. They know to clean the place and not to say shit. I'm not sure if you should have Ollie meet you there or if you should walk away now."

"'Twas a thought I had myself. 'Twould be odd indeed for me to be seen walking the street though."

As we were speaking, Hugh and Higgs put the corpses into the back of the SUV.

I said, "I think I should remain here until my ride arrives."

"Get those bodies out of there, Pip."

"My thought was to destroy the car and contents."

"I'll text you the address of one of the disposable mules homes. There's a large garage in back. Behind that, there's a fenced in junk heap with lots of old cars and crap. Burn it there. The police might not even show up if you tell the mule to put the fire out."

"Is Julia—"

"No change. Doreen just pulled in."

"Call me with news."

I hung up and went to tell Higgs where to meet me.

Chapter 54

My mule listened intently, nodding as I gave directions.

Higg's had brought the car full of corpses as ordered.

I set the spelled napkin on a corpse, closed the car door, and activated the spell.

Flame burst through the roof of the car before I'd run three steps away.

Higgs hadn't had time to make a sound, which I thought was too good for him.

I ran back to my car.

Ollie said, "You're sure there's no cameras here, boss?"

"Julia would've ensured it," I said absently as I scrolled through my texts.

Doreen had advised that she accompany Ryu to monitor Julia, which he'd done.

I said, "Stan won't be happy to see me. He might be angry enough to pull a weapon. If he does, leave me. If I wave you away, drive down the road a bit and wait for my call."

"You shouldn't go in alone if you think he might shoot you."

"I shall be fine. See to your own welfare. Call Bent and Smalls and see if they need anything and remind them that they're to return directly to the house after disposing of the cars in London. If they do require anything, send Tate or one of the others."

I glanced back to see smoke billowing into the air. It didn't worry me unduly. We were far enough on the outskirts of town that there'd be few to notice. The fastest responders wouldn't arrive for a good ten minutes. The car would be reduced to molten metal by that time and my mule would be busily throwing additional pieces of trash into the fire for a further ten minutes until he put out the fire. I cared not a whit if he were arrested or fined or whatever happened to people who set such large fires.

Stan's wife, Paige, opened the door when I knocked. She had a faint rind that I knew was from an abortion four years prior.

She looked unhappy to see me, forcing a smile, saying hurriedly, "Lou, I was just on my way out. I'll call the moment I get a minute."

I grasped her arm, pressing my anger on her as I said, "Is Stan here?"

"No. He's at the office."

"Where are you going?"

"Nowhere."

"Why send me away?"

"He asked me too."

"How silly of him. My illness isn't at all contagious. Brent has invited Julia and I out on his boat this evening. You're going of course."

She nodded.

"Did Amber call and tell you we were all meeting there?"

554

The pinched look on her face faded as she nodded again, this time more naturally.

"I think you should change quickly to whatever you'd planned to wear on the boat, grab your bag and run out to the grocery store to buy the things to make some snacks and Amber's favorite drink. Brent tells me a dinner cruise is so much fun. I'll see you there after you're done shopping."

I debated a moment then said, "Why don't you call Stan so I can be sure he knows Brent changed the time."

She took out her cell and made a call.

I was beginning to think he wouldn't answer her when she said, "Honey, Lou is here and wants to speak with you."

She handed me the phone.

"Leave her the fuck alone," Stan said.

"I shall. We can discuss it like civilized people on the boat tonight."

"Like hell I'm getting on a boat with you."

"I don't see why you wouldn't when 'twould just be us aboard... or did you mean to take yourself off to the wilds of Australia or some other godforsaken spot for the rest of your life?"

"What do you want, Lou?"

"For us to have a cordial dinner. I know my illness has made our friendship difficult. I think it will be lovely to clear the air between us. My lady was happy to take Amber under her wing. The two were discussing some investment scheme or another and quite excited about it. I think your wife would also benefit although, in truth, I have no head for business anymore. I leave that all entirely to Julia."

"Are you fucking saying you had no idea what your wife is up to?"

"I'm sure whatever she's doing is for my—our—benefit."

"And if I don't go?"

"Then I shall have to alter my plans. I hope to see you at Brent's in a few hours."

"My wife can't go, man."

"I'm certain she'd be happy to wait for my own to arrive while we get some fishing in. I quite like Paige. I find her company... relaxing."

She beamed at me.

Stan growled.

"Of course, if no one else shows, the two of us could always try our luck."

"We'll fucking be there."

He disconnected.

I said to Paige, "Drive safely and don't let your husband or anyone else talk you out of going. I look forward to seeing you."

"I won't be long," she said happily.

I was dying to question her more thoroughly, but that would need to wait until I was certain there were no recording devices.

The one on the doorbell here would've recorded this exchange.

"Where too?" Ollie asked when I got into the car.

I gave him the address of Brent's oceanside cottage, then called Ryu.

"She's still sleeping," he said as a greeting.

"It occurs to me that I need to erase the recordings of Palma's arrival at my home."

"I can handle that when we go home. It will take police at least a day to demand a warrant even if they were certain you were involved. You'll probably be back before they even know she fell overboard. Which reminds me, make sure Ollie stops for gas somewhere you can buy beer and chips on camera. Leave it with Brent and then make sure you call someone as soon as you leave. Stay on the phone so your cell will ping towers as you drive away, and if you can think of somewhere to go that will seem normal and get you on camera, do it."

Sandra called me on Ollie's phone as we stopped to buy chips at a convenience store right down the street from Brent's.

She said, "I disabled the cameras at Brent's and at Hugh's. Brent and Lief are both there and I heard them talking. They know something big is going down between the three of you but not what. They knew the plan called for killing Amber, but they didn't think it was really going to happen."

"We're they upset about it?"

She snorted. "They're worried but not about that. Brent joked about it saying if we're getting rid of them that we should've done them all at once, which pissed Lief off. He said his family was out of bounds and it got heated for a minute. Leif went to the bathroom, called his wife, and told her to go visit her sister. They don't trust each other at all. Julia and I can fix that at our next meeting."

"I don't care if they trust each other only that they obey."

"I agree. Give me a week and Julia and I can have them locked down."

"'Twould be better to dispose of them."

"I agree, but they won't be a problem, Pip. Julia can find a mule to send to Australia and take care of Stan, but it needs to be done subtly because we can't afford an investigation. We're cleaning up your involvement with Shipley, but that's taking time."

"Stan has no rind for me to grasp."

"We can control him with the fear of exposure. I think we should have the other three buy him out. Let him think he's washing his hands of them. If we do it in a way that he thinks he's winning, we'll get the time we need."

"He's likely to try to kill them all. I think 'twas his intent tonight."

"Then call him right now and tell him he can't. That you're handling it. Offer him a payoff or something. Do whatever you need to stall him long enough to reach him."

"I'd trust no command on his black heart."

"That's where blackmail comes in. He'll cave to save himself."

I called Stan who said angrily, "What the fuck did you say to my wife!"

"That it would be a fun trip. 'Tis most vexing to arrange these things. But all has been arranged to my satisfaction. Paige will truly believe Amber is aboard, which is all you need to know about that. If anything untoward we're to happen to the boat or people thereon, you become the prime suspect. I shan't trouble myself with anything you might have to say to the authorities about my involvement because no reports will make it to any ears that could do ought. I think this partnership is done now. My wife will be in touch to clear up loose ends. For sentiment's sake, the affection I must have one time held you in to agree to such a scheme, I'll arrange that a fair price is offered—one time. I can't however guarantee that my various associates will react in a likewise manner. I suggest you plan to relocate, but if you do so without first wrapping things up to my wife's satisfaction, I shall have no choice but to take further, perhaps harsh, action."

I disconnected.

He would hide, I was as certain of that as I was that he'd also plot. But 'twould take him at least a day or so to determine the best course of action when he couldn't be certain who else was in my pocket.

I called Ryu, "Set someone on watching Stan."

"Way ahead of you. I've got someone on his house, his real job, and Shipley."

"When Julia wakes, have her speak with Sandra forthwith. If you can do so without angering her, attend that meeting. Sandra has requested time to get me out from under whatever suspicions might fall on Shipley. 'Twas a profitable venture, one I'm willing to forgo, but 'tis my thought that Sandra might think it worth a risk. Not to say I think she works against us, but I haven't the knowledge to navigate the world of finance and law. I've told her, and she agreed, that they must all be dispatched posthaste. Her concern is an investigation could turn up something unsavory in Lou's past. I'd like to encourage Julia to send Stan at least away, Australia, the States, somewhere we have no connection and then send a mule to handle him but in a way that seems accidental. Ideally, 'twould remove them all..."

"I'll talk to her. We'll figure something out. Sandra's right that we don't want too many deaths connected to you. Make sure public perception stays that you're friendly with them. Distant but friendly."

"I shall. And you have my most sincere thanks for guarding Julia so well."

"Don't say that. I screwed up and almost got her killed."

He disconnected before I could demure.

Brent and Leif were waiting when I arrived at Brent's home. I'd expected armed strangers or Stan, but no one was around when Ollie parked.

I approached slowly, concentrating on the feel, but sensed no hostile regard. Brent answered my knock and he and Leif stepped outside. Both glanced around, looking angry but I didn't think it was with me. I didn't think Stan had told them the entire plan. I thought perhaps Hugh was right when he'd said Stan meant to kill them all, which they surely must sense themselves, or perhaps not. Perhaps greed had blinded them—or mayhap the remembrance of friendship that had surely been the cornerstone of this wicked endeavor when it was first purposed.

Lief said angrily as I approached, "When the hell are you coming back to work? Stan can't do this shit, man."

"It's a stupid fucking idea," Brent said angrily. "Tell me you have a better one."

"I do."

I stepped into the cloud of their anger, pressing mine on them as I said, "When it gets dark and you're at least a half a mile offshore, you're going to yell for Leif to toss you a beer then say loudly, Amber ready for another. She's going to stand and fall over the side. All four of you will see it happen. Don't think about it until you see her fall and then do whatever you would normally do when something like that happens. You'll all know it was a tragic accident and you'll be trying to find her. You truly believe she fell. You'll call for help immediately and be upset that your friend is missing. Get on the boat and behave in a normal manner, eating, drinking, laughing as friends do. Amber will be there sitting beside Paige wearing white pants and a dark blue shirt. She and Paige were drinking heavily, but you weren't paying much attention to them while you were fishing and talking."

I gave them directions again when Hugh arrived, which he did about ten minutes after me and repeated it until Paige arrived fifty minutes later. I told her the same thing with the addition that she was to make two drinks, and when she finished hers, she was to dump one overboard and make two more. Making people forget actions they hadn't taken yet was tricky. Some people forgot to perform the action and some people forgot to forget but I had no choice in the setup since I wouldn't see them after.

I took Paige's hand, pressing my anima on her as I said, "Amber sat beside you and drank with you. You'll drink at least four drinks. You won't remember dumping the drinks out. You'll truly believe that she drank them. You can see her laughing as she leaned on the rail. Remember, you'll truly believe she fell by accident. I can't accompany you all because my wife is feeling unwell. We're all friends and will go again another time. Go now and have fun until the accident, which will shock you all."

They went.

I returned home.

Chapter 55

Leif called me the next day to inform me that Amber had fallen overboard. He seemed honestly distraught. I wasn't certain if that was fear of discovery or if my commands had held.

Julia and Ryu hadn't yet returned although she'd woken a few hours ago and called me.

I called her as soon as I hung up on Leif.

"Leif tells me the search is ongoing with divers, but they have little hope."

She snorted angrily. "I guess you should go see Hugh and offer support. Have Kathleen make some food to take with you. I'll meet you there."

"Are you... able?"

"I'm pissed as shit but in control of myself."

Ryu said something in the background.

She huffed in annoyance, saying, "He thinks we should make the visit quick. I think we need to play it by ear because even casual friends would probably show up for something like this. Speaking of which, you should call Reg."

"Me?"

"Yes. The police might check our phone records. It would be more normal if you call him seeing as you all used to be friendly."

"If you think it best."

"If the police ask, you went from our house to Brent's to go on the boat but didn't go with them because I called you on the way there to say I wasn't feeling well. My phone will have pinged towers in London, so I'll say I went to the apartment meaning to have a quick lie down before returning home and fell asleep. You got a call from Ryu saying I was sleeping but thought it was too late to return to go on the boat."

"How distraught should I act?"

"Not overly. Distant concern. Polite like you'd be for anyone you barely knew who had something like this happen. You'd be sorry for him and her but not for yourself."

Ryu said something that made her snort in amused annoyance.

"He says just be yourself. Call me when your half an hour out so we can meet up."

"I shan't be long."

"Bring Bent or Smalls."

"Keep Ryu with you."

Her voice softened as she said, "I love you, Pip."

She disconnected.

I called Kathleen to request a basket of food prepared and then Vicky.

"I've just received word that a wife of a friend has been lost at sea. I'd like you to accompany me on a condolence visit."

"Me, my lord?"

"Yes. Dress in business attire and bring a few of the listening devices. We depart in an hour."

"Yes, sir," she said happily.

I called Smalls to tell him to dress appropriately and then Ollie to tell him to ready the car and speak with Mrs. Roman about the food.

Reginald answered, saying briskly but without hostility, "What do you want?"

"I'm calling to inform you that Hugh's wife Amber was lost overboard last evening."

"What!"

"I don't know the particulars. Leif was quite distraught when he called me, which I believe he did out of politeness or perhaps reflex as something he would've done when I was Lou."

Reginald snorted.

"I thought perhaps Leif would've assumed that I would call you, him being aware that we were particular friends."

"He knows about us?"

"I'm unsure. 'Tis certain Stan does—or at least that he believed it to be true. I'm unsure if it was purely surmise or if he has proof of some sort."

"You don't sound too worried..."

"I'm not."

"You're not... what the hell does that mean?"

"'Tis my belief that homosexual relationships are common now. Anything that happened between us happen 'ere I was wed, so while it might be titillating gossip, it could hardly be more."

"You goddamned bastard!"

"I meant no disrespect. I meant only that Stan could have nothing of note to say that any would give undue credence to, besides ourselves, I mean. 'Tis my belief that he thinks us still... embroiled."

"Ha! That fucker wants to ruin me!"

"I shall do my utmost to learn what proof he might have. Meanwhile, 'twould probably serve us both best if our denials were made with some humor so that latter if proof were offered, we could then recant."

"Stop fucking acting like you don't give a shit who knows about us when I know you do!"

"Truthfully, I haven't given the notion much thought at all. On a personal level, I mean. My thoughts have all been on how 'twould affect you and Julia, neither of which I wish to embarrass in any way. I might not be as savvy as some but even I can see how such a thing were it known publicly would be embarrassing for all parties. I haven't the knowledge to know if the fact that the affair was a homosexual one would be as damning as one with the sibling of a spouse..."

"Knock it the fuck off."

He hung up on me.

For the first time I truly contemplated how hurt, how confused he must be. Whether Lou was manipulating him or not, 'twould surely be distressing to lose the affections of a lover.

Kathleen knocked lightly on my door, saying, "My lord, the car has been brought around."

I put thoughts of Reginald to the back of my mind and hurried out.

I closed the privacy glass in the limo to say to Vicky, "These men are dangerous charlatans. 'Tis possible they mean to implicate me in this in some way."

"Were you involved?"

"My wife and I were supposed to be aboard."

Her eyes widened. "You think he killed her and meant to kill you all?"

"I think it wouldn't trouble him to do so. She was an unpleasant woman. I hardly knew her at all and have no idea if Lou and she were truly friends or if we were merely polite acquaintances. Not that I believe they were friendly. I'm speaking of public perception."

"Were you maybe more than friends?" she asked worriedly.

I contemplated that for a moment.

"I doubt it. There's nothing that makes me think so. I haven't spoken to her or him either really, except for two short visits. My wife saw them more frequently. 'Tis my thought that the police should have no interest in either of us, except that Julia had lunch with Amber just prior and I'd gone to Brent's meaning to go on the boat until my lady called me to say she was unwell."

"They'll be questioning you for sure."

I nodded.

She continued, "I can't imagine it will be a problem though with so many witnesses who can say you were home."

"I'm unsure what would be considered normal interest or reactions by the constabulary. Which is where you come in. My thought was I could say I'd brought you to facilitate whatever needs doing as one would do to be polite. I don't wish to appear to be too friendly or overeager to help."

"Ahh... I get it. You want me to be helpful because you don't want to be bothered but don't want to seem like it's a bother, except you do, subtly of course."

I snickered.

She said, "I can do that. Just don't be too disinterested. Maybe fake a headache to leave but only do that if it'll play naturally and won't draw attention. You should be a bit high handed with me as if you're used to the help hopping to and can't wait to brush this all off, but make it clear it's because you have no real memories of him, no friendly feelings."

"'Twas my thought as well. I brought Smalls so I could leave him to help if needs must, but I'd prefer to leave none of my household there. I'd like to distance myself as much as possible."

"Your wife should accompany you."

"She'll be meeting us."

"You should arrive together and let her take the lead because she knows these people."

"My wife is… angry. Furiously angry with all of them. Her temper sometimes gets the better of her."

"She's too smart to do anything that would worry police. Unless maybe we want to worry them. What's the downside of making the police think he did murder her?"

"An investigation could uncover some crimes I committed while I was Lou. The trouble is I have no recollection of anything I did then, so can't say how well I covered my tracks."

"Ahh… you think they're trying to clean up loose ends. Will they try again?"

"'Tis a certainty that Stan will. The rest I have well in hand."

"Lady Julia knows?"

"She knows all that I do. She never liked them much but hadn't been aware that they or Lou was involved with any shady dealings."

"Do you know what you were involved with?"

"Julia is handling all of that and had straightened it out, except for Stan. He was away and hadn't been showing much interest in what was happening here. If anyone is going to cause a problem, it will be him."

Vicky and I picked Julia up at a local market.

Three police cars were parked in front of Hugh's house, blocking an assortment of vehicles in the drive. The street was lined with cars on both sides, which was normal for the neighborhood, but I thought most of the cars didn't belong to the local residents but to visitors that were heading to or from his home.

Julia said to Smalls who sat in the front passenger seat, "Drop us here and circle the block until you find a place to park."

"Yes, ma'am."

"Will do," Ollie said cheerfully.

Julia, Vicky, and I exited the car.

Vicky took the basket our housekeeper had prepared and led the way to the front door where she knocked.

A man I didn't know answered it.

She offered the basket to him as she said, "Lord and Lady Blackwood.

Julia said, "Is Hugh in? God, I can't believe this! I just saw her yesterday."

"I'm Detective Gordon. You better come in. He's right through here."

"I'll take this to the kitchen, shall I?" Vicky said as she took the basket back and walked past the detective.

Julia and I entered.

She headed directly to Hugh who was sitting on a couch holding Paige's hand beside Leif on one side and Brent the other.

Julia gave them all hugs while I scanned the room.

An older couple who I assumed to be Amber's parents were sitting at the dining table in an adjoining room. Both looked shocked and heartbroken.

A policewoman wearing a uniform was sitting with them taking notes while another officer was standing by the doorway that I assumed led to the kitchen.

Brantwold nodded a greeting, turning away a bit to speak on his cell.

Gordon headed directly to Brantwold to whisper for a moment. Both men returned to me.

"Lord Blackwood, we meet again."

Stan stepped into the dining room, glaring at me for a moment before his expression smoothed.

"Lou," he said as if we were the best of friends and he was happy to see me.

I stepped past the detectives, offering Stan my hand.

"Such a tragedy."

He shook it then gave me a quick one-armed hug.

I said, "I hadn't the chance to get reacquainted with her really..."

I was afraid to say more because my anima was so thick around me.

Julia said, "People are found all the time. Surely the police are still looking!"

The woman officer said, "We are, ma'am."

Brantwold said, "Unfortunately, the chance she's found alive is slim, seeing as how we know right where she was lost and have been searching all night. We have divers searching as we speak."

Paige burst into loud sobs.

Stan rushed past me to crouch to hug her.

Hugh said, "This can't be happening. What am I going to tell the kids? There has to be more we can do!"

Vicky said, "Their lordships have offered assistance. If more divers are needed, I can arrange that."

She handed the woman officer a card.

"Vicky Atkinson, Lord Blackwood's personal assistant. If we can be of service..."

The officer took it, offering her hand as she said, "Gail Jax, family liaison officer."

Brantwold said, "Lady Blackwood, my colleague tells me you had lunch with Amber yesterday?"

"Yes."

"Did she seem... normal."

Julia's eyes widened. "You think she threw herself in? Don't be ridiculous! She'd never do something like that! Never! She was perfectly fine. Happy even. We were both excited to begin working on a fundraiser for a charity she'd recently gotten involved with. We were both looking forward to catching up a bit..."

She trailed off, ducking her head and dabbing her eyes.

I said, "My accident has made socializing awkward. My wife was trying to rebuild those broken ties."

Hugh said gruffly, "I've been a shit friend... I should've made an effort before all this, but I thought you'd get your damned memories back..."

Leif clasped his hand quickly, "Don't worry about it now, Hugh. Lou isn't the sort to hold a grudge and I'm sure that hasn't changed."

He smiled a sickly smile at me, releasing Hugh to stand and give me a quick hug.

"We've all been shit friends. None of us kept in contact like we should've. But it wasn't personal, man. We just thought you'd be back when your memories returned, and meanwhile you needed the peace and quiet to recuperate."

"I've been meaning to call," Paige said. "Time just always got away from me what with the kids and work... Amber told me how excited she was to work with your wife. We hoped we'd all become good friends again..." she trailed off crying again but quieter now.

Stan said, "Come on, darling, let's get you home. You've been up all night and need some rest. Hugh, I don't know what to say, man. If you need anything at all..."

Paige released her husband to hug Hugh.

Julia stepped closer to Stan, saying, "Stop by and we can catch up."

Stan stilled staring at her with a fixed blank look of a mule until she turned her face away to smile at Paige. He smiled too, a sickly parody of her smile.

I was positioned to awkwardly to see what if anything the police were noticing of this exchange,

Leif and Brent both hugged Paige and escorted her and Stan to the door.

Another woman entered carrying a casserole dish.

"Hugh, I just heard! I couldn't believe it! I warned her about wearing those shoes on a boat!"

She thrust the casserole at Lief and rushed to hug Hugh, crying and babbling about Amber's choice of footwear and then rushing to the dining room to hug Amber's parents and gush over how wonderful she was.

Vicky took the casserole from Leif during this and headed to the kitchen.

Julia sat beside Hugh saying polite comforting things and apologized for missing the boat while I patted her shoulder occasionally.

Vicky returned from the kitchen with a fresh pot of coffee and a plate with danish that she set on the table.

She served Amber's parents and then offered drinks and danish, saying to Hugh, "I took the liberty of placing a few of the casseroles in your freezer."

"People have been stopping by all morning," he said dully.

Julia said, "We should let you rest. Call me if there's anything we can do."

She kissed their cheeks again.

I shook their hands and followed her out.

Vicky and Brantwold trailed us.

Vicky called for the car.

Brantwold waited for the house door to close to say, "You didn't know Amber, my lord?"

"We'd met a few times since my accident. She seemed a nice woman..."

Julia said, "He doesn't recall any of them."

"Amnesia, *huh*? I didn't think people really get that."

His demeanor made it clear he still thought that.

She shrugged at him, "Me neither until it happened to us."

"You don't remember them at all?" Brantwold asked.

"No."

"My husband has almost no recollection before his accident. I'm just thankful the headache and seizures have stopped." She stepped closer, her anima surrounding him as she added, "His test results show some improvement, so we still have hope that his memory will return. The damage can be seen in the tests so there's no possibility that he's faking it. It was just a freak accident and nothing to do with any of this. Amber's death was a tragedy and nothing to do with us or anyone really. It was just an accident."

She stepped away.

Smalls pulled up, blocking the road on one side.

Brantwold said, "They tell me that you were supposed to accompany them last evening."

She nodded, saying, "Amber had come to Horsham to see me, and we went back together, but by the time we got back I had a horrid headache. I get them occasionally. Mostly when I drink vodka, which I hadn't realized was in the drinks she'd ordered. Well, anyway, I went to the apartment we have in London for a lie down, hoping it would pass."

I said, "You have to stop worrying about me, my love. In time I'll make new friends or renew old acquaintances."

She smiled wanly.

Brantwold said, "How often do you socialize with Hugh and his wife?"

"Never since my accident."

Julia said, "He finds it awkward when he has no recall of the incidents that they all recall. It's easier for him to make new friends."

Vicky murmured, "My lord, if we want to meet the bankers, we need to be going."

We headed to the car.

Julia said, "If you'll excuse us…"

"Of course."

Vicky offered Brantwold a card.

"If I can be of help."

She held the door for Julia.

I circled the car to the door that Smalls was holding open.

As we drove away, Julia said, "Vick, find out why Brantwold was there. This should've been out of his jurisdiction I'd have thought."

"That was a lot of police for a drowning," Smalls said. "They must think he whacked the bitch."

Julia said frostily, "Never refer to a woman again in such a disrespectful way."

Her anger was a red cloud that flowed in thick streamers to all of us.

I said, "Love, I think our talk needs to wait until we're somewhere private."

She nodded.

I kissed her hand, keeping it in mine until we reached home.

Ryu was waiting and let us in.

I said, "Escort my lady to my study. I shall be right up."

She stomped up the stairs.

He winced at me and followed.

I said to Vicky, "Did you hear anything of note?"

"No. I planted one of the bugs though. I can retrieve it by dropping another meal off. Smalls was right about all of the police though, boss."

"Find out who's in charge of the investigation and then find out when he or she can be approached privately."

"If you try to bribe him and it fails, you'll be in seriously deep shit."

"I wish only to be prepared if needs must. Find me a spot I could run into Inspector Brantwold for a private talk."

"Boss, arranging for that sort of privacy will mean a serious coverup if the talk doesn't go in your favor. He's a police officer, which means if he reports you tried to bribe him or threaten him that he'll be believed. We couldn't take a chance that he told anyone he was planning to meet you or anyone else for that matter. Cops watch each other's backs. If he goes missing after your little chat, they'd pull out all the stops looking to see what happened."

"I've no intention of doing anything, except speaking to him. It needn't be a secret meeting. Only private. A bar perhaps? Somewhere I might run into him and chat a few moments."

"Then people will see it, which could lead to more problems even if he agrees and he's questioned about it."

"Then think of something harmless that we might have chatted about."

"If you say so... just be careful approaching officers. They sometimes wear cameras and they have them in their cars. And like I said, they'll be believed the way an asshole like Tussaud wouldn't be."

"Understood. Perhaps a coffee establishment or dinner. I need a mere minute of his time."

I could see she wasn't happy with the idea, but she nodded agreement.

I headed upstairs to speak with Julia.

She was pacing and yelling in our study, which looked odd from the open doorway because I couldn't hear her.

I stepped over the threshold to say, "When you leave the door unlocked, be sure to watch it in case someone else opens it to look in. 'Tis best to keep it locked to ensure they knock."

"Stan's going to run! I know it! I should've asked him to help me in the kitchen or something!"

I said, "I was afraid to speak at all... we were both too angry. Even condolences could've been awkward."

She grimaced at me, nodding agreement. "I was worried about it too. I think it was fine though."

"You should've brought me," Ryu said.

Julia flushed.

I said, "Vicky was able to snoop about unnoticed. And 'twould surely anger me greatly to see Stan glower at you or even sneer. I despise that man! He must pay for her murder! He must!"

Julia nodded in agreement.

Ryu said, "I cleaned up the security tapes at the house. I'll take Smalls and Bent back to the club and check that again. We can send another cleaning crew in or painters or something. I'm worried they were able to track her car or phone there."

"Her car!" I said, struck with horror that I'd forgotten it.

"I had Doreen bring it to Hugh's yesterday."

Julia said, "Even if the police tracked her here, I can just say we talked about the club and stopped in and I'd forgotten."

"'Twill be suspicious that both Brent, Hugh, and ourselves had malfunctioning cameras."

Ryu said, "Ours have real footage. I inserted a generic clip for that time frame. Unless they can somehow check the mainframe at that alarm company, which Sandra assures me can't be done, we're all set. Is all you need to do is tell the guard at the gate to forget he saw anything. I already spoke with Frank."

"I'll make sure all of our employees will listen to you," Julia said as she stomped to the door.

I waved Ryu away, saying, "'Twill be a good use for her anger. When you return, you can show me how one inserts fake footage."

"Don't try it until I'm sure you can do it," he called back as he followed her.

Chapter 56

Blackwood," Inspector Brantwold said sounding surprised and suspicious when he turned around.

"Good morning, Inspector."

"What brings you here?" he asked, eying me with a weighing glance that told me that he didn't believe for a moment that this was a chance encounter.

"The coffee. I'm glad I ran into you though. I'd been meaning to call and ask if there was any news on Amber?"

His lip lifted the smallest amount and his eyes hardened. His tone was polite though and just slightly mocking as he said. "News? What sort of news?"

"Hugh asked me to call and see what I could find out on the state of the investigation."

"Did he, now..."

"Latte with caramel," I said to the girl at the counter.

Brantwold and I stepped to the side to let the next man order.

I placed my anima coated hand on his as I said, "Is the case closed?"

"It was ruled an accidental drowning."

"Do you believe that?"

"No."

"How come?"

"No corpse and there's something off about the husband."

"Off how?"

"The money. His attitude…. although they all passed polygraphs."

He looked confused now.

I pressed more of my anima on him as I said, "Hugh might be an ass, but you know he had nothing to do with his wife's death."

"Your latte," the server said.

I released Brantwold to accept the cup.

He followed me from the store.

Vicky exited the car to open the car door for me.

I said, "Why were you there at Hugh's house? Isn't that outside your jurisdiction?"

"Your wife's involvement."

That angered me enough to make my anima appear to me.

I stepped closer to press my anima on him, saying, "How do you think she's involved?"

"Those men she hires."

"Her charity does good works. She might be naïve thinking she can help them, but her efforts are sincere. She's a good woman."

"She's a good woman," he agreed in the tone that said it was my idea he think so.

I continued, "Everyone knows it has naught to do with us. It has naught to do with us," I repeated.

"My lord," Vicky said worriedly, and I realized I'd said the last bit loudly.

I pasted a smile on my face.

"Have a pleasant day."

Brantwold watched me go. The weight of his regard followed me to the car. I wasn't sure if that was his lingering desire for my anima or his natural suspicion.

As we drove away, I said to Vicky, "I shall want to speak with him again in a week or so."

"It isn't smart to confront him like that. He isn't going to believe your protestations. Saying you have nothing to do with it will tell him you have something to hide."

"Find another such place," I said firmly but without using anima on her.

She heaved an annoyed sigh but nodded.

"You can trust that I know what I'm about."

We drove in silence most of the way home.

She finally said, "It could work to discredit him, but it's a risk, boss. I'd drop this but I know you don't really know how things work now. It's never smart to mess with the police. If you really think we need to control what he does, then you need real leverage."

"What would you do?"

"I guess I'd try to set him up. If you could prove he was doing something illegal, he might back down. But that's always risky because he might rather fight you in court. It'd be best to find something real on him, something you're sure he'd want to hide. Killing a cop won't work even if you do it in such a way that everyone believes it's an accident because someone else would just take over the case and then you're right back where you started. The only sure way would be to get a corrupt cop on the case, but the cop has to want to be corrupt if you know what I mean."

I nodded, saying, "I do appreciate your insights. I'll know better after my next meeting whether further efforts are needed. You don't perchance know of any such officers?"

She snorted softly as she nodded.

"Your wife already has the list. She's smart enough to leave them alone though, boss. You don't want to get involved with them or they'll own you."

That made me laugh.

She laughed too, shaking her head.

"I really wish I knew how you do that," she said wistfully.

"I do too."

She laughed again.

I hadn't been jesting. My lessons with magic had become frustrating in the extreme. No matter how hard I tried, I couldn't make my written spells stronger. My anima just wasn't strong enough for the type of spells I had in mind.

"I wonder if the lack is true anger? Perhaps I need a subject not under my control at all..."

"What are we talking about?"

"Ignore my ramblings. 'Twas nothing of consequence although, perhaps, you could help me locate such a man. One who no one would miss or mourn. An evil man full of anger."

She huffed an angry laugh, nodding agreement, saying, "I've got a list."

Chapter 57

"God's teeth!" I exclaimed as I jumped away from the blaze Julia's interruption caused.

I hadn't realized she'd returned from Dubai. My studies had distracted me utterly.

I was glad the heat of the fire would disguise my guilty flush. She'd be irate to know I'd only slept twice since she'd been gone.

My conjured flame shot to the ceiling, reacting to my startlement. My anger at letting myself be so startled as to lose control fueled the spell. It took me a few seconds of concentration to regain control of it.

I stepped from the summoning circle.

Julia said, "Sorry, Pip. Sandra just called. A mage calling himself Zayvion showed up to... I actually don't really know what he wanted. He confronted Drew. Sandra wants us to keep an eye on Cass. She's sending her to our apartment in London."

I began gathering a selection of my spell materials.

She continued, "I told her to send Drew here. I think we should bring Cass here as well."

"A mage... Silah?"

"No. Or at least I don't think so. I think she knew him. He's from her realm. His arrival here made the news."

"Good grief!"

I stepped back into my summoning circle, holding my hands out to make a circle, focusing my will and envisioning the fire spell that I'd just cast breaking as I separated my hands.

The fire dwindled and disappeared.

"That's great, Pip!"

I grinned over my shoulder at her.

She said, "I'll go pick her up."

"Have Smalls drive you and make sure he's armed too."

I gave her a quick hug and handed her a fresh packet of binding powder.

"Give it to him and tell him he's to pour it on his left hand and then grab this Zayvion fellow. It'll only hold for five minutes, so you'll need to be fast. Did she say... never mind. He must be very powerful if he formed a portal. I should come with you..."

She kissed my cheek, giving me another quick hug.

"He wasn't after Cass. And he didn't try to hurt Drew. She just wanted her daughter away. I'll be fine. It'd be better for you to stay here and prepare."

"I'll call Ryu and have him arm the guards. We better send all the staff away."

She ran for the stairs.

I ran to my spellbooks.

My small spells would likely do nothing at all to a mage who could form a portal. I couldn't imagine he'd have the least problem dispelling one—and he could likely turn it back on me like Sandra could, but I still carefully withdrew two fire spells and the one levitation spell I had prepared, folding them and putting them into my pocket.

I grabbed the larger spellbook that held my holding spells. The book contained ten spells that when unfolded to their full size would form a holding pentagram large enough to hold a horse, two twice that size, twenty smaller sizes, and an assortment of much smaller parchments that could be placed on door handles and window latches.

I didn't bother with any of those because I could make door locks in moments if I was angry or with someone else who was— or had a rind of stolen anima.

I took the entire book of larger spells and hurried up the ladder, letting myself through the spell-locked trapdoor, which Drew had locked to open for only Ryu, Julia, and myself. The entire lab was protected by a holding spell to keep our magic contained. It also kept noises out and we had no cell service inside. The ladder emerged into an empty stall.

I jogged to the house as I called Ryu.

"Hey, boss," he said cheerfully when he answered. "Are we—"

I interrupted to say, "Sandra called. Julia has gone to pick up Cassandriel. Arm the guards and send the staff away. Meet me in the downstairs study."

I hung up so he could get started making his calls.

John was waiting at the front door when I arrived.

I said, "Gather the household help and call the barns and Mr. Roman. I want everyone off of the estate within an hour, except for our security people. You're to go through the buildings personally to be sure there are no workmen or students lingering. Then return to your rooms and call me."

"The adjoined estate too?"

"No just the main one."

"Yes, sir."

He headed for the kitchens, reaching for his cell phone.

I left my spellbook in my reading room, then ran to the security room, which was above the ballroom.

Frank Carver, the guard on duty, greeted me at the door to the security room by saying, "Mr. Poole informed me to alert all of the guards, sir."

"I want them armed and outside the house, watching the entrances. Lady Blackwood has gone to retrieve a guest. No one except her enters the estate. Stop everyone else at the gate, including staff. Notify me the moment anyone at all arrives. Lock all of the back gates and deny entry at all of them. Any deliveries need to come to the front gate or be rescheduled."

"Do you expect an armed assault?"

"I sincerely hope not but it's my duty to be sure that my guests are safe here. A dear friend was just accosted in the street by a person who we believe might attempt to forcibly get him to accompany him. We've offered the safety of our home while the situation is sorted. I've sent the staff home on the very slim chance that we need to retreat to our safe room. If you spot anyone on the cameras, call me at once. I'll be in my library should you need me."

"Do we have an ID on the suspect?"

"Not even a description yet. As soon as I know more, I'll inform you."

His tight expression became one of bland politeness.

I was fine with him thinking I was overreacting as long as he did his job.

Frank had been a soldier, a good one. His rind was acquired in an incident that lost him the use of his left arm. He'd killed four men protecting the ambassador he'd been ordered to protect. He was glad to get this job when he'd been dismissed from his majesties service. We were glad to get him.

I thought he'd do everything in his power to keep the household safe without me needing to use his anima to make him, but to ensure it, I grabbed his arm and his anima and said, "No one gets near the house without you calling me first."

"No one gets near the house, sir."

I ran back to my library where I found Ryu, John, and Asa.

Ryu said, "Lady Blackwood called me. We have a tentative description of the man. She warned me that he's delusional and probably very dangerous."

I said, "Call the description in to Mr. Carver. He's manning the desk right now."

Ryu took out his cell.

"Frank, we have a tentative ID. The man is a raving lunatic. He calls himself Zayvion."

He listened for a moment, "No. I doubt it's his real name. Mrs. Alder would've told us if she knew it. I'm sure her security is already looking up his record. He's got long black hair, a long beard, is wearing a red cape, leather vest, and carrying a sword. Yeah, I said sword. I told you he was crazy."

My phone rang with Sandra's ring tone, so I stepped into the hall to answer it.

She said, "I need you to meet me at Stonehenge. If we act fast, we can hide his arrival here."

"I'll get there as soon as I may."

"Bring some muscle."

She disconnected.

I returned to the library.

"Ryu, call Bent and have him bring the car around—make it the Mercedes. John, Asa, my wife will be back with our guest in two hours or so, so make sure there's a hot meal waiting, and the white guest room is ready. Ready the green room as well. Give staff tomorrow off—a paid day. Asa, you and your wife can have that day off as well just be sure there's enough fresh foods that we can prepare lunch and breakfast for ourselves tomorrow."

"Should I leave one groom on duty or a cook?"

"No. My footman can see to the animals for one day. John will remain on duty. I'm sure he's capable of making sandwiches and coffee for the guards on duty."

John nodded.

I continued, "I'd intended to remain, but the call was urgent. Allow Mr. Drew Shangrün inside should he arrive. Call Lady Blackwood or Mr. Poole if anyone else requests entrance. Ensure that no one at all, even yourself, enters my lady's study."

I took my spellbook into her study and closed the door. It took me a few minutes to rearrange the furniture. I placed the two chairs that normally sat in front of her desk to the left, leaving just enough room between them and the wall that you could walk past them. Then I put the potted plant from the corner to the right of the door, again leaving enough room you could walk around it.

I then removed one of my larger holding spells from the book and spread it onto the carpet in front of the desk.

Light appeared to flow from the fingertip I placed on the bottom point of the pentagram. The light flowed across the spell dissolving the writing as it did so. Within seconds the spell had sunk into the carpet.

Goosebumps pebbled my arms. Seeing magic—especially magic that I had done—was still astounding. I didn't do many spells of this power. It had taken me days to cast that spell.

Effort we'll worth it, I thought in satisfaction as I crumpled the now blank paper and tossed it into her trash can.

I let myself out of her study, locking the door behind myself.

In the backseat of the car with Ryu, I called Julia.

"I left my strongest holding spell directly in front of your desk. Don't forget and step into it. Walk around the plant or the chairs, not through the center of the room. If he arrives, send Cass to our safe room and get him into your study. He might not be prepared for guns, Jewels. Tell them all to shoot him but keep Smalls close to you because I'm sure he knows how to use that sword. But don't attack him at all if you can just get him to leave. Maybe if he thinks we're just people, he'd just go? I hate the idea of you fighting a mage!"

Julia said, "Sandra is going to send Drew to our place. She says he can handle Zayvion."

"...that's terrifying. The man ripped a portal from another realm. I'm glad Drew can overpower him but..."

"I know. I'm trying not to let it worry me."

"You *must* study more."

"We'll talk about it later. I love you. Be careful. I don't like the idea of you going alone to help her. You're nowhere near ready to fight a mage of his skill."

"I'm not alone. Ryu and Bent are with me."

"As much as I love him, Ryu won't be helpful in a mage fight either! Send him home."

"I'd not let harm come to him."

"I don't need no babysitter," Ryu said angrily.

"Just... please don't get hurt. Either of you."

She disconnected.

Ryu face was flushed when he handed me his phone.

"It's on the news."

We watched the news until we arrived in town just a few miles from Stonehenge where we met Sandra.

She said, "From what I could tell, there's only two people we need to adjust. Karen Hunt was the passenger in the second car and saw Zayvion step from the portal. She's the main target. If we can make her report unbelievable..."

"And the second?"

"Was at Stonehenge filming the stones when Zayvion arrived. He caught the formation of the portal on film. I have his camera. If you could adjust his memories of the event to recall black smoke instead of a black hole, which is how he initially described it..."

"Where is he now?" Ryu asked.

"Ranting at the police about his camera, which he believes a reporter stole. I can text you his home address. I think as long as we catch him today it should be fine as they'll expect him to be calmer about it for a follow up interview."

She handed me the camera, which was a digital one. Ryu and I examined the images.

"Holy shit!" Ryu said. "That... can that damage our reality? Can he explode the earth or anything doing that?"

"I have no idea since I don't understand the science of how it works. I doubt it though. We use portals all the time in my realm. They sometimes destroy whatever is passing through them but never harm the ground where they form, except for making a matching rune. If you have that matching rune already in place, the portal works quicker with much less effort and is less likely to damage whatever is being transported. I erased the rune here."

"So he's trapped here?" Ryu asked.

"He could always redraw it. It would take him time to gather enough magic to power it unless he came through with enough, which I don't think he did because according to Karen he wasn't carrying anything at all, except a glowing white ball. Since he showed up by Drew seconds after he arrived, I think we can safely assume that ball was a keyed portari. It would've used the power from the ley line to bring him to Drew—unless they've found a way to take a charged portari through a portal, which, I suppose, is possible. Portari aren't commonly used as they take a lot of power. One the size he held could've teleported him much farther than he went. It could've been keyed to bring him back to where it was cast. So it's possible he returned through the portal when Drew sent him away."

"It was engulfed in fire by then," Ryu said.

"A mage of his caliber wouldn't have been bothered by a little fire. If I'd made that portari, I'd have set it to encapsulate the caster in the strongest protections I could've when the return trip was triggered. He'd have teleport back to the runes and then through the portal within seconds."

"But you don't know for certain?" I asked.

"No. But since he didn't do anything to Drew, and he clearly gathered all the power from the node there, I think he really was just delivering a message."

I said, "What will whoever sent the message do next?"

"Hard to say. My guess is he'll send a few of his minions to try to force Drew to return or at least force him to say where Shangrün is."

"Does Drew know where this person is?"

"She isn't a person and yes."

Ryu said, "Maybe you should just tell him."

"Maybe... I'd hoped I'd have a few more years because I think it'd be smarter for me to go back and deal with Kazimir and Shangrün myself. Giving him what he wants will just encourage him to come here. I shudder to think of the chaos that would ensue. This realm isn't ready for a being like him."

I said, "Can we stop him from coming?"

"I can—but the cost..." she heaved an annoyed sigh. "That's a worry for another day. I'll see what I can do to get access to the police reports. We might need to encourage the investigators to believe a bomb was planted, but I need some details first to build a plausible story. Make an excuse to visit the morgue where they sent the bodies in case you need to go back to adjust some reports there.

"I hadn't heard the police gossiping about anyone else claiming to have seen anything that we'd need to worry about, but maybe check that if you get a chance."

Ryu said, "Julia texted me to say she's with your daughter and they're on the way to the estate and that Andre is arriving at nine tomorrow."

"Damn!"

Sandra gained a pinched expression that I knew was worry over her daughter. Andre's arrival worried me as well because I knew it would limit Sandra's actions. She'd be afraid Cassandriel would see something that would make her believe that magic was real, which reminded me how dire this was for us to cover up before Cassandriel could begin to dwell on those thoughts.

"Julia will keep watch," I said as reassuringly as I could.

"I'll think of something. Let me know how you make out."

She returned to her car.

Ryu and I did the same.

"Take us to the hospital," Ryu said to Bent.

When we arrived, I said to Ryu, "Walk through to see how many people are about."

"She might not be able to speak to you at all. I'll find out her condition and text you."

He got out.

I said to Bent, "Find a spot nearby to park."

"What are we doing here, anyway?"

"None of your business."

Angry anima sparkled through his stolen rind.

Bent sulked and I worried while we waited for Ryu to call.

He called me twenty minutes later.

"She's got a private room on the fourth floor. A police officer just left her. He should be leaving any minute."

"See if you can stop him outside. We'll be right there."

I hung up and said to Bent, "Come with me. Don't speak unless I tell you to."

His anima collided with mine hard enough to knock me back a step.

I maybe shouldn't have kept him so angry so long without commanding him, I thought ruefully. Keeping our anima apart as I'd done had made his denser than normal. 'Twas an effect I wished to study when I had time.

By the time we reached the sidewalk in front of the hospital Ryu and the officer were already there and the officer looked angry.

As we got closer I could see angry anima sparkling on his words.

I said haughtily, "Tell me what Karen Hunt told you."

"She claims she saw a man wearing a cloak, carrying a glowing orb step from a black hole in the sky."

Ryu said, "Did you write that down?"

I said, "Show me your written report."

The officer handed me his notebook.

Bent tensed, inhaling sharply.

I handed the book to Ryu as I said, "You spilled your coffee on your notes, so need to rewrite it. Karen reported seeing a man in a red hoody with a flashlight running from the crash site, but it was so smoky she isn't sure if he came from one of the crashed vehicles or was just someone who stopped. He was six feet tall or so with black hair and a beard."

Ryu ripped a page from the man's book and handed it back to me.

I said, "What do the police think happened?"

The officer said, "That one of the cars contained a bomb meant for Stonehenge and it detonated early."

"What sort of bomb would do damage like that?"

"I don't know."

"Don't forget to rewrite that report right away and forget we ever met."

I handed him back his notebook.

Ryu, Bent, and I headed into the hospital.

Karen was sleeping when we arrived.

Ryu shook her shoulder. "Wake up!"

"Who are you?" she asked muzzily when she finally opened her eyes.

I said to Ryu, "Watch the door. 'Tis clear she's been sedated. I shall need Bent for this."

I took his arm, saying to him, "Hold her hand."

He grinned at me.

I returned it then shuddered in revulsion that I had. *The warmth of his anima was growing too familiar*, I thought in dismay.

"Who are you?" she repeated, bring my attention back to her.

I grabbed her hand as she reached for the call button.

"The man you saw earlier, describe him to me."

"The man... you mean the one in the cape?"

I pressed Bent's anima rind on her as I said, "Yes. He was wearing a red hoody and carrying a flashlight like he thought he was a superhero, but it was too smoky for you to see him well. He had black hair and a long black beard. You aren't sure where he came from."

"Pip," Ryu said urgently as a woman said, "Can I help you?"

I released Karen's hand.

"Let her go," I muttered to Bent.

I said to Karen, "I'm so glad you're feeling better and that you enjoyed our little visit."

I leaned down as if to kiss her cheek and whispered, "You won't remember that we spoke of the man you saw. He wore a red hoody and carried a flashlight. It was too smokey to see much."

"Ms. Hunt?" the nurse who entered said, glaring at me suspiciously. "Is this man bothering you?"

"We're having a nice visit," Karen said. But she looked confused.

I said to the nurse, "There's nothing to worry about."

Repositioning Bent's anima so far from us took a lot more effort. I'd been practicing but it still made me feel lightheaded and a bit giddy as if I'd just woken from a drunken stupor.

Bent grabbed my arm, pulling me up and I realized I'd stumbled into the bed, which made me laugh again.

I giggled as I said, "There's nothing of note going on in here. You won't even remember this. You can go check on another patient."

She left without another word.

I turned back to Karen. "When I leave, you won't remember I was here. If anyone asks, tell me what you'll say about the man you saw."

"You have brown hair—"

"Not me! You didn't see me!"

Bent staggered, catching himself against the bed.

"I didn't see you," she agreed.

"Describe the man you saw right before the crash."

"It was smoky..."

"He was wearing a red hoody and carrying a flashlight," I prompted.

"Right. He was wearing a red hoody like a cape and had flashlight, a round one."

"Pip," Ryu said again. "She's got this. Let's go."

Laughter bubbled up my throat.

"A regular flashlight. It wasn't round."

"A regular flashlight," she agreed.

"He wore a red hoody and carried a regular flashlight. You aren't sure if he came from one of the cars or was walking past. Forget I was here. Go back to sleep."

She immediately closed her eyes.

Ryu grabbed my hand.

"Come on."

He tugged us from the room.

Two men in suits were approaching the door of Karen's room.

The taller one said, "And you are?"

Ryu squeezed my arm as he said, "Lord Blackwood. We came to see if there was anything we could do to assist, but Ms. Hunt was sleeping. We'll return another time."

"Friends of hers, are you?"

Ryu stepped closer, lowering his voice as he said, "His lordship has a bit of thing against terrorists. He's that determined to help. In fact, he wanted to offer all of the victims a bit of financial aid for the funerals."

"It hasn't been determined that it was terrorism. It could've just been an accident."

I said, "Still—they must be buried, mustn't they? We shall go and offer our support."

I grabbed Bent's arm and marched out, fighting giddy laughter, which I knew was caused by overusing the anima, but the knowing didn't make it easier to suppress the laugh that I could feel building in my throat.

To quell it, I bellowed imperiously, "Martin, attend!"

"Toffs," one of the men muttered.

I pretended not to hear it.

Out on the sidewalk again I stopped, saying to Ryu, "Are they taking the deceased to the morgue here?"

"Yes and New Hall."

"What sort of thing should I offer to do?"

"I don't know. We could pay for the burials but that could get pricey, and it would set a precedent. You'd have all kinds of people asking you to give them money."

I said, "Let's just take a quick walk through. Hopefully we don't run into anyone, but if we do just tell them we're starting a fund to help with the expenses."

We headed back inside, passing records, the morgue, and three different laboratories.

The giddiness had worn off by the time we returned to the car.

I called Sandra to report, "We've taken care of Karen and scouted as you requested. The police officer we spoke with thought it had been a bomb meant for Stonehenge."

"My sources say it's being ruled an accident since no accelerants were found."

"The crack in the ground?"

"They're saying the roadway collapsed and the crack was from the construction crews burying trees and shrubs there years ago when the road was put in. They're claiming that the damage was caused by the crack in the ground, not the other way around."

"Who is being blamed for the crash?"

"The driver of the first car, who's deceased."

"And Drew?"

"Is at your home with Cassandriel. They'll be coming back tomorrow."

"You're certain 'tis safe for her?"

"As long as Drew or myself is with her. And, Pip, I want you and Julia to know how much I appreciate your instant support."

"Of course. Cass is one of my dearest friends. She's welcome to stay with us as long as needed."

"We appreciate it. I'm really hoping to receive information tonight that will make it much easier to keep her and Andre from consummating their relationship."

"I like him."

"He seems a nice boy."

"You don't sound sure."

"I'm not sure he's right for her. I'm not sure what I can do about it—other than reveal a truth that she isn't mature enough to hear."

"Could you take her back to her realm—not forever just until she can safely live here?"

"I could make a portal but to traverse one is dangerous. I believe the charms she wears would keep her safe but the journey there is the least of the danger. It wouldn't be safe for her there. The moment her existence was known, she'd be hunted, and they'd be looking for her kind there. She could be killed easily. We'd have a better chance of hiding her here but only if she cooperates with us."

She laughed a dark bark of laughter. "I'd have a better chance of protecting her here with my magics than there where they have magic too, especially when you consider I'd need to spend a large portion of my stockpile to make a portal."

"Then we shall just need to ensure that she keeps this shape."

Chapter 58

The next day, Ryu and I escorted Cassandriel and Drew to Sandra's estate and then headed to Oxford where we browsed the garden centers, stopping any angry people we ran into to send them to our shops and hear the gossip about Stonehenge.

Sandra had seemed certain that Zayvion had gone, which was a relief. Most people believed the official explanation. I didn't think we'd need to do anything, except prepare for his return.

No one who'd come through a portal from another realm to send a message was going to take no comment as an answer. I was certain Zayvion would be back. But Sandra had assured me it would take him years to gather the power to form another portal.

I knew that was hopeful supposition on her part. We both knew he might already have the necessary power squirreled away, but I also knew she only needed a year or so before she could tell Cassandriel what she was.

And since there was nothing I could do about it anyway, I'd determined to continue as we had been although I also intended to make more of the larger holding spells as time permitted.

Sandra had given me permission to browse her library, which I headed to immediately when we arrived at her home.

Cassandriel said, "Thanks for the ride home, Pip. I'm going to go shower and change if you'll be okay here."

Her eyes danced with mirth because she knew how I adored the books.

"I shan't be long. We have business to attend although I'm at your complete disposal. Perhaps we could meet latter for dinner?"

"I'll call you," she said. "Andre has to get back soon, so we might take a rain check."

She ran from the room before I could press her.

I began to browse Sandra's books, jotting down titles that I thought might have some insights. I really needed to figure out how to hold and condense my magic like Sandra could.

"Pip!" Ryu called and I reluctantly set my notes aside.

"Coming!" I called back as cheerfully as I could.

We planned to visit Stonehenge and ask what people thought had happened, planting our story while sending people to our stores. I found sale days tedious, but they were necessary to build our brands, and it made sense to use this opportunity even though it wasn't a planned sale day.

Ryu held the car door for me saying, "We could find our marks while visiting the greenhouses around Oxford and visit Stonehenge in the afternoon. It'll give the rumors time to really circulate."

I snorted with laughter, and he winked at me.

He grinned at me as he said, "I'm really enjoying growing our own plants. I never imagined I'd like anything like that but there's something really satisfying about it."

"I've always enjoyed it," I agreed. "Our gardens were extravagant... I wonder if my father was attempting alchemy as well?"

"Probably."

"'Tis frustrating searching for the key to my magic..."

"Maybe there isn't one?"

"There must be! I feel it when I write the spells and can almost grasp it."

"You think she knows what it is and just isn't telling you?"

"Perhaps, but if so, I'm certain she doesn't withhold the information for nefarious purposes. Knowledge gleaned by intense study teaches more than a mere fact told as *the* truth. I see there are many ways of doing things. The search has value. 'Tis just frustrating to be relegated to the weak spells I can manage without that key."

"Maybe it isn't a plant either."

"Dragons excrete gems and can infuse them with their magic. They can infuse any gem because gems are an essential part of them. It makes sense that humans can do the same with plants."

"True, but you aren't a human—not really. I think we'll find more plants that can boost the power of various spells, but maybe that isn't the right medium to hold your magic because anima isn't mana. Maybe a seethe can't make a spell like a dragon or human mage can?"

"I *can* make a spell though and I can do it faster and make it more powerful than I could a month ago. I feel that I've mastered the writing of the fire spell. 'Tis only the strength of magic that's lacking. Sandra wouldn't be able to cast an inferno strength spell if she didn't have her gems and it took her years of study to hit upon the method she uses now to infuse them with her magic. It can be done. I just need to find the knack of it. I know it."

"Then maybe spend more time casting and less reading? I mean, if the answer was in a book, wouldn't that be the same as having Sandra tell you the answer? If it's the spell, then study the spell."

"The books are priceless. You both should be reading them to gain your own insights. But you're absolutely correct. I should spend more time learning to cast spells."

"Ha! No weaseling out of this. Jewels was serious about this. She wants the opening to be sold out. If we don't find our fifty marks, we'll have to go out again. And don't forget to tell them to talk about the book and to tell their friends how good the beer is."

"Do you have the business cards for the salon and nightclub?"

"Yeah."

"Then we'll go out tonight when we go home and hand them out. What's needed is a few stores here and in London. Something we can send the locals to. Have you considered opening another club here?"

"I haven't, but you're right."

"Leandro could use a place to showcase his art and perhaps Ollie could invest? We could open three new clubs, one in Oxford, one in London, and one in Dubai. Have the footmen begin looking to see who the trend setters are."

He began laughing, saying, "I love this idea."

"I as well. It will only take me a few days to speak with the clients we need and 'tis a simple command that 'tis their favorite club. If Tate or any of the others want to invest too, 'tis fine with me. Remind them that all investing needs to be done on the books. We would co-sign their loans for them."

"You think Mary would help with the design?"

"Yes, if she does that sort of thing, not that you need a designer, do you? All of the nightclubs I've visited seemed the same to me..."

"Leandro might have ideas..."

"I'm sure Mary would be glad to help or at least tell you who to call for it."

"Yeah..."

"What worries you about that?"

He flushed, shaking his head.

"Nothing."

"If you're worried that you have to ask her, I don't think Julia would care. I can't imagine Mary would be insulted either if you used a different designer. I can't imagine she has much nightclub experience…"

He snickered, reaching to squeeze my knee.

We pulled into a nursery parking lot, and he parked before saying, "I just want her to like me is all. I'll ask her and Leandro and see who else in the crew wants in. Thanks for doing this, Pip."

"'Twill be simple and fun. Julia will approve. She adores going to such places. I'll be happier letting her go when I know the staff will be watching out for her. Now, let's see what we can find for our gardens."

I ignored his flush, hoping his dismayed expression wasn't for asking for the simple favor of finding him patrons—or worse, that he was resenting me for butting in at all.

I thought the dismay was over Mary though. It was going to hurt his feelings if Mary didn't want to be involved. *I'd speak to Julia*, I decided as we entered the greenhouse.

Julia would know how to smooth things between them if this wasn't the sort of project that interested her mother. And she could speak to Reginald who I was certain was behind this new worry of Ryu's. Reginald's worry over his mother working with criminals was understandable, but Ryu probably found it insulting.

I hadn't noticed any new tensions between them, but I hadn't been looking either. I'd need to make more of an effort with all three of them.

"Look," Ryu said happily, "They have Red Helleborine."

"Outstanding! Find the shop girl and see if we can buy ten of them."

The orchid was on the endangered species list and Sandra's list of plants that could repel demons if prepared correctly.

"See if she has advice on how to propagate them," I called after him."

An older man browsing the aisle said, "My gran used to say a glass of red wine once a month in honor of Dionysus was a sure-fire way to get your orchids to bloom and she raised some beauties."

I stepped close enough to feel the heat of him and said, "Tell me more."

By noon I was starving, so we headed back to town and my favorite pizza place where we ran into Rourke.

"Join us," I said. "Or at least sit with us while your order is prepared."

"I'll put our order in," Ryu said.

Rourke followed me to an empty table.

I said, "We've been at the garden centers. 'Tis the God's honest truth that I shall never grow tired of plant shopping!"

"Have you been to Notcutts? My grandmother loves that place."

"It's our next stop after this."

Ryu joined us and handed me a flyer he'd taken from the counter. "Maybe we should see about developing a mailing list of our own?"

Rourke said, "Julia has one already. We're sending tickets out for an invitation-only preview night."

I said, "Don't let this distract you from your final exams."

He shrugged. "It seems like just yesterday that I was dreading graduating and now I can't wait."

"Dreading it? How come?" Ryu asked as he pulled up a seat.

Rourke grimaced ruefully. "I was imagining doing some awful job my grandmother would approve of while living at home..."

"She doesn't approve of this?"

"She's thrilled."

He grimaced at me as he leaned forward to add, "She wants me to steal your ideas—maybe even your artists."

"They have contracts, so they can't be stolen. As for the ideas, there's any number of art studios. 'Tisn't really original. Julia's connections is what make it work. They like her… not to say they wouldn't like you as much, but she spends a great deal of effort making those connections. We both spend a good portion of our time chatting and touting our products."

Ryu said, "You could have the same sort of connections if you wanted to develop them what with you being a future duke."

"That's more Honey's line…"

I patted his hand as I said, "Then you'll be a good partnership. My wife enjoys socializing and doesn't seem to mind at all that I prefer more scholarly pursuits. The trick is to never be late when she requests your presence and to hire scads of good help."

Ryu laughed as he said, "You and Jewels have a good method of sharing the work." He turned to Rourke to say, "They make it look easy, but it's a lot of hard work running all of their businesses."

I said, "Speaking of which, we do appreciate your help. Julia will be completely understanding if you choose to replace any of the help she sends your way just give them a two-week period first."

"I've no problem with any of them, which is weird when you think about it. No offense, Ryu, but some of your friends would've terrified me, but at Pip's place they seem perfectly normal."

Ryu snorted.

I said, "They *are* normal. 'Tis my belief that people everywhere are very much alike. 'Tis just language and dress that sets us apart."

Ryu said, "I don't know about that. I think culture is a huge hurdle."

"'Tisn't really. The cultures that oppress minorities or enforce law that differs from what we're used to still have those same people. The people just learn to live hidden. I prefer cultures that allow people to live more freely without hiding, although I do prefer when the people hide their violent natures as it makes me uneasy to see it too boldly, although, I suppose, a case could be made that forewarned is forearmed. Still, I think most people aren't prone to sudden fits of violence."

Rourke said, "I prefer when people don't look on the verge of violence either..."

I said, "How is the refurbishment of the store going? Are Mary and Isa working well together?"

He nodded. "It's a miracle but they are. I like Honey's mother, don't get me wrong, but she can be a bit much. I was worried when Julia suggested it, but she and Mary have hit it off famously. The stores are coming along beautifully."

He handed me his phone.

I leaned closer to view the images.

"Very nice," I said in approval. "Did Julia speak to you about our idea to open an equestrian store? We were thinking of opening it here in Oxford. Cassandriel was considering buying the Stansfield Estate and turning that into a public riding ring as a place to house some of her horses. It has enough parking to hold shows there and it's close enough to town to get tourists. Julia and I were looking at the adjacent property for a winery—not that we expect to make much actual wine. 'Twould be more for people to spend the afternoon admiring the horses in the fields and the views. But it was our thought that a store specializing in all things equestrian would do well in conjunction."

Ryu said, "He wants the sort of place that will tailor your riding clothes for you."

"And sell hats for the ladies," I agreed. "We need to find a saddlery to have our own brand. It must be top of the line stuff."

"She hadn't mentioned it, but it sounds great—just the sort of place my grandmother would love."

I said thoughtfully, "Perhaps we should put a tearoom next to it? I know just the artist I'd love to commission for some paintings."

"Andre's aunt?" Rourke asked.

"You've seen Cass's painting then?"

"It's amazing."

"We should hang a few in both stores and then match those color schemes at the winery. I bet we could talk Cass into matching our theme for the house as I believe she intended to rent the rooms. Or maybe we should buy the house and her the stable... I'll speak with Sandra. We need a prime spot here in town for the store though."

"I'll call around and see what's available."

"And I shall send out my footman to see if any businesses are floundering and might consider selling out their lease."

Ryu leaned closer to Rourke to mock whisper, "He's always like this. He gets an idea and runs with it. Make sure you tell him if it's a horrid idea if you think it is. I don't know enough about the horse world to have an opinion."

Rourke said, "I really do think it's a great idea. I think we should offer a few items that anyone could wear and maybe some other types of leather goods. The tailor should have their own entrance and it should be very posh with a really fancy waiting room and windows so the people waiting can be admired—or imagine they're being admired—by the people passing."

I laughed in delight and then felt a sharp pang of sadness. My sister had adored visiting the seamstress and the shops. She'd always been admired everywhere we went.

I said, "Speak to Mary and tell her that this one I'd like to be involved with. I know exactly how I'd like it to look. In fact, we'll get a copy of Violet's portrait made and it shall hang in the place of honor. The tearoom will have a painting of her in the woods and one of her dog at the tea table. 'Twas a beast like my Pansy in looks but much smaller. She'd often serve her Pansy tea..."

Ryu clasped my hand for a moment. "I'm sure we can find an artist who can do it if Andre's aunt won't."

I winked as I said, "I shall offer her an exorbitant commission."

I called Julia later that evening from the apartment.

"I've bought the winery and spoken to Rourke about the stores in Oxford. I was so inspired that I called and spoke with Andre's uncle, he being the only one I could reach, to beg his aunt to make me a painting of Violet in the woods and a few other pictures. I offered a ridiculous amount, but I think they'll be well worth the money."

"Then I hope she says yes."

"Rourke will begin looking for a saddler and a suitable location in town. Do you have a preference where we put it?"

"Whatever you like is fine with me. It's nice to hear you so excited."

"'Twill be just the sort of store I'd loved to visit. I shall have a candy counter and a barrel of wildflowers by the door! With bolts of lovely wools and silks to gaze longingly at in the windows!"

She giggled and my heart expanded.

I said, "'Tis wonderfully to build something so special with you."

"Will you be home tonight?" she asked.

"I'd meant to, but time got away from us. We'll go out tonight for a late meal and to acquire a few more promises to come to the opening. Speaking of which, Ryu had a great idea, but 'tis one I'm unsure can be done. I'll need to speak with Sandra."

"Sandra...."

"Maybe she can show me how to embed a command into a flyer?"

"*Hmm*, that would be handy."

"'Twill likely cost a great a deal to learn..."

"I'm not against you studying, Pip. I just don't want you spending all your time doing it and missing out on the fun."

"It *is* fun!"

"It's interesting but not what I'd call fun."

"I truly enjoy it. I know you don't but 'tis needful for you to have at least a small degree of proficiency."

"I know. Tell you what, we'll compromise. You work with me in the office for eight hours a week and I'll work with you for eight. We can do two four-hour sessions or all in one day, whichever suits."

Eight hours was better than none, but it would take her a very long time to master a spell that way.

I said, "'Tis a deal."

"I'm tempted to come join you two for dinner..."

"Do! 'Twill be fun."

"I'd have to come back here though because I'm meeting with the contractor tomorrow."

"Have Ollie bring you. He can join us and drive you home after or in the morning. We've had another idea to open a chain of nightclubs that the boys can invest in. I was hoping your mum and Leandro could design it together?"

"I'm sure she'd be thrilled. The two of them are thick as thieves."

"Ryu will be so pleased. He was worried Mary wouldn't be interested in working with him."

"He said that?"

"Not in so many words. I thought maybe Reginald's worry had insulted him..."

"I'll speak to him."

"And I'll speak to my footman about finding a good location and who I need to whisper to."

"I'll give the contractors a heads up."

"Don't forget to tell the contractor we'll be wanting him to work on the winery as well."

"See you in an hour or so."

She arrived with Vicky.

"Vick," Ryu said, and the two bumped fists.

Julia flushed as she said, "I thought maybe you could keep Vicky with you, and I could take Ryu? I was thinking about what you said, and I agree, I should study a bit more and since I find that tiring, it'd be best if he was at the estate—"

"Of course!" I said eagerly.

She laughed as she said, "Relax, darling. We aren't going back tonight. I brought Ollie as well. He's moving some things into an apartment right down the street. The building isn't as secure as this one, but it has more rooms. Our staff can stay there when you're in town and still be handy. Ryu and Vicky can have the two main bedrooms."

She turned to Vicky to say, "You should install a lock on your door, not that I don't trust Ollie, but his room will be shared by whichever driver is on duty."

She took my arm, leading me to the elevator as she said, "I hadn't realized how sexist I was until I imagined asking Vicky to sleep on the sofa like we do Ollie. I realized we should've provided him a room here long ago."

Ryu said, "He doesn't mind, Jewels. He's crashed on my couch more nights than not."

"Still, he should have a private place of his own for when he's off duty."

I wondered if Ryu had asked her to arrange him a private place because he was very flushed and avoiding my gaze.

She got into the back of the car with me, saying to him, "Drive down here and take a right. I'll point out the building to Pip. Then drive back toward the river. I bought another new rental. We can take possession in two weeks but it's going to be a few months before we can use it as I intend.

"I'm having secret entrances and exits put in between the rooms. Vicky will have a real apartment there, one she doesn't have to share with anyone. Ryu, you'll have to drive Vicky around later and show her all of our rentals just in case she ever needs to drop anything off, not that we have too much to do with any of our tenants. Jacob oversees all of that, but we do occasionally need to approve one of their requests to paint or whatnot."

"Do we have a tenant in mind?" I asked.

"Yes. Ryu and I can handle it."

I tried to keep my expression bland.

To complain of her practicing after I'd just asked her to practice more seemed churlish. It just worried me how tipsy she got when using another's anima like that.

I gave Ryu a speaking glance when he caught my eye in the rear view, and he nodded uncomfortably back.

She didn't seem to notice our exchange, leaning forward to say, "Vicky, accompany Pip to our temporary greenhouses so you can talk him out of rebuying plants we already have."

"Ha!"

Ryu and Vicky laughed.

Julia kissed my cheek.

"I'm just teasing, darling. Buy however many bushes you like."

Shopping in all the garden centers made me almost giddy with delight. Of all the things the future had I appreciated the libraries and plethora of plants available the most, well that and hot running water and the amazing amounts of food available.

I could imagine my sister's joy, which made me both angry and wistful. She'd have loved them as much as I did.

I said, "We'll call the store in Oxford Violet's and offer a custom brand of clothing. I shall invite Delphine to the opening."

"Pip..."

"I know she won't be able to attend, but still... it must hurt her heart as well to lose so many she'd held dear. Mayhap I'll even commission a portrait of her. I can see her clearly astride her lovely horse with her scandalous shoes..."

"Scandalous shoes..." Vicky asked laughingly.

"'Tis nothing, just a personal jest."

Julia said, "Tea at Delphine's... we better make it an incredibly posh tea house."

"I can hardly wait!"

Chapter 59

The next morning, I was just leaving the studio in London when Sandra called. I knew by her tone that she was in more trouble than the simple request, could I come at once, revealed.

I knew it was very bad when she didn't take time to explain but said to call her when I was on the way.

I called Ryu.

"Where are you?"

"At the bank. What's wrong?"

"Reschedule. Sandra called and needs me there urgently."

"Where are you?"

"We were on the way to the studio, but we're headed back now."

"Tell Ollie to come pick me up here."

I'd reached the car while we were speaking and lowered my phone to say to Ollie, "We're picking up Ryu at the bank and step on it!"

On the phone, Ryu said, "Did she say why?"

"No. She just said to call when I'm on the way there. I better call Julia."

I disconnected to call her.

"Hello, love," she said, "I've spoken with the caterers—"

"Sandra called," I interrupted. "Something is wrong. I'm headed there now but I think you should come to London just in case."

"In case of what?"

"I don't know yet. But if I need help... bring my bag from the upstairs study. I'll call as soon as I know anything."

"Be careful, Pip."

"You too."

I was tempted to call Sandra but didn't because I wasn't officially on my way there yet.

The fifteen minutes it took to get to the bank felt like an hour.

Ryu got into the back with me and leaned over the seat to say to Ollie, "Get us to Oxford pronto, mate."

I was calling Sandra as he rose the privacy barrier.

It rang ten times before she picked up.

Ryu's expression became pinched, and we both loosed relieved sighs when she finally answered.

She said, "I haven't time to talk long. I need you at the estate. Andre's cousin's wife has just been kidnapped and the woman holding her is planning to murder her live online—unless she reveals her werewolf shape."

"Does she have an alternate shape?"

"Maybe—probably."

"...Andre?"

"Probably. We've suspected. It's a long story. One I don't have time to tell. Cassandriel has no idea, about it being true, I mean. She's aware of the kidnapping and extremely upset—so upset that I'm worried she'll lose her shape too. If that happens, I need you to make people leave or forget they saw a thing. I have no idea how to fix this..."

"I'll be there within the hour. I've sent Julia to London. Should we see about renting a plane or cargo ship or..."

"No. I couldn't get her on one if she didn't wish to and she's too young... if we have to move her, Drew will need to levitate her, but if she fights him...."

"Could I order her?"

"...maybe. It would be very dangerous for both of you. Don't try it lightly, Pip. Her temper would be fierce, much more powerful than a human's. I give her pills to control it, not that she knows that. She thinks them vitamins." She laughed a harsh bark of laughter. "Listen to me, I'm babbling. I'll text you the web address."

"What will we do if this girl shifts her shape?"

"Pray no one believes it's real."

Ryu said, "If we act quickly enough, Pip could make whoever's putting it online claim it's a hoax."

"I doubt we can reach them before authorities do, although maybe we could reach them in prison. It's a good idea but I think we need to brace ourselves for some level of panic within our community."

"I'll call Vitus and Trujillo and offer assistance should it be necessary. Should I call Andre?"

"No. I haven't decided what to do about him."

"Do?"

Ryu grabbed my arm hard, shaking his head at me.

"I'd hoped to find out whether he was a werewolf, and if so, if they're truly immortal as spirit creatures from my realm are before revealing myself. If he is, then I can warn him about my daughter, and if he isn't, I can warn him away."

Ryu shook his head at me again.

I said, "I understand that he's potentially a problem, but I believe he really does love her."

Ryu released my arm to take out his phone.

Sandra continued, "Fenra from my realm are immune to magic. They appear as wolves, but they can reason like a man. I believe the werewolves here are descended from the fenra. Fenra are completely immune to magic. You couldn't sway one and I can't cast on one. Andre is immune to spells. Believe me, my last option would be force. I've no wish to make his pack my enemies, nor upset my daughter. But she isn't going to be easy to hide or contain. It would be much easier to hold him away from her then to let him upset her and then have to deal with her."

"I better call Julia. Should I call Cass?"

"...no. I suppose not. It would be best to speak to her in person. I've got to go."

She disconnected.

I checked my texts, holding my phone so that Ryu could read it with me.

He typed in the web address as I called Julia.

"Jewels, I'm texting you a web address. Pull over though before trying to look it up."

Ryu had found the site. Tears burned my eyes. The poor girl looked terrified. It made my voice rough with anger as I told Julia what Sandra had told us and our plan so far.

"I'll make the phone calls," she said.

I said, "Prepare a spot to hold Andre if necessary. I want to be able to truthfully tell Sandra that we're prepared to keep him there. Not that I don't trust her, I do, but she's sounding panicked and he's a friend. I'd feel much better if 'twas us who take him if he must be held away from Cassandriel."

"Pip," she said breathlessly.

"I know, love, but we can't turn our backs on him, and not just for his sake, but our own. If we let her do this unhindered, then she'll feel that we can be made to do anything."

"Pip's rights, Jewels," Ryu said. "We'll respectfully offer our help. If she's telling the truth, she should be grateful that we're willing to hold him, which is crazy of us. But Pip's right that it's better us doing it than her. We can explain and ask him to cooperate. But I think we need to prepare for the consequences of kidnapping him regardless of our motives in doing so."

"His family is bound to be pissed," she said worriedly.

"Let's worry about that later. Put the cage in our lab, or maybe build another underground room near it, whichever you think best. Make sure 'tis strong."

"Really strong," Ryu interjected. "And we'll need another one in the barn or something in case he needs moonlight. Make sure you use someone you have complete control of because we're bound to be suspects if he goes missing here, and god knows what abilities a werewolf has to make people talk."

"I'd think just being a werewolf would do it," Julia said dryly.

I laughed nervous agreement.

I said, "I'm a bit… miffed that she didn't warn us."

Ryu said, "She said she wasn't certain. Don't be angry over that, Pip. Both of you try to stay nice and calm."

"Call me when you get there or if you hear anything. Love you."

She disconnected before I could answer.

I called Delphine using my burner phone.

"*La longue nuit,*" a man said in French when he answered.

"This is Lord Blackwood. I'd like to speak with Lady Delphine. It's quite urgent."

"One moment."

"Should you…" Ryu trailed off, shaking his head and heaving a put-upon sigh. "Never mind. Of course you would. Just don't promise anything rash, Pip."

I was on hold for ten minutes before the man returned.

"My lady is here." A moment later Delphine said, "*Mon pépin,* what is amiss?"

I explained what was going on ending with, "If I can be of assistance…"

"*Mon Cherie*, how sweet of you to be concerned. My house will be safe under my protection."

"I meant no offense."

"None was taken. We've planned for this day. Should the need arise, we're prepared. If you need a safe place, my door is always open to you."

"As mine is to you."

"*Au revoir, mon doux pépin.*"

The woman who answered the number for Vitus promised to have him return the call at his earliest convenience.

A man answered when I called Trujillo and asked me to hold a moment.

Trujillo, or someone pretending to be him came on the line quickly.

"Trujillo here," he said in a whispery voice.

I'd never spoken to nor seen him, so had no idea if it sounded like him or not. I didn't think it mattered though.

I said, "I'm sorry to disturb you but I'd thought you'd be interested in an incident that is even now taking place in America. I'll text you the information I have on it. If you believe I could be of assistance, don't hesitate to call."

I disconnected.

"Will he call?" Ryu asked.

"Probably not. I'm sure he has his own means of protecting himself and his family. But Julia and I are trying to be good neighbors, as it were."

As I was speaking, I texted Trujillo the web address.

Cass's fear and confusion made my heart hurt for her. It angered me to perpetuate the lie, especially when I, of all people, knew how badly it would hurt once the truth was known to her.

I offered the only comfort that I could, my pledge of support.

Drew was obviously upset as well, which surprised me by making me jealous. I literally couldn't image my father rushing to my side to offer comfort, although he might have rushed to my side to prevent me from exposing him.

We'd gathered in the barn outside the stall that held Cassandriel's favorite mount, Laude. She was quite worried that the horse was injured, I knew the injury had been inadvertently caused by her, but she didn't.

Drew looked at me as he said to her, "The horse will be fine Cass. Don't worry so."

I took the groom, Laura's, hand in mine and said, "Thank you for taking care of the horse. It must have been a simple stomach upset and nothing to worry about. Everyone here is just so upset over this. To think, Cass knew that awful girl! She's truly crazy!"

Laura nodded agreement.

Cass gave me a wan smile.

Drew, Ryu, and I walked away.

Ryu leaned closer to whisper, "I'll take a walk around the estate and make sure no one is around."

As soon as he left us, Drew said, "Pip, can you get animals to follow you?"

"Yes."

"We'll need to feed her right away if she loses her shape. She'd eat just about anything, but it would upset her later to know she'd eaten one of her horses. Can you see if you can entice one of the neighbors' horses or cows closer? I can grab it and drag it, but I don't want to leave her."

"Yes."

I climbed the paddock fence and ran across it to reach the woods.

It took me an hour to find a suitable animal, an elderly draft horse that I was certain was being kept as a pet of her grace. It made my stomach squirm with guilt to steal it because if she was letting it graze and lay about, she obviously felt affection for it, but I couldn't afford to be squeamish.

It followed me willingly. I left it in the stable by Laude and told Laura to forget she'd seen it there.

When I returned to the house, both Sandra and Cassandriel were much calmer. The girl had been rescued and Cassandriel thought it had been a horrible hoax.

She was worried about her friend but in the way one would expect.

Sandra was furious. A dense cloud of red lit with gold sparks appeared whenever she spoke. I thought it for the unknown fate of the children.

She spoke calmly but I could see the angry anima swirling about her whenever she mentioned them. It had a denseness that human anima lacked. 'Twas so dense that I worried that it would become visible.

I said, "I think perhaps more tea is in order. I shall prepare some forthwith to calm all of our nerves."

I spent the day watching the news with them.

Sandra calmed when it was announced the child had been born alive. The people responsible called themselves the lupine society. Their leader was Cassandriel's neighbor, Stacy Anderson, the sister of one her friends who'd married Andre's cousin.

The reporter was gleefully talking about Stacy's arrest record, which was a long one that included arrests for theft, prostitution, drugs, and assault. Stacy was wanted for questioning for two murders and was suspected of drugging minor girls without their knowledge.

"I know she murdered Carrie! I know it!" Cassandriel said angrily.

"It seems likely," Sandra agreed.

"Anne shouldn't stay there. It isn't safe."

"I agree, darling, but it isn't up to us."

Sandra gave me a speaking glance.

Drew said, "Cass, I'll call her and if she won't see sense, I'll go to make sure the guards we hired for her have done everything possible."

"I shall accompany you," I said. "Perhaps she'd be more willing to believe someone who isn't as involved. And I can assure her of entrance into the school of her choice, perhaps even talk her into attending college here."

Sandra nodded approvingly.

Cassandriel said, "Thanks, Pip. She just makes me so mad with this! Anyone can see that it isn't safe there!"

"We own a large security force. Id happily put it at your complete disposal."

Sandra said, "I'll speak with Jewels if my team tells me they need more people."

I said, "I think a second opinion would ease all of our minds. I shall send our team at once to ensure the proper equipment is in place."

Cass smiled a real smile full of relief.

I kept her busy talking over the options with our security firm, which wasn't as relaxing as I'd have wished for her, but 'twas easing her mind.

Julia joined us for dinner.

Cassandriel picked at her food, which I could see was worrying Sandra.

I said to Sandra, "If your work will keep you here, I'd be happy to escort Cassandriel home to speak with her friend."

Julia said, "Pip and I were considering opening a library of our own in the village. We'd be more than glad to offer Anne's mother the position of librarian. And I'm certain a job could be found for her father. Plus we have the housing available. Send her the pictures, Cass. I know just the strings to pull to get Anne accepted at Oxford. If she absolutely has her heart set on Harvard, I have a friend on the faculty there as well. I could find out if a job at the University for Anne's mother is possible."

I said, "There are plenty of libraries in Massachusetts. I'm sure a large enough donation would procure a posting at the library of her choice."

Sandra nodded her approval. "I'll call and speak to her mother myself, darling."

Cassandriel said angrily, "It's just so stupid to stay there when they know that bitch murdered Carrie! It doesn't matter if they grabbed the wrong girl or not. She's a psychopath!"

I flinch back from her angry anima. 'Twas darker and denser than normal even from a furious man. It lacked the cohesion of Sandra's, which told me that Sandra had been making an effort to keep her anger contained.

Sandra said, "She's been apprehended, darling. I really think the danger is over. But if it's truly worrying you, I could always fire Irene. I'm sure I could arrange for her father to be fired as well. It wouldn't guarantee they'd leave the town though..."

"Don't do that. At least not yet. I'll invite Anne here. She can go to Florida with me and then to Germany. I'll hire private detectives to find out who else in that town might be working with Stacy."

"I'll handle that, darling. I think it's a good idea to get Anne away for a spell. Soon she'll be in college safely away from Stacy's influence."

"I want guards to accompany Anne there."

Julia said, "I have just the men. Come tomorrow and meet them."

I forced a laugh as I said, "You can send your Thompson as well and let Anne believe he's the only man guarding her. These men will be unnoticed by Anne; hence she'll have no cause to demure."

Julia said, "These are good honest men with years of experience. Not that I don't think your man isn't up to the task. It just worries me that he'll become distracted by the co-eds seeing as he's just a few years older while the men I've been recruiting are more mature and happily married."

Sandra said, "I think it's a great idea. Thompson can be on call for Anne should she feel the need for an escort, and we'll hire three men who she isn't aware of to work in shifts watching her around the clock."

"Can we send them now?" Cassandriel asked anxiously.

"Sure," Julia said. She turned to Sandra to say, "Maybe you should give them Query Inc identification just in case they need to call in for assistance. They'll have access to Black Whit, but your company has better contacts for finding information in the States."

Sandra said, "You're certain their training is adequate?"

"Completely. I won't need to give them direction personally again as they understood my requirements perfectly."

"Then that's settled. Consider them hired."

Ryu and Drew joined us after dinner.

Cassandriel retired early.

Sandra sagged in relief when Drew closed the sitting room door. "Thank God!"

Drew said, "I think that crisis is over. If you'll excuse me, I'll go retrieve her horses and give our thanks to the staff there. The quicker things go back to normal for her, the better."

He left.

Sandra said, "I don't think we'll need to force Anne's parents to leave, but just in case, I'll find a place to relocate them." She turned to Ryu to say, "If Pip does need to force them, make sure you get them to remove their wedding rings. She won't be able to ask them

621

too. You might need to use force. Once they're removed, she should be able to make them forget..."

He nodded that he understood.

"Will you go speak to Andre?" I asked.

"As soon as I can, but I darn't leave her or take her there quite yet. Take her home with you tomorrow and do what you can to distract her. I need some time here to finish some spells I'd been working on for you. I'll pick her up and drop off the spells. How long until the cage is ready?"

"A week or so assuming the parts are available," Julia said.

"When it's done, I'll come put a holding spell on it. Meanwhile, I'll write up a few and drop them by along with a few inferno spells, just in case. Zayvion will be able to dispel one and maybe move it, so use care, but if he was distracted enough or careless an inferno spell could kill him in moments."

Ryu said, "Can you key it for me to set off?"

"No!" Julia and I said together, which made us both laugh.

She said, "Don't be crazy. If he turned it on you, he'd fry you like an egg."

"Maybe but it leaves me vulnerable if I can't use the weapons."

"Pip?" Sandra asked.

"What do you advise?"

"That he has access to spells if you think he can handle them safely."

I reluctantly nodded.

Julia said, "Just don't be a knucklehead and rush in. It would be better for Pip and me to be hurt than you."

Sandra said, "They're correct. A seethe can heal even bad burns with enough anima. It's dangerous though because they'll suck in all of the available anima if they're too hurt, which could leave them drunk or in a stupor. It could also kill the person whose anima they're stealing if they can't stop themselves in time."

"Can we heal him if he's burned?" I asked.

"Some seethes can, and some can't or maybe they just didn't choose too... I'm not certain. I think it must have hidden costs they don't speak on because they so seldom do it. I've never met a seethe with more than three close human companions although it's possible they had more that they'd hidden away."

Ryu said, "And what about this Stacy Anderson chick? Is she a witch like she claims?"

"In a way."

Angry anima flared from Julia.

Sandra continued, "She isn't a powerful one or trained. I know she can't read Salazar because she approached me about translating some books she had."

"She has spell books?" I asked.

"Diaries from her mother who I believe was descended from an inou."

Julia said, "Do they know of you?"

"No. At least I don't believe so. I didn't know of them either until recently."

I found that hard to believe as did Julia judging by the way her anima surged.

Ryu said doubtfully, "You live right next to an inou and didn't know it?"

"It isn't as unlikely as you'd think. I think John, her husband was descended from green dragons."

"You missed a dragon and an inou right next door?"

She wrinkled her nose at him.

"Green dragons have a plant natura. Where they live, life flourishes. Inou have something very similar. Both John and Alice are very weak, and I think completely unaware of what they are. I think they have so much human ancestry that he's mostly human. I picked that spot because it was so beautiful and peaceful. The effect is so subtle as to be almost unnoticeable. They were good neighbors in that we were polite, but we kept to ourselves for the most part, exactly like I liked it.

It wasn't until I saw a werewolf stalking Stacy that I got suspicious. But I didn't realize what she was until that first girl went missing. I immediately began looking for her but inou are naturally immune to that sort of spell. Anyone living with them would also be immune. I think she inherited more of her ancestors' inou nature than her mother has or maybe her mother is more powerful than I think and just perfectly content with her husband and children. But I truly think Alice has no idea and that Stacy is just beginning to come into her power."

"But the wolves knew of her…"

Sandra said, "It worries me too. I think maybe Stacy isn't lying when she says that her sister was bitten by a werewolf. In my realm, all sorts of spirit creatures would be attracted to a green dragon's forest. The dragon would let the ones it liked live there but they usually didn't allow many because it could be dangerous. That's a lesson for another day though. But my point is that a dragon's forest would be enticing to everyone because crops would grow in abundance, water would be fresh, fires would be easily contained, that sort of thing. Werewolves would've been as attracted to it as I was, and maybe like me they hadn't realized why.

"Kelly was bitten when she was just a girl. It's possible one realized she was other and lost control of itself. Who knows what it intended. How she ended up in Montana with Andre's family is anyone's guess but it's possible that family has more family all over. I think she's happy there though. I've seen pictures and spoken to Alice about her.

"She'd be an inou too," Ryu said thoughtfully.

"Maybe, but she's more like her father. She liked to be out in the woods and spent most of her time there alone, which is a green dragon trait, not an inou one. Her sister Stacy had a more amorous nature. She kept multiple lovers, which is an inou trait."

"So her sister could be a dragon?"

"I seriously doubt it. Kelly was so young that she wouldn't be able to control herself. She was scared enough to lose her shape if she had one to lose. She hadn't started a hoard either. In fact, she'd left most of her childhood possessions behind when she eloped and had been giving her money to her sister, which isn't something a dragon would do. I think she's a human woman with enough dragon blood to cast spells and she probably heals quickly."

"So the wolves might've taken her for their own reasons," I said.

Julia leaned to grab my hand.

"We can't afford to get involved with that, Pip."

Sandra said, "She's right. It's too late for Kelly anyway. If her husband is a fenra, he'd hunt you to the ends of the earth if you take his mate. If he isn't but has fenra relatives they would probably do the same because I'm sure if they knew about her, they'd want her for inou ancestry. They wouldn't give her up easily. But they'd also treat her kindly at least until they were certain that she's powerless, which will take them years, centuries even to be sure of. They would have to if they wanted her magic to work for them."

Ryu said, "She has the children, Pip. She won't want to leave them, and you saw his face. He isn't letting those kids go."

Julia said cajolingly, "Let it go for now. Sandra will find out what's going on there and then we can talk about it."

"We should send an assassin after Stacy," I said.

Drew said, "Maybe. It might be better to wait though and find out what she knows."

Ryu said, "If we whack her, we need to really cover our tracks because for sure Andre's family will be looking to see who sent him."

Sandra stood and headed to the door, pausing to say, "Let me get to work. Drew will watch Cassandriel to be sure she doesn't try to slip away and join him."

I said, "I can keep watch. Let him rest."

She nodded and left.

Ryu said, "I'll go help him settle the horses."

"Me too," Julia said as she leaned to kiss my cheek. "You can stay and covet her library," she added laughingly.

I laughed with her because I did covet it.

Chapter 60

Sandra was showing me a Salazar primer the next day when Cassandriel ran into the room.

"They've stolen the baby," she said breathlessly.

We all immediately headed for the television where we, like the rest of the world, watched the drama unfold.

We remained there for days.

Cassandriel was angry but not frantic. I thought it unlikely she'd lose control because she believed the kidnappers to be crazy.

I was furious.

Sandra was furious.

Drew pressed tea on us continuously, which I refused to drink.

When Cassandriel was safely abed for the night, I joined Sandra in her study.

"She must be stopped," I said.

Sandra said, "And quickly."

"Don't rile her," Drew murmured. "This wasn't Stacy. Or at least not directly."

Julia said worriedly, "The police want to catch them as badly as you do, darling."

Sandra said, "This is how it starts. They begin hunting us and at first humans are outraged. They feel sorry for us but then they begin to see the profit to be had and soon we must hide or be murdered..."

Drew said, "It hasn't come to that yet. No one believes them."

Sandra said, "They drained his blood—they know it's use. Imagine how much more they'd want the blood of a purebred! We should kill them all now before they can raise more followers!"

"I agree," I said. "Any group that would kill a child for an evil rite deserves to be hunted."

Ryu said, "I hate to say this, Jewels, but he's right."

Drew said, "Those wolves will handle it."

"Don't be ridiculous!"

Sandra stomped to her desk to grab her phone. The curtains billowed as she waved her hand, canceling the spells on the room so that she could use the phone.

She barked into the phone, "Find out everything there is to know about the Lupine Society. I want the name and address of every member. I want the names of their friends and family. I want their bank records, school records, police records. I want to know who they speak to online and by phone. Let's find out who really believes that bullshit and is willing to act on it and who just wants to be a murderous bastard. You have a budget of five million and I want the info presented in an organized manner by September. Send me weekly updates. Prioritize the members who have a real link to that bitch. Notify me at once if you have reason to believe they have another target. Keep this search as confidential as we can." She listened a moment then said, "The usual rates plus bonuses."

Her anger appeared muted to me. It was thick but faded into an almost colorless mist. I wondered if that was from the tea but didn't ask.

She threw her phone down and began to pace.

Drew said, "The wolves will be looking. You're drawing attention to us."

"We're already on their radar. Andre would expect me to look for my daughter's sake, not to mention Anne."

I said, "I shall go look."

Sandra grimaced at me.

"Not yet. Drew's right. Anyone who knows the truth is going to be watching those assholes—and human police will be looking to see who shows up. I'll go. No one would think it odd that I offer support. In fact, the opposite is true. It would be suspicious if I didn't seeing as how I know them all. Andre would expect me to show up. We can't wait any longer."

Drew's expression tightened.

"I can be back in half a day. She's calm enough for me to go, and I think my going will relieve her mind as well."

"She'll want to go too."

Sandra shook her head. "She'll understand it's too dangerous. I'll call Andre and tell him that he's to tell her not to. He won't want her there."

She turned to me to say, "Nothing remains to be done here. She needs to return to her classes. Everything must be as normal as we can make it for her—and anyone who might be watching to see if Stacy might be right."

Ryu said, "You think the Lupine Society is following Andre?"

"I think everyone from our town will be under scrutiny. Andre's connection to Mark will assuredly bring us to the attention of those who are investigating such things. Our wealth will cement that interest. If I were purely human I'd still be alarmed, which is why I'll increase her security like anyone would expect."

Drew said, "I agree. Go for that visit but don't stay long because anyone who knows you would know that you'd never leave Cassandriel for long at a time like this. Go and come back. You can return home in a week or so. I can take Cass to the Florida events, and you can go then for a longer visit. No one would think it was odd at all if you returned to the States for a short visit if she was doing her normal thing."

He said to Julia, "You should continue as normal too. I'd assume I was being watched if I were you but there isn't much to see if you're careful, which you should be anyway."

He turned to me to say, "We'll show you that report on the Lupine Society when we get it, and we can decide then what's to be done. I've no intention of letting anyone involved with murdering that child go, but maybe we can use them to flush out more. So don't be hasty or reckless. It might be simple to go there and tell them to kill each other but it wouldn't be smart—yet."

The next morning we made our goodbyes to Cassandriel.

As soon as we were in the car, Ryu said, "Will we kill them?"

"Yes. I shan't wait for them to hunt me, which they *will* do if they'd harm a child like that."

Julia said, "Should we talk to the vampires?"

Ryu said, "No. Not until we have real information anyway."

I said, "They've probably all been hunted at one time or another..."

"All the more reason we shouldn't say anything until we know what we're going to do. I bet every one of them is already planning a hunt of their own. It's going to be a mess... we should lay low and stay out of it."

Julia said, "At least until we get that report. I'll start looking for a business or two we can buy that would take us there. We need something that looks legit so when we go ask our questions, no one thinks it's odd."

I said, "No one would think it odd if we visited our friend at her home."

Ryu said, "Those assholes ain't all going to be there. Look at the group in Cali. I bet they're all scurrying away, but Sandra will find them. What we need is a reason to travel around. You could schedule a showing for Leandro almost anywhere without it being weird. Maybe he does a tour of the States? We could get a few more artists and hit all the major cities. If we time things right, we could travel from the show to another event, say a charity event or horse show or something and stop off almost anywhere we wanted to have a little chat with no one the wiser."

"Ingenious," I said.

Julia nodded in agreement.

"I'll start lining things up."

Ryu said, "It might take Sandra more than a few months to find the heavy hitters."

She shrugged as she said, "So we do it every year. It'd be good for us to do it anyway. We should be going to as many high-end events as we can to get our product base firmly established. I'd planned to do a lot of that in Germany while attending the horse events."

I said, "Are you sure you can take the time away?"

"I can always pop back home if I need to, but I can work remotely. Besides, there'll be plenty of new contacts there to keep me busy. I think it'll be fun, Pip. People always get angry at these sorts of events when their favorites don't win, and no one would think it odd to see us whisper for a second or two just remember to tell them they're having a good time so they smile."

Ryu glanced at me in the rearview, which made her heave a heavy sigh.

She said, "I won't get drunk because I'll simply be telling them to vacation at our hotels if they're considering a vacation or to buy our products if shopping for nice gifts or tiles. We'll just use small nudges. Tell them they love our beer and whisky or want one of Leandro's pieces. Just simple things that it wouldn't matter if anyone heard you say."

I knew she'd be making careful note of who might deserve to be ordered to spend more aggressively at her charities, which I heartily approved of and did myself. And those sorts of people would have rinds she could manipulate.

I said, "Leave the unrinded for me."

She nodded absently.

Ryu said, "Will we contact the wolves?"

"Maybe. Let's see what Sandra finds out. Our priority is keeping Cass calm, so we'll go back this weekend and encourage her to come riding with us. Hopefully her new stable will distract her if we're enthusiastic enough about it."

I must've frowned because Julia laughed, saying, "You'll have plenty of time for reading your new books. I think we should both get on a normal sleep schedule though just in case we're needed again."

"'Tis a good idea."

We talked over our sales strategy until we reached home.

I headed directly to the study upstairs to place my new books.

I'd just sat at my desk when someone knocked on the door.

I opened it to find John.

"Lady Julia asked if you could pop into her office when it's convenient."

"Thank you."

I hurried back downstairs.

She grinned when she saw me. "Sorry to alarm you. I forgot to ask Sandra what animals we should stock up for a peckish werewolf. I think we should expand our farm to table anyway so I'll add more chickens and smaller game animals but if you could research that…"

"I shall read those texts at once."

"Let me know if there's anything good," she said absently as she reached for her day planner that was almost hidden under a stack of unopened mail.

Her phone rang.

I said, "I shall," and let myself out.

Allison, her head footman was in my old office.

I stopped to say, "I'll be in the upstairs study if I'm wanted. Please make sure that Julia's riding clothes are packed and ready for this weekend."

Allison smiled crookedly. "She asked me to see who's hosting casual hunts next weekend too. I think she really means to attend."

I snorted softly.

Allison laughed.

We both knew that Julia liked to attend the party afterward and not the ride. Forgetting to pack riding clothes was her favorite excuse to sleep in. Not that I thought she planned to avoid this trip. I thought she was likely to truly forget because of the amount of things she needed to catch up on.

"If I can be of assistance to her..."

"I'll text," Allison said. "None of that mail is urgent if that has you worried. It's just the summer seasonal invites and spring balls and things like that. She already informed me that she plans to be in Germany for a good portion of the summer. It won't take her long at all to go through them. I can send her regrets."

"Very good. Thank you, Allison. I'm delighted with the job you do."

"Thank you, my lord. I love this job. I never thought I'd be able to get such a good one again..."

"'Twas criminal how you were treated."

Her eyes filled with tears.

Allison had spent nine years in prison for second degree manslaughter after killing her husband who'd been trying to kill her. She'd been barely more than a child, only twenty-two when she'd killed him. She'd asked repeatedly for help and been turned away despite the clear evidence that he'd been seriously hurting her. She might still be in jail if Julia hadn't whispered to the parole board. The unfairness of it was enough to make me angry when I contemplated it.

I must do something about his horrible parents, I thought angrily. They'd used their influence to keep her incarcerated even though they'd known she was the victim.

She said, "Of everything Lady Julia has done for me, believing in me was the one that's helped me the most. It makes me so goddamned mad that he got away with everything he ever did! If I could kill him again, I would."

"As would I, but 'tisn't smart to say so."

"I know... I'm sorry. It won't happen again."

She was still angry enough that it showed on her anima.

I said, "Perhaps we could do more to tarnish his reputation though..."

"Like what?"

"I know not. Think on it. Mayhap he had other victims who could come forward? Or even a friend of a friend of someone he might've dated and has since passed on? Or perhaps he had a male acquaintance of ill repute that he might've confided in? I can be most persuasive..."

She snorted with laughter, saying eagerly, "I'm sure he did. I wouldn't want you to get into any trouble though. It isn't worth it when no one cares except me."

"I care. Never think I'm not truly angered by his actions or that of his foul parents, or that I don't understand the need for vengeance. It matters not that he won't know when *you* will."

"It isn't me so much as my parents. They get so embarrassed, which always pisses me off so much."

"Unfortunately, even if the truth be known there will always be those who'd choose to use you to harm them."

"I know…"

"Of course, I could persuade them to look elsewhere for their amusement as well. Notify me if anyone is being especially pugnacious. Me, not Lady Julia."

"Thank you, my lord."

Her smile glittered with anticipation.

"Not at all," I said and went to find John to tell him to bring Julia tea and a snack.

I knew well how being seen, truly seen, was a gift beyond price.

I wondered if Andre knew what he was and worried about being seen. I thought he must hate hiding himself from her. 'Twould be an unbearable sorrow to know your true love would die in a human span of years when you would not.

I hurried my step upstairs to my books. So much rested on whether he was truly a creature of sprit or not, but perhaps if not then I could help him and thereby help her. But first I needed to master my magic.

Chapter 61

Julia called me as I was just sitting at our rented table in the library at the museum in London. We'd leave here in two days to join Sandra at her home in the States.

My research over the past weeks had shown me that I needed to be able to harness my magic or my spells would be limited in power. More often than not the magic wafted away before I could finish a spell. Saying a spell too quickly didn't allow me to press much anima into it. Saying it too slowly let the anima escape. I'd begun experimenting with the anima of my mules, which worked better to a degree but twice now I'd made myself completely drunk. I needed a better method.

This book had intriguing insights on how I might do that. I was tempted to steal it because I didn't wish to ask for copies on the slim chance that Stacy Anderson had a confederate watching me because of Cassandriel. I had the sort of money that attracted her and didn't wish to give her further ideas. 'Twould be easy to make the librarian forget she'd given me this book. 'Twould be impossible to hide it being copied when so many forms and people were involved unless I snuck in to do the copying myself, *which I might do*, I thought as I set the book aside to take her call.

Julia said, "Sandra called. Cass and Andre have broken up and she wants me to meet her at the airport."

"Does that mean he isn't..."

"Apparently Andre told Cass what he was, and she didn't believe him, which he had to know she never would without proof."

"Does that mean he isn't?" I asked again. Because if he was a werewolf I assume he'd have shifted his shape to prove it.

"Sandra doesn't know. She hadn't had time to speak with him. She intends to speak with his father, but she's heading back too."

"Why his father?"

"I assume because it's probably a family trait. Maybe Andre is too young to be able to lose this shape or change his?"

"You don't think she means to threaten the man..."

Julia huffed in annoyance.

"Of course she will. She'd do anything she needs to keep her daughter safe and who could blame her? I'd do the same. But right now she's worried about stopping Cass from doing something stupid like finding a rebound guy."

"What is that?"

"I haven't time to explain now. You can look it up. I need to finish our packing in case she goes home again, and I haven't much time to do it if I want to meet her flight."

"I could return home to pack our bags."

I knew our clothing was the least of her preparations but I was woefully ignorant about what needed to be done to prepare our home for a prolonged absence, which this would be seeing as we'd intended to stay in America until Cassandriel went to Germany and then accompany her there to watch her compete, assuming we didn't need to help Sandra force her to Africa, which was our last resort plan.

Julia would be seeing to those last-minute details too.

She'd started construction in Africa, but that hidden lair wasn't nearly finished yet. We'd have to go in person to ensure no humans we didn't have control of got near.

We had no idea how long it might take to force Andre away, so had cleared the schedule for two months, which made no real difference to me—I could study anywhere. But it complicated her work immensely.

She said, "I've got this, Pip. Stay and have fun at the library. I'll call as soon as I know anything. I'm sure Sandra will call if there's anything you can do."

Julia joined me the next day, having sent one quick text the night before saying it was under control.

She settled into the seat beside mine, saying sadly, "Cass is heartbroken. Sandra asked us to stay close, which shouldn't be a problem seeing as how we planned to attend her events anyway."

"Did Sandra say if they were fenra?"

"She's certain some of his family must be and plans to investigate it, but she can't leave Cass right now. I'll need to slip away for a few days to check on the African project. I'll take Ryu and Jean just in case I need a mule and get sleepy. Sandra should be able to handle things if you get sleepy."

"Where's Drew?"

"With them. He plans to come to Africa with me if he can get away. Sandra isn't sure if this is a good or a bad thing. She's really on edge. Really really on edge. I'm a bit worried that *she* might lose her form."

"I hadn't considered... what can we do to help?"

"Keep Cass as distracted as we can. It has to be worrying Sandra that Andre is perfect for Cass and that she's blowing it for her daughter. So the quicker we can get Cass under control, the quicker Sandra will be comfortable leaving her to investigate, maybe it'll be soon enough that she doesn't need to tell too many lies to her."

"She can't lie to her. Cass can see it on the aura."

"Unless Sandra can block her aura somehow, but I wasn't speaking of actual lies anyway. I meant the huge whopper of withholding the truth of what Cass is. Cass really loves Andre. Someday she's going to realize that we all lied about this and even though she might understand, she's bound to be angry and hurt."

"I think her hurt will be one we cannot mend. She will lose all that she holds dear. 'Tisn't something that one recovers from. For us, the pain is one we see and become accustomed to. For her, it will be thrust upon her and perhaps made cruelly worse if her natural self possess the abilities to prolong a human life if she'd but known."

"Oh God, Pip!"

"'Tisn't something we should worry over now when we lack the means to prevent it."

Tears filled her eyes. I thought her considering her beloved parents and mayhap her villainous brother.

I kissed her brow, taking her hand to say, "The temptation to act despite not understanding the repercussions are great. But this thing we can do might be a fate worse than death. I beg you do nothing until we're assured that our actions would be their salvation and not their damnation. Once lost from this realm, they'll remain out of reach. I'd not have us be the cause of their eternal torment in Hell."

"We risk that with Ryu," she said breathlessly.

"He chooses knowingly."

She grimaced at me.

"If you tell your parents, they'd think you quite mad. If you show them, will they think you an evil thing? Or mayhap a thing that should be examined? Would we need to protect ourselves? Would you be willing to force their obedience? Could we force them, or would they too be immune to us? Would knowing our secrets put them in peril? Think on it, beloved. 'Tis no need to rush. Every day I learn more. I'd do whatever you wished."

I didn't mention the unknown number of Blackwood seethes about. *What might they do if they thought we were attempting to turn the Whitmores into seethes?*

She said, "Cass has gone to a friend. Do you remember Liam?"— I nodded, and she continued— "which has Sandra all in a twitter. I've ordered him to remain a gentleman, but I'll need to follow up on that."

"It shouldn't be difficult."

She nodded in agreement.

"Sandra said she'll tutor you when she gets a chance." Julia thumped my book with a finger. "We're both going to the events and to the activities. You need to get out more and make friends too."

"I detest nightclubs."

She narrowed her eyes at me.

I heaved a dramatic sigh that made her laugh.

"Fine. You win. I shall attend two such gatherings a week. Our footmen are perfectly able to keep unsuitable types away from her as is our Ryu as long as you keep a clear head."

She snorted indignantly.

I kissed her flushed cheek.

"We're taking Pansy. 'Twill be the perfect excuse for me to take her dog, Luna. I'll see to her training."

Julia hugged me.

"It'll be fun, Pip. You'll see. You'll enjoy the events and there'll be lots of places to explore."

It occurred to me that it wasn't a selfish desire to go out that was prompting her but an attempt to give me a stockpile of happy memories should I once more be trapped in the bardo. Maybe it was an attempt to give herself such.

I held her tighter.

"Maybe I'll like the music there better."

She laughed in delight.

Chapter 62

I hated the music here even more than the music at home if that were possible. The crowds were too noisy, the dancing ridiculous, the lights annoying.

Julia was having a marvelous time though.

Cass was faking a marvelous time.

I thought her new girlfriends were fooled—or perhaps they didn't care seeing as how Sandra was footing the bill nearly every night.

I stayed long enough that Julia wouldn't complain.

She didn't even roll her eyes when I said to Ryu, "See my lady safely home, please."

Back at the hotel I let myself into Sandra's hotel room, where we met nightly to discuss our concerns and for quick lessons.

"Well?" she asked as she turned from the papers spread across the table. Her penthouse suite had two adjoining bedrooms, one of which she'd made her office and given me a key to. The main room had a sofa, two chairs, a television and a small table just like our own room did. Cassandriel had a matching suite across the hall that she had been sharing with Anne until Anne returned home.

Drew had the room on one side of her and Ryu the other. Our room was by the elevator. Sandra and I both had staff staying on this floor as well. She'd rented the entire floor to make it easier to keep an eye on who came and went.

I said, "I'm certain Liam is just a friend. He knows Cassandriel isn't at all interested romantically. Julia has mildly beguiled him, which will keep him happily occupied in a way that keeps his romantic interest from Cass. Jewels can keep him from coming back, but you don't need to worry even if he does come back. She's certain he won't attempt to seduce Cass or force her. He truly likes her. Before Julia spoke with him, he'd have tried to seduce her but I'm also certain he won't now. Cassandriel is still deeply upset though. It doesn't take magic to see it."

"I know. I think this will be your last lesson here, Pip. You and Julia can return home."

Sandra had been tutoring me every chance she got. She'd been showing me how she was making the amulet that would translate Salazar, which was a complicated process of writing the word atop the correct runes that would infuse it into the chosen vessel, which in this case was a gold bracelet. The word had to be written while speaking it and thinking of the meaning of the word while infusing it with her will. When done correctly the runes lit and faded into the gold. She'd been working on it for weeks.

She handed me a thick book and the bracelet.

"I hope you never need this, but just in case Zayvion returns, the bracelet will let you speak and read Salazar. I'd meant to teach you to read it the traditional way so that you could read the texts I'd brought with me. But you won't be ready for that level of magic for years, and meanwhile who knows when Zayvion might show up again?

"He might not come prepared to face your kind. Seethes are rare at home, and he'd have no reason to believe they would be more common here or even here at all. But you'd need to be able to speak with him—and so the enchant. That book is the history of Salazar, and it includes some basic information on making and storing spells. Use caution if you try any of them, Pip. I'm not giving you the book as a teaching tool but as information on that realm because you couldn't face Zayvion without the risk that he'd form a portal to escape, which would take anything within its radius with him.

"There are nine perfect diamonds inside that bracelet that I've enchanted as best I know how, which should protect you if you were thrown into a portal. You have my word that once I was certain Cassandriel was safe, I'd follow to bring you back here. It could take a hundred years or more to make her safe here, but I swear I wouldn't leave you trapped there. I'll show you everything I know about making a portal and all of my protection spells, which are too advanced for you now, but given time you could probably bring yourself back here. I know I'm asking a lot..."

I gave her a quick hug, saying, "You have my word that I'd do my best to stop Zayvion, but only me. I want your word that you won't ask Julia to face him. She can help in other ways, but we never risk her facing a mage or, God forbid, being thrown into a portal. Julia is too accustomed to the machines and conveniences of this realm. We do nothing that would make her face the bardo!"

"You have my word. If anything were to happen to you, whether it was on account of me and my daughter or not, I promise to do my best to help Julia prepare, not that there's much I *can* do except what I'm already doing. The best preparation is all mental. Training to focus your will is the only thing that I know of that can help a seethe change hosts or escape the void."

"She could live a long time in her own body if she could master a shapeshifting spell."

Sandra said, "I'm sorry, Pip, but she's nowhere near ready to master that."

"I know. She's agreed to study more. If she thought she might someday be able to master it if she practiced more, maybe it would encourage her to do so?"

"I'll show you the steps, but don't try it on a whim because to try and fail would almost certainly—" she paused pursing her lips at me— "I was going to say kill you, but if you had a mule or two handy you might live through it. A bad transformation can leave you crippled, horribly disfigured, maybe even with brain injuries that you couldn't recover from. My teacher recommended I have enough magic stored to transform a few times before he let me try it once."

"How do you know if you have enough?"

"You practice transmuting. I practiced with plants for a good fifty years before I attempted to change my own shape. Plants naturally become other—from a seed to a sapling. You learn to gauge how much magic it takes you to guide that change. Then you learn how to change a sapling into a tree. Then you learn to change the tree into a different species of tree. You learn to impose your will on what is to what *can* be. It's much easier to hurry the natural order along than it is to impose your own vision. And during those years, I studied anatomy. Not like the humans here do. I studied how a woman walked, what their skin felt like, how their hair grew, I watched closely until I could envision myself wearing the shell I have now, which meant I had to know my own body, every part of it. And that's the easy part for my kind. Learning to harness the spirit of yourself in a new form without losing yourself is the difficult bit."

"So you become a human—not just appear as one..."

She hesitated the merest second then nodded. "A seeming is much easier to master and much less dangerous. Here, though, with all of the recording devices, it would be hard to pull off, for my kind at least. You could probably do it as long as it didn't matter if your real face was caught on camera. I've been working on a spells to fool cameras. They work, but they're not really practical for me. Besides, I can easily keep this shape but it took years for me to certain of my control. Cassandriel will need to practice for years..."

"Will she have another shape if she was born human?"

"I'm sure of it. Her aura isn't a human one. The pills I give her help keep her in this shape. Her ignorance of what's possible is what truly keeps her human though. That and her youth. I keep her perfectly satisfied to keep her inner self calm. But eventually, no matter what I do, that inner self will grow too large for a human shell to contain. Only her will can keep herself contained and she'll need magic to do it."

"Will she be able to?"

"I dearly hope so. Some mages never master even simple transmutations and some, like Kazimir, can impose their will on others and change their shapes."

"Like turning them into a toad?"

"I don't think he could do that unless he made the toad person-size. I've never seen him make a person that small. I *have* seen him turn one into a large dog."

"A real dog?"

"Yes. The man afflicted retained his intellect for about four years. I'm not sure if he gave up or still retained it and pretended not to or if he fought the loss of intellect and gave into his animal instincts. Kazimir regularly gave his subjects horns or tails or wings or made them scaly or changed the color of their skin. Sometimes it was meant as a punishment and sometimes a reward."

"I can't imagine I'd feel rewarded..."

She barked a harsh laugh.

"Nor I. But he occasionally rewarded someone by making them beautiful or frightening or giving them thick skin or sharp nails."

"So in theory, I could perhaps learn to shift Julia's shape for her?"

"In theory," she agreed with reluctance. "Kazimir killed a good many of his subjects. I believe it was accidental a lot of the time. He grew better at changing them over the years and few die of it now, but it's something you should do with extreme caution."

"But first I need to learn to store magic..."

"I wish I could help you learn it but the only way to learn that is to study *your* magic. Cassandriel is my daughter and she and I don't see magic the same way. It's my belief that no one sees it exactly as anyone else does. There's similarities but the only advice I can give is to pay close attention to everything. Yours can be a subtle power. A seethe's mood can affect some people and leave others unaffected. Some seethes could use it purposefully, and some didn't seem to be able to do it all. Or maybe they just preferred to keep all humans away from themselves. My point is you need to learn to see how and why you affect people."

"Julia and I have been practicing. She takes careful notes, and we have a control group. She gets tipsy much easier than I do but I'm not certain if that's because she lacks the patience to take small sips or lacks the ability to. Or mayhap she just grows angrier easier?"

"Be careful practicing, Pip. Is all it would take is one drunken episode to ruin everything you've built. You could convince police to look the other way for a lot of things, but a massacre isn't one of them—assuming you lived through it yourself."

"We're careful."

"The translation amulet is meant for emergencies. Learn to really read and write Salazar before attempting spells using it. When I get a chance to get home, I'll bring back a copy of my book of runes for you. The Salazar runic system has fifty-six symbols which make up all spells. You could make your own symbols, but this is a tried-and-true system that took centuries to perfect. Learn the symbols and the meaning of each. Practice drawing them until you can perfectly reproduce them and then you'll be ready to begin writing your own spells."

She sat at her desk and took a piece of notepaper from a drawer then picked up a gold pen.

"The pen is infused with my magic. I could draw the symbols with my finger, but the spell would be much less potent, I can store more magic in the pen than I have. My natural magic regenerates but it's always quicker for me to take the magic from other sources like it is for you to use the rind of a killer."

I nodded that I understood.

She set the gold pen down and picked up a marker.

"If I were to trace the runes I'm about to draw, I can infuse them again, strengthening it, but if you trace it too many times you'll actually begin to leach the power back out. To my knowledge, there's no known cure for that. After you've done this a few times you'll be able to see or sense when the spell is as strong as you can make it. On average, I can trace something four times before it stops gaining power. This is the rune of beginning—the light of creation."

She drew a symbol that vaguely resembled a G. "It's the power source. Notice the line at the top of the circle? That will become the rune of ending—the immovable force or the wall. Without it, the spell would have no end and the power would leak away. I'm not empowering these runes just by drawing them, but a powerful mage could empower them by shifting his magic to them. That can be dangerous because I might have hidden a trap in the spell, a hidden rune."

She set down the marker to pick up a pencil.

"Pretend that the pencil marks are runes drawn with my finger."

She drew in the rune of fire, connecting it the rune of beginning with a sideways u.

"The Rune of Fire connected to the beginning by the Rune of Continuation." She picked the marker back up and drew a wavy line like a loose W with three small dots along the inner line that she connected to the rune of continuation.

"The Rune of Air." She drew another sideways u and then an upside-down t with a slanted bar that crossed the top of the Rune of Beginning.

"To someone reading the written marks, it would appear to be a rune of air. If you poured your magic on it, the magic would flow through the runes, empowering them as I'd willed them to be empowered. So what you'd really be doing is setting off a rune of fire along with air. A careful mage would trickle his power along the runes, and he'd see the runes light up and know he was triggering fire. A really skilled mage could impose his will on that rune, shifting it be something else."

"Like what?"

"That would depend on his skill and the spell. The simplest thing to do would be to insert a continuation and then an ending which would halt the spell dead, but maybe he'd prefer to insert the rune of return along with the rune of auctor which would send the fire to the person who wrote the rune."

"So the more complicated the spell, the harder it would be to stop?"

"Again, it depends. Some processes take longer than others to get going. Plus I could've intentionally empowered the fire rune and left the beginning and end weaker. It's difficult to do that, especially if you need it to be unnoticeable, but if I'd done it correctly, the power would gather there like a deep spot in a puddle making it harder to stamp out or control. It isn't enough to know the rune. You have to be able to shift the power in it by either taking that power and making it yours or removing and replacing it before the spell can fall apart or activate in a way you didn't intend."

"Because you drew it in with your finger, you wouldn't be able to trace it, so it would be weak?"

"*I* could trace it, but I've practiced for centuries. Also, fire *is* my power so it would be the strength I willed it to be. But in general, hidden runes lack the strength of written ones. Now, did you wonder where the pentagram is?"

"It's in your mind as you're drawing the rune."

"Very good! Each rune is written on a point. Novices will draw out the pentacle and write their runes upon it to help them keep the spacing and flow of the spell. A spell always has a beginning and an end. The pentagram and pentacle are visualization aides that help you time the drawing. You need to learn your rate.

"Channeling magic takes a toll. If you go too fast, you'll tire yourself before you can finish, which, if the spell is half done and lacking the rune of ending, could be disastrous. But it's always wasteful to let the magic trickle out even if the broken spell has no backlash. So we learn to trace that shape either on paper or in our mind while writing out the runes so that we pace ourselves to our known strength. Because we all cast at different speeds, we all have different methods. Your method will evolve over time as you grow more adept. Tracing that shape is also a good way to train your magic that the rune is done. Watch closely as I write that same spell, this time I'm empowering it."

She'd showed me before how to write a rune of fire. I hadn't known the names of the different swirls or that it was even three separate symbols I was writing. I peered closely as instructed. The runes lit as she wrote them; one flowing into another. I realized the spell would be missing the crossed x I used.

"Wait! Won't it activate when you draw the rune of ending?"

She winked at me and drew in the x.

I realized the x wasn't crossed but linked to the circle which was the holding spell with a rune of continuation that was linked to the rune of ending.

"The rune of agere—to set in motion. This one can be modified to need a specific reagent or left as is to just require your will to start it. What else did you notice?"

"The smallest hesitation in the way the light flowed from one rune to another."

"I'm very skilled. That hesitation is the tracing of the pentagram. It will take a novice much longer to lock off each rune because if you don't, that rune will activate then and there. That lock is never written. It's always mental. It's your focused will on the rune—your intent. You write that rune to the cadence you've learned of the tracing of the pentagram. You trace that pentagram again and maybe many times until you have the magical power to write the next rune. That rune needs to be written and finished with agere before you can stop again but the pace needs to remain regular or the magic could think the rune is done *without* the rune of ending, which means nothing is holding that magic inside the spell. It would just be a bunch of separate runes, not one spell. At best the magic would just slip away, at worst the magic was confused and linked random parts of the spell."

She traced the line of the pentagram, saying, "Orange light, heat, white light, smokey scent, fire—the way that I learned to cast fire, traced along the pentacle in my mind's eye then ending with a mental crooked x atop the rune, the rune of agere."

"So—two symbols at one time..."

"Writing the rune while envisioning the pentagram ensures your focus. It also keeps you from attempting spells beyond your skill. If you attempted to write a new spell, you'd quickly lose the thread of it unless you already had a very solid base. Now, imagine you wanted your fire spell to go off at a set time or for certain conditions, you need to have that base to work with because that's a complicated set of symbols to match a complicated idea. The magic is yours. It has no independent thoughts. So it has to be trained to do what you want it to, and it has to be trained so well that it always does the same thing when told. I haven't yet thought of a spell that I'd like to do that couldn't be managed with the Salazar runes. Using those runes makes the spell a measure of magnitude stronger because so many people have focused their will upon them in the same way that the runes have been trained to hold power—the magic recognizes the runes in a way that it wouldn't for a symbol you'd just invented."

I nodded my understanding. This was the key that had been missing from mine own attempts. I was amazed now that I'd managed to write the spells I'd written at all and excited to try again with this new insight.

I'd no longer need to trace it continually to keep the magic contained although doing so had taught me much about my inherent abilities, which had likely been her intent. Well, that and keeping the strength of my spells weak.

That she was showing me now told me just how worried she was that I would have need—a need she wouldn't be here to help with. *She was planning to return through a portal...*

Over the next eight hours she wrote out all of the separate runes and told me their names.

"This is an alphabet the same way the letter A can be used to write Cat or Ant and each word has a different meaning, so too is the rune. It is always the same but the meaning it gives is different. My book at home will explain it better and in more depth than I can."

"You think he's coming back, don't you?"

"I hope not. This is too advanced for you, Pip, but I'd not have you ignorant of what you might face. I bumbled around for a century or more figuring out small bits and pieces. Knowing that there's a method and *why* there is should help you tremendously.

"It would be very dangerous to attempt any of this though without study and practice. The only reason I'm telling you now is because your life might depend on you knowing. But don't try unless it's truly life or death.

"Knowing what a mage meant might be enough that you could ruin one of his spells although Zayvion tends to say his. Spoken spells generally lack the power that a written spell can have unless they're magnified by talismans. Not that a mage need to actually write. A mage need only make the gestures of writing like I do when I write the spell with my finger and not a pen. One with good control could imagine those gestures but that can be a very dangerous practice because you could then cast spells without meaning to while thinking on them. Interrupting my cadence would interrupt the spell.

"Mages that intend to use their magic in battle usually opt to say the spells because it leaves their hands free to fight. They'll have prepared spells on paper or things meant to be thrown that can be activated by will or blood, that sort of thing. His sword is a powerful talisman. Likely everything that he's wearing has been enchanted to empower his spoken spells. Talismans have limits though."

She grimaced ruefully.

"Basically we need to keep him quiet, unable to write, and unable to concentrate. Cutting his head off would do it nicely."

"How skilled is he with that sword as a sword?"

"I actually have no idea."

"If I were to take that sword, would it be just a sword?"

"Again, I don't know. It likely has protections on it to prevent it from being stolen. I've only ever seen him point it or swing at men already overpowered by his or Kazimir's magic. Zayvion is Kazimir's minion. Kazimir controls him completely much like one of your mules."

"Is Kazimir a seethe?"

"No."

She didn't volunteer what Kazimir was, so I didn't ask.

I said, "I haven't practiced with a sword in ages, but perhaps I ought too?

"And order him to impale himself?"

"'Tis, after all, the family motto."

A wicked smile lit her eyes.

"I'll make you a sword—an enchanted one. Won't he be surprised to face you!"

"If it be within my power, I shall bring you his head."

"Don't try to face him alone if you can help it. I'll make you another spellbook as soon as I get a chance, but I'm not sure when that will be. I darn't leave her and have much to do."

I realized as she said it that it wasn't only Zayvion that she was worried about but the wolves as well.

I said, "I shall begin writing out the rune of fire again. 'Tis good practice and Julia can set them off too—and mayhap Ryu."

"Practice the holding spell. It would at least slow him to have to dispel it, maybe enough that he could be shot. My advice would be to try to hold him and place other holding spells in front of yourself, set off as many fire spells as you could on him, have your expendable mules shoot him, and while doing all of that try to order him, but act quickly. I don't think you'd have time to question him. I think he could resist you if given time to gather himself. It might be better to pretend to help him and ease him into a position where he could be overpowered. It depends on the enchantments he brings with him and what he does. He can't bring too many unless Kazimir is willing to waste a ton of his magic to take the enchants across the void."

"Can he cross the ocean with a portari?"

"If it's strong enough, but it wouldn't work again to find Drew unless Drew wanted to be found. Which might be the better option. We haven't really decided. The portari is blocked now but we might allow it in the future.

"I plan on taking Cassandriel home when she's finished here. I'd like you and Julia to join us there to stay with her and Drew while I go speak to Andre's father and maybe Andre himself."

"If Andre must be held, then Julia and I will hold him."

"Are you sure you want to do that?"

"If it needs to be done, than 'tis better that we do it so that you can truthfully say that you don't know where he is. When the time comes that we can release him, she won't then be angry with you—the one person who can help her most, and I believe in time they would both forgive me."

"I wouldn't count on that. My daughter can hold a grudge—it's a family trait."

"I truly believe he loves her. He'll understand the necessity of staying away from her—or perhaps *not* staying away just behaving as a gentleman ought."

"I'm sure you have your own affairs to see to, so I'll put the jet at your disposal. I think it's safe for you to leave her now."

"None of our affairs are more important than the life of a friend."

"I sincerely appreciate you coming—more than I can say."

"And I sincerely appreciate your patient tutelage. My Julia is content with our holdings now. She's still interested in learning the secrets of stocks and finance, but I think her fears have eased enough that she's willing to slow down."

"Be careful showing her the runes. More than one novice was killed by their own enthusiasm."

I knew that warning was also intended for me.

"We shall both be most careful."

I'd learned much and knew there was still more—much more—for me to learn. I was excited to do it, more confident in my abilities and in myself.

My mistakes had taught me much as had Julia's. I'd no wish to repeat them but couldn't truly regret them either since they'd brought me here to this life. I much enjoyed being Lord Blackwood. Perhaps someday I'd learn to enjoy being a man, a true man in every way.

I suppose I should study modern men, I thought in amusement. Mimicking my father had served me well but 'twould take a more modern attitude if I wished to find a male companion to share my life with, not that I was ready for that. I wasn't yet certain that I wanted a lover of either sex, but male or female, a more modern approach to sex would serve me better than the outdated manners of my youth.

Maybe, in time, I could love Julia as a man did.

This world had so much to offer, so many choices. I could be anything I wished.

"Pip?"

I laughed as I said, "I was just thinking, I've come to enjoy being Lord Blackwood. 'Twill be most enjoyable to learn these arcane arts. I think Julia too will spend more time in study now that we have our mundane affairs more in order."

"Remind her to keep as low a profile as she can. It's always a good idea that no one truly knows all of your assets. She's doing a good job of hiding yours but greed can get the better of anyone. Just keep an eye on that, Pip. Not only is it too time consuming to manage huge companies but wealth always brings enemies— thieves and opportunists."

"I think her content with what we have now. There's still some organization needed but I think soon she'll be able to work behind the scenes as it were to do all of the charity things she so enjoys instead of finding all of these unpleasant mules."

Sandra nodded agreement.

"Keep an eye on that too though, Pip. It's fine to be successful but don't be flamboyantly successful even with fundraising."

"We shall both be quite content to manage our town. We see how it will need constant supervision and how difficult it becomes when so many people become involved."

"You're doing a great job as Lord Blackwood. Let's see how you do at being, Pip."

"I shall truly enjoy being Pip the mage."

THE END

NEXT BOOK IN THE SERIES

ANIMA WHISPERS

Realms ♥f Man

C.M. CONNEY

Published by
Ace Lyon Books
LLC

www.ingramcontent.com/pod-product-compliance
Lightning Source LLC
Chambersburg PA
CBHW030738030726
47497CB00001B/30